By the same author:

The Well Travelled Road

The Leenane Inspector

All Along The Barrow

Brian Grehan

Brian Grehan

Published by New Generation Publishing in 2019

Copyright © Brian Grehan 2019

First Edition

ISBN: 978-1-78955-847-0

www.newgeneration-publishing.com

 New Generation Publishing

"If I could be of any service in saving souls in any part of the globe, I would willingly do all in my power."

Nano Nagle (1769)

Acknowledgments

A sincere thank-you to all in the Longtable Creative Writing Group for their enduring encouragement and feedback , and their all-for-one attitude, and my daughter Joanne for helping with the computer bits, and lastly to my grandmother for her inspiration from on-high.

All proceeds from this book will be donated to Sightsavers Charity

For my Grandmother

Prologue

"Part of human torso found by dog beside river Barrow near St. Mullins."

Exclusive story by Ignatius Purcell.

Last Saturday, Walter Gough from Graiguenamanagh went hunting rabbits on the west side of the river Barrow near St.Mullins. Mister Gough was shocked when his dog returned with a human bone in its mouth. He searched the area for further remains but found nothing. There had been flooding recently further up the river. He immediately reported the incident to the Garda.

Garda spokesman Sergeant Nick Hackett stated he was sending a team with cadaver dogs to investigate. Sergeant Hackett also gave details of recent missing persons in the area, all male, but said he was puzzled, as forensic tests indicated the bone was from a female body.

A good one for "The Carlow Nationalist" and for me, Ignatius Purcell mused, putting the newspaper, dated 28th July 1982, back in the file. It was a front page scoop for the paper. Sales went up as the story grew. He was promoted, happy days. Now, after retiring, he was compiling an album of the major stories in his twenty five years with the newspaper. He'd decided this story, the one he called The Barrow Conundrum, was top of the heap.

His mind drifted back to the time of the story, when he first met Nancy Hackett.........................

Chapter 1

The Far Hills

Ned Rooney stretched his muscular, six-foot frame as he left the Astor cinema in Bagenalstown, blinking in the brightness. Those bloody wooden seats, he muttered, no wonder I'm stiff. His pals had gone for the cheap seats, payday being a few days off. Still, it was worth it, he reckoned, even though the film stretched over two hours. John Wayne's finest effort, Ethan Edwards in "The Searchers". He hoped his hero "Duke" Wayne would get an Oscar for it. That'll be the day. He felt Wayne should have got one for Sergeant Stryker in the "The Sands of Iwo Jima", the year Broderick Crawford won out. This time justice would be done, he hoped. Better to win an Oscar in the mid-nineteen-fifties than never. He enjoyed that his pals said he looked a bit like his hero. He never told them that he deliberately walked pigeon–toed like Wayne.

Autumn was not long away, the evening balmy, a saucer-moon pale in the sky, swallows darting every which way. He spotted his pals among the crowd leaving the cinema, heading for the pub, and waved to them. John Riordan shouted over that they'd meet on Sunday, ten o'clock sharp, at Ned's house. Sure, Ned called back, saddle the horses and we'll round them up and head them off one last time. Yeah, the final roundup, he thought grimly. The weekly rabbit hunt had always been the highlight of the week for him and his three best friends. The four musketeers, they always called themselves. Then Myxomatosis had struck the rabbits and virtually put paid to all that. Sunday coming would be the final hunt before he headed for London. He felt sad about that even though the rabbit-disease had killed off most of the enjoyment at home. His pals all knew he'd handed in his notice at the bakery. His future was set, for better or worse.

The night before they'd celebrated his news in the pub, where all his pals agreed, though sorry to see him go, it was the best and only way for him to make a go of his life. Laughing, he'd joked that he'd come back and paint the streets gold. The hell he would.

But tonight he had other things on his mind. His girl friend Nancy Hackett had said she'd see him when the film had over. He'd asked her to come with him, but she'd refused, saying she hated Westerns, they were too violent. She'd seemed cool that he'd still gone with his friends. Maybe he shouldn't have gone, he reflected, but John Wayne held sway. He wondered then if she might stand him up. She was a sister of one of his pals, and they'd met a month earlier at a dance in the McGrath Memorial Hall.

What a night that had been, he remembered, with Mick Delahunty and his orchestra playing the night away. Immediately he was smitten by her good looks and charm, and felt easy in her company. She made him smile and relax. Soon they were dancing close together, and when he'd asked her outside she didn't say no, handing her fags to one of her friends, ignoring the catcalls as they left the hall.

Outside in the shadows of the pine trees they'd kissed long and hard, as if they'd known each other for a time, and she'd let him go further than he'd ever gone before with a woman. His heart was pumping with excitement. He'd never felt this way before, and wondered if it was the same for her. She seemed more experienced than him, and seemed to understand him, helping him when he was fumbling to undo her buttons. He'd never had a sister, and lacked confidence in a woman's company. He wished someday he'd be able to make love to a woman the cool way John Wayne did. That'd be the day. That night she'd pulled away from him suddenly, saying.

"It's time we were getting back to the hall, Ned. I know them in there, they'll be timing us. We'll have to walk the gauntlet when we go back in. Is my lipstick smudged?"

He'd told her it *was* smudged, but she still looked beautiful. She'd laughed, her face flushed, before making a beeline for the bathroom inside the hall. It was the best night he'd ever had at a dance. The hell it was. She went home that night with her brother, but they'd kept in contact afterwards. One time they'd gone to a Doris Day film in the Astor, but had never been as intimate as that first night outside the dancehall. He knew she knew he was leaving town, but he had never spoken directly to her about it. Tonight he would.

He saw her standing at the corner of Station Road, a few hundred yards from the cinema. Black scarf on blond curls, yellow dress buttoned up the front, her nyloned legs shapely in black high heel shoes, a red cardigan draped over her shoulder. She looked alluring in the distance. He moved towards her, holding his breath.

"Howdy Nancy, didn't see you there, I was waiting outside the picture house."He said as he approached. Up close he thought she looked even more beautiful, her eyes bluer than the sky above, her skin pale, a smile curling her lips. His heart began to pound.

"I'd never wait there Ned. People might think things."

"They might I suppose. Say, how about us going for a drink and a chat in the pub?"

"Thanks, but I'd rather go for a stroll, maybe down by the Barrow. There's still a stretch in the evening, and it's better for talking, and other things." She smiled shyly as she spoke.

"That's a good idea. More privacy there and we can talk too."He nodded, his eyes fixated on the curves in her dress.

She sat on the wall, and bent to take off her high-heels, putting on her walking shoes. As she lifted her leg he stared at the line on the back of her nylons, following it right up her leg. She seemed unaware of this, as she lifted her other leg. He held his breath as he watched.

Soon they were ambling along towards the Barrow, under a mackerel-coloured, swallow-swooping sky. He circled his hand round her waist as they strolled by the Fairgreen, onto Regent Street, past the Sawmills, along by the mill-race, and over the drawbridge, onto the far side of the river, and she seemed easy with that. A tingle went through his body as he felt the contours of her body on the way, her breath moving in and out. They stopped on the far bank of the river, near a boathouse, where he told her of his plans to leave for London. Her face was solemn as she listened in silence. Finally she spoke.

"The far hills are green Ned."

"I suppose they are Nancy, and there's long horns on the cows in the far away fields. And they say too that there's gold in them thar hills. Well, they can say what they like, but I have to go. There's no future, and no chance of any, in this place. There's no two ways about it. Maybe you'd like to come over and visit sometime, when I get to know the lie of the land, and have a few bob jingling in my pocket?"

"Perhaps I might do that Ned, but I've got my job here in O'Reagan's chemist shop. It's not great but it's steady. And I have to look after my mother at home. She's crippled with arthritis. Dad works all God's hours in the beet factory in Carlow. My three brothers are worse than hopeless when it comes to doing anything in the home. You probably don't understand, being an only child. And what about *your* mother, she's a widow, a lovely lady by all accounts, but not in the best of health I believe?"

"Yeah, you're right there, ma's a saint. She knows I'll be home as often as I can. And I'll write to her every week and send money. Sure I could be home for good in a couple of years, with my money made. She agrees I have to give it a go, for better or for worse. If it doesn't work out, she says she'll always be there. And so will the house. It's one of the Soldiers' Cottages off Kilree Street. My dad got it from the British Government. He was a soldier in the First World War. Ma's got a widow's pension from them

4

too. She got nothing from the Irish Government when she needed it."Ned spat on the ground after speaking.

"It's good to have the house Ned. Still your ma will miss you a lot."

"Yeah, and I'll miss her too. And I'll miss you too Nancy."He spoke, his lips pressing hers hard until they opened, his hands exploring the curve of her back, desire a river rising inside. Then she pulled back.

"Ned, hold your horses, it's still bright, and there's people walking along the far side of the river. "

"So what?"

"So they might recognise us. It's a small town."

It's a small town all right, a small town with no jobs, he thought ruefully.

He surveyed the boathouse nearby. It belonged to Lar Murphy. He'd often fished with Lar and knew it was rarely locked in the summer. He suggested they go in there, but she hesitated, saying it might be scary inside. He hugged her hard, saying everything would be fine. After a few minutes she relented and they approached the boathouse. When they got there, it was unlocked, as he'd hoped. The door creaked as he opened it, and they entered.

Inside it was gloomy, light filtering through the wooden slats, water lapping against the side of the moored boat. Outside, ducks quacked and splashed in the water.

"It's spooky in here Ned. I'm shivering."She said, grabbing his shoulder.

"Come in closer Nancy, a good cuddle and you'll feel warmer."He said, putting his arms around her, kissing her long and strong, pressing her back against the side of the boat, his hands feeling her from behind.

"Ned, do you love me?" She asked, as his fingers unhooked the catch on the back of her dress.

"Sure I do Nancy, and I'm going to come home from London and marry you, when I've scraped enough money together, I swear it."He replied, kissing the side of her neck.

"And I love you too Ned, and I'll always be here waiting for you. You will come back won't you?"

"Sure I will Nancy, let's lie down here. I'll put my coat down."

"I'm not sure this is the right place Ned. It's scary. It's dark as a dungeon. There might be rats in here. I'm scared of rats."

"Don't worry, its fine here, and there ain't any rats. I'll look after you." He said, kissing her lips, guiding her down onto his coat.

In the dark he fumbled with the buttons on the back of her dress to the noise of the boat creaking in the water, and water hens splashing outside in the river.

When they left the boathouse later, purple gloaming shadows lay on the river. Her head was down and she seemed to be shivering. She buttoned her cardigan.

"Are you ok Nancy?"He asked, putting his arm around her. It was then he noticed the tear marks streaking the make- up on her face.

"I'll be all right in a few minutes Ned. It just wasn't what I expected it to be. The earth didn't move, I suppose. Maybe I shouldn't have expected it to. Nothing to do with you, it's just the way I feel. I'm just a romantic fool."

"You're not a fool Nancy. You're beautiful, and I love you."He said, kissing her lightly on the lips.

"That convent across the river, that's where I started school. I suppose that was on my mind all the time, why I don't know. Sister Philomena would hardly have approved of our carry-on in the boathouse."

"Unlike Sister Philomena, you're not going to die wondering, are you?"He said, laughing.

"It's no laughing matter Ned Rooney. You're being disrespectful to the nuns. They do a great job. Only for them I'd never have been educated. *And* I have an aunt who's a nun. And she's someone I really admire, always looking out for others, and always decorating the river with flowers. God, I'd love a drag."

They lit up, and strolled in silence along the bank of the river, crossing the drawbridge to the other side, back past the mill-race gushing beneath the shell of the derelict mill building, before they stopped outside the convent.

"You did mean what you said about loving me, and writing to me, and getting married, Ned?" She broke the stillness.

"Sure I did Nancy, sure I did, as God is my judge."

"That's good, and I'm going to miss you, even though I hardly know you." She said kissing his lips.

"I think you know me pretty well after tonight."He said, grinning.

"Well, that's different. Oh look, there's a grass stain on the front of my dress. My mother will suspect we were up to something."

"And what if we were? What's the harm in that? Once you love each other."

"She'd say that you're supposed to wait, until you're married, if you really love someone. And that's what the church says too."

"They don't want anyone to have fun Nancy, just because they're not allowed. I suppose you'll have to go and confess what you did?"

"Yes I will. The rules have to be obeyed whether you like them or not. You have to respect the church. It's for your own good."

"I suppose, but why should you feel guilty if you love someone?"

"I don't make the rules, Ned."

"No, but you sure can question them." He muttered, stamping his cigarette butt into the ground.

When they reached the garden gate of her house, she turned to face him.

"I suppose you're still going to London?"

He hesitated a while before replying.

"I love you Nancy, really I do, but I have to go, there's no other way to make a decent living in this town."

As she opened the gate and ran crying towards the house, he called after her that he would write and send money for her to come to London, when he'd settled in. His words echoed in the silence. The door slammed shut.

Chapter 2

Sweet Sorrow

The old lady's heart was sad. Her only son Ned had told her earlier he was leaving home to work in England. Her worst nightmare had happened. She sighed as she squinted behind her glasses in the half-light. Removing the globe from the brass lamp, she put it on the oil-cloth-covered table, checked there was oil in the lamp, turned up the wick, struck a match, and lit it. After turning the wick down again, she replaced the globe. Careful not to leave it on too high, she thought, or the glass will crack. After a few minutes she touched the glass. Feeling the globe had warmed, she turned the wick up again, and light seeped into the shadows circling the room.

The brightness shone on her thin, frail body, on the clips pinning her wiry, greying hair. It shone too on the range, where the fire glowed warmly, and on her slippered feet, warming on the fender. The tic-toc of the clock on the mantelpiece, balanced between two identical clay dogs, broke the silence in the room. She took a packet of five Woodbine cigarettes from her bag, leaving them on the table beside her book. Now was the time of day she enjoyed the most. A couple of cigarettes, and a Zane Grey book, *Riders of the Purple Sage*. Even though she'd read it before, it was long years back. Her reading choices were limited now, as she couldn't go to the library anymore. Her collapsed lung had put paid to all that.

That afternoon, Ned had picked up the battery from the garage, recharged for another five hours, and hooked it onto the radio on the sideboard. Soon she would be able to listen to her favourite nightly programmes. The Irish Hospital Sweepstakes show would be on at half-past ten, with Bart Bastable. *Makes no difference where you are, you can wish upon a star.* She loved that tune from

Pinnochio. Afterwards would follow A Book at Bedtime, with John Wyndham's *Day of the Triffids*. It had the living daylights frightened out of her, but she couldn't wait to hear the next episode.

She lit her cigarette with a piece of paper, flamed from the top of the lamp globe, inhaled the fumes, relaxed, and opened her book. Although her eyes kept reading the words, her mind would not stay on the page. It was filled with the bad news Ned had given her that day, when he told her he was leaving the following week to work in London. He said he'd be going with his best friend Francie McDonnell. His job in Connolly's Bakery had absolutely no prospects, he'd said, even though he worked day-in day-out as hard as two men. With his strength, he said, he could hump sacks of flour around on his back like Hercules, instead of using the trolley. He did it that way because it was quicker, but said he got no thanks for his efforts.

There was plenty of work in London on the building, he'd continued, what with the new motorways and all the rebuilding after the War. He'd said he'd write to her every week, and send money home. *And* he'd be home to see her at Christmas, and in the summer for his holidays, *and* when he'd enough money saved, he'd return home for good, and settle down. He'd handed in his notice and would finish in Connolly's the next Friday, and be on the mail boat to Holyhead a week later. She'd just nodded her head in agreement, saying it was God's will, but inside her heart was in turmoil. He'd said he was only going as far as London, but for her it was as far away as Timbuktu.

After a while she left her book down, put the butt in the ashtray, and stood up. Moving closer to the fire in the range, she poked it, and filled it with turf. Then she went into the scullery, filling the kettle from the pail. Going back to the range, she put the kettle on the fire. It was cosy by the fire. By the time I'm going to bed, the water should be boiling, she thought.

She lit up again, took a drag, opened her book, and continued her attempt to read. But in vain, her mind kept drifting elsewhere. The day she'd dreaded had arrived, though she'd prayed it never would. The scourge of emigration had finally hit her house. But she knew Ned was now twenty years old, and wanted to do something with his life. He was a fine, handsome lad, popular with everyone. *He was* her life up to now, and she would miss him more than anything. She feared too that *her* life would change utterly. Her wish had always been that he would meet a nice girl from the town, fall in love, and settle down at home. It seemed that was not to be, though she knew he'd lately gone out with a girl from the town called Nancy Hackett. Yes, she remembered her, a sister of one of Ned's pals, a lovely girl, from a lovely family. She would pray later that they might fall in love.

She felt the scourge of Myxomotosis, as well as killing all the rabbits in Carlow, had killed off any hope of Ned staying. It had changed everyone's way of life in the area. Hunting rabbits every Sunday with his pals was what he'd lived for. Ned was happy once he had the rabbits to hunt, though he often complained about his job, and the pittance he was paid. They used sell some of the rabbits they'd catch, to make the price of the pictures, or buy a pint in the pub. Now all the rabbits were being wiped out, dying a cruel, slow death, eyes bulging from their sockets. Damn and blast that man who brought the disease in, all the way from Australia, she muttered. He's first taken away the people's way of life in the country, and now he's taking away my son. Tears rimmed her eyes, and one trickled down her face, falling in a blob onto the page she was reading.

And he's done you poor hounds out of a job, she thought, eyeing Ned's two greyhounds, Sparky and Babes, stretched on the floor in front of the fire. She remembered that Sparky, a brindle, had been the fastest hound Ned ever owned. He'd had plans to race him. But all that went up the spout when the dog broke its leg one winter's night, when they were out lamping for the rabbits. She recalled the incident a few weeks after the accident, when Ned had left with the other dogs on the Sunday hunt. Sparky was in plaster and left behind, and going frantic, yelping his head off. Then she looked around to find he had vanished. The window had been left half open, and the hound had jumped onto the sofa, plaster and all, and out the window in a flash, following the hunt a mile up the road. Ned had to carry the whimpering hound back in his arms, before heading off again. She wondered what would become of the hounds when he left. She would miss their company, and felt more secure when they were around. Someone would have to exercise them every day. But who?

And she wondered who would take the empty pail to the pump at the bottom of the road, fill it, and bring it back to the house, after he was gone? Not to mention the slops. There had been talk of running water coming, and even electricity, but when? She doubted if she'd ever see either. She worried. Even the priest had to call to the house to visit her in recent years. Her only trip outdoors now was every Friday to the Post Office to collect her pension, when she'd dress up in her mothball-smelling fox fur, like the lady of the manor. Mister Mitchell the retired vicar next door was kind, often offering to do messages for her in the town, banging with a rock on the back wall between their houses, to get her attention. God will provide, she thought, there's no sense in worrying. But she did worry, as she continued staring at the pages of her book.

Later, she put down the book, took out her rosary beads, and said a decade of the rosary. Afterwards she felt better. Putting the beads back in their purse, she looked at the clock on the mantelpiece. Twenty-five past ten. The kettle began singing on the range. She shuffled to the bedroom, returning with a stone jar. Removing the stopper, she filled the jar with boiling water from the kettle. Then she wrapped it in an old nylon stocking, and left it to heat in the oven on the range.

As she clicked the radio on, she wondered how she was going to get the radio's battery charged each week. The battery was too heavy for her to carry to the garage, but then she thought again of the vicar next door. He might help her out. And there was the methylated spirits for the primus-stove that she cooked on. Maybe the vicar would help her out there as well. He was a gentleman. Soon the voices on the radio had lulled her into a world where her worries ceased to exist.

Near midnight she clicked off the radio. Can't run the battery down, she thought, there's only four hours left. Ned was late, probably celebrating his big decision with his pals in the pub. He'll put the hounds to bed out in the shed, and put the bar on the back door, when he comes in. The house was always left open, even at night. Not much to rob in Maggie Rooney's house, she mused.

Maggie took the stone jar from the oven, went into the bedroom, and placed it beneath the sheets on her bed. She returned to the fireplace with the red-globed Sacred Heart lamp in her hands. She lit it, and brought it back to the bedroom, leaving the large lamp, with the wick turned down, on the kitchen table for Ned.

The Sacred Heart lamp was placed on the table beside her bed. It would give enough light to read her bedside book, before falling asleep. Before starting to read it, she knelt by the bed. She gazed up at the hand-carved Stations-of-the-Cross picture hanging above her bed, and said her night prayers, adding an extra one for Ned and his girl friend, Nancy Hackett.

In bed, her feet resting cosy against the jar, she read her book, feeling more contented. Maybe they would fall in love. Maybe he would stay. Maybe..... Her eyelids became heavy, and she closed her book, reaching to turn down the wick on the Sacred Heart lamp beside the bed.

Chapter 3

Forgotten Farewell

In Nancy's mind the month after he left seemed to stretch to infinity. Every day, around when the postman was due, she'd peek out through the front window, hoping Ned Rooney's promised letter was about to arrive. Nothing came. Usually, after this happened, she'd slink out of sight to dry her tears. Her mother, arthritic, bent-over, would sometimes ask her if she was all right. Of course, she'd reply, trying to mask her feelings. But she reckoned her mother suspected that something was amiss. Nancy was hopeless at pretending. Her mother knew about the dates she'd had with Ned before he'd emigrated, but she never mentioned him by name. God, but he was the handsomest fellah in the town, she remembered, and all the girls mad after him. But the only things that seemed to excite him were his hounds, hunting rabbits, and being off with the lads.

After nearly six weeks Nancy gave up hope of a letter ever arriving, and resolved to get on with her life. Her foolish expectations were driving her to distraction. His loss anyway, she convinced herself.

A month later, she missed her period, and began feeling nauseous in the mornings. Dear God, I might be pregnant, she thought, panicked, feeling she had the symptoms of morning-sickness. She had to stay out sick from her job in O'Reagan's chemist shop, during the first week of the nausea, and worried she might lose her job. The money wasn't much, but it helped to pay some of the bills. Her mother said nothing, but Nancy felt she was looking at her in a funny way. Her father was either working in the beet factory in Carlow town, or down at the pub each evening.

The ensuing weeks confirmed her worst fears, she *was* pregnant. The night with Ned in the boathouse was ingrained in her brain. At night she went over it constantly. How could I have been so stupid? She thought. But it all seemed so right at the time. He loved me, I loved him. I was smitten by his good looks and charm, and I thought he felt the same way about me. My mistake, stupid me, what will I do now? She knew that being nineteen and pregnant in a small town in Ireland in the fifties was not a pleasant prospect. Being youngest of a respectable Catholic family of three girls and three boys only added to the problem. Nancy racked her brains. She even considered following Ned to London, but later dismissed the idea. She felt furious at him for leaving her in such a predicament, and him off gallivanting now in the bright lights of London. He hadn't kept his word. He'd let her down, pregnant or not.

Who could she turn to? She wondered. Her mother was first to come-to-mind, but she had her own health problems and Nancy didn't want to burden her. Her father, no, he was out of the question, she couldn't face him. All that'd worry him would be what the neighbours might think. And there was no way she'd speak to the Monsignor in the church after the way he'd berated her when she went to him in Confession, the day after she'd been with Ned in the boathouse. She recalled the reek of drink off his breath in the Confession box. And then him wantin' too much information. She was afraid if she spoke to any of her sisters or friends, the news would be all over the town in no-time. She racked her brains again. And she prayed. And she prayed. And she racked her brains. And then it came to her who she could turn to. Clear as a bell.

Next morning she walked down Regent Street to the Presentation Convent, beside the Barrow. Her aunt, Sister Roberta, ushered her into her office. She was tall and wore glasses, forbidding in her black habit, narrow face framed in her veil, with a crucifix entwined in her fingers. Nancy looked around. On a wall opposite the window, hung a wooden crucifix. Over the fireplace, was a picture of a nun named Nano Nagle. The room reeked of beeswax polish and incense.

"Do sit down Nancy, my dear niece, and to what do I owe the pleasure? I haven't seen you since last Christmas."A smile creased the nun's lips.

"That's true I suppose, but I kept meaning to call. Every time I see the beautiful flowers you planted on the river banks near the convent I think of you, and what a nice person you must be to do something like that, something of rare beauty. And when you taught me for a year when I was twelve, you were never cross, but always understanding and kind. I always felt I could come to you if I had a problem. "

"My dear child, you don't look well at all. You surely need help. Please tell me your problem, tell me what it is that ails you?"A frown came on the nun's face, and as she took Nancy's hands in hers, Nancy burst into tears, and blurted out her story.

"Oh my dear, dear girl, how awful for you, and you not being able to share your troubles with anyone close in your family." The nun spoke kindly to her, her hands resting upon Nancy's shoulders. Nancy immediately felt she understood, and was not judging her.

"I didn't know what to do, Sister Roberta. I prayed and prayed, and I believe God sent me here."

"I'm sure He did, and I am so glad you came here. We must think how best to handle this delicate matter." The nun stood and paced the room for a few minutes, her lips moving in silent prayer. She stopped and gazed awhile out the window, towards the Barrow, to the place where her flowers adorned the river, before turning to Nancy.

"The first thing you must do is tell your parents what's happened."

"I can't, I've tried, but it's not easy."

"I didn't say it was easy child. Pray, and God will show you the way. I will pray too for you, and when you've done that, come back and see me again. Now I must hasten, I have a class at twelve."

The nun stood up, flattened the creases in her habit with her hands, and swished out the door.

Nancy left the convent feeling better, but dreading how she would break the news to her parents. That night she prayed again for guidance, and was rewarded.

Nancy's eldest sister Kitty was married, with two children, and lived on the outskirts of the town near Dunleckney. Her husband was a carpenter, hard working, and a good provider. Kitty used to joke he never had a real job, but was never out of work. Nancy walked by the Barrow towards her sister's house, having decided to confide in her, realising her pregnancy had to be revealed, and that she needed her sister's help to do so.

On the way she passed the place on the river where in her youth she and her sisters used catch pinkeens in a jam-jar. The ruin of an old mill loomed on the far bank. In the distance she saw the Cannons, where they swam in the summer, daring each other to swim to the far bank, when the river was low. Later, she passed the spot where her brothers used fill jam jars full of jellied frogspawn in the springtime. They'd place them on window-sills at home and wait and watch until the growing dots burst into swimming tadpoles. They could tell the weather by the frogs. They went yellow in the sun, and brown in the rain.

When Nancy called, Kitty was busy washing clothes, the kids at school, but she stopped straight away to hug her, before putting the kettle on the range.

"Well Nancy, this is a surprise visit. A lovely surprise, I like surprises like this. And how is everything going with you? You look a little pale, I have to say." As Kitty spoke she poured the tea, smiling, using her best willow-pattern china. She had flaming red hair and freckles, and wore glasses.

Nancy told Kitty of her situation, and asked her if she would break the news to her parents. Kitty's eyebrows arched, as she replied.

"But why can't you tell them yourself? Surely it would be better if *you* did it."

"I know you're right, but I can't. I can't explain it, I just can't."At that moment a wave of nausea hit Nancy, and she dashed to the bathroom.

When she returned, Kitty put her arms around her, and hugged her hard.

"Poor thing, don't you worry little sister, I'll speak to Mammy and Daddy, they'll understand, I'll make sure of it. Don't you worry your pretty little head, sure amn't I your big sister? I'll look out for you, isn't that what big sisters are for?"

Nancy wasn't sure her parents would understand, but she didn't care now, she was relieved, and hugged Kitty, shedding tears of relief. Before Nancy left, Kitty asked if anyone else knew about her news. Nancy said the only one was their aunt, Sister Roberta in the convent. Kitty said nothing for a few moments, before nodding her head and saying it probably was a good thing that the nun knew, as she had only the height of respect for Sister Roberta, but it might have been better if Nancy had come to her big sister first. After a few moments, Nancy agreed Kitty was right, saying she should have come to her first, but she wasn't thinking straight. They hugged again, smiling.

Kitty kept her word, speaking to her mother the next day about Nancy. She took the news calmly, but fretted how their father would react, saying he was worried about being made redundant at the beet factory, and was stressed out. Nancy's mother came to her later, telling her not to worry, that everything would be alright, that she would sort things out with Nancy's father. But Nancy doubted if she ever would.

A week later Nancy and Kitty met for tea in Doorley's Hotel, alongside the river. Kitty told her she had spoken separately to Sister Roberta and their mother on several occasions, and had come up with a proposal.

"And what is that?" Nancy asked, dreading what she might say.

"Because Mammy is afraid to tell Daddy just now, we had to come up with something straight away. We couldn't wait, just doing nothing."

"I know Kitty, I know, but what is it?" Nancy asked, desperate to know.

"Well, nothing is perfect Nancy, but you know Mammy has an unmarried sister, Agnes, who lives in Manchester?"

"I do."

"Well, the idea is for you to go and stay with her until the baby is born. We would come and visit as often as possible. Also, Sister Roberta's Presentation Order have a convent in Manchester. She said they would help out as much as they could, and she herself would travel across to visit you as regular as she could."

"And what about after the baby is born?"Nancy asked.

A silence fell before Kitty replied.

"The baby would have to be adopted Nancy, then you would return to Ireland. The only other way is for you to have your pregnancy terminated in Manchester, but that's not what you'd want. Is…is it?"

Nancy hesitated awhile before replying, shocked by the words she'd just heard.

"No, no…..of course not…I wouldn't want that at all. I….I want my child to live."Nancy sighed as she spoke.

"I guessed you would say that Nancy, but maybe you should sleep on it, at least for a few nights, before any final decision."

Kitty put her hand on Nancy's shoulder as she spoke. They parted, agreeing to meet again in two days.

Nancy walked home by the river, her head spinning. The smooth flow of the river, eternally eddying, soothed the panic pulsing through her. Passing the Sawmills, she turned left at the convent, her spirits lifting when she saw Sister Roberta's flowers blooming all along the river there. She mulled over Kitty's words that night, restless, sleeping little. She knew people were trying to help her, but felt adrift in a sea of darkness, with no landfall in sight. She prayed to God for guidance.

When she met Kitty again, Nancy said her mind was made up, and that she agreed to the proposal. Kitty was relieved and hugged her, saying it was the right thing to do, and that she would get things moving with Sister Roberta and Mammy. They finished their tea and left, agreeing to meet again soon. The sooner things get going the better, Kitty said, before tongues wagged. Nancy nodded.

Leaving the hotel, Nancy headed for the river. She wasn't elated, but felt a worry had been lifted from her. When she reached the riverbank she stopped, staring into the swirling waters. She saw cobalt dragonflies hover above the rushes where the butterflies fluttered. Swallows swooped and skimmed above the water. Poplars, stately, lined the far bank, leaning in the wind, leaves shimmering in the sun. Birds sang unseen in the trees. The river had a mesmeric effect on her, and she continued walking until finally reaching the convent. Stopping there, she took out the bread roll she'd brought from the hotel, breaking it into crumbs, throwing them into the water. The ducks and water hens squawked in delight. That gave her a fillip. She continued home, her mind filled with her visit to the doctor the next day, accompanied by Kitty. All went well.

**

Kitty and her mother accompanied Nancy to Manchester. Afterwards, she couldn't remember saying goodbye to her father. She wondered how much he knew at that time.

Her aunt Agnes was a kind person, and did all she could, but the months dragged. When Sister Roberta came over to visit she took her to visit the Presentation Order house in Manchester, and Nancy got to know some of the Sisters. They were kind and understanding, and she took to visiting them regularly on her own. She felt at peace there.

Nancy had only a hazy recollection of the pain before the birth. It all vanished when the nurse washed the baby down, placed the child in her arms, and told her she had a healthy seven-pound boy. A feeling of wonder hit her, looking at the sleeping bundle before her, realising she was a mother, and had a baby who depended utterly on her. Although fatigued, she was overcome by the emotion of love, something she'd never felt before. The nurse instructed her on how to breast-feed, and she fed her baby for the next two weeks, until he was taken away from her.

She was distraught when he'd gone. She had a sense of loss, but felt that was the way of the world. She felt the loss of love. The baby was love and she had lost love. And she knew she had changed. In the months before the birth, she'd had time to reflect on her life and on many other things. She felt her country had deserted her, that there was a lack of love and compassion there, which had forced her to flee to another country for the birth of her child. Yes, for sure her sister and mother had done their best, but she reasoned that it was the society in Ireland that lacked understanding and love, and had let her down. She felt it deep in her heart's core. Her feelings for Ned Rooney changed after the birth. She forgave him his going away, but felt aggrieved that he had.

Sister Roberta and her fellow nuns radiated the love she felt her soul yearned for at that time. And so she stayed on in Manchester afterwards, in the company of the nuns of the Presentation Order. And after some months of prayer and meditation about her future, Nancy decided to follow in the footsteps of her hero, Nano Nagle, and become a nun.

Chapter 4

Epistle

When she became a nun, Nancy decided to take the name Brendan, after her father. Though never close to him, she respected how hard he'd worked to get his family reared and educated, and deep down felt love and respect for him. Maybe it's my way of thanking him, she thought. He'd crossed the Irish Sea many times to visit the Manchester religious house with her mother, when Nancy was a Novice there. Their relationship improved, and he now treated her as an adult. He also seemed to behave better with her mother when they were away from home, bringing her to the shops and the cinema. Her mother said the breaks abroad made him forget the stresses of his job in the beet factory. He would try to arrange the visits to coincide with a Manchester United game in Old Trafford, during which her mother would spend the time with her sister Agnes. Her mother said coming over to the UK added a new aspect to his life. He was chuffed about his daughter becoming a nun and calling herself after him. He liked to brag about it in the pub at home, like it was some kind of status symbol. Sometimes Nancy wondered if he knew the full story of her vocation, but if he did he never let on. In truth, she preferred it that way.

In the beginning she worried if she had a true vocation, or was it just a reaction to the whole affair, the birth and adoption of her son, an escape from reality? Would she stay the course? She believed so. Many didn't, she knew.

One day she was called to a meeting with the Mother Superior, Sister Martha. Plump bodied, bespectacled, with a friendly demeanour, the elder nun spoke first about life in the community, but later probed Nancy closely about her calling. From here onwards there will be only one person in your life, and that's God, she'd said, you will forever be a bride of Christ. You must devote yourself body and soul to him, and no one else. You must understand that. The Devil will put temptation in your way, in dark and devious ways. Our Order works within the community, and we are not sheltered from the ways of the flesh. Are you sure this is the life for you? Sister Martha's eyes narrowed and she stared into Nancy's eyes, as if she suspected it might not be. Nancy replied that she had no doubt it was the life she wanted.

Good, Sister Martha concluded, I've enjoyed our little chat, and we must do this again Sister Brendan, I will pray for your intentions. She thanked the old nun, saying she would pray for her too, and left with an uneasy feeling, but still confident of her vocation. Anyway she knew that the Presentation Order had its own way of assessing new entrants, a period of discernment they called it, where you were put into situations in the local community and judged on how you reacted. She had already been tested in this way, and had come through with distinction.

During this period she'd read up on the history of the founder of the Presentation Order, Nano Nagle, and was enthralled. This was a person she'd come to admire. This was the person she wanted to emulate. This was a person whose story convinced her she had made the right decision in becoming a nun. **(see Note 1).** Nancy was sad when she read that Nano Nagle died of TB in 1784. What a woman, she thought, a doer, a leader by example. She wanted and prayed to be like her. Her hero.

Nancy loved her life among the poor people in Manchester, many of them Irish, who had fallen on hard times. Their spirit was inspiring, and it brought a purpose in her life, trying to improve their lot. From an early stage she realised that most people in Manchester had a passion for two things, football and cricket. If she mentioned either Maine Road, or Old Trafford, their eyes lit up. Reading up on both sports, she became hooked, and started following Manchester United's matches, and listening to John Arlott, "the Voice of Cricket", on the radio. The "Busby Babes" were in their prime then, and probably the most famous soccer team in the world. And when Lancashire played Yorkshire in cricket, it was the real "War of the Roses" all over again. Not only did her new-found knowledge help to "break the ice" with strangers, but, to her surprise, she found herself enjoying both sports.

Her life was happy there, she prayed hard, and passed through the probationary period, before taking her first vows, becoming a Novice for two years. It would be a further three years before she took her final vows of Poverty, Chastity, and Obedience. She couldn't wait. The English people, including the nuns she lived and worked with, were kind and helpful. When she thought back on her prospects in Ireland, in a dead-end job in a chemist shop in Bagenalstown, she'd no regrets in being where she was. Now she was going to do some good with her life.

Her thoughts never strayed far from her family though, and her home town in Carlow. She missed them, *and* the silent, sinuous flow of the Barrow snaking through Bagenalstown, and the vista of Sister Roberta's flowers gracing its banks. And she sometimes wondered if she might end up back home there, teaching in the convent beside the river, and that notion kept her going, whenever she had those longings.

The Order had advised against travelling home, except in emergencies, and she abided by their wishes. She also had a problem in returning home, while wearing a habit. She preferred to stay anonymous. On and off she would think about her adopted son, wondering if he was happy, and what he looked like, and she would pray for his health and happiness.

In her final year she had another meeting with Sister Martha, who again quizzed her about her vocation, saying it was for life, that there was no going back, and asking Nancy if she was happy with her decision to become a nun. Although assuring the head nun again that she had no doubts, she afterwards felt unsettled, wondering if the elderly nun knew something she didn't.

Her parents were in attendance at her final profession in Manchester. She knew they were proud of her, and she couldn't have been happier. Part of the ceremony involved dressing up in white, like a bride, before switching to the habit. She thought it the happiest day of her life.

Years slipped by, and after graduating as a teacher, she taught young children in the Order's local school. Aunt Agnes passed away when Nancy was twenty nine years old, and her parents' visits became less frequent. When she was thirty five, she returned to Bagenalstown for the burial of her mother, who had reached the age of seventy one. This was a trip she'd always dreaded. Prayer and her family helped her cope. This was the first time she'd worn a habit in Ireland. She was heartbroken. While there, she met many elderly sisters from the Presentation Order, including her aunt, Sister Roberta, from the local convent.

"We're all getting older." Sister Roberta said to her on one occasion.

"Maybe we need an injection of new blood on the banks of the Barrow." The old nun added.

"Perhaps you do, Sister Roberta. I'll pray for your intentions."Nancy replied, guessing what she was alluding to.

She worried then how her father, who was long retired, would now cope alone, but her sister Kitty assured her he would be well looked-after by his family. One of the advantages of having a big family, Kitty added.

On her return to Manchester, after her mother's funeral, Nancy requested a meeting with Sister Martha. When she entered her office, overlooking the cloister, the sun was dazzling through the stained-glass window, adorned with the image of a lantern. Sister Martha was very old then, well past retirement age, it seemed to Nancy, but, like the Pope, nuns never seemed to have a retirement age, going on forever and ever. Although Sister Martha's body had aged, her mind was still razor-sharp. The old nun sank into her chair, propped her walking-stick against her desk, and peered at Nancy over the rim of her glasses.

"Well Sister Brendan, first please accept my sincere sympathy on the loss of your mother. A mother's love's a blessing, and a mother's love is irreplaceable. I have said a novena for her soul. May she rest in eternal peace and happiness." The old nun blessed herself with her rosary beads.

"Thank you Sister Martha." Nancy replied, a tear trickling down her cheek. She wiped it off with the back of her hand.

"Is there anything I can do for you, at this difficult time?"The old nun asked.

"Well yes there is. I…I would like to request a transfer to one of our schools in Ireland."

"So you're not happy with your life here? Had you anywhere in particular in mind?" The old nun leaned over across her desk, one eyebrow arched.

"Yes, my heart's desire is to return to Ireland, to Bagenalstown in county Carlow, where I was born. I've just been there for my mother's funeral, and many of the nuns teaching there are elderly. I believe I've got enough experience now to adapt to teaching there."

"Just because you reach a certain age doesn't mean your little grey cells cease to function." The elderly nun harrumphed.

"Yes, of course Sister Martha, I didn't mean it like that. It's just that I know I'd be happy there."

"Are you saying you're not happy here?"

"No. I'm very happy here, but I…I feel it's time to move on. All of my family live there."

"*We* are your family now. Remember your final vows. You are doing a fine job here, believe me, we would hate to see you leave us. Your dedication and work have been exemplary, even *I* must admit I was wrong in that respect. I *will* look into your request, and see what can be done. Now is not the time for quick decisions, with you still grieving for your mother. We'll let the dust settle for a while. I'll pray for your intentions, God bless you Sister Brendan." The old nun got up slowly and reached for her walking-stick.

After two years the dust had well settled, but still there was no response from Sister Martha. Instead Nancy was switched to teaching in an orphanage in Manchester. She prayed hard for guidance, but all the time the longing to return home festered within her like a cancer. Thoughts about her adopted son also occurred more frequently, usually at night, disturbing her sleep. Sister Martha has hardly forgotten, she thought, I'll have to see her again.

But before she'd worked up the courage to ask for a meeting, a letter arrived from her sister Kitty. It was loose inside a large envelope, which contained two other letters in smaller envelopes. Kitty's letter, said that their aunt, Sister Roberta, had died recently in Bagenalstown, but before she'd passed-away Kitty had visited her. The old nun was very weak, and had spoken in a whisper, asking Kitty to pray for her, and to send Sister Brendan the two letters, after she passed on. It was her dying wish.

Nancy picked up the two envelopes. One had a lantern embossed on the outside. Guessing it must be from Sister Roberta, she sliced it open, and started to read.

"Dear Sister Brendan,

My dearest niece, I hope my epistle finds you in good health. My own health is waning, and I am writing this while I still have the strength to do so.

You are always in my mind and heart, and I pray constantly for your intentions, ever since you came to me all those years ago, when you needed my help. I was so proud of how you handled everything at that difficult time, and how you have progressed in the Order afterwards. Sister Martha always kept me informed of your progress. She is always caring, and looking out for you.

Now I am old, too frail even to tend to the flowers at the riverside, and I pray that someone will keep them flowering after I'm gone, in my memory, and in memory of the Presentation Order of nuns. I often think of you as that person, but may whatever God wills be done.

You may be upset by the news I have for you, and that is why I've refrained from telling you before. Believe me Sister Brendan, I always have your best intentions at heart in all my actions. I also consulted with Sister Martha at the time, before making my decision *not* to tell you this information previously. The right time is now, I believe, although Sister Martha would not agree...she felt the news should *never* be divulged. So I asked your sister Kitty to send this letter to you.

Before your aunt Agnes, my sister, passed-away many years ago in Manchester, she wrote a letter to me. It contained information about the adoption of your son, acquired through a friend who worked in the Adoption Board in Manchester. Agnes wrote down the details of the adoption, and these are contained in the letter in the other envelope. At that time you were about to take your final vows, and Agnes was afraid the information might distract you from your studies. She may also have consulted Sister Martha at that time. When I received her letter, I too was reluctant to pass it on immediately to you. I spoke to Sister Martha, and we both felt it wasn't the right time then to burden you with this information. We both thought and prayed a lot about this decision. You were happy then, and making good progress in your life in the Order. We felt at that time it would be wrong to possibly make you unhappy, and more preferable to wait until you had more experience in your life as a nun, and all the sacrifices involved. I have some regrets now about this decision, but anyway I am now passing on the information while I can. I prayed to God a lot about divulging it, and I believe this is what He wanted to happen. The Lord works in mysterious ways.

Believe me, I had only your best interests at heart, as had Sister Martha. Please forgive me if you feel deceived, it was not intended, and I am sorry if I have made you unhappy in any way. Please pray for my soul, and if you ever pass this way again, take some of my flowers from the river, and put them on my grave."

The letter was signed by Sister Roberta.

Nancy put the letter back in the envelope, hands trembling, brushing away the tears, and knelt by her bed. Mind spinning, heart thumping, she felt as if she was drowning in a river, gasping for breath, entangled by streeling weeds, about to be sucked under. Kneeling, she prayed for the memory of Sister Roberta, and for Sister Martha's intentions, and for God's guidance on what she should do. When she stood up, she had no desire to open Aunt Agnes' letter, but felt her life had somehow utterly changed. She realised the letter could hold the key to her tracing her son's whereabouts, but was afraid to confront that issue just then, afraid it might jeopardise her vocation, afraid Sister Martha's reservations about her vocation might prove to be correct. Sometime afterwards, she hid the large envelope in her wardrobe.

(Note 1):

Born Honora Nagle in county Cork in 1718 to a wealthy Catholic family, eldest of six, she was soon called Nano by family and friends. In the era of the Penal Laws, and under the first "Act of 1695", it was unlawful to open a Catholic school in Ireland, and forbidden for Catholics to travel abroad for education. Nano attended a "hedge school" close to her home, before being sent to Paris, with her sister Anne, to complete their education, assisted no doubt by the family's business ties with the French. A high life of glamour and sophistication followed, with balls, parties, and theatre outings the norm. But when Nano later saw the wretchedness of the poor in Paris, and the contrast with her own privileged life style, it preyed on her conscience, and she was determined to do something about it. On her father's death she and her sister returned to Ireland in 1746. Nano was appalled at the poverty she found there. Soon she had secretly set up her first school for the poor in Cork, in defiance of the law. She felt education was the only way the poor could better themselves, and within a few years, she was running a network of schools all over Cork.

After school, she would visit the sick and elderly, and soon opened homes for aged women, and began adult classes. She would go from hovel to hovel each day, gathering the neediest to teach, and then minister to them by night. This led to Nagle being nicknamed the "The Lady with the Lantern". The lantern later became the symbol of the Sisters of the Presentation worldwide. A symbol of hope, that lit up the lives of the poor everywhere.

At that time, religious sisters were required to remain enclosed in their convents. Nagle's schools expanded, without her establishing a formal religious congregation, and so were free to work for the poor in the community, without being enclosed. Finally, she founded and opened the first Presentation convent in Ireland in Douglas Street, Cork, on Christmas Day 1775, and her organisation spread countrywide and worldwide over the years.

Chapter 5

Decision

Sleep was erratic for Nancy in the weeks after receiving Aunt Agnes' letter. At first she was furious with Sister Roberta and Sister Martha for not informing her many years before about the adoption information. She resolved to confront Sister Martha, but later hesitated to do so, as she recognized her own mind was in tatters. Her son had come back into her life too, although she'd tried to block him out, as if he'd never existed. The reality that she *was* a mother remained ingrained in her being, despite the vows she'd taken. Prayer was her only resort, and she prayed in earnest. *Dear God, forgive me my trespasses, and show me what I should do, always your will not mine, and guide me , a poor sinner, to do what is right in your eyes, and not offend you further.*

At night her mind sometimes drifted back to Sister Martha's questioning about her vocation when she was a Novice. She knew now what the older nun had been alluding to in her questions. Sister Martha *was* right of course, Nancy reflected, the knowledge of her son's whereabouts *would* have affected her when she was taking her vows. But by how much she wasn't sure, the choices were stark. Life as a single mother in Ireland in the fifties was not an appealing one, compared to devoting your life to God as a nun. Things that were not socially acceptable were swept under the carpet. Nevertheless, a feeling of guilt racked her body, subliminally at first, as if she had abandoned someone who was part of her being, just for appearance's sake.

Blood binds deep, and she wondered about her son, and what he might look like now as a teenager, and if he was at all like her, and where he was living, and if he was happy. She even worried about his health, and if he suffered from any afflictions. The questions burned into her mind and her sleep. Her concentration began to lapse in her work in the orphanage. Times out of mind she would end up staring out the window, her mind a blank, until one of the sisters would shake her back to reality. Sister Brendan, daydreaming of Ireland again, soon we'll be calling you Sister Daydreams, they would tease her.

Her appetite went and she began to lose weight. Each day and night she prayed for guidance. She abandoned her plan of returning to Ireland, it no longer seemed important. Sister Roberta's flowers could go to rack and ruin on the banks of the Barrow, for all she cared. The decision whether to open Aunt Agnes' letter or not, tormented her brain. In the end she still decided *not* to open it. Maybe she was afraid to face the decision posed if she did, or maybe she just hoped that life would eventually revert back to what it had been before the letter came. Her mental health continued on a downward spiral.

Eventually Sister Martha called her to a meeting, enquiring about her health, saying she looked unwell. Perhaps you need a break Sister Brendan, she said, maybe a week in Rome or Milan? You have been working too hard. She assured the old nun that she would be fine, that it was probably just a middle-age problem, nothing more, but agreed she *would* consider her offer. Saying that they would pray for each other's intentions, they parted, promising to meet again soon.

Afterwards, Nancy reflected on how her initial anger at Sister Martha about the letter had abated. Her decision to put Nancy working in the orphanage had also proved correct. Initially she'd resented it, thinking the old nun wanted to dissuade her from returning to Ireland, but the children were a joy, and she soon came to love her life there. When one of the children smiled, it made Nancy feel good, and she'd smile too. Maybe Sister Martha was right about the letter too, she thought, maybe the mental strain would have been too much for her at that time. She seems to know me better than I know myself, Nancy reflected.

Though Sister Martha had still not mentioned her request to return to Ireland, Nancy no longer cared. But when she looked in the mirror her face was gaunt. She grimaced. Sleepless nights had become the norm. Her mental state was worsening by the month though she was reluctant to accept the fact. That is most likely the reason behind her later bizarre behaviour.

Three years had elapsed since she'd first started working in the orphanage. It was meant to be a temporary arrangement, but *tempus fugit*, and she loved working there with the children. Each had a tragic story to tell, each dealt a bad hand by fate, but never a day went by without one of them bringing a smile to her face. Sometimes she wondered how they came to be there, abandoned without love by their parents, then the fact that she too had done the same to her own child would hit her, and her mood would change from happiness to melancholy. Aunt Agnes' letter had exacerbated her dilemma, and even though she prayed hard for strength and guidance, the sleepless nights, guilt-ridden, continued.

It was a mixed orphanage, with boys and girls of all classes and creeds, usually from age two upwards. They were taught in a Catholic ethos up to their teens, when, if not adopted, would be placed for work outside in the real world. At weekends, visitors would come. Some children never had any visitors, and this saddened her. And when she saw the looks on the faces of the lucky ones, after their visitors had left, she felt even sadder. In particular, she worried about the girls, afraid that if left too long in the artificial life of the orphanage, they would end up on the streets, prey to the pimps of the Devil.

In the six months after the arrival of the letter, a new child arrived at the orphanage. This child was different, in being only a few months old. And beautiful, having a mop of frizzy dark hair, brown eyes, and brown skin. A veritable living doll. She was the youngest child ever taken into the orphanage, and Nancy took her under her wing, literally, and even had her sleeping in her room at night. With hindsight, this may not have been a wise thing, but she'd become besotted with the child, whose name was Anne. Anne's mother had lived in Ireland, in the midlands, and had several other children. She'd worked in a local hospital, where, after an affair with a foreign student doctor, Anne was born. Her mother refused to take Anne home because of her skin colour, that being the way it was in Ireland at that time, and eventually Anne ended up in the Manchester orphanage.

Nancy's spirits rose after Anne's arrival. Even Sister Martha commented on that fact, and allowed her to continue minding Anne exclusively. This continued for a few years, until it was approaching the time when Anne would be put into a class with other pupils. It was then Nancy hatched her plan. As she was allowed to bring Anne outside the orphanage for walks, she had a letter stating she was the child's guardian. In fact Nancy liked to think she was her Guardian Angel.

On the day in question, Anne was dressed in her best Sunday clothes, a pink coat, cardigan, and black bag and shoes, while Nancy wore her lay clothes. Placing her suitcase on the floor, she knelt in front of Anne.

"We're going for a little holiday, Anne."Nancy said, settling the pink bow on Anne's frizzy mop.

"Where we going mammy?" Anne beamed.

"To Ireland, on a big boat. It's very green in Ireland and full of flowers and animals. You'll like it there."

"Yes I will, I will." Anne said, hugging her rag doll.

They took a taxi to the bus terminus, waiting an hour for the bus to Holyhead. On the way, Nancy pointed out the animals in the fields, telling Anne there were many more like these in Ireland. Anne smiled, hugging her doll and gazing out, and Nancy was happy and sure that everything would work out for them. Silently she prayed it would, believing it was God's will.

They reached Holyhead, shrouded in mist and damp, two hours before their boat sailed. Seagulls wheeled and shrieked about, scaring Anne. Entering a dingy cafeteria they had tea and scones, before joining the queue for tickets. When they reached the ticket office, the man there seemed to glare at Nancy awhile before excusing himself, and exiting the office. Within minutes, he'd returned, accompanied by a security man and a policeman. They ushered Nancy and Anne into an adjoining office, and Nancy felt the eyes of the irritated queue scrutinising her as she passed by, as if she was a criminal.

In the office, Anne was taken away by a female officer, while Nancy was accused of attempting to illegally abduct a minor. She pointed out that she was Anne's guardian, and only taking her for a short holiday, but as she spoke she knew the dreams she had for both Anne and her were gone, vanished like the mist on a river on a hot summer morning. It transpired the taxi driver had informed the orphanage of their trip to the bus terminus, after the staff had discovered they were both missing. The police had quickly tracked them to Holyhead, waiting there until they were spotted. They certainly stood out in a crowd, a white woman with a black child.

The Police officer was polite, but asked if Nancy knew what she had done was a criminal offence. She replied no, that it was not, that what she had done was an act of love, and the will of God, *and* He had told her to do it. The policeman paused, scratched his head and peered at her for a while, before asking if she had any medical problems, particularly in the area of mental health. Nancy suggested he speak to her Superior, Sister Martha. He said he would.

When he left the room, Nancy started praying, it was all she could think of doing. Returning about an hour later, the policeman said no charges would be made on this occasion, although he was not happy with that decision. Nancy was to be taken back to the orphanage in a police car, and report to Sister Martha. When she enquired about Anne, he said she had already been taken back. Under her breath she thanked God for delivering her from a prison cell and worse, but felt a tremor in her bones at how it might go with Sister Martha. She dried her tears as she left.

When Nancy later entered Sister Martha's office, the old nun was already seated, her walking stick propped against the desk. A younger nun stood by her side. Sister Martha introduced her as Sister Veronica, who would soon be taking over from her, as she was about to retire. The younger nun had a narrow face and lips, and after nodding condescendingly towards Nancy, excused herself, and left the room. Nancy wasn't sorry to see her go, and had a bad feeling about their future relationship.

"I wanted to speak to you alone, Sister Brendan. I feel I understand you better than anyone."

"Oh please forgive me for what I did today, Sister Martha. I don't know what possessed me. It was a crazy thing to do. I am truly sorry for all the trouble I've caused you. And thank you for getting me released."Nancy dabbed her eyes as she spoke.

"In a way, I'm as much to blame. I should have known better, letting you become too close to that child. Never let your heart rule your head was always one of my credos. But I saw the difference in you when she came into your life, how the sparkle returned to your eyes, and I did nothing to break the spell. I failed in my job, may God forgive me." The old nun sighed, clasping her fist to her forehead.

Nancy wondered then if Sister Martha's generosity to her with Anne was to atone for not informing her of Aunt Agnes' letter about the adoption.

"What happened was entirely my fault, Sister Martha. *Mea maxima culpa.* You have always been so kind and understanding since I joined the Order. In fact, you seemed to read my mind better than anyone. Almost as if you had a sympathetic streak."

"Yes, you're right Sister Brendan, I did have a special interest in your life, from the beginning. You were always like a daughter to me. I somehow saw myself in you, just as I had been when I was young." The old nun leaned over and took Nancy's hand in hers, her face wrinkling in a frown, her eyes moistening, something Nancy had never witnessed before.

"I don't understand, what do you mean?"Nancy asked.

"I mean I understood exactly how you felt. To be a mother and have your baby taken away from you."

"But how could you have known all about that?"

"Because I too was a mother, before I joined the Order." The old nun's eyes had a faraway look. A tear slid down her cheek.

"You mean your baby was adopted too?"Nancy asked, shocked.

"No, she died at birth, in a Mother and Child home in Manchester. She's buried in an unmarked grave there. I used visit the grave every week in the beginning. That's how I understood how you felt." She dabbed her eyes with a hanky, and released Nancy's hand.

"Oh, I'm so sorry." Nancy said.

"Don't be sad Sister Brendan, that's all in the past. Life goes on. We all have a cross to bear in our lives. Mine was my baby dying, yours maybe having your baby adopted. We must now deal in the present and the future. You must now leave the orphanage and return to your previous teaching position in the convent. You must have no contact with Anne in the future. You understand this is for your own good, and I always have that in my heart. I will pray for your intentions."Sister Martha rose, took her stick, and went slowly towards the door, paused there, turned and spoke.

"You should think about a short break somewhere abroad, Sister Brendan. I will be retiring soon. Better to do it before that happens, may God bless you." Sister Martha then tapped her way out the door.

It was the last time Nancy saw Sister Martha. And she never saw Anne again. That broke her heart. She eventually convinced herself it was God's will, and for *her* own good.

Chapter 6

Il Cenacolo

In Milan, all roads led to the *Duomo*. Following one, Nancy stopped at a cafe on the edge of the *Piazza Duomo*, shadow-split by the slanting morning sun. Ensconced beneath an umbrella she relaxed, breathing easily, happy to have left the Manchester rains behind her, taking in the scene, dressed anonymously and modestly in civilian clothes. Sister Martha would hardly have approved of her dress code, she mused, but she was in Italy now, far from the convent's strictures.

She ordered coffee, and as she waited, gazed in awe at the Gothic masterwork on the outside of the cathedral, with its mass of spires, saints, and gargoyles. An army of architects and sculptors had apparently been involved in the *Duomo's* construction over five centuries, she'd read. She had a problem with such buildings, deeming them an edifice to an ego, and wondered if Jesus would have approved. But she had to admit it was impressive, towering proud above the *Piazza*.

Sipping her coffee, her mind went back to the day before, when she'd first visited the *Duomo*. After praying awhile at a side altar, she'd rambled around the vast cathedral, with its maze of giant pillars. But it was another item there that had intrigued her. Carved along the floor, in black and white marble were the signs of the Zodiac. She wondered what they were doing there. The signs seemed amiss in a religious building. What was their meaning? She shook her head, baffled.

The waiter's arrival to re-fill her coffee cup cut through her reverie. The *Duomo's* magnificence, the busy chatter, the stylish dress of the thronging people, brought an inner peace she'd not felt in ages. Sister Martha knew best, and Nancy was glad she'd taken her advice about taking a break before the old nun retired. Sister Veronica would then be in charge, worse luck. That was something she felt uneasy about.

Poor Sister Martha, she reflected, all along she'd been on my side and I'd been unaware of it. She sighed in disbelief at her own lack of appreciation, recalling her Superior's final words written to her before she left for Milan. Be careful dear Sister Brendan, evil lurks everywhere. Satan stalks in many guises. The difference between good and evil is only skin deep. Scratch the surface, and evil may emerge. Be careful. A flock of pigeons fluttered nearby. She threw some bread crumbs to them, and smiled as they fought over them.

Before leaving Manchester, in the same note she'd got from Sister Martha, the old nun said she was glad to hear Nancy had heeded her counsel to take a short break, as she expected to be retired by the time she returned. Sister Martha also stated she'd visited Milan many times, and gave a list of places to visit. But there was one place *not* to miss. *Leonardo da Vinci's* masterpiece, The Last Supper(*il Cenacolo*), in the church of *Santa Maria delle Grazie*. It had to be booked in advance, and Nancy was to look out for the 16-sided lantern in the church, because of the significance of the lantern in the founding of the Presentation Order. She had a ticket to see it at four that afternoon. That gave her enough time beforehand to visit the museum of the *La Scala* Opera House, a ten minute walk from the *Duomo*. She called for the bill.

Leaving the cafe, Nancy sauntered across the piazza, entering the *Galleria Vittorio Emanuele 2*, resplendent with its enormous iron-and-glass dome, strolling by the fantastically expensive shops and famous restaurants, before exiting onto the *Piazza della Scala*.

Inside the famous *Teatro* she stood beneath the crystal chandelier with its multitude of lamp bulbs, breathless at the architectural beauty of the place. La Scala was the Mecca for all operatic singers and composers, she knew. Maria Callas was her favourite singer, beautiful in looks and voice. The place abounded with pictures of the diva, and the many other musical legends.

The opera *La Boheme* was playing currently, with Pavarotti starring, but was booked out. She fumed, it was her all-time favourite, and she regretted not checking and booking it in advance, thinking she might never get the chance again. Leaving the museum she sighed, glancing at her watch. It was time to head for *Il Cenacolo*.

Outside the *Teatro* she boarded a vintage tram, which left her near the church of *Santa Maria delle Grazie*. With half an hour to spare, she entered the church, viewing the lantern, praying for Sister Martha, thanking her for watching over her, and guiding her to such a wonderful place.

Near to four o'clock, a crowd had assembled at the entrance, and a guide led them into the refectory to view *da Vinci's* five-hundred-year old fresco. They had fifteen minutes to see the masterpiece, before moving on to view the other items on display.

"One of you shall betray me." That was the moment portrayed. The words tore into her heart, sending a shock through her as if Jesus was accusing *her*, instead of one of his disciples. The effect on them was etched in their faces, and she was stunned that a wall painting, much damaged over the years, including bombing in WW2, could still carry such power.

"Impressive, isn't it. Powerful scene, amazing use of space and perspective, and stunning use of the signs of the Zodiac." A man had sidled up beside her.

She turned to look at him. Medium build, middle-aged, piercing grey in the eyes, greying at the temples, wearing a Panama hat and white jacket. A moustache crowned his smiling lips. His voice seemed to have a trace of an Irish accent, she thought, but she wasn't sure. He was a handsome man.

"Yes, utterly." She replied and turned back, continuing to look up at the fresco.

"Your first time?" He asked.

"Yes."

"I'll leave you then to savour every moment. I've been here many times."He said, bowed, and drifted away into the crowd. His voice *did* have an Irish twang, she reckoned.

About a half hour later, as they filed out the door, he was back again at her side.

"Pardon me for being a nuisance, but I thought you were from Ireland when you spoke earlier. I could be wrong but I hope I'm right, but one way or another I'd like to buy you a coffee, as I'm from Ireland myself, and we're supposed to be friendly to strangers. I'm Martin Maher by the way, they call me Martino over here, and I do hope you enjoyed *Cenacolo Vinciano*."As he spoke he grinned and removed his hat, bowing in mock chivalry.

She hesitated, thinking what harm could there be in having coffee with a stranger, especially one from her own country. And after two days on her own she felt the need to speak to someone.

"I'm Nancy Hackett, and you're right I am Irish, and yes I *was* mesmerised by The Last Supper. Yes thanks, it would be nice to have a coffee and chat with someone from back home, but I must be back at my hotel by six."*No need to tell him I'm a nun. Keep it simple.*

"Oh, so you have an evening appointment?"

"Yes."*No need to tell him either of my evening prayers every night at six o'clock.*

"Pity, but don't worry, I'll have you home to your hotel in time."He said, beaming.

Over coffee she learnt he was from Kilkenny, and had been in Milan five years, spoke Italian, and worked in the *Ospedale Maggiore*.

"Oh, is that the one where Hemingway was hospitalised when he was young and an ambulance driver in the war?"

"The very place." He nodded.

Time slipped by, agreeably, and she enjoyed his company. He asked if she liked Milan, and she replied positively, her only regret being she hadn't booked a seat in advance for *La Scala* Opera House. Her favourite opera was playing, she said.

True to his word, he hired a taxi and had her walking into the hotel as the church bells tolled six o'clock. She was about to bless herself, remembering the Angelus bells, but decided not to. As she turned to wave goodbye, he left the taxi, bounded up the steps, and spoke.

"Say Nancy, I'm working all day tomorrow in the hospital, but I'd love to take you to dinner tomorrow evening. There's a very nice place called *"Pietro's"* near the *Duomo*. I'm sure you'd like it." As he spoke, his hand rested on her shoulder.

After wavering a few moments she agreed, nodding her head. She told him she had booked a trip to *Lake Como* the next day, returning at four o'clock.

"Great, pick you up then at eight *domani sera. Ciao.*"

As she turned, his hand slipped off her shoulder, and slid down the side of her body, brushing her gently. She started, as a tingle shot through her bones, and she wondered if his touch was deliberate or accidental. Later she reckoned it was accidental, that life in the convent had made her far too fastidious.

The trip to Como, rounded off by a cruise around the lake, was pure delight. Majestic mountains framed by an azure sky, lake-waters mirroring mountains, sun-splashed, bordering ancient villas bedecked with bougainvillea, breathtaking to behold. Heaven must be like this, she thought, entranced.

Later she visited *La Rinacente* store in the Galleria, and bought a dress. White, laced, knee length, modest neckline. The girl in the shop complimented her when she tried it on, and she felt good. A tremor of excitement tingled through her. Hold on, she thought, viewing herself in the full-length mirror, don't get carried away, you're just a nun on holiday, and you've taken a vow of chastity, so you're not supposed to feel any other way. She calmed down then, thinking it's just dinner with a person from Ireland, nothing more. She paid for the dress, and a matching pair of shoes, and left the store.

Pietro's restaurant was down a winding side street off the *Piazza Duomo*. It was popular and packed, and they sat outside in the warm night air, sipping glasses of *Chianti* from *Montepulciano*, perusing the menu. He asked her how Como was, and she replied, beautiful beyond words, her eyes glazing as she remembered the beauty of the lake.

She ordered a jug of water with the meal. Swallows dipped and ducked in the dying sky. Later, as she gazed at the winking stars mottling the night sky, worshipping a saucer-shaped moon, she thought God must be approving. The owner, *Pietro*, was known to Martin and came to their table as they ate, serenading them on his mandolin. Martin informed her it was a Neapolitan tune, *Core Ingrato*. She remembered it well. Ungrateful heart.

Martin proved a charming host, prone to showing off his fluency in Italian, and the night flew. After the meal, they ordered coffees and relaxed. She'd gone easy on the wine, drinking lots of water.

"I must say you look stunning Nancy. *Bellissima*. A veritable Botticelli beauty. New dress?" He spoke, lifting a glass to his lips.

"Yes, it's a one-day old dress. I'm afraid I hadn't come prepared for being entertained somewhere as nice as this."

"I like this place, but there are many similar restaurants in Milan. Still, it's one of my favourites. *Pietro* is a charming host."

"Yes Martin, you must be an expert on Milan after five years?"

"I wouldn't say that. By the way you can call me Marty. My Irish friends do. It's Martino to the Italians. Can I call you Nancy?"

"Sure Marty, why not? Tell me, what part of Kilkenny are you from?"

"Graiguenamanagh. It's a beautiful place. Seven-arched

bridge over the river Barrow. And you?"

"Bagenalstown, it's also on the banks of the Barrow. No bridge, only a drawbridge, but we're Barrow cousins, you might say."She said, laughing.

"Yes, that's a good one Nancy, I like it. *Buono*. My star sign is Scorpio the scorpion, by the way." He raised his glass again.

"Is it? Mine is Pisces the fish."

"Really? So we're both water-creatures. I'm supposed to be loving but moody, jealous, enigmatic, volatile. *And* controlling. Never take no for an answer. Pisceans are compassionate and understanding, and into healing and helping others. They're also talented, artistic, and musical. We're also supposed to be attracted to each other, I'm glad to say."He smiled as he spoke.

"You seem to be well versed in astral matters. Maybe you can tell me the connection between *da Vinci's* Last Supper, and the Zodiac signs?" She asked, remembering his words at *Il Cenacolo*.

"Good question Nancy. *Da Vinci* spent many years preparing his masterpiece. Twelve Apostles. Twelve signs of the Zodiac. Divided the Apostles into groups of three, for the four seasons. Jesus, in the centre is the sun. He also used the signs to portray the character of each apostle in the masterwork. A stroke, or strokes, of genius. It's one of the reasons I tend to re-visit it, to study these details. I'm interested in these things you know. "He seemed animated as he spoke.

"That's fascinating. So perhaps you can also explain about the Zodiac signs on the floor of the *Duomo*?"

"Well, as much as I can, Nancy. On the floor of the *Duomo* is located what was once the largest sundial in the world. Through a hole in the roof a light shines daily, focussing on each sign, at exactly the time of year it refers to. For example on the 19th February each year the light will shine the image of Pisces the fish on the floor. Ditto for the Equinoxes. It's very accurate. Many in Milan set their watches by it."

"Amazing, but it hardly seems appropriate for a place of worship."

"*Correcto*. Some say it has satanic overtones. There's a lot of that going on in Italy, even today. The *Duomo* goes back a long way."His face was now solemn, and his eyes had a faraway look.

"I suppose, strange, I never knew. And are your family still living there, in Graiguenamanagh? I hope you don't think I'm prying?"

"No I don't, not at all Nancy. I'm an only child. My mother lives there alone. People watch out for her. I get home as often as I can to visit her. And tell me, what about yourself?" He asked, draining the dregs of his wine glass.

"My mother died some years back, and my father lives at home with my younger brother."

"It's good to have someone living at home, someone you can visit. By the way, I have a little surprise for you." He took an envelope from his inside pocket.

"Something nice? Oh good, I love surprises." Her face lit up, as she spoke.

"I hope you like it." Smiling, he handed her the envelope.

She tore it open, excited. Inside were two tickets to *La Scala*, for a private box, dated for the following evening. She gasped with joy.

"Oh Marty, that's wonderful, but it's too much. I don't know how to thank you."

"It's nothing, a gift from one of my *Mafiosa* friends at the theatre. I take it you're free, it's my pleasure, I'd like nothing better than the pleasure of your company there." As he spoke, he reached over and took her hands in his, lifted them to his lips, and kissed them.

"Yes, I'm free, I wouldn't miss it for anything, but I insist on paying my way."She replied, elation filling her.

"Nonsense my dear Nancy, we don't do it like that in Italy. Maybe in Holland, but not here."

"Ok then, I'll have to go shopping again, but I'm not complaining."

"Good, that's settled, care for a nightcap?"He asked, calling the waiter.

She declined, as he ordered a *grappa* for himself, at the same time releasing her hands. As he did so, his hand rested momentarily on her thigh, and he winked as he squeezed her leg, at least she thought he did, before he removed his hand. She was too excited about the tickets for the opera, to think anything more about it then.

"You must have had many suitors over the years, Nancy?" He asked, sipping his drink.

She guessed he was alluding to her ringless fingers.

"Of course Marty, but I'm very happy in my solitary life. And you?"*No harm in a little peccadillo.*

"Exactly the same as you, I'm happy with my own company. And tell me Nancy, if you don't mind, what do you work at?"

"I'm a teacher. And yourself?"

"I help people in the hospital."

"In what way?"She asked.

"In different ways, a bit of everything. Tell me, have you ever been to Venice?"

"No, it's my first time in Italy."

"It's the most romantic of places. Casanova lived there. When do you return to Ireland?"

"In three days." *It was a lie, she left in two days. She didn't know why she blurted out the lie, maybe she was afraid of the unknown.*

"It might be possible to visit Venice, a fleeting visit, it's only a few hours by train, you never know. Anyway thank you Nancy for a lovely evening. I'll call a taxi." He stood up, snapping his fingers for the waiter.

This time he didn't accompany her back to her hotel, saying he lived near the restaurant, and would walk home. As she turned to enter the taxi he muttered *Ciao Bambina, Domani Sera* at six, and kissed her lightly on the cheek, and she felt his hand slide down her back as she bent to sit down.

Later in the bathroom, she examined her body, but found no mark on her thigh. I must be paranoid after all the years in the convent, she thought. After saying her prayers, she tossed and turned throughout the night with excitement, visions of *La Scala* bedevilling her mind.

Chapter 7

Opera

The girl in *La Rinacente* store recognised her. Madam is going to the opera? The girl beamed. *Benissima.*

Nancy nodded.

"And what does Madam wish to wear this time?"

"Something nice, but inexpensive, and modest." As she spoke, Nancy worried Sister Veronica might make a song-and-dance about her expenses when she returned to Manchester. She made sure to keep the receipts.

Eventually she bought a blue, sleeveless, high necked, knee-ength dress, with matching high-heels. She couldn't remember wearing high-heels since going to the McGrath Hall in Bagenalstown, donkey's years earlier. The girl assured her she would look *fantastica*, and escorted her to the door. As she left the store she felt uplifted. God was good. The sun shone in the Piazza. People were smiling.

Clutching her shopping bag, she strolled across to the *Duomo,* joined the queue, and entered. Inside in the coolness she prayed, her daily breviary, before seeking out the star signs, embedded in the floor. She found the one for Pisces, then Scorpio. Her eyes were glued to the icons for several minutes. During her studies she'd learned that astrology was perceived as satanic, and in contravention of the First Commandment *"Thou shall not worship false Gods."* How could the Church allow such signs in one of its foremost buildings? It didn't make sense. Bewildered, she shook her head as she left for the hotel, excitement mounting, images of *La Scala and La Boheme* building in her mind.

That afternoon Marty rang. He'd had a difficult day and felt wrung-out, but was looking forward to seeing her again, and *La Boheme*. In that order, he said. He'd booked a pre-theatre dinner at six, near the theatre, and would pick her up at a quarter to six. He said he'd go easy on the drink in case he fell asleep during the opera. She laughed, replying nobody goes asleep during *La Boheme*, and if *he* did, she'd disown him. *Ciao bambina*, see you later, he'd replied.

A while later, she decided to try on her new dress and shoes, and entered the bathroom. Yes, I do like it, I hope he does, though I'll probably never wear it again, she murmured, as she surveyed herself in the full-length mirror. Yes, blue did suit her, the dress fitted like a glove, and was not revealing.

The restaurant was expensive but convenient. Everyone there seemed glamorous, sophisticated, and dressed for the opera. The fashion was spectacular. She gasped at the style of the ladies' dresses. Money seemed to be no object.

She felt like Cinderella. But Marty was charming, her prince, swearing she was the belle of the ball. Beauty is skin deep, he said, you can't buy it, you either have it or you haven't got it. You *do* have it Nancy, by the way.

Bellissima, he said, smiling, pecking her on the cheek. You must have had too much wine, she said, laughing. It flashed through her mind that he'd finished off the bottle of Chianti with the meal, while she'd had only one glass. Still, he'd been so generous, and he'd had a rough day.

The booth was for two people, private, in a prime position, with entry by a door at the back. She squeezed the programme in her hands in anticipation, as the curtain went up. Soon she was lost in the music and tragic story of love and loss in Bohemian Paris. Pavarotti was in his prime, his voice perfection.

There were two intervals. During the first, many strolled about the foyer, holding champagne flutes. Marty said it would be a sin not to do the same on such an occasion, and went to the bar, returning with a glass in each hand. Who am I to disagree? She thought, sipping the sparkling, fizzy liquid, enthralled by the atmosphere all around her.

Back in their box, she again became immersed in the brilliance of the music and singing. In the middle of "*Musetta's Waltz*", she felt his hand resting on hers. Initially she ignored it, her mind transported to another place. When, after several minutes, he made no effort to remove it, she lifted it and placed it in his lap. As she did so, she saw him smile at her and wink, and she smiled back, apologetically.

Soon the second interval arrived, and they sat at a table in the bar beneath a glittering chandelier. Marty produced a small bottle of champagne and two glasses, uncorked the bottle and filled the glasses. They toasted each other, declaring it a wonderful night. A *bella notte*, Marty said. She sipped her glass, deciding it would be her last drink.

"I'm popping out to the ladies, Marty, leave some for me." She said, thinking the break would give her less drinking-time.

"Ok Nancy, but don't be too long or it'll all be gone." He laughed, sipping his drink.

When she returned there was a brimming glass on the table.

"Down the hatch Nancy, the bell has gone, we've only a few minutes left before the next Act." He said, his glass empty in his hand.

She took a mouthful. It tasted good, different from her earlier glass, but just right for such an occasion, she reckoned. As she gulped the remains of her glass, she saw that Marty had consumed the rest of the bottle. She wondered if he drank a lot. Maybe it's the climate, she mused, but he certainly has champagne tastes. She left the empty glass on the table, and they rushed back to the auditorium.

The Third Act tugged her heartstrings, Mimi's health deteriorating, and Rodolfo having abandoned her. The champagne had mellowed her. She was so lost in a beautiful aria, she hardly noticed him putting his hand on her knee. Or a few minutes later, when he tugged her dress above her knee. Or a few minutes later as his fingers inched up her leg. Behave yourself, she hissed as she pushed his hand away and smoothed her dress. When she glared at him, his face was focussed on the stage, as if unaware that anything had happened. She turned again to the stage.

***

Next morning she was dreaming of a giant chandelier sparkling and swaying above her head as she awoke to the glare of the sun, dazzling into her room. She felt hot and sticky, her head throbbing. Then she remembered an earlier dream. It was like a mixture of Cinderella, Beauty and the Beast, and Phantom of the Opera. Memories of the opera the previous night then shot into her head. But she had no memory of returning to the hotel.

She gazed about. Her clothes were strewn about the room. The blue dress was draped over a chair. Her shoes lay at the door. She saw then that she was wearing her under-garments in the bed. Strange, she always wore a nightdress. She checked beneath her pillow. Her nightdress was there. And she always tidied away her clothes. She stood up, feeling dizzy, a sick taste in her mouth. I must have drunk too much, I must be hungover, she muttered, grimacing.

She ran to the bathroom, a wave of nausea hitting her, and retched into the toilet, before flushing it to clear the vomit. She stared into the mirror and gasped. Her face was wan, her hair tousled, streeling down her neck. She felt and looked wretched. And all for a few glasses of champagne, she fumed. Dear God, I hope I didn't make a show of myself after the opera. And Marty was so kind and generous. Dear God, forgive me. She blessed herself.

Afterwards, Nancy stood awhile in front of the full-length mirror, inspecting her body for bruises, afraid she might have fallen somewhere. She spotted a small bruise on one thigh, then another, larger one on the other, and thought she must have stumbled into the furniture. Somehow she felt unclean, and had guilt pangs, as if she'd let herself down in some way. After a lingering bath, she emerged from the bathroom, feeling better. Picking her dress from the floor, she noticed it had been slightly soiled and wondered if this had been caused by her being sick earlier in the night.

She dressed and tidied her room, said her morning prayers, then packed her suitcase for the flight to Manchester that evening. She remembered she'd told Marty she was leaving the next day, but had no regrets about that lie. She just wanted to get back to the sanctuary of her convent, without seeing or speaking to anyone. She decided to go for a last walk around Milan before taking a taxi to *Bergamo* airport, hoping it would clear her head.

As she left the hotel, the concierge called to her, waving an envelope. In it was a message from Marty. He said he hoped she was feeling better. After the opera, he said she'd felt faint in the taxi. He'd escorted her to the door of her hotel room, before leaving. Luckily it hadn't happened during the performance, he continued, although she had complained of feeling dizzy before the end. It must have been the drink he reckoned, as he too had suffered later that night, and he apologised if it had made him misbehave in any way. He hoped she'd enjoyed the night, as he had, in spite of the ending. He wished to see her that night, if she felt better, as it was her last night in Milan, and he gave his phone number. She stuffed the envelope in her handbag, and left the hotel.

Outside in the glare, she put on her sunglasses, and walked around the *Duomo Piazza*. One last time, she muttered, as she entered the *Duomo*. After praying she surveyed the star signs again and left, still puzzled by their significance.

Afterwards, at a café on the edge of the *Piazza*, she sat outside under an umbrella, and ordered a bottle of water. She took Marty's note from her bag and studied it again. She knew she had deceived him by not telling him she was a nun, and also by saying she was returning to Manchester a day later than she had booked. He had been a gentleman, and made her trip so enjoyable. But she could not meet him again to continue the deception, deciding it was too complicated. Instead, she would leave a note at the hotel later, explaining she had been unwell and had left for home a day earlier. Keep it simple.

In the afternoon, she visited a museum near the *Duomo*, and on leaving saw a sign for *Ospedale Maggiore*. She recalled Marty worked there. On impulse, she decided to visit him and say farewell, face-to-face. Face the music and dance, not run and hide. But she would still not divulge that she was a nun.

Inside the hospital, she went to the information desk.

"*Parla Inglese?*" She asked the thin, stooped, old man behind the desk.

"*Si, un piccolo.*" He smiled.

"I would like to see Martino Maher."

"Ah, Padre Martino. The Padre, he is occupied all day at a funeral."

"You called him Padre. Is he a priest? What is his job in the hospital?" She asked, startled.

"*Si,* he is a priest. His work here is that of a Chaplain. He will talk to people who have had a loss, and also he performs the work of a priest, saying the Mass, and performing other duties. Shall I give him *un messaggio?*"

"No thank you, I'll see him another time." She dashed from the building, shocked.

Back at the *Duomo Piazza*, she sat outside a café, ordered a coffee, her mind reeling, and reviewed the revelation. Marty a priest? He had deceived her, just as she had deceived him. But why were they both either ashamed or afraid to admit what they were? It didn't make sense, God knows. Anyway, it probably explained why he was middle-aged, unmarried, and living in Milan. And she had been worried that he might have a drink problem. If she had known he was a priest, she probably wouldn't have lied about her return date, *or* about being a nun. She would have trusted him more.

Anyway, there was no going back now, she reckoned, better to let the hare sit. She would write to him when she got back to Manchester, and tell him the truth. Maybe they could still be friends, pen friends. She rose, decision made, mind clear, paid the bill, tipped the waiter, and headed for her hotel. The taxi would arrive in one hour. On the way back, she saw a small church, and stopped to pray. Prayer always made her feel better.

Later that evening, as the plane circled above Milan, Nancy looked out the window, down on the city to see the majestic *Duomo* diminishing in the distance. Her Italian interlude had ended. She was glad she had come, but she was also glad to be returning to Manchester, to the safety and sanctity of the cloister. She would miss the ancient attraction and glitter of Italy, but not the champagne. In a strange way, she would miss Marty too. He made her feel important.

She smiled, her lips moving in silent prayer. She worried about how she would get on with Sister Veronica, and said a prayer it would go well. Sister Martha had been like a mother to her, but somehow she felt things would not be the same from now on. Perhaps she had crossed some sort of Rubicon by coming to Milan, but maybe that was what Sister Martha had in mind for her to do, when she'd suggested the visit? She continued praying silently, rosary in hand.

Chapter 8

Chastisement

Back in Manchester, Sister Veronica *had* taken command. Sister Martha had already been despatched to the Order's retirement home in Scotland and was now history. Nancy was summoned to a mid-day meeting with Sister Veronica, on the morning after her return from Milan. She's not wasting any time, Nancy muttered, as she trod the polished parquet floor down the corridor to the Head Abbess' office.

On the way she felt a knot tighten in her stomach. Sister Veronica had a reputation. A brilliant mathematician, she ruled with a rod-of-iron. Even the parents of the pupils were in awe of her. Not someone to cross. Inside, Nancy's nerve-ends jangled. Outside, in the cloister, the bells tolled noon.

She knocked softly on the door, and entered. The light inside was dim, odour of incense wafting about. A wooden crucifix hung on one wall. Through a stained-glass window, a shaft of sunlight lit the dust motes in the air, and shone on a statue of the Virgin Mary, giving it a celestial aura. A tall, elderly nun pored over a file on her desk, reading glasses perched on the end of her aquiline nose. The nun looked up, thin -faced with thin lips.

"Ah, Sister Brendan, please be seated." Sister Veronica spoke, gesturing to the chair in front of her desk, and continued.

"I trust you had an enjoyable break. Milan is a place I've always wanted to visit. But work has always got in the way, unfortunately. Perhaps someday, who knows? I want to apprise you of changes in your absence. I've spoken collectively to everyone, while you were away, about my objectives, and that of the Presentation Order here in Manchester, which I am honoured and proud to lead.

People say I can be hard, but I want to assure you that beneath this habit I'm wearing, I *do* have a heart. That is, as long as all rules and procedures are obeyed. Those who break the rules will be chastised. I believe Sister Martha may have been a little lax in this area. But things have changed, I trust you appreciate that? Would you like some water?" The older nun asked, pausing to fill a glass on a tray before her. Her voice seemed as cold to Nancy's ears as the water she was now pouring.

"Y..yes, thank you." Nancy nodded, intimidated, uneasy inside.

The elderly nun took the jug, and filled another glass, placing it carefully on a coaster on the desk.

"We don't want to wet the desk, do we?" Sister Veronica asked rhetorically, a smile slicing her lips.

"N...no." Nancy stammered, lifting the glass to her mouth.

"Well, let's move on Sister Brendan. I've been studying your file. Hmm, it's interesting to say the least. Not the normal type of vocation, I must say. But your inter-personal skills seem exceptional. Good singing voice in the choir too. But then we have this strange incident of you trying to run away with a young girl from the orphanage, and your subsequent banishment to working within the walls of this convent. Have you anything to say now, Sister Brendan, about this matter?" The older nun's left eyebrow arched as she spoke.

Feeling like a criminal in the dock, Nancy replied.

"I *am* truly sorry for what I have done, Sister Veronica. I don't know what came over me when that incident with little Anne occurred. I had a lot of things on my mind then. But that's all in the past. I would dearly love to return to teaching young children. It's what I long to do, and it's what I do well, in spite of everything." As she spoke, Nancy felt a headache welling in her head. It wasn't going well. A bad start. Definitely.

"Yes Sister Brendan, I can see that you *are* repentant, but it *was* a major breach of the Order's rules, and must be punished accordingly. The past is often a precursor of the future. Of course, all chastisements and sufferings in this life must be endured, and offered to God, in atonement for our sins, mustn't they?" The tall nun's eyes were slits of steel as she spoke.

"Y…yes Sister Veronica, of course. I suppose we're all sinners one way or another."

"Yes I agree, but some more than others I'm afraid. I need more time to reflect on your situation. In the meantime you will be restricted to remaining inside the walls of this convent. You will help out in gardening duties, and in organising the choir, until further notice. I will pray for your intentions. I must leave now, as I have a maths lecture at one o'clock." After speaking, Sister Veronica rose, nodding that the meeting had ended.

Trudging back to her room, Nancy felt dejected. The euphoria she'd felt after Milan was gone, evaporated into the ether. It was a new regime, but not *her* type of regime. Maybe things would improve, she reflected, but maybe not. It was going to be difficult, but she'd no choice but to suffer on, and offer it up. Offer it up, she fumed, why do we have to endure so many things in this life, if they're not right, and try to make it right by offering it up to God? The days seemed longer after the meeting. Nancy prayed each night that things would improve.

A week passed, and she was summoned again to Sister Veronica's office. Sister Amelia, a pleasant young nun, gave Nancy the message, warning her that the Head Abbess was in foul humour, winking and saying maybe it was a case of the Monday-morning blues. Nevertheless, as she walked to the office, Nancy felt a twinge of hope inside. Perhaps the old nun might have relented in her attitude.

Inside the office, papers were strewn over the desk. Sister Veronica was glancing at them, and waved her to sit down. After a few minutes, she looked up, scowling.

"Sister Brendan, I've been going through your Milan expenses, and they seem particularly high. Personally, I'm not in favour of such trips, and I will be banning them in future. After all, we take a vow of poverty when we enter the Order. We cannot afford the luxury of such overseas trips, no matter how well-intentioned they are. And they certainly were not part of Nano Nagle's vision for the Presentation Order. I have receipts and invoices here for two dresses, and I also have the dresses in question here beside me. The blue dress, in particular, seems very expensive. Perhaps you could explain?" After she spoke, the elderly nun's lips curled in anticipation, as she leaned back in her leather swivel-chair.

"I…..I….I can explain." Nancy stammered, taken aback.

"I'm sure you can, dear Sister Brendan. Today, I'm not in any hurry, so please take your time. In fact I've all the time in the world." Sister Veronica's lips were pursed in a smug smile after she spoke, seemingly relishing Nancy's discomfort.

Nancy was furious that someone had searched her room. She'd left the dresses bundled in a bag in her wardrobe, intending to bring them to the dry-cleaners. Maybe it was the cleaning lady who found them, she wondered. Or was it?

"Well…well…I……I met someone in Milan…… in fact he was a priest, an Irish priest, working in a local hospital….he…he asked me out to dinner…..and he bought me tickets for the opera….*La Scala*….he knew how much I liked the opera. I couldn't refuse his hospitality. I didn't have anything suitable to wear. If you think they were inappropriate expenses, I will pay for them from my allowance."

"And the blue dress, was that the one you wore to the opera?" Sister Veronica asked.

"Yes."

"And did you have an enjoyable night?" Sister Veronica appeared to smirk as she spoke.

"Yes, it was most enjoyable."

"Indeed, it appears it was too."The old nun bent over to open a drawer in her desk, pulling out a plastic bag. From it, she pulled a blue, creased dress, and flung it on the desk.

Nancy started, recognising the dress.

"Is this the dress you wore?" Sister Veronica said accusingly.

"Yes, but why do you ask?"

"Because there are stains on the dress. I won't go into any more detail now, but they don't look like food stains, and they do look inappropriate. I will have them analysed. *And* there are two buttons missing from the part of the dress that goes around the neck. Hadn't you noticed? And hadn't you noticed the bruise on your neck, behind your ear? I had, last week, as you left my office. If the man you were with behaved in such a manner, he could hardly have been a priest, could he? And in any case, whoever he was, he obviously didn't meet much resistance to his behaviour, did he?" Sister Veronica said, leering in triumph, leaning across the desk.

"He….he…was a priest…I'm certain of that…and he behaved impeccably. I….I… don't remember too much about the night after the opera, because I became ill. I may have fallen when I returned to my room, I don't remember. I still can't remember, but the bruise may be due to a fall."

"Could there have been drink involved?"The elder nun continued, gloating in triumph.

"N…no, not for me. One, perhaps two, that's all, nothing unusual for such a night in such a place."

"I'm sure, but you did take drink, and it appears your friend *did* indulge himself. Not normal behaviour for a priest, you must agree. But you must accept, based on the evidence there, something untoward did happen." Sister Veronica nodded towards the ruffled dress on the desk, like a lawyer making a winning disclosure in a case.

"N…nothing untoward h…h...happened, you have my word, as God is my judge. I…I was ill that night in my hotel room. That may have caused the stains."Nancy stammered, her voice quivering, feeling like a fly trapped in a spider's web.

"That may be your opinion, Sister Brendan, but the Presentation Order does have certain behavioural standards. I suggest you go and examine your conscience, and if anything occurs to you which might change your recollection of that night, please let me know. In the meantime, I will reflect on the whole matter. It's not a time for quick decisions. I will pray for your intentions, and I will retain the dresses." Sister Veronica rose. Case closed.

Nancy returned to her room, head spinning, tears streaming. From the wall of her room a crucifix looked down. She dried her eyes as she knelt before it, saying five decades of the Rosary, before finishing up with the *Confiteor. I confess to Almighty God…….*

Later, she rose and sat on a chair, facing the crucifix, feeling slightly better, but still reeling from what she'd just experienced. Guilt and remorse overwhelmed her mind, although deep down she felt she'd done no wrong, and was angry. The words from the Last Supper spun through her brain. *One of you will betray me.* Maybe somehow she *had* let Him down, and *had* betrayed Him. She rushed into the bathroom with a hand-mirror. Using it, and looking into the one on the bathroom wall, she saw the bruise behind her ear, faded, but definitely there. Her hair must have covered it before, she realised, when she'd checked her body, the day after the opera. Maybe Sister Veronica was right, she pondered. Still, it could have been from a fall. Then again, maybe not. And a person is innocent until proved guilty, and so far nothing had been proved, everything was conjecture. Sister Veronica could be trying to make an example of her to the rest of the nuns, in order to assert her authority. The older nun's words revolved endlessly like a windmill in her mind.

Slowly she came to realise Marty's behaviour could be in doubt. What if he'd entered her bedroom that night? He'd drink taken, for sure, but he'd always behaved like a gentleman, and he *was* a priest, someone you could trust. If you couldn't trust a priest, then who could you trust? No, he would never behave improperly. Yes, he had put his hand on her leg at the opera, but she put that down to him being carried away by the drama on the stage. No, whatever happened, if indeed anything did happen that night, it was *her* fault. It must have been. Sister Veronica had implied it, and God had forecast she would betray Him. She wished she could remember more about that night, maybe it would come back to her later. She prayed that it would. Marty and Milan were in the past. Sister Veronica was in the present. Nancy knew she needed to figure out what lay ahead for her career, if indeed she had one at all.

Sister Veronica would probably be glad if I quit the Order, she reflected. I'm an embarrassment to her. If I don't quit, she'll make life hell for me. *Her* problem is she's never been a mother. She has no feeling for how a mother feels. Sister Martha did, but she's in the past now. Nancy felt alone now in her world.

In the following weeks, she went through the motions of carrying out her duties in the garden and the choir. She found the gardening exhausting, but still enjoyed the singing and organisation of the choir. And the other nuns couldn't have been nicer, but she knew they knew she was being punished, and inside her spirits dropped, bit by bit.

Sister Veronica had made no contact with her. She felt ostracised, and knew that was her chastisement. Then the sleepless nights returned, and her health regressed into the downward spiral it had been in, before her trip to Milan. Her energy levels dropped, and she took to the bed more and more, and did not want to go out. It was not her norm, and she realised she had to do something before she had a breakdown. She prayed hard for guidance.

One evening after prayer, thoughts of Aunt Agnes' unopened letter came back to her. Maybe she should leave the Order, and try to find her adopted son? Anything would be better than the life she was living now. After retrieving the letter from her wardrobe, she sliced it open, and scanned the contents. The adoptive family name was Robert and Emily Jones, with an address in Salford, Manchester. Great, she thought, realising the address was not too far away. She would take a bus there next weekend. Her spirits soared.

It took her a lot longer to find the house than she'd expected. Red-bricked, semi-detached, in an estate full of red-bricked, semi-detached houses. Middle-class suburbia, in the old, industrial town, with the horse-drawn barges on the canal. Not the image of the song *Dirty Old Town* she used to sing. As she rang the bell, a dog barked inside.

A lady, grey and aged, peered out through the chain-lock on the door. When she saw it was a nun outside, she opened the door. No, the lady had no idea where the Jones family were. They'd bought the house from them fifteen years ago, and she thought Mister Jones worked with a large retailer. It might be worth checking with the Estate Agent involved in the sale. Nancy waited in the hall, while the lady scoured the house for the name of the Estate Agent. Eventually she returned, handing her a business card for Atkinson & Co, in the Salford Docks area. Nancy thanked her and left. The polite lady closed the door and put the latch back on.

***

She returned to the convent, tired and disappointed, fell into bed, and had her best night's sleep for ages. The next day she awoke determined to follow up on her son's whereabouts. At least she had an objective in her life now.

That week a letter arrived from Ireland. It was from her sister Kitty, who said their father Brendan's health had deteriorated. Their brother Nick, a Garda, was now living at home with him. Kitty needed to talk to Nancy face-to – face about the situation, and wondered if she could get leave-of-absence on compassionate grounds, to come home for a few days?

Nancy didn't hesitate to apply for compassionate leave of absence. A week later, Sister Veronica summoned her to her office, saying the application for leave was granted, and she would pray for Sister Brendan's father's recovery. That gave Nancy a fillip. The thought of going home excited her. She wrote immediately to Kitty to say she was on her way. She would deal with her other problems when she returned to Manchester. But before she left for Ireland, she resolved to make one more attempt to contact the family who'd adopted her son.

Chapter 9

A Family Matter

Next day Nancy wrote to her sister Kitty, saying she would return home the following Friday. A few days day before departing, she tried once more to contact the Jones family. A last effort to see my son, she murmured, as she travelled to Atkinson's real estate office in Salford. The salesman, young and blond, appeared surprised to be dealing with a nun. She regretted not wearing ordinary clothes, thinking she was typecast in wearing her habit, thinking that people thought she belonged to an alien world.

"I'm afraid this transaction goes a jolly long way back, m…m..madam, fifteen years to be precise. All our old records are microfiched, and archived in a warehouse in Manchester. Ever so difficult, and *rather* expensive, to go back that far. No guarantee either, I'm afraid, that anything will be found. Might I ask *why* you need this information? "He enquired politely.

She bridled, suspecting he just didn't want to be bothered, there being nothing in it for him, no sale just a time-wasting query.

"You may indeed enquire if you must. The reason is a personal matter, a family matter, and I need to contact them urgently. It's as simple as that."

"Rather, I understand, but it will be ever so awkward going back so far into our archives."

"Yes, I'm sure it will, but I do need to contact that family urgently. And because I'm a nun, I don't have any money. So can you help me, or have I got to talk to somebody else, even to Mister Atkinson himself?"

"No…no need to do that madam, anyway Mister Atkinson is long gone from this business and this world. I'll initiate a search straight away. I must warn you though, it may take some time. *And* there will be no fee, you can be assured of that. And your name is Sister…..?"The young man beamed a smile he normally reserved for paying customers, as he waited, pen poised in hand.

"Brendan."

"I beg your pardon?"The young salesman cleared his throat.

"Brendan, its Sister Brendan."

"But…but that's a man's name."He stammered.

"Correct, it's my father's name. He lives in Ireland. It's an Irish name."

"Of course, well of course, I see, hmmm, but of course. And your address?"

She gave her Irish address, but left feeling she had come to a cul-de-sac. She had no hope that this source would help in tracing her son. She felt he was giving her the polite brush-off. Nancy trudged back to the convent, despondent.

In the middle of packing her bags for Ireland, Nancy was summoned to Sister Veronica's office. She quaked, wondering if the old nun was going to change her mind about granting her compassionate leave. Knocking on the office door, she felt the muscles contract in her stomach. She feared it might be the end of the road, that she might be about to be thrown out of the Order. Sister Veronica was capable of anything.

Do come in, a voice loud and stern commanded. She entered and saw the elderly nun bent over her desk, folding a file. This time Sister Veronica had a thin-lipped smile on her narrow face.

"I've been meaning to speak to you Sister Brendan, since our last talk, but so many things have intervened. So many issues to set right, there's not enough time in the day."The old nun sighed as she spoke.

"I'm sure, Sister Veronica, but I suppose it's all about priorities."

"Indeed. First let me say dear Sister Brendan, you may take leave as long as you wish to take care of your father. It's the kind of work our founder, Nano Nagle, would have approved of. Families first, is part of our ethos. And you and your father must have been very close, seeing you took his name." The old nun smiled, the sunshine through the window glinting off her wire glasses.

So she has a heart after all, Nancy thought, thanking God, sighing with relief, as she replied.

"Thank you Sister Veronica, yes, we were close, very close. You are most understanding, may God reward you."

"And pray tell me, have you had any further recollections of your experiences in Milan?"Sister Veronica asked, head cocked, left eyebrow arched.

"No...no, not so far. But I will keep trying. I pray to God and rack my brains daily."

"Good, please keep doing that. And remember...... be careful in your travels, dear Sister. Evil lurks everywhere. The difference between good and evil is only skin deep. Scratch the surface, and it can emerge. The Devil has many disguises. Beware of wolves in the clothing of sheep. Please be careful. I will pray for your intentions." After speaking, the elderly nun turned away. The meeting was over.

The words of advice resonated in Nancy's mind, and she recalled Sister Martha giving her a similar warning before she went to Milan, and she wondered if it was just something old nuns did.

Returning to her room, Nancy reflected the meeting hadn't gone badly. She could leave for home with a clear conscience. Deep down though, doubt lingered, nagging her mind. Perhaps it might not be all so rosy–in–the–garden in the future with Sister Veronica. Anyway, she'd cross that bridge later, now she was heading home. A surge of excitement went through her, as she restarted packing her bags.

After taking a train from Manchester, she boarded the car-ferry in Holyhead, suitcase in hand, shivering in the dank air. A mist had enveloped the port. Gulls squawked ghost-like, invisible in the gloom. Inside, she sat down in the warmth of the boat lounge. Memories of her aborted trip to Ireland with little Anne came back to her. Sad memories. I need to think about something else, she decided. *Anything*. I better find out what's going on at home, she muttered, buying a copy of *The Irish Independent* in the onboard shop. I've been sheltered from events in Ireland for so long. That has to change, she vowed. She sat back, unfolding the paper, gasping when she saw the headlines.

Bobby Sands dies after 66 day Hunger Strike. Large bold type. Picture of a young man with long hair, unkempt and dirty. A poet and musician. Dead by choice at twenty seven years, nine in prison, leaving a young family behind. She thought Maggie Thatcher's callous comments on his death would surely make him a martyr and a hero, and he a sitting MP for her own Parliament. She read some of his sayings, mesmerised.

"They have nothing in their whole imperial arsenal that can break the spirit of one Irishman who doesn't want to be broken."

"Our revenge will be the laughter of our children."

"Never will they label our liberation struggle as criminal."

"They won't break me because the desire for freedom, and the freedom of the Irish people, is in my heart. The day will dawn, when all the people of Ireland will have the desire for freedom to show. It is then that we will see the rising of the moon."

She read the paper, cover to cover, stunned by the death of one man on 5th August 1981, in the Maze Prison in Northern Ireland. Surely giving his life for a cause, namely political status for him and his fellow-IRA prisoners, would lead to many more espousing that cause. Even though Bobby Sands was a republican, who had used violence in the past, she admired his courage and commitment. He was different. And like Jesus, he'd given his life for a cause. That impressed her. His legacy would last.

Later she dozed off, and woke as the boat passed the Kish Bank lighthouse. On her right lay the cliffs of Howth, with Bray Head looming to the left, burnished by the afternoon sun. Behind, in the distance, the Sugarloaf Mountain stood, brooding like a volcano, a few wispy clouds bearding its summit. Ahead, the jaws of Dun Laoghaire's horseshoe harbour yawned. Inside, she felt excited, a sense of homecoming she'd never felt before. What it meant she wasn't sure, but there was hope in her heart, and she resolved to do her utmost to find out, *and* sort out her life. She twisted the rosary beads between her fingers as her lips moved in silent prayer.

***

"Welcome home, it's great to see you again, my favourite sister. I nearly didn't recognise you, without your habit on." Kitty hugged her as she spoke.

"It's great to be here, you don't know how much. I feel more comfortable dressed like this."

"I'm sure you do, and you look the better of it too. Tonight you're staying with me. I want to fill you in on the situation with Daddy, and all the other gossip in town, and all the other scandals."

They both laughed heartily, as they left the granite-facaded railway station, and headed down Station Road towards Dunleckney in the old Ford Anglia Kitty had inherited from her father. Nancy felt elated at being home again. She and Kitty had always got on well. They understood each other.

"Jim's away all week, nearly every week, a carpenter has to follow the work. He's on a big job in Waterford for six months. He gets home on the weekends. I like the space, I can do other things. The kids are reared, and have fled the nest. We've got the place to ourselves now." Kitty said, grinning, as she drove the car.

Later, after dinner, Kitty produced a bottle of red wine, and offered Nancy a drink. She declined, saying it was too early. Kitty poured herself a glass, at the same time informing Nancy of the imminent closure of the Presentation Convent for girls in Bagenalstown. Talks to amalgamate with the De La Salle Brothers boys' school were ongoing. Nancy was gob-smacked.

"It's a lack of vocations. All the older nuns, like Sister Roberta, have either passed away, or are in nursing homes, and there's no one to take their place. Who'd have thought years ago, of a co-ed school in a place like Bagenalstown? But then why not? Times-they-are a-changin', as the song goes."Kitty explained.

"They are for sure. I must visit the Sisters in the convent, before it's gone forever. I wonder why nobody wants to become a nun nowadays?" As she spoke, Nancy was riven with regret that she'd never returned to work in the convent, and feared that now it was too late. But on reflection she realised that she alone could not have averted its demise. Visions of Sister Roberta's flowers, withering in the Barrow, shot into her mind.

"It's the same for priests. Vocations are on the wane. Maybe if priests were allowed to marry, their wives could be the nuns of the future." Kitty said, giggling, sipping her wine.

"Revolutionary talk, still you never know." As she said the words, Nancy's encounter with the priest in Milan flashed through her mind.

"I want to talk about Daddy. I'm worried sick about him, that's why I wanted you to come home."

"Sure Kitty, go ahead, tell me more, I'm dying to know."

"Well, Daddy's had a good innings up to recently. He got a good pension from the beet factory, and he's coped well since Mammy died. But a couple of months back, he took a stroke, as you know, a mini-stroke they said, and now he's in a wheelchair. I didn't tell you the full story when I wrote to you before, as I didn't want to worry you. He's lost the use of his left arm. He may have other mini-strokes in the future, the doctor says. Not terminal, but each one will make him worse."

"That's terrible. But how is he coping?"

"A carer calls every day. Ditto for Meals-On-Wheels. His mind's gone a bit slow, but he's got good recall. His hearing's not great. The eyesight's ok, and he's still a great reader. We'll all be that way I suppose, someday."

"Perish the thought. What about night time?" Nancy asked.

"That's a difficulty, Nick covers that area. He moved back to live in the house a year ago. By the way, he got promoted to Sergeant in the Guards a few months ago."

"Good for him. I thought he was engaged to a girl from the town, Sheila Hynes, a nurse?"

"He was, no ring flashing though. They lived together for two years in Carlow, while she was studying."

"What happened then?"Nancy asked.

"About a year ago, Sheila Hynes was employed in a hospital in Kilkenny. *She* now lives in Kilkenny City. They broke up, or appeared to, but I believe he still sees her. Anyway, around that time he moved back into the house with Daddy."

"That was great for Daddy."

"In theory yes, but *I* do most of the donkey work in the house. It's like in most Irish families, the daughters always end up looking after the ageing parents. He's a lazy sod. I never minded looking after Daddy, but I was damned if I'd look after Nick as well. He's a lazy pup, and I told him so."

"Why are you so vehement about Nick? Surely he's company for Daddy?" Nancy asked.

"Yes, he is a little, I'll give you that. Daddy thinks so, too, but the reality is, Nick's hardly ever there with him. Being the youngest, he was always a spoilt brat. I still think he has it for that lass in Kilkenny, and he visits her several nights a week. Says he's away on assignments, but I don't believe it. I'm there with Daddy every day, and it's getting to me, me doing all the work in the house."

"You're great Kitty, but you must have something else in mind, to ask me to come home? What can I do, that you're not already doing?"

"Yes, there is something else. Since Daddy had the stroke, Nick's been agitating to have him moved to a Nursing Home. That's the nub of it."Kitty said, frowning.

"Oh, why does he want to do that?" Nancy asked, surprised.

"He says he can't cope. Incontinence, and all that. Believe me it's not that bad. I should know."

"Then *why* is he doing it?"

"I believe he wants Daddy out of the way, so his girl friend can move in, and they can live rent-free in our family home. Squatter's rights. It wouldn't be the first time it's been done."

"I see Kitty, and have you spoken to the rest of the family?"

"Yes, and nobody's happy about what's happening. That's why they asked me to contact you. It's a family matter. Everybody would be happy if you could stay with Daddy, even for a few months. What do you think?"

After a few minutes pause Nancy replied.

"Well, I can see the problem. I would like to help, and if the rest of the family are up for it, so am I. I'll stay as long as I can. Indefinitely, in fact." Nancy said, feeling relieved. She was happy to be home, and now she had a reason to stay. Sister Veronica would not be featuring in her life anymore, thank God. She felt her prayers had been answered.

"You're the best, I do love you, I knew you wouldn't let me down. I'll tell the others. Nick won't like it, but tough shit. Daddy's welfare is more important than him, and it will stop a rift coming in the family." After speaking, Kitty put her arms around her sister, hugged her tight, and continued.

"God I'm so relieved Nancy. But I never asked you about your life in the Order. I always envied you, and I was so proud of you, when I was raising my family, through all the blood, sweat, and tears. And now look at you, with not a wrinkle in your face, and me with the grey streaks showing through my once-lovely mop of red hair."

"And I was proud of you too, Kitty, always envying you, raising such a fine family here on the banks of the Barrow." Nancy said, deciding not to confide in her about trying to trace her son. *Keep it simple*.

They stayed up until the wee, small hours, reminiscing, and Nancy felt happy to be amongst her family again. And she prayed that night for their intentions.

Chapter 10

An End to Something

Nancy was taken aback when her brother Nick opened the door at her father's house. She hadn't seen him in some years, though Kitty had told her all about him. Come in, come in big sister, he exclaimed, wrapping her in a bear hug. After embracing, she pulled herself away and looked at him.

Standing over six foot, curly-blond, blue-eyed, oval-faced, handsome in his Sergeant's uniform. When he smiled, his lips revealed a mouthful of snow-white teeth, matching his hair. When born he'd been named after the Wexford hurling ace Nick Rackard, his father's hero. He'd hurled for Carlow, Kitty had informed her. No mean achievement to hurl for your county, I'm sure Daddy is proud of him, Nancy thought. An Achilles-tendon problem had put paid prematurely to his sporting career. When it came to marrying he'd always said, according to Kitty, why buy the book, when you can join the library? He was thirty three, living at home, and unmarried. Kitty reckoned he was a spoiled get. Nancy wondered how she would get on with him.

"God, it's been so long. Too long, I can't remember when. Look at you now, still pretty as a picture. Let me get you a cup of tea, you know, I'm getting' better at the cooking and the housework, since I started looking after Daddy. He's asleep now, he sleeps a lot these days, you know. Gives me a break, gives me a chance to organise the house. Hold on, while I put the kettle on."He said, doing his best to impress her.

She smiled to herself as he searched in vain for the tea bags.

"Sorry Nancy we've run out of tea. Looks like I need to do some shopping today."He grinned, shrugging his shoulders.

"No problem Nick, I'll be going to the shops later. Tell me all about yourself. I heard you got a big promotion lately."

"Yeah, but even on a Sergeant's wage, it's not easy to make ends meet these days in Ireland."He sighed and shrugged.

"I suppose, but at least you're living rent-free at home." She remembered Kitty had told her he drank and smoked a lot.

"That's true, it helps, but you do like to have your own place."

"So they say, but there's no gain without pain, and you can't have your cake and eat it too. Any romance in your life? Anyone special?"

"Yes, there *was* someone in my life a while back, but it's all over now. She's a nurse in Kilkenny. We're still friends. Still talking." He sighed again.

Nancy thought Nick seemed to regret the affair had ended.

"Good to hear that. And how is Daddy?"

"To tell the truth, Daddy's going downhill slowly. I'm finding it hard-going trying to look after him properly, what with the work pressure I'm under, and the lack of back-up. But he's our Dad, the one and only. I love the bones of him, and I'll always do my best by him. Since Bobby Sands died, we've all been on red alert in the Force. The whole security situation North and South is out the window. And to cap it all, I'm having a visit soon from an Inspector from Kilkenny. About what, I'm not sure. Frankly, it's tough going coping with Daddy and all that."After speaking he paced around the room before sitting on the sofa.

"And now tell me all about yourself, your life in the monastery and your plans." His face furrowed with concern as he listened.

"Not much to tell I'm afraid. They said I'd been suffering a bit of a mid-life crisis, and it was affecting my mental health. A change of scenery was prescribed by the Order. Then I heard Daddy was unwell, and it'd been years since I'd seen him. So I asked for leave-of-absence to come home. Kill two birds at the one time, kind of. I can help you out in looking after him for a few weeks or more. Pay for my stay that way." She smiled at the end, wondering how he would react to her presence in the home.

"That would be grand Nancy, it really would. It'll sure take the load off my back, and Daddy's looking forward so much to seeing you. I'll go and fetch him. Be back in a few minutes."

She tidied around the room while he was gone. The place was topsy-turvey.

She started when she first saw her father in a wheelchair. Nick had wheeled him into the room, then excused himself and left, saying there was an urgent incident in Carlow town, a large retailer having received a telephone warning of a bomb in the store. He rushed from the room, buttoning his uniform, cursing the IRA.

Her father was thin and bent over a little, and seemed frail and vulnerable. His eyes lit up in recognition.

"Ah Nancy, the apple-of-my-eye."He smiled as they embraced.

She was glad he hadn't enquired about her not wearing her habit. She wondered if the stroke had affected his memory.

"I'll be staying here for a few weeks Daddy. It's my first holiday in years. I'll be able to look after you, and I'll take over some of the workload from Nick and Kitty."

"Great Nancy, now I'll have someone to talk to." He paused and coughed, before continuing.

"It can be lonesome here betimes. It'll be better having a woman around all the time too. Nick's a grand lad and tries hard, but housework isn't his cup-of-tea. Only for Kitty the place would be in a right tip. Sport, and the great outdoors are more up Nick's alley. *And women*, he was always a great one for the women." He seemed breathless when he stopped talking.

"I'm sure. Strange, none of them have hooked him yet. Have they?" Nancy asked.

"Well, he has it bad for a young one, a local girl, Sheila Hynes. First time ever for him to fall head-over-heels for a girl, I think. I believe she's a nurse in Kilkenny. She's even spent a few nights with him here in this house over the past few months, and they thinking I knew nothing about it. She'd be gone early in the morning, but I noticed a few things in the bathroom, and some bits of clothing around the place that gave the game away. I said nothing." He paused again, gasping for breath a little, before speaking again.

"Beware of the old dog, he may not bark loud any more, but he knows all the tricks." He smiled, tapping the side of his nose with his finger.

"Can you walk at all Daddy?" She'd seen a walking-stick propped in a corner. It gave her hope. She knew he was a fighter.

"Not since I had the stroke, love. They said I should get my mobility back, and I was to attend the Physio daily in the clinic down the town. But I've only been able to go there a few times. Nick has been so busy, since he got promoted to Sergeant. There's a session on this morning at twelve."The effort of speaking left him breathless a while.

She took her time as he sucked in air, before speaking.

"Righto Daddy, I'll have you there with the Physio straight after breakfast." She saw his face brightening. Things are going to change, she muttered to herself.

The weeks slipped by, and her father began getting around the house with the aid of a stick. He slept downstairs. She saw little of Nick, but Kitty called daily. Nancy looked forward to her visits, for a cup of tea and a chinwag. Her father's progress gave her hope, and she enjoyed the time spent helping him. Her life now seemed to have more purpose.

Every day she would push him in his wheelchair along by the Barrow, serenaded by birdsong and the water gushing at the weirs. They both loved that. People would come up and talk to him, and he loved that too. They'd start their walk from the old Minch Norton mills building where the river divided, one part diverting to a lower level, while the upper level became a canal. Following the canal they passed the Sawmills, before going by the convent up to the lock with the old hand-operated drawbridge. There they could see the divided river far off on the right side, and the weir water rushing through the deserted mill on their left. Nearby, lily pads flowered flat on the water, and the poplars swayed on the far bank. From here they'd turn and head home by Regent Street.

She felt content, thinking this might be what she was destined to do with her life. Sometimes her father would get out of the wheelchair, walk a little and sit on the low wall, staring into the swirling, mesmeric current. His spirits slowly picked up. Sister Veronica was a world away. The only thing that still rankled Nancy was not hearing of the whereabouts of her son. Well, she hadn't expected much, had she? She prayed hard, day and night. She believed in the power of prayer. Prayer opened doors of hope. God was good.

One day, weeks later, around mid-morning, there was a knock on the front door. A young man, smiling, stood outside in the sunshine, holding a large bunch of flowers.

"Interflora at your service, delivery for you madam. Please sign here."He beamed.

She hesitated at first, then signed the docket, took the bouquet, and in seconds he was gone.

She gazed at the flowers. Twelve roses. Red, pink, and white, four of each. They were beautiful. She smelt the flowers, wondering who could have sent them. Maybe it was a mistake. Then she spotted an envelope sellotaped to the back of the cellophane wrapping. Rushing back into the kitchen, she took a scissors from the drawer, cut the envelope free, and sliced it open. She put on her glasses, sat on the sofa, and read the letter.

"Ciao Nancy,

Or should I call you by your adopted name? Fancy us both pretending to be what we're not. It must be a feature of those born under a Water *star sign. Anyway, you've been on my mind, since I discovered you'd left Milan for home a day earlier than you informed me. Time out of mind, I've thought about you. I don't blame you leaving me the way you did, after you found out I was a priest (the receptionist at the hospital told me the next day that you'd called). I had deceived you, and for that I am truly sorry and do apologise. I was smitten by you at first sight. Believe me it was not normal behaviour for me. I would have told you later that I was a priest. I was afraid if I said anything at first it would scare you off, and we would never have had those wonderful hours together in Milan.*

After I'd checked at your hotel, and discovered you'd gone, I found out your address through a contact in the hotel, and finally rang the convent in Manchester last week. It cost me something to find out your address but it will be money well spent if it means I end up seeing you again. The convent eventually told me you had taken leave to look after your father in Bagenalstown in Ireland, and they gave me your address there. I had to put some friendly persuasion on them to get the information, but I can be very persuasive, that's part of my star sign. You can imagine my shock Nancy, to discover you were a nun. I hoped it might help you to understand why I didn't level straight away with you. Anyway it hasn't changed how I feel about you. In fact, it's very much the opposite. I would love to continue our relationship as friends, without compromising our vows. I hope you will agree. I love your company, and hopefully it's the same for you. I hope to return to Graiguenamanagh in a few months to see my mother and take my summer leave. Maybe we could meet then, and go kayaking on the river, or take a trip on a barge. Or just walk and talk.

I apologise again, if I have offended you in any way. It was not intended. You are always in my thoughts. Please write anyway, I'd love to hear from you. My address is on the enclosed card.

Ciao Bella,
Marty.

She was numbed. She read the letter again, and again. Before she could gather her thoughts, she looked out the window and saw Kitty coming up the road. She quickly placed the flowers in a vase on the table, and put the kettle on.

"What beautiful flowers, Nancy. Are they for you? Have you a secret admirer?" Kitty asked later, smiling, sipping her tea.

"None of your business, dear sister. Actually, they *are* for me. A friend I met in Italy. He's from Graiguenamanagh. He's also a priest, so don't be getting any ideas. It was a purely platonic relationship. But he did take me to the *La Scala* opera house in Milan. You know how I love opera. It's the shortest way to my heart. He hopes to come home in a few months to visit his mother and wants to meet me, if I'm still here."Secretly she felt happy that someone had sent her flowers.

"He sounds very nice. But you'd better tell Daddy they're for him. You know how he feels about the clergy. He never got on with the Monsignor here, especially after the furore about your baby all those years ago."

"Good idea Kitty, I'll do that. I'll say they're from the nuns in Manchester."

"Will you still be here in a few months? Daddy seems much improved since you came. I do hope you'll stay." Kitty's brow furrowed as she spoke.

"Don't worry, I'll be here, I can stay as long as I like."

That night in bed she read Marty's letter again. She had written him out of her life, after her meetings with Sister Veronica, but here he was, intruding into it again. What to do? She knew it wasn't on for two people devoted to God, to be keeping company. But what harm was there in a casual friendship? We're not even living in the same country, she mused. Sister Veronica's words of warning shot through her head. She needed time to mull over things. She needed God's guidance. She needed to pray for it. She'd not reply to him for now. She'd wait and pray for guidance.

During the next week a letter arrived from Sister Veronica. It was curt, expressing hope her father was doing well, and asking if she could return urgently to Manchester. She held the letter in her hand, trembling, wondering what could be behind the old nun's command. She dreaded what it might be. Her stomach tightened with worry. She told Kitty she had to return to Manchester for a few days, and asked her to hold the fort with their father till then. Kitty agreed, hugging her. Nancy packed her bags and left the following day, still apprehensive over the reason for her recall.

***

Nancy knocked three times before entering the office, the door squeaking shut behind her. This time she'd resolved she would not be cowed, she would fight her corner. Inside it was gloomy, rain spattering on the window, smell of incense in the air. Sister Veronica's eyes were closed in prayer, her rosary clutched between her fingers. The old nun's eyes fluttered open after hearing the door squeak shut.

"Ah Sister Brendan, there you are. I was lost in prayer. Please be seated. I trust your father is well?" The old nun seemed solemn and concerned, with an earnest look on her face.

"Much improved thank you, Sister Veronica."

As she sat down, Nancy noticed a bundle on the corner of the desk. She started, recognising the blue dress she'd worn in Milan to the opera. Her heart sank. She knew she had to act or react. A sour taste came in her mouth.

"Well, you're probably wondering why I called you back to Manchester, Sister Brendan." As Sister Veronica spoke, she pulled the bundle containing the blue dress across the desk, and left it in front of her.

"Actually I'm glad you did summon me here Sister Veronica, because there's something important on my mind that I needed to speak to you about."Nancy's voice was firm.

"Really, have you recalled something about that night you went to the opera with the priest, presumably the person who recently rang the convent here, to enquire of your whereabouts?"The old nun asked, her voice gloating.

"No, there's nothing further to report about that, Sister Veronica, but I've decided to request a dispensation from my vows, so I can leave the Order. After much thought and prayer, I've decided it would be best for me, my family, and the Order." There, better to get your spoke in first, she thought as she spoke.

The old nun's mouth sagged open. She was speechless for a while. Finally she replied.

"If that is your wish, so be it, Sister Brendan. I will make the necessary arrangements. But I would like you to take some time to reflect on your decision, say at least six months. If you change your mind in that time, I will not finally process your request. You need more time to reflect on your decision."Sister Veronica snapped, annoyed Nancy had got her spoke in first.

Curt. No thank you. No good wishes. No empathy. Heartless, Nancy thought, before replying.

"Thank you Sister Veronica, I'll go now and pack my bags. I will think it over as you advise. Thank you for your forbearance. I will pray for your intentions." Nancy rose, bowed, and turned for the door. As she reached to open it, the elderly nun called after her.

"You know I've some experience with bodily stains, having worked in an orphanage with teenage boys and girls. There was nothing conclusive to relate on the dress stains, one way or another. I'm not going to say any more about the matter, but if I were you I'd be very careful about having anything to do with that priest. That's *my* advice."

"Thank you Sister Veronica, I appreciate your concern." After speaking, Nancy went out the door.

She would say that, Nancy fumed, always has to have the last word, implying the priest had anything to do with her decision to leave, always suspecting the worst. She closed the door behind her, and trod the corridor back to her room for the last time.

Back in her room she prayed long and hard. Afterwards she made her way around the convent, saying her goodbyes to the other nuns. Most reacted with shock, eyes glazing over, all wishing her well. She was no longer part of their life, she had moved on. Some joked she was escaping to the real world. She would miss some of them. And some parts of her life there. She would miss the children she used to teach. Mist in the early morning, in the garden, autumnal, dew dripping on the grass leaves, she'd miss that. The peace and tranquillity pervading the convent, yes, she'd miss that too. And she'd no longer be a bride of Christ. How she'd miss that, she sighed. Then she heard the choir practicing in the chapel. *Monteverdi's Vespers*. A work of genius, she would miss that very much. It was when singing, that she felt closest to God. Overall she felt relieved, like a weight had been lifted off her, but her heart was heavy. A new beginning beckoned.

After packing her bits and pieces, she went to the Chapel to say her last prayers there. She returned to her room, uplifted.

Her return journey was next day. Before leaving, she decided to make one last effort to contact her son.

***

The young man in the Estate Shop recognised her.

"Never forget a face madam. Rather. Mind you, you nearly had me fooled, not wearing your habit. I *was* expecting you though, Sister Brendan isn't it?"He beamed.

"I like a change of dress now and then. But why were you expecting me?"

"Well, I rang the convent a while ago, and left a message for you to contact me."

"Oh, when was that?"

"Let me see, three to four weeks ago."

"Oh, and who did you speak to?"

"Can't say for sure, spoke to more than one, but the last one, she said she'd pass on the message."

"Did you give her any information?"Nancy asked, fuming that she'd not been informed.

He paused, thinking, before he replied.

"In hindsight, I may have. She did quiz me what it was about."

"And what did you say?"

He hesitated again.

"I probably said it was a family matter. Rather I shouldn't have jolly well said anything. I do apologise if I've embarrassed you, or anything."

"That's all right, you *were* trying to help me. And what news have you got?"

"Fifteen years ago, the Jones family moved to Wilmslow, in Manchester, 54 Hackshaw Crescent, that's all the information I've got. We were involved in the purchase. I do hope it helps you to contact your son."He beamed with satisfaction.

"Thank you, you have been very helpful."

She wrote down the address, and left. Outside was a park, which she entered, sitting on a bench, her mind spinning. Children played all around, and in the distance lay a lake, brimming, with ducks and swans swimming in it. Nearby, flower beds blossomed, blooming in myriad colours. She felt angry in spite of the beauty all around her. Why had she not been told about the phone call? Who had blocked the information reaching her? It must have been Sister Veronica, she reckoned. She felt betrayed. Somebody could even have told her in secret, when she was making her goodbyes. But they'd all closed ranks and said nothing. Anyway it was now an end to all that, there would be no going back. Later, she rose and hailed a taxi for Wilmslow. Less than a half hour later it had stopped outside 54 Hackshaw Crescent.

A middle-aged lady opened the door. From her doorstep, the lady informed her that she had rented the house for two years from the Jones family, who were now in Dublin. Mister Jones worked for BHS, she said, and was managing their new store in O'Connell Street, in Dublin. A dangerous place to be, the lady added, with the IRA bombing the place to bits.

"I suppose so, thank you so much. That's all I need to know."Nancy smiled as she spoke.

She made her way back to the convent for the last time, stepping with a lighter tread. At last she had a lead, something definite, something to follow up on, and in Ireland too. Yes, things were indeed looking up.

Chapter 11

Back to the Barrow

Soon Nancy sank into the rhythm of life beside a large river, the Manchester bustle a faraway memory. She felt relaxed, happier in herself. People seemed friendly, non-judgmental. Time went peacefully by, and it hit her that most of her reservations about coming home were non-existent. She liked the symmetry of the laid-out town. Everyone greeted her with a smile and a welcome, no questions about her past life as a nun. No prying.

Summer heat was on the river, fish rising for flies, boats floating lazily, kayaks skimming along the water, river-levels dipping lower, bare bodies crowding the swimming places. She reminisced on the summertime long ago, when she'd swam to the far bank of the Barrow for a dare, a coming- of- age moment. She smiled, thinking maybe she'd do it again.

Corn yellowed in the fields, workers sweating there with handkerchiefs on their heads, people moved by the frenzy of the hurling and football championships, even though Carlow were knocked out of both early on. In the hurling her father followed Wexford, she Kilkenny. On their daily walks, they'd argue-the-toss about who'd come out on top that year. Sunday mornings, she'd bring him to watch the locals playing Pitch-and-Toss near the Fairgreen, while in the afternoon they'd trek to the McGrath Sports Grounds for the football or hurling. The McGrath family were benefactors to most of the sports facilities in the town, he told her.

Her father's health had perked up, the Physio sessions helping, and he said he looked forward to these weekend trips, swearing they were the highlight of his week, saying he'd played a bit of all sports in his youth. Badly, but he *had* played them. Even if the hurling or football these days isn't up to much, he'd say, there's bound to be a punch-up involving the crowd, especially if the locals are losing, and that'd liven things up. Each week his mobility improved. She hoped and prayed that someday he'd make his way unaided to the matches.

One Sunday afternoon, on their way to the Gaelic grounds, they passed the cricket pitch, a match in progress. She was tired, and rested on a wooden bench, glad of her hat and sunglasses, the sun scorching the grass brown. She told her father that the scene brought back memories of summer times in England. He wasn't impressed.

"For God's sake Nancy, I haven't a clue what's going on out there, but it's not much that's happening by the looks of it. There's no action atall, atall. And what about all that padding on their legs, and them gloves on their hands? For God's sake, it's a cissy's game played by a bunch of cissys, and it's boring the pants off me. Like watching paint dry. Sure didn't Groucho Marx once say it was the best cure for insomnia that he knew?" Her father grinned as he spoke.

"There's more to it than meets the eye Daddy. You need to know the rules."

"I suppose, but it still looks like a cissy's game compared to hurling."He harrumphed.

"Maybe you're a bit biased, seeing you used play hurling? Have you never heard the expression, it's not cricket?"

"No, what does it mean?"

"Play up, play the game. Fairly, with no cheating. Not bashing each other over the head with a hurley stick."

"Ok Nancy, I get it, but what about the rules?"

She rummaged in her handbag, producing a piece of paper.

"I have a brief set of rules here, written for just the likes of you. Do you want to hear them?"

"Ok, go ahead."He said, listening intently.

"You have two sides, one out in the field, and one in. Each man that's in the side that's in goes out, and when he's out he comes in, and the next man goes in until he's out.

When they are all out, the side that has been out comes in, and the side that has been in goes out, and tries to get those coming in out.

Sometimes you get a man still in and not out.

When both sides have been in and out, including the not-outs, that's the end of the game.

Alternatively, two men in white coats go out into the middle of the field, and set up two sets of three sticks, with smaller pieces of wood balanced on top.

*When they have done this, it rains. Understand now?"*After speaking, she put the paper back in her bag, smiling.

"Clear as mud them rules, but please don't repeat them. I do like the idea of it though, so maybe we'll stay a bit longer until all those latchicos that are in are out." He said, laughing.

The next day he asked her to get him a book on cricket from the library. She did, envisioning the day when he could walk over to the cricket ground alone and sit down there enjoying the game. The book was called *All on a Summer's Day*, by Margaret Adelaide Hughes.

One day she visited the home of the Presentation nuns in the town, finding out where Sister Roberta, her aunt, was buried. After praying at her grave, she left a bunch of wildflowers in front of the headstone, before wandering back to the river to check out where her aunt's flowers had once flourished. The flowers were no longer in the water, the convent derelict and decaying. It's almost dead too, she muttered grimly, soon it'll be gone completely, consigned to oblivion. She vowed to start work that week on restoring the flowers in the river in memory of Sister

Roberta. She also resolved to enquire about a teaching job in the new school on the Royal Oak Road. She thanked God her father was making good progress.

Next morning she read that Dublin was on high alert in the aftermath of Bobby Sands' death. The newspaper was filled with reports of IRA protest marches in Dublin, through O'Connell Street, ending with rallies outside the GPO. According to the headlines, the British Home Store (BHS) shop nearby, was having serious trading problems due to the rallies. Nancy feared the company might shut down and leave Ireland. She knew she had to act now to contact the Jones family about her son. She put down the paper, turned and asked Nick about the security situation in Dublin.

"Why would you want to go to Dublin at all for, Nancy? It's dodgy up there at the moment."His face wrinkled in a frown.

"I want to go to the BHS store."

"Why's that?"

"To go shopping of course. Actually, I've some things I bought in the UK that I'd like to exchange, and I'd like to browse around the other shops. I was thinking of going next Thursday. Kitty said she'd cover for Daddy."Nancy replied, not wanting to tell him the real reason.

His face lightened then.

"Ok, I'll check if there's any rallies planned for that day."

Later Nick confirmed Thursday should be ok. As far as the Garda knew nothing was planned by the IRA. But all that could change in a flash, he added. There was also the ongoing possibility of evacuations due to bomb warnings. All the big stores in the city centre were on high security. Sometimes, he said, there are advantages in living in a place like this, a little backwater on the Barrow.

"I'm sure, and what about your meeting with this Garda Inspector from Kilkenny?"

"That's next week, here in the town."

"I hope it goes well."

"Me too. It's been giving me grief, and a few sleepless nights."

She thought Nick seemed nervous, not his usual cocky self.

"I'll pray for your intentions, prayer is a great healer."

"Thanks Nancy, you do that, I must be going, there's been a road accident on the way to Borris."

He grabbed his hat and dashed from the room.

***

As the train moved forward Nancy looked out, admiring the granite Italianite grandeur of the Bagenalstown station, before settling back to enjoy the journey. She had phoned BHS in Dublin the previous day, and they'd confirmed Mr Jones would be in the store all week. She wondered what he'd be like, if he'd be welcoming to her, and she worried what she'd say to him. She remembered too that she hadn't replied to Marty's letter. She must do that, she muttered, got to stop putting things off. Maybe I'll do it next week, when I've got this over me. As the fields and towns flitted by, the clicking rhythm of the tracks lulled her asleep.

Dublin's main street was drab and dirty, litter blowing about, smell of sick on the streets, winos walking freely around, flagons in hand. It had a multitude of fast food outlets on it, ugly neon signs garishly lighting the scene. Some capital street, she thought. She'd read that every week security incidents clogged up the city centre traffic. Everyone seemed edgy, as if something was about to happen. The whole place seemed like a no-go area. She hastened to the store.

Security men checked her bag as she entered. Inside only a handful of customers roamed about. I'm not surprised there's so few, she muttered, with all the hullabaloo going on outside. She went to the Reception desk, and asked to see Mister Jones, the Manager.

"May I ask what it's in connection with, Miss Hackett?" The girl enquired.

"It's a personal matter, a…a family matter."

"Does Mr Jones know you personally?"

"No, but he knows *of* me."Nancy said.

"Please take a seat while I contact Mr Jones."

Nancy sat down, her stomach tightening.

A few minutes later the girl informed her that Mr Jones was on a long distance call to London, and would see her in about fifteen minutes. She picked up a magazine and browsed through it, agog at the fashion styles, realising how out–of–fashion her own tastes now were.

His office was big, overlooking O'Connell Street, and when Mr Jones stood up from behind his big desk, *he* was big too. A mane of thick, greying hair hung over his blue eyes, his face creased in a welcoming smile, blue suit immaculate. He removed his glasses, placing them on the desk.

"Please sit you down there Madam, and may I offer you coffee or tea?"He waved her to a table in the corner as he spoke.

"T……t……tea……thank you."

"And to what do I owe the pleasure of your company?"He beamed as he filled the cups, and put a plate of scones before her.

"Firstly, t.. thank you for seeing me so readily, Mr Jones."

"It's my pleasure my dear, please do go on."

"Well, I know this may come as a shock to you, but I've come about my son."

"*Your* son? Please do continue."His eyebrows arched in surprise.

"He's now *your* adopted son. I hope you don't mind, but I *do* want to see him. I've been wanting to visit him so much these past few years. It's something I feel I have to do. I…I hope you understand." She said, hesitant. There was a silence. A frown came on his face.

"But of course I *do* understand. Of course I do, so you're Liam's mother?"He said, seemingly taken aback.

"Yes Mr Jones, my name is Nancy Hackett, and I'm from Bagenalstown in County Carlow. I came up on the train today. So his name is Liam?"She asked, excited.

"Super, yes he's called Liam, and I'm so delighted to meet you Nancy. Please call me James. Jean and I have spoken many times about the possibility of you contacting us. Still, it's a bit of a shock when it happens out of the blue, you will appreciate. Yes, his name is Liam, called after Liam Whelan who played for Manchester United. My hero. We always liked that name. *And* we knew you were Irish. It's so lovely to meet you at last."After he spoke he grabbed both her hands in his, and shook them, smiling.

"And how is he?" She asked, a nervous twinge shooting through her.

"He's fine, Liam's absolutely fine, but he's not staying with us at the moment. Ah yes, I can see the resemblance around the eyes, and he's got blond hair just like you. Tell you what Nancy, how about you coming with me now to meet Jean in our house in Killiney? She's at home now, it's a chance to break the ice with her, and things are not that busy here, as you can see. I'll get some cover organised in the store, and have you out there and back in time for your train, or shopping as the case may be. Excuse me while I ring Jean, she's going to get a bit of a shock."He left the room to make the call.

After what seemed ages he returned. Everything's fine, he said, Jean was a bit panicked at first, but after a while she settled down, and she's happy to see you now, if you wish.

"Oh yes, that would be lovely." Her voice appeared calm, but inside her stomach was churning.

Within the hour, she was sitting in the living room of the Jones' large detached residence, backing onto a golf course. Jean was a frail, gentle, friendly lady, grey-haired, in her fifties Nancy guessed, always with a smile on her face. Her hands seemed gnarled and misshapen from arthritis, but she never mentioned any discomfort from them. Jean poured the tea into her willow china tea cups, holding the teapot delicately in both hands.

"I'm *ever* so glad you came, Nancy. I felt nervous when James rang, but I'm sure it's the same for you as for us. Anyway here we are after all the years. We've always wanted to thank you for all the joy that your boy Liam has brought into our lives. James and I met many years ago you know, when we were both working in the same store in Wilmslow for BHS. We were ever so happy together when we married. All we wanted was each other, and children around us. And we *did* have children."

Her eyes were moist. James held her hands in his.

"Really?"Nancy asked.

"Yes, a boy and a girl. But they both died at birth. The medical team said I had a rare genetic defect, and advised against becoming pregnant again, after the first baby died. But we ignored their advice, we both wanted a child of our own so badly. Sadly, they were right, it was not to be. It took us a long time to get over these experiences. A long, long time, as if you ever really get over that kind of thing. I don't really think you do." She dabbed her eyes with a hanky after speaking..

"That was terrible for you."Nancy felt for them both.

"It *was* terrible, there were times when I was very low, very low indeed. James, he was my rock. Without him, I don't believe I'd have survived the trauma. He suggested us adopting around this time. It took a long time, before finally Liam came into our lives, but he changed everything straightaway, for the better. He became the light in our lives."

"Oh, that's good to hear, I'm so glad of that. Tell me, what's he like, and what's he doing now?"Nancy asked.

"I should think he's jolly well singing or playing music somewhere. He's a fine, strapping six footer, fair haired and brown eyed like you, and ever so well-behaved. Never gave us any trouble, a model child. He was always into sport and music, passionately. He'd a good voice, and got involved in folk music groups in Manchester. Two years ago, he asked if he could go to Trinity College in Dublin to study music. We agreed reluctantly, as up to then we had all been so close together, holidays and all. Then James got the chance to come to Dublin this year with his job in BHS, and we jumped at the chance. Seeing more of Liam was an added bonus. On the other hand, there are the security risks. Kidnapping by the IRA is a big worry for James. He has to be ever so careful."

"And does Liam know about me?" Nancy asked, anxiety stabbing her stomach.

"Yes my dear, he does, we informed him when he was about twenty. He always wanted to meet you sometime. Maybe he felt his coming to study in Dublin would lead to that. We don't know, he's a very independent lad."

"And where is he now?"

"Oh, he's touring around Ireland with some folk or traditional group or other. He calls every week to say where he is. He's writing a thesis on the history of Irish music for his University studies. He says he's never been happier. And what about yourself my dear, tell me what do you do?"

Silence. A wave of relief swept over Nancy. The end of her mission seemed nearer, and the Jones family couldn't have been nicer. She thoughts for a few moments and replied.

"I…I was a nun in Manchester for over twenty years. I resigned this year to devote myself to minding my father at home, after he had a stroke. When he recovers, I hope to take up a post teaching in the town." There it was, the truth was out, for better or worse. Nancy sighed with relief.

"Oh, how lovely, Liam will love to hear all about you. And what town is that?"

"Bagenalstown, in County Carlow, it's beside the river Barrow."

"Super, how lovely, when we hear from Liam, we'll write to you with his whereabouts. I'll need your name and address."

Nancy scribbled these down on a piece of paper, handed it to Jean then stood up. It was time to go. They hugged, and she thought there was a tear glistening in Jean's eye as they parted. James dropped her to Heuston station. He was a perfect gentleman. She'd decided to forego her shopping plans, the tension in the city being too much.

What lovely people, she thought, sitting in the railway carriage on the way back. Liam is so lucky, I'm so happy for him. They've probably given him more opportunities than I ever could. Tears came in her eyes then. She sniffled, rummaging in her bag for a hanky. As she dabbed her eyes she looked out the window at the fields of green flashing by, filled with animals frozen in their footsteps, while birds of all shapes and hues cavorted like crazy in the sky. The train trundled on. A smile came to her lips. I feel closer to him now, she thought, all I wish for now is to see his face.

Chapter 12

A Matter of Honour

As the weeks slipped by Nancy had more time on her hands, her father's health improving gradually. She asked Kitty if there was any part-time work going in the town, adding she'd do any kind as long as it was convenient. Kitty replied she'd heard Major Burgess, owner of a large house in Dunleckney, needed a cleaning lady two days a week. His wife was invalided, and had recently entered a Nursing Home. Sounds perfect, Nancy said. Within days Kitty had confirmed the job was Nancy's, starting the next Monday.

Burgess told her he'd been a tank commander in WW2, in North Africa, under General Montgomery. Grey hair and moustache, medium-build, ruddy-cheeked, square-shouldered, he walked with a limp, and carried a walking stick. Early on, he explained his limp.

"*El Alamein*, where we knocked the stuffing out of Rommel, the Desert Fox. Damn fine General, Rommel, master strategist. I was scouring the desert with my binoculars, half-in half-out of the tank, when a shell hit directly below me, right in the belly of the tank. Got blown sky-high, damn lucky to still have my legs, luckier than the poor blighters below, they never had a chance. I alone survived. Hence the bloody limp." He grimaced and his eyes glassed over, as he emptied his whiskey glass.

He explained that he coped with the loneliness caused by his wife's departure through writing and gardening. One day he'd write his memoirs of the war, he said, but at the moment he was completing a history of nearby Dunleckney Manor, ancestral home of Lord Bagenal, after whom Bagenalstown was called. Writing was what kept him from jumping into the river, he said.

In the following weeks she saw very little of Burgess when she worked there. He mostly stayed in his study, writing. She had never cleaned his study, but he had never told her not to. One day she saw him out in the garden, the study door ajar. Armed with her duster, she went in. An open manuscript lay on the table, beside a typewriter and a half-empty whiskey bottle. Curious, she went over, and started reading it.

***

Darkness was down as Bagenal Harvey flicked the reins across the sweating rump of his horse. He urged it up the rutted track to Dunleckney Castle, home of his cousin Beauchamp Bagenal. The horse struggled to move on the last leg of its journey, carriage wheels stuck in the mud. Harvey swore, cracking the whip repeatedly, before alighting at the Castle and handing the reins to the groomsmen.

Two bonfires blazed outside the castle, lighting the entrance, casting eerie shadows about the building. Harvey stood in the heat of the blaze, warming himself. It had been a long day, and a hard one. He'd left in early morning drizzle from Bargy Castle in Wexford, passing by Mount Leinster at Bunclody, then on through Borris, before finally arriving in mist-shrouded Bagenalstown.

It should be worth the effort, Harvey thought, after all, his cousin's parties were legendary and lavish, and this was his first time to be invited. It might last the entire weekend, they normally did. His cousin had quite a reputation, being reputedly a notorious playboy, with delusions of royalty, who liked to be addressed as" King" Bagenal. Harvey had done his homework. After all, he was going to need the" King's" help in the future.

Nancy became engrossed in the story and wanted to finish it. Looking out the window she saw Burgess bent low, pruning the roses at the far end of the garden. Good, she thought, and after placing her duster on the desk and sitting on the swivel-chair behind the desk, she continued to read.

Bagenal Harvey went upstairs to his room, servants carrying his trunks. It was spacious with a four-poster double bed, overlooking the gardens. A room fit for royalty indeed, and room for a visitor too, he mused. After washing and changing, he left his room and was escorted to the dining hall.

Braziers blazed at both ends of the long, rectangular oak table dividing the hall, and torches flamed high along the walls. Lit candles adorned the laden table, and wine casks lined both sides of the table. Harp strings plucked the air. A goblet of mead was put in his hand by a young lady servant, comely and attractive in a green dress. Compliments of his majesty, she murmured, smiling, curtsying, showing a birds-eye view of her well-shaped body. If you need any more later, she said, smiling again, before fading back into the shadows.

Harvey drank the mead, feeling it warming his blood, and relaxing the tension in his body. Already the hall seemed to be acquiring a heady atmosphere. He decided to go easy on the mead, and keep his wits about him for when he would put the big question to his host. He reckoned he'd only get one bite at that cherry. A gong sounded, and people were told to take their seats. In the distance, Harvey observed a handsome man sitting on a throne, piled high with cushions, at the top of the table. That must be the" King", he thought. Indeed they are right, he is remarkably good looking, Harvey mused.

He was seated next to Beauchamp Bagenal, who nodded to him as he shook hands with the other guests lining up to meet him. On the table in front of Beauchamp lay a case containing a pair of flintlock duelling-pistols. Also in the case were bullet mold, a powder-measure, and ramrod. Harvey knew Beauchamp had a reputation as a duellist. In the gentlemanly art of legalised murder, the burning question of the day was" Did he blaze?" In his profession, Harvey had dealt with many such matters. Beauchamp finally turned to greet Harvey.

"Please be seated dear cousin from Wexford. You are welcome for the first time to our revels. And how was your journey?"

Harvey bowed, and sat down, before replying.

"Rather tiring your majesty, the rain was steady all the way."

"Glad you know my title, dear cousin. Do refill your cup. We'll have you in fine form before the night is done."Beauchamp said, tapping the cask of wine beside them with a duelling-pistol.

"And why, may I ask your majesty, do you have your duelling-pistols beside you?"

"Right you are to ask. One I use to tap the cask when I want to drink. The other is a warning to all my guests to drink up, or else they may have to put up with the consequences."

"You mean they'd have to duel with you?"

"Yes, but that would be a foolish thing if it were to happen."Beauchamp said, snapping his fingers at the servants.

As Harvey refilled his goblet, servants entered the hall, bearing the banquet food. A roast pig was sliced and served, along with salmon, and other delicacies. Three female harpists, all young and beautiful, attired in striking costumes of different hues, sat before the dining table, and sang "Aileen Aroon", followed by other beautiful Irish airs. Beauchamp's wife had now joined them, and Harvey was introduced to her. She had a pretty face and a friendly smile. After a polite welcome she excused herself, saying she had to welcome one of the Kavanaghs of Borris House. Beauchamp turned from addressing some female guests on the far side of the table.

"So you are one of our esteemed legal profession, dear

cousin? Do fill your goblet, I do love the sight of a flowing bowl." Beauchamp smiled, supping his drink.

Harvey obeyed with haste, disregarding his earlier decision, as he seized the chance to converse with the "King", hoping to find out if all the stories he had heard about him were true. Beauchamp, he knew, had inherited his father's estate when only eleven years old, and some years later had gone on a Grand Tour of Europe, spanning several years.

"Pray tell me your majesty, about your Grand Tour of Europe. It must have been a truly great experience." Harvey said, raising his wine goblet to his lips.

"It was, everyone was so impressed that I had a town called after me. That of course was my father Walter's doing. A big improvement he thought, on its previous name of Muine Beag, which means little hedgerow in Irish. My father had delusions of modelling the town on Versailles in France, with the river Barrow becoming like the Seine. But of course that never happened, although the Court House is a fine building. Little did the people in Europe or Carlow know I had to sell off part of my father's estate to finance my excursion to Europe."

"Oh, and did you find your European trip very educational?"

"Yes, but not in a way my parents might have approved of."

"Really, and how was that?"

"Well, with my name and money, I socialised at the highest level, and was many times in the company of royalty. And believe me dear cousin, most of my education was in the area of debauchery, and rake-like behaviour. And believe me too, when it comes to that kind of behaviour, royalty are second to none. But what could I do if beautiful and rich ladies threw themselves into my arms?"

And other parts of my body too, he added, patting his groin.

"Our cups are empty." Beauchamp said, snapping his

fingers, and within seconds one of his lady servants had refilled them.

Harvey noticed that while Beauchamp spoke to him, he was approached many times by beautiful lady guests who curtsied before him, and kissed his hand. It seemed the man had a magnetism that was attractive to women.

"I believe you once jilted a Princess on your travels?" Harvey said.

"Charlotte of Mecklenburg-Strelitz. I remember her clearly and dearly, how could I not? Yes, she was a beauty, and we had a passionate affair, but there were so many other fish in the sea, beckoning. Still, she didn't do that badly. She ended up marrying King George the Third of England."

"Not a bad second choice. And I heard you carried off a Duchess from Madrid, and also scaled the walls of a convent in Lisbon?"

"Dear cousin, you are bringing back memories of my youth, happy memories in the main. Nothing like a bit of adventure to lend some spice to your love-making eh?" Beauchamp scratched his groin as he spoke, his eyes glazing over.

"But your adventures were not always with the opposite sex. I believe that you also fought a Prince, intoxicated the Doge of Venice, and fought a duel in Paris?"

"Hah, noble cousin, you seem to have done some homework on my life. Please refill your goblet. I'm enjoying our conversation, it's stirring old memories." Beauchamp said, tapping the cask with one of the duelling-pistols.

"Pray tell me how you became involved in the Paris duel. I'm fascinated to know how one might arise. You obviously were successful." Harvey raised his refilled tankard to his lips, happy at how the evening was progressing, and that Beauchamp Bagenal was giving him so much time and attention.

Harvey felt the moment nearing when he could ask Beauchamp the question near to his heart.

"Duelling is a matter of honour. A gentleman must defend his good name at all costs. Sometimes it can be because of a woman, sometimes about money, sometimes even about your appearance." Beauchamp spoke, wiping his lips with the back of his hand.

"And what pray was the reason for the duel in Paris?"

"A woman was the reason. She was engaged to be married. He travelled much. We had our liaisons when he was away. The frisson was magnifique as they say en francaise, and she was hot-blooded and demanding. One day he returned to her house unexpectedly, when we were in flagrante delicto, a common occurrence for us. A duel was the obvious solution, but he added fuel to the flames by dishonouring my family, and my physical constitution."

"Did he die?" Harvey asked, wondering why his cousin's physique would be called into question. After all, he was extremely handsome and attractive to the ladies.

"No, but he was wounded in a place which would severely restrict his marriage prospects. In fact, they never married." Beauchamp rubbed his groin for emphasis.

Harvey now felt in awe of this man, his cousin, who had packed so much adventure and romance into his life. And shot a man, something he had never done.

The tables had now been cleared, and a band of musicians commenced playing. Soon couples were dancing to the music in front of the blazing braziers. Beauchamp remained seated. He turned to Harvey.

"You know dear cousin, women are the most beautiful and desirous creatures, and you should always love them when you can."

"Yes, but when you're married all that has to change, hasn't it?"

"No, once you look after them properly." Beauchamp snapped, a frown creasing his face.

"Of course, your majesty." Damn, Harvey thought, I shouldn't have said that, it must be the wine. He knew *from Beauchamp's reaction, that he thought Harvey was alluding to the illegitimate daughter, Sarah, whom Beauchamp had fathered with a local woman.*

Harvey froze inside. He was afraid he had offended Beauchamp's honour. But he decided to go for broke. It was now or never.

"Your majesty, there is a matter on my mind, of the utmost gravity, which I would like to discuss with you."

"Yes, my dear boy, what is it, having a problem with women? Balancing multiple affairs? Or is it money? Out with it, you have aroused my curiosity for sure. "

Beauchamp's wife then asked him to join her in socialising with the Kavanaghs of Borris, but he waved her away, saying he would join them later, and asked Harvey to continue talking.

"It's none of those your majesty. It's about something that's bigger than either of us. It's about Ireland. For five hundred years we've been under the yoke of England. Raped, plundered, persecuted. Ireland is a separate island, and should be governed by the Irish. "Harvey spoke slowly, his face set serious.

"Of course you know my grandfather came over in 1601 under Queen Elizabeth, and was given these lands for his loyalty and courage. Are you asking me to cut off the hand that fed me? And how do you propose to achieve what you are proposing?" Beauchamp leaned forward, agog with interest.

"For centuries there has been unrest, rebellions and wars against English rule, but to no avail. I have formed the Irish Volunteers in Wexford, to fight for Irish freedom. I would ask you to support our cause. You are as Irish as anyone, and you must see that one day rebellion has to happen for Ireland to achieve independence from the yoke of England. Are you on?"Harvey asked.

Silence. Harvey waited anxiously. Minutes dragged by. Beauchamp was deep in thought. A frown framed his face and his eyes bulged. He picked up a walking stick that lay beside his throne, pushing himself upright. Harvey gasped. Beauchamp was lame. He was unable to stand upright without the aid of his stick. No wonder he was not interested in socialising and dancing, Harvey thought. The man, so irresistible to women, was a cripple.

"Sir, you have dishonoured me in my own house by asking me to become a traitor for your cause, and making other insinuations which I chose to ignore. We will settle the matter by duelling at ten o'clock in the morning. You are a scoundrel. "Beauchamp was trembling, but spoke in an even voice, which was not heard by others, above the music and chatter in the hall.

Harvey froze. He had been challenged to a duel for the first time. He quaked inside. It was a nightmare outcome for him, but there was no way out now.

"I am no scoundrel, and I will defend my name. But I have no duelling-pistols with me, and no second."

"I will provide you with a pair of pistols, and a second. He will collect you at nine in the morning, and bring you to where the duel will be held. Be ready sir. "Beauchamp snarled.

"And pray, where is the duel to be held?"

"It will be in Killinane graveyard, near Dunleckney." Beauchamp muttered, and hobbled away.

Harvey retired to his bedroom in a state of shock. He couldn't believe what had happened. All his fine plans gone for nought, and he now faced a life-or-death duel with his cousin. In a graveyard too. And he had little experience in using duelling pistols. He wondered if Beauchamp had been wounded in a duel. He knew from his legal work that these pistols were inaccurate in inexperienced hands. He paced the room in a panic. A knock came on the door.

"Yes, who is it? "

"It's me Hannah, your maid-servant. May I come in?"

"Yes."

She entered. Harvey recognised her as the girl who had served him mead earlier.

"I've called to see if you needed an extra pillow on your bed, sir."

"Thank you Hannah, but I don't need one tonight. "

"You're welcome sir, good night. " She bowed and vanished out the door.

Later he realised he had been tetchy with Hannah. She may have had other things in mind when she called about his pillow, but her timing was unfortunate. He should have gone easy on the mead, but Beauchamp was a persuasive person. Maybe there was method in his madness in getting one drunk. Harvey's mind was addled, and he tossed and turned until the dawn came, grey and wet.

***

Dewdrops lay trapped in a large cobweb on a tree beside Harvey, as he stood in Killinane graveyard. The morning was dank and misty. High cypress trees framed the cemetery, adding to the gloom. He shivered as he surveyed the scene, wondering if there was a vacant grave plot earmarked for the possible fatal outcome of the duel.

Harvey's second checked his pistol, while Beauchamp's second marked out twenty paces from where Beauchamp sat propped against a flat gravestone.

"I like the support of a tombstone. A graveyard is the perfect location for a duel, don't you agree, dear cousin? It makes one think of the hereafter, before one possibly goes there. You should say your last prayers." Beauchamp sneered as he adjusted the cushion beneath him on the tombstone.

Harvey said nothing, but shivered as a sliver of fear slid through his body. He knew Beauchamp was using psychological tactics to unnerve him, and he was succeeding. He wondered how many others had been lured to their deaths in the same graveyard.

"My second has marked the distance you can walk away from me, as I cannot walk. Please commence the duel." Beauchamp spoke in a nonchalant manner.

Harvey started walking away from Beauchamp. He knew that the less steps he took the better chance he had of hitting his opponent. He counted the paces, one, two, three, four, five, six, then turned and raised his pistol. Beauchamp Bagenal still sat on the gravestone with his pistol by his side. Harvey cocked his pistol, took aim, and pulled the trigger. The sound exploded in the eerie quietness, frightening the birds in the trees into a raucous cacophony of sound. Harvey peered through the cordite cloud at where Beauchamp had been sitting. He had missed. By a country-mile or two. Beauchamp pushed himself upright from the gravestone, raised his pistol, and aimed at Harvey. Harvey stood frozen in fear for several minutes. Then Beauchamp lowered his pistol, and spoke.

"Damn you, you villain, do you know you had like to kill your own godfather? Go back to Dunleckney, you dog, and have a good breakfast ready for us. I only wanted to see if you were stout." A smile edged Beauchamp's mouth as he spoke.

Shocked and relieved, Harvey hurried back to Dunleckney. The man was indeed unbelievable. And to think he was his godfather. After breakfast they shook hands, honour restored, and later that day when the sun had burst through, they went hunting around Dunleckney, and fishing in the Barrow. During this time they again discussed Harvey's plans for forming The Irish Volunteers. Finally Beauchamp said he would give tacit support to Harvey in his venture but not in an open way. He agreed Ireland should be for the Irish, but for the moment he had to make a living with the status quo.

That night the party continued late into the night. Harvey finally staggered into his bedroom, shattered by the events of the day. A short time later a knock came on the door.

"Yes, who is it?"

"It's me Hannah, your maid servant. My master said to ask you if there was anything you needed. May I come in?"

"Yes Hannah, please do."

She entered the room and closed the door behind her.

Postscript: Beauchamp Bagenal Harvey, leader of the rebellion in Wexford in 1798, was hanged on Wexford Bridge in June 1798.

***

Nancy had barely finished reading the last words when she felt a hand squeezing her right breast, and heard a voice saying nice tits. She swung around to see Major Burgess standing behind her, leering, wearing a bathrobe, bare-chested beneath. She didn't know what to say. Did you touch me? Was all that came out from her mouth. He denied doing anything, saying he stumbled when his walking stick caught in the carpet. She fumed, detecting a whiff of whiskey from his breath.

"I hope you liked my story of Lord Bagenal."Burgess said, trying to defuse the situation.

"Y…yes." She mumbled.

"He and I have something in common you know, we're both cripples. That rules out being attractive to the opposite sex. Still it didn't stop Lord Bagenal trying to have his way with the ladies, did it? Because you're on a diet, doesn't mean you can't look at the menu."

"I suppose." She muttered as she left the study and went home, a sour taste in her mouth.

Her suspicions were confirmed a week later, when he pinched her bottom, while she was bent over the fireplace emptying the ashes. She handed in her notice straight away and stormed home, furious.

Dirty lecher, and his wife in hospital, some people have no sense of honour, Kitty commented when Nancy told her the story. Nancy nodded in agreement, thinking it was the way of the world and that Sister Veronica's words of warning had been vindicated.

Chapter 13

Inspector

Nick Hackett's week started badly. The day before his meeting with Inspector Cornelius Doogan, Sheila Hynes had written to say she was breaking off their relationship. After two years it was going nowhere, she reckoned, and now was the right time for them both to move on. She apologised for doing it in writing, but felt it was the best way for them both. She said it hadn't been an easy decision, and hoped they'd remain friends.

He was shocked. For the first time in his life he'd been dumped by a woman, and he didn't like being on the receiving end. No, not one little bit. What piqued him most was her not doing it face-to-face. If she had, he was convinced he could have persuaded her to change her mind. Maybe that was why she had done it in writing, he mused. Ironic too, given he'd done all the chasing with Sheila from the word go, but maybe he'd got complacent of late, thinking they could drift along in a cocoon, like he'd done with his previous girlfriends. It was nice and cosy when they had the house to themselves, when his Dad was in hospital. His sister Nancy's return from England had put the kibosh on all that. He felt deflated.

He wondered if Sheila now had another boyfriend. He realised then he was still gone on her. It was stupid he knew, but he was hurting, and rued not having proposed previously and splashed out and bought the ring to cement their relationship. Too late for all that now, he reckoned, but maybe not too late to try and make up. But how to do it? Her going to work in Kilkenny had been a bad move for him. Out of sight..... He'd slipped up, he realised, but maybe all was not lost. He resolved not to give her up without a fight.

Entering the Garda Station on Kilree Street for the meeting with Inspector Doogan, his mind was distracted. He felt nervous. He tried to focus on the facts he'd gleaned on Doogan the previous week. Forewarned is forearmed, he'd found out the hard way in the Force. He'd learned from his colleagues that the Inspector was in his late thirties, unmarried, ambitious to become a Superintendent. Political too, not well-liked in the Force. An arse-licker, known to have done favours for local politicians, off the record of course. Doogan was sharp. Nick knew he needed to be on his toes, and put Sheila Hynes out of his mind. It wasn't easy.

The meeting room was bare and sparsely furnished, white paint flaking off walls and ceiling, the air musty, reeking of stale smoke. It had a table and six plastic chairs in the centre, with pad, pencil and ashtray on the table. Two neon strip lights dangled on wires overhead. It was the room normally used for interrogations. Nick wondered was that an omen, was Doogan going to grill him? When he entered the room Inspector Cornelius Doogan stood at the window, staring out onto the street, hands clasped behind his back. He swung around to face Nick.

A blocky six footer, Doogan had black wavy hair, blue eyes, moustache, with a pipe protruding from the corner of his mouth, giving him an intellectual air. He had two distinguishing facial features. On his right cheek was a birthmark, hairs protruding. A beauty spot, which he no doubt thought attractive to the ladies. The other a dimpled chin. Shades of Kirk Douglas the movie star, Nick mused. Doogan's raincoat was draped over one of the chairs.

"Ah, Sergeant Hackett, good to meet you, I've heard a lot about you, mostly good I'm glad to say."

Doogan smirked as he shook Nick's hand, and sat down. He took the pipe from his lips, tapped it on the ashtray, emptied the dottle, then stuffed it with tobacco and lit up, puffing peacefully toward the ceiling. A smile creased his face, displaying two rows of even white teeth evenly gripping his pipe, as he leaned back in his chair. A silence came.

"I believe you were a decent hurler once, Sergeant? Wexford have put paid to the Cats this year. Might be the Yella Bellies year?" Doogan broke the ice.

Beating about the bush, Nick thought. Waiting to strike when you're off guard, like a snake.

"Maybe, but they'll have their work cut out against Offaly. Still, they've got the tradition, Offaly have never won an All-Ireland in hurling, so maybe 1981 is their year."Nick replied.

"You're probably right there Sergeant, tradition and experience count for a lot in sport. In the Force too. Anyway we haven't met today to discuss hurling, have we? See this pad here, I'll take a few notes on it of our meeting. In pencil of course, so I can rub out anything I don't like later on, ha ha." Doogan seemed amused at his own humour.

Rumours about him deleting Summonses for Road Traffic offences sprang to Nick's mind. He's checking me out, Nick reckoned, bristling inside.

"That's fine Inspector, once I get a copy of everything."

"Of course you will Sergeant, of course, everything will be done *kosher*. Now to brass tacks. My Super has put me on a special assignment. Even though I complained bitterly about how much pressure we were under, what with the IRA and the fall-out from Bobby Sands' death, but he was having none of it. Said I'd have to find the time. He must be looking for promotion, or else he's under political pressure. He conceded I could have a team of four to help me. That's why I'm here. I want you on my team, Sergeant Hackett. I've done my homework, I want young, ambitious types, who get things done. I want this project to succeed. "Doogan eyeballed Nick as he spoke, puffing smoke clouds at the ceiling.

"And what exactly is the project Inspector? You appreciate we're completely snowed under at the moment."

"I do appreciate that fact. He wants a new investigation into a number of unsolved, suspected crimes in Carlow, Kilkenny, Wexford, and Kildare, over the past twenty years. These incidents involve people vanishing in all sorts of mysterious circumstances, and its felt bringing a fresh focus onto such occurrences should throw up new clues. That's the gist of it. A new brush sweeping clean, like." Doogan replied, pipe clenched tightly between his teeth.

Doogan then took his briefcase from the floor, propped it on one knee, removed a large number of files, and dropped them on the table.

"There you are Sergeant Hackett, twenty in all for starters, probably all unrelated, but who knows? You'll need to go through these with a fine-tooth-comb. I've given the others on the team their own cases to study."

"You mean there are more cases than these?" Nick gasped, incredulous.

"Yes, the situation in the North of Ireland has added to the numbers. Some of these cases may just be people doing a runner, for whatever reason. We need answers. The families involved are still suffering, that's the bottom-line. We'll meet again to discuss these in a month's time Later, we'll have a full team get-together. Ok?" Doogan asked, eyeballing Nick.

Silence. Then Nick nodded. A grin crinkled Doogan's mouth edges as he stood up, shook Nick's hand, retrieved his briefcase, and within minutes had left the building.

Dismayed, Nick stood staring at the pile of documents on the table. As he picked up a file to browse through, it struck him Doogan had never bothered to ask him if he wanted to take on this job, on top of everything else he was doing. It was just assumed. Bloody hell it was. Nor had he got much choice if he wanted to get on in the Force. Nick shrugged. Anyway I guess I'll have more time on my hands, with it being off with Sheila for the moment, he mused. He sighed as he flicked through the files, realising that sifting through and analysing the mass of reports was a mammoth task. He wondered if Sheila would ring. They always did. Damned if *he* was going to. So he waited. And waited. But she didn't ring.

That night he burnt the midnight oil, poring through the data. At the end of it, he was still stuck into the first file. This wasn't going to work, he realised, a change of tactics was needed. Over the rest of the week, he skimmed through all the files when he got the chance, taking sketchy notes, hoping some clue would leap off the pages and slap him in the face. The week passed. Nothing arose. He was getting anxious, he needed something for Inspector Doogan. Soon.

He worked late each night on the files, as it was impossible during the day. He'd never worked as hard. His Dad had told him he should ease up, saying he was getting edgy and losing weight. Life was for living, he said. You're right Dad, Nick replied, this will soon pass.

The next week, he did get a slap in the face. Not the one he was hoping for. On the day in question, his sister Kitty had called. His Dad was resting in bed, and Nancy was in the kitchen making tea, when Kitty spoke.

"Nick, I hope you don't mind me saying this, you may think it's none of my business, but it's something I think you should know about."

"Sure Kitty, fire away, we're family and we'll still be friends, I promise." Nick crossed his heart, grinning.

"Good. It's just we're all a bit worried about you since you split with your girlfriend, and after the meeting with that Inspector Doogan from Kilkenny, you've been working morning, noon, and night. It's not good for your health you know."

"I suppose not, but what is it you want to say?" Nick asked, bemused.

"Well, not to put a tooth in it, and you can call it small-town gossip if you like."

"Get to the point Kitty, the suspense is killing."Nick said, impatiently.

"Well, it was on the day of your meeting with this Inspector."

"And?"

"After your meeting with Inspector Doogan it was observed he had lunch in the Railway House Bar with a female companion. None other than Sheila Hynes herself. And they appeared quite friendly, holding hands and the like. I'll leave it at that. I'm sorry if this upsets you Nick, but Nancy and I felt you should know."

With that Nancy entered the room, carrying a tray of tea and biscuits. The conversation changed to other things, and Nick was glad of that. He felt dazed, like he'd taken a right hook from Mohammed Ali.

That evening his mind was in tatters, so he hit the pub for a few pints instead of working late on the files. Later in bed, his mind churned. He was furious with Doogan, and could see now why he'd selected him. He'd probably told Sheila of his plans before she broke it off, he guessed, and probably advised her to do it in writing. She must think Doogan's Mister Big now, he fumed. He has me over a barrel for sure. His mind filled with ideas on how he'd knock the smirk off the Inspector's face. But he realised there was now no way back for him and Sheila. That hurt the most. A restless night ensued.

***

Nancy stared at the blank page in front of her. It was weeks since the letter and flowers had come from Marty, but since meeting her son Liam her mind had been distracted. She knew she had to reply now one way or the other. Marty wouldn't give up on her she knew, it was decreed in his birth star. Controlling. Persistent. He was like a dog with a bone. She feared he might arrive anytime, unannounced, on her doorstep. Sister Veronica's warnings about him still irked. She didn't believe them, thinking they were just the typical rantings of someone who led a closeted life, and she was determined to prove the old nun wrong. And she would do so she vowed, but not just now.

She wrote, thanking Marty for the flowers, saying she was unable to see him at the moment, her father needing full-time care. Maybe in the future, when things improved they could get together, perhaps in Graiguenamagh, and maybe go boating down to St. Mullins. She would like that. She hoped his mother was well, and looked forward to meeting her. After stamping and posting the letter, she felt satisfied.

Her father was progressing well, and she now was looking forward to getting on with her own life by the Barrow. Her only worry was her brother Nick, as she saw the effects of work pressure and the breakdown of his romance etched in his face. She wished she could do something to help him, but all she could do was pray. And she did. That week she wrote to the new school on the Royal Oak Road, applying for a temporary teaching position.

Chapter 14

Ned Rooney's Story

Looking back, it was Ma I missed the most. God, there was no doubt but she was a saint. Never complaining, always praying and looking out for others. People like her deserved a fairer deal in life, but they had to make do with the lousy cards they got dealt.

She'd been married twice. Like my Dad, her first husband was in the First World War. They were both from Carlow town and got married in 1919, a year after the war ended, after he'd spent four years as a prisoner-of-war when his regiment, the Royal Irish Rifles, was almost completely wiped out early on in the war. My step-sister Mary was three when he died in 1923 from TB. Ma said he loved music and played the fiddle on his death bed, dying during the winter the Barrow flooded up the stairs of their house in Montgomery Street. She always kept his war medals in a drawer beside her bed. Ma was left with a three-year-old daughter and no pension as they got married after the war, but she kept fighting on and went to live with her sister in Blackrock in Dublin.

No doubt about it but she spoiled me too, there being only the two of us most of the time after my Dad died, except when my step-sister Mary's kids stayed with us in Bagenalstown while on their holliers, or when Mary was unwell. There was a baby born before me but she died. Ma was nearly too loving, so she was.

Dad died when I was ten years old. He'd fought with the Dublin Fusiliers in the First World War. After the war he'd worked in Booterstown in Dublin as a gardener. It was there he met my Ma, and it was there in the church on Booterstown Avenue they eventually got married. Late onr they settled in Bagenalstown in Carlow, courtesy of the British Government, he being entitled to one of the

Soldier's Cottages there. My teenage step-sister Mary had stayed on in Dublin.

I remember Dad being good with his hands, and he built us a wooden birdcage. He'd catch singing birds, chaffinches and linnets, and the like. He'd trap them by putting sticky stuff on a stick beside some bread in the garden. He owned a ferret too, and would take me out with him and the ferret to catch rabbits. I never liked ferrets, they'd bite the hand off you, but man could they catch the rabbits. The deeper the rabbit hole the better Dad used say, catch more rabbits. The ferrets were probably the start of my love for hunting rabbits. Anyways when I grew up I only hunted rabbits with dogs, it was fairer I felt, no ferrets or snares. The rabbits always had a chance to escape.

Dad died a slow death over six years, nursed by Ma to the bitter end. She had to put up with a lot. I heard later he was fairly fond of the jar. I suppose I followed him in that regard.

And there I was leaving Ma all alone. Leaving her to cope with the hefting of pails of water from the pump down the road in all weathers, getting rid of the slops and all that, and the other chores I did. I felt guilty, but what else could I do? There was no future in Bagenalstown, it was a dead-end one-horse town, but there was work aplenty in England, and most of my mates had skedaddled there already, and they all said they'd help me get started if I followed them over. The building boom had been going great guns over there since the war.

And finally there was the bloody Myxomatosis killing off all the rabbits at home, and the fact it started locally only made matters worse. That was the last bloody straw.

The bright lights shone, and I was rearin' to go, and make my fortune abroad. Sure weren't the pavements there paved with gold just like the song said? I promised Ma I'd write, and send money home every week, and when I'd saved enough I'd be back for good. She'd nodded, saying she'd think of me every night in her prayers. Always thinking of others she was. A saint.

Sometime later I was bound abroad, sitting on the Mailboat's wooden seats outside on the deck, somewhere between the Kish Bank and Howth Head, moving with the swell, stomach churning, clutching my brown suitcase, a belt strapped about it to stop it bursting open, when Nancy Hackett's face flashed into my mind.

Guilt hit me like a wave. I reckoned I should have been nicer to her before I left, damn right I should've been, but I just didn't know how to handle things. Affairs of the heart weren't my cup of tea. John Wayne, he was my hero, and like him I reckoned I'd always come out on top in the end. Dang right I would. Life was complicated enough leaving, so why string her along too? I'd liked her company a lot for sure, she was fun and pretty too, more than pretty, she had a sense of humour and we'd got on great, but she just didn't fit into my plans at that time. I was mixed up in myself then I guess, and I sometimes wondered deep-down if I was making a mistake.

Her last words stung hard, and are still stuck in my craw to this day. Ned Rooney, I remember her saying, better you just go your way, and I'll go mine, and then we'll both be happy, very happy, won't we now? That's exactly what you want anyway, isn't it? She'd spat the words at me. I'd nodded in silence. Going over things again on the boat, I wondered if one of the reasons I was escaping abroad was to dodge a decision about our relationship. I'd promised her I'd write, but wondered if I should just let bygones be bygones. Anyway I'd moved on and had to make the most of it. There was no going back or looking back. The door was closed behind me, and I was on my way.

I was glad of the help of my Irish buddies in getting started in the building abroad. Not all builders in London then wanted Paddies working for them. McAlpine had a sign up "No Irish Need Apply". And me thinking they'd all be queuing up for me, and me used to humping sacks of flour on my back around Connolly's Bakery, carrying twice the weight of anyone else, and never bothering to use the hand-truck. For all the good it ever did me.

Anyway I got a start over there and worked for a few years with the same builder in High Wyckham. First thing I noticed was that you got tax deducted from your weekly wages. Have to admit I probably owed tax in Ireland when I left. I intended to sort it out, but kept long-fingering it. A lot of my mates were in the same boat tax-wise. They didn't talk much about it though. It was probably a reason in some of them leaving too. I couldn't believe it when we got paid for doing nothing, that was when it rained, and we got "wet-time payments" from the gaffer. This is the life, I thought. Mind you, it went quick enough in the pubs, so the rain ended up costing you money. I soon learnt that lesson.

I got home to Ma that first Christmas, silver jingling in me pockets, and she seemed happy enough. Mind you, I hadn't written her much, as I'd promised her and Nancy, but she never said anything about that, she was just happy to see me. She told me that Nancy Hackett had joined the nuns. I told her I was surprised at that. She said so were half the people in Bagenalstown.

I told Ma the work was good, and the craic too, and I was making good money, and saving hard, and would be home when I'd saved enough to settle down. She said the house would always be there for me anyway, and she prayed I'd come back again soon. She always backed me even when I was wrong. I suppose she just loved me.

By the time I got home the next Christmas, I'd fallen into a cosy pub-life in England with my mates. It seemed the thing to do. We drank, backed horses, did the Pools, and life slipped by in a hazy cocoon of drinking and gambling. We worked hard, played hard, and drank hard. The Irish navvy was appreciated now by the English builders. In the pubs we sang "McAlpine's Fusiliers", or "Paddy worked on the Railway", or "Hot Asphalt", and all the Irish Comeallyes. We were young and none of us saw that eventually the jar would take over our lives. Or maybe we didn't want to see it. We thought it was the life, with no worries. *O mother dear I'm over here, I never will come back, what keeps me here's the rake o' beer, the women, and the craic……………*

The next time I came home was for Ma's funeral. I wasn't proud of that fact. She'd been ill for some time, living with my half-sister Mary, but had said nothing to me, not wanting to worry me. All the lads I used go hunting rabbits with were at her funeral in Carlow. They loved her too.

Before I'd left London to come home for Ma's funeral, one of my mates from Bagenalstown, Feargal Hynes, asked me if I'd deliver a message to his older brother Aengus when I was home. I agreed. It was money he said, and he trusted me, and there would be a generous payment for doing it. He handed me a small brown parcel, stared me in the eye, saying if it wasn't delivered intact I'd be brown bread. I knew by the weight of it there was a lot of money inside, and breathed a sigh of relief later when I handed the parcel over to Aengus. The Hynes family were well-known IRA people. Not to be crossed. I cried bitter tears at the funeral, but afterwards couldn't wait to get back to the UK, and see Feargal for the pay-off. It was generous as promised, and I made a beeline for the *Rose & Crown* pub. The money didn't last long.

After a while I moved to Beaconsfield, following the builder, with some of my mates. The gaffer had a lot of work going on there, and the years slid by. My savings were nil, but so far I'd avoided "subbing" from the boss, that was getting' advances on future wages. A lot of guys had fallen into that trap. Then you could never leave to earn more money from another builder.

I'd been staying in the same digs in Beaconsfield for a few years, and fell for a lovely blonde living there. Her name was Angie. Her mum was the landlady. We got married when she got pregnant. It seemed the natural thing to do, or so I thought. We'd be living rent-free, and everything would be rosy-in-the-garden. Her mother was the fly-in-the-ointment. When James was born, blond like his Mam, he was the apple of our eyes. But soon Angie's mother started interfering, and starting rows over my behaviour, saying I was spending far too much time in the pubs, and telling me to mend my ways. I'd say back that this was the way I'd always lived my life, but I promised to try and change.

But I couldn't change. I tried, maybe not hard enough, and finally Angie kicked me out, probably at the instigation of her mum. I got digs not far away, and started visiting Angie and little James every week, slipping gradually out to a fortnight, and then to a month. I used give her money when I called.

A year had hardly passed, and the builder was moving again onto a new job in Ruislip Gardens, and I had to go with him, the work being scarce then. I didn't know it at the time, but I'd got more into the drinking, and was now subbing my wages from the boss. I'd finally fallen into the trap. He was a fair man, but I owed him too much then to be able to leave him. I had to cut back on what I was giving Angie for the child.

Angie had got into another relationship, and I didn't blame her, I'd been a lousy husband and provider. She now just about tolerated my occasional visits, while her mum ignored me completely. The feeling was mutual with her mum. The drink was now my best friend and worst enemy, and my life continued on its downward path. After moving to Ruislip I only saw Angie and James now and again and afterwards hardly at all.

Over the next few years the builder moved on to other parts of London, following the work, and I followed too, getting digs locally. Over this time I lost contact with Angie. She could have been married again for all I knew.

Drink helped a lot to blot out the past. I was neglecting myself, not eating properly, but I was still fairly fit, though losing weight, but luckily I was never out sick from work. No matter what drink I'd taken, I never missed a day's work because of the drink. That was probably why I was always in work.

Anyway, I was spending more than I was earning, and the gaffer refused to advance any more wages. Ned Rooney, he'd said, you're one of the hardest-working men I've ever employed, one of the best and most popular too, but you've got to control the drink mate, or it'll be your downfall. I've seen it all before. No Ned, I can't advance you any more money, you're already way over the limit, you'd be better advised to find some other source of income, sorry mate. He was a decent bloke the gaffer, and I knew he was right.

I was desperate and needed more cash for drink and debts. A West Indian friend, Cliff, said he could get us work on the weekends, and we went out scavenging for copper on dumps outside the city. I tried this for a few months. It was hard work, but I reckoned I could handle it. The money involved wasn't great, but beggars can't be choosers. The problem was the poisonous fumes, and I could feel them eating into my lungs, on top of all the smoking I did. I couldn't keep it up, it would kill me in a year, I realised. I packed it in, but I knew I was cracking-up then. That Christmas was the lowest of the low.

On Christmas Eve I hit rock-bottom. I'd got back late from the pub, and remember crawling up the stairs, not knowing if the crawling was due to the drink or my lungs. I opened the fridge door to find just a piece of stale bread and a lump of hard cheese inside. Something clicked in my head then. I knew I had to get home, or I'd be found dead, deserted in some lonely digs, another forgotten Irish lost cause. But I hadn't got the fare. I hated doing it, but I tried begging the money from my mates, promising to pay it back, but they couldn't help me. Finally, I believe it was my poor Ma up in heaven who did the trick, once more coming to my aid. Heavenly aid it must have been. I'd always prayed to her every night, and went to Mass every Sunday.

Most of my mates had dropped their religion when they left home, but I never did, and I have Ma to thank for that. I went to see Father Delany. I used chat to him every Sunday after Mass, before heading for the pub. Luckily when I called to the Parish house he was in. We sat inside, in a polished room, me clutching my cap in anguish, as I begged him for the fare home, swearing I'd pay it back as soon as I got a job there. Before answering he asked if I'd like a cup of tea, and some fresh scones. I nodded. I hadn't eaten properly in weeks. I was famished. He left the room, and was back within minutes, with a tray in his hands. He put it on the table before me.

"There you are Ned, help yourself. Then we'll talk about the money. "

I scoffed some biscuits and scones, and washed them down with a cup of tea. Father Delany said nothing then, he just kept staring at me. He must have been alarmed at the state I was in. Unshaved, with frayed clothes and worn-out shoes. Finally, he spoke.

"Ned, I've known you these past few years, and I've always been impressed that you've kept up the practice of your faith, when most of your friends have dropped theirs. In that regard, you stood out. I also know that you work hard, and are good company. But, unfortunately, like many of your compatriots you are overly fond of the drink. Would you not agree?" The priest paused.

"I would agree Father, but there's not much else to do when you're on your own." I said, nodding in agreement, but inside I'd a sinking feeling I wasn't going to get the lolly.

"No, I suppose there isn't a lot else, in any case not at this stage of your life. Look Ned, I'm going to lend you the money for your fare home out of my own savings, because I believe it's the right thing to do, but I'm doing it on two conditions." He eyeballed me then.

"Yes, Father?"

"First, that you do not spend one penny of the money on drink. Second, that you try to make a new start with your life back home, and control your drinking habits, and not let them control you. Agreed?" His face was solemn. He took an envelope from his inside pocket, and placed it in my hands.

"T..t..thank you Father....may God bless you....I will buy my tickets home straight away... and I'll pay you back as soon as I can....and I will mend my ways when I'm back home."My heart leapt, I couldn't believe I'd got the cash.

"Ned, I trust you, It's my personal money, and I don't expect to be repaid....I don't want to see you back in England again, but if you wish you can make a donation to some charity in the future. " The priest said, smiling as he led me back to the door.

At the door he stopped, and placed his hand on my shoulder.

"Ned, I wish you well, and remember, this is our little secret, nobody else is to know about the loan. Ok? Mum's the word." He placed his finger on his lips.

"Yes Father, I'll always remember your kindness."

The priest smiled again as he closed the door.

I dashed to a telephone box and rang my step-sister Mary in Dublin. She said I could stay a few weeks with her in Dublin, before heading home to Bagenalstown on the bus. She'd guessed I wasn't in good health. I agreed to her offer. Afterwards I headed straight to the travel shop and booked the tickets home, leaving in two days. There wasn't much packing to be done, all I had to my name was a travel bag. After all my years abroad, I was going home penniless, bust, but I didn't care. So much, I thought, for all my high-falutin' notions of making my fortune in far-away places. Anyway it didn't seem important then.

That night I told the lads in the pub that I was off home on the next day. They wished me well, and bought drinks to celebrate. Another one bites the dust, they toasted. None of them had been in my first group of pub-friends abroad.

Word got around fast, and the day before my leaving Feargal Hynes rang me in my digs. He'd heard I was heading home for good, and asked would I deliver another parcel to his brother Aengus. Same terms as before, and Aengus himself would settle with me this time. I agreed, telling him I was staying a few weeks first in Dublin with Mary. That news didn't please him, as the money was wanted urgently by Aengus in Bagenalstown. Feargal wanted Mary's address and phone number. Aengus would ring in a week and arrange a rendezvous in Dublin to collect the money. I agreed. I needed the money too. Desperately.

Mary was shocked by my condition when I arrived at her door. She said I was just skin and bone, and on death's doorstep, and she fed me the first proper food I'd had in a long time. She was so kind, just like Ma, and she set me on the road to recovery. I felt like the Prodigal Son returnin' home.

The country was buzzing with the news that Bobby Sands had died on hunger strike. Each night I took the bus to Dun Laoghaire, and drank in O'Loughlin's pub. I liked it there. But then I did something I regretted. I took money from the brown parcel I had to deliver to Aengus Hynes. At first, I intended to only borrow what he owed me for delivering the package, but I kept dipping in, intending to put the money back later, but not really knowing how, or really thinking too deeply about it. The pull of the pub had taken over.

Then the call I'd been dreading came, a week later than I'd expected. Aengus Hynes said he'd been up North on urgent business, and would meet me that night in Dublin in Ryan's pub on Parkgate Street at eight. Be there, with the money, he said. I said ok I would. We were to meet in a snug at the back. I was sick with worry before I went.

"Is this some sort of sick joke Ned? Half the money is missing. What the fuck's going on? This better be good." Aengus spat the words at me, fuming, with his eyes out-on-sticks.

I knew then the night wasn't going to go well.

"Jesus Aengus, I'm awful sorry, I had to borrow me fare back, I hadn't a bean, you wouldn't deny me that, I'll pay you back as soon as I get home, and I'm going to sell the house in Bagenalstown." I lied in desperation.

"Going on the amount missing you must have travelled first class. No Ned, I don't believe you, not for one minute. The people I work for have ways of dealing with people who cross them. Usually it means ending up at the bottom of the Barrow. Or worse. I believe you drink every night in O'Loughlin's pub in Dun Laoghaire." His eyes were slits as he spoke.

"I do Aengus, but I'm going to change all that when I get home, I swear it. Remember the times we used go hunting rabbits around Borris and Fenagh? I'll not let you down , as God is my witness. I'll get a job too and I'll give you something each week, while I'm selling the house. Just give me another chance Aengus, please, for old time's sake."I begged.

Silence followed. A dead silence. Then Aengus leaned across the table.

"Ned Rooney, you always had a persuasive way about you, the gift of the gab some might say. But your mother was a good woman. My Ma always thought highly of her. She's your saving grace. I don't believe you'll do what you say you will. Graveyards are full of people with good intentions. Look Ned, we go back a long way, but I don't make the rules, you understand? In fact I'm moving soon to a new job in Dundalk, waste disposal, and I'll be out of the area for a while. I can maybe get you a four week stay of execution, and that's exactly what it is. After that, it's out of my hands."He shrugged after speaking, and stood up, leaving his whiskey untouched.

"Thanks Aengus, I won't let you down."

"You better not, for your own sake." He snapped as he turned, pushed the snug door open and left.

After he'd gone, my hands were shaking. I finished off Aengus's drink, ordered a double whiskey, and knocked that back. That helped. Then I had another drink, telling myself not to panic. But I did. The reality of the situation gradually hit me. I panicked as I couldn't see any way out. I regretted ever getting mixed up with the Hynes family. Then I realised I was just feeling sorry for myself all over again, when what had just happened was all my own fault. I had another whiskey, paid the bill, and took the number six bus back to Blackrock.

Mary saw how worried I was when I returned, and she asked what was up with me. I told her the story.

"Jesus Ned, why did you ever get involved with an IRA family?"

"I was in a hole, I was broke, I needed to get home."I never mentioned Father Delany's generosity. I wasn't proud of lying to Mary.

"You were right to come home Ned, you'd be dead by now otherwise. But by the sound of what Aengus Hynes said, coming home is only a short stay-of-execution. At least you're getting back to your old self health-wise. I'd help you if I could, but raising five boys isn't easy, and I don't have any savings. Vinny and I are put to the pin-of-our-collars to make ends meet. "Mary said.

I knew too she'd have smelt the drink off me.

"I understand Mary, I know you've both been more than generous to me. I'll head back to Bagenalstown this weekend, I feel strong enough now to work. Aengus Hynes has worried the hell out of me. I've only four weeks to pay him back."

"I'll pray tonight for you Ned. Maybe God will show us a way."

"Maybe." I said, and left the room. That night I slept little. Fear has a way of getting' in on you. I suppose it's just like what a rabbit feels when it's cornered. No way

127

out.

Next day Mary spoke to me.

"Ned, I had words with Vinny about your situation, and you're in luck about the house in Bagenalstown. We'd rented it out after Mammy died, but it's been vacant since last month. You can stay there. If you like we can sell it and you can take your share of the proceeds".

I thanked her and said I'd think about it.

That night I had second-thoughts about selling the house. It was a two–edged sword. Yes, I could pay Aengus Hynes off, but I was afraid of drinking the rest of the money, and then having nothing left. And I felt Ma wouldn't like it either, and she looking down on me like my Angel Guardian. And I remembered all the happy times I'd had there. No, I wasn't going to sell the house. I'd be letting everyone down, including myself. No, I'd go get a job and pay Aengus Hynes back the hard way.

On the first day back in the old homestead in Bagenalstown I had a weird feeling. I kept seeing Ma's spirit everywhere. The memories flooded back. It was eerie. A lot of the furniture in the house was the same, and it now had running water, and electricity. A radio but no TV. I spent the day cleaning and sorting out the garden which was overgrown. I felt like someone who'd returned from the dead.

That night, my mind returned to the problem of paying Aengus Hynes. I realised I had only three weeks left to raise the money. I had to do something. After turning things over in my head, I came up with only one plan of action. I looked out the window and saw it was raining. I took my cap from the back of the door, put it on my head, and headed for the pub.

Chapter 15

Brendan Hackett's Story

I was always a church-going person, though truth to tell, my wife Brigid, I called her Breeg, was the mover and shaker for my religious rituals. Sunday mass, weekly confession, monthly sodality, the annual retreat, we used attend them all. Then when our Nancy got pregnant, and the Monsignor started preaching from the pulpit at the Sunday mass about the scandal in the parish, and everyone in the church knowing what and who he was referring to, I stood up, marched down the aisle, and out of the house of God, fit to be tied, swearing never to set foot in the place again.

And I didn't ever go there again, though Breeg kept attending, saying I was over-reacting, and that God was bigger than the people that ran the church. I didn't care, I was hurt to the quick, and from then on I did my praying at home, and if I ever saw that Monsignor approaching me on the street in Bagenalstown, I'd cross to the far side of the road. And him with his high colour, not due to excessive sun, but to a fondness for the liquor and left-over altar wine. And him being the self-same fellow that banned Bingo in the Parish Hall, saying that gambling was Satan's handiwork, even though the proceeds of the Bingo were going to help the poor in the parish. And then the people telling him what they thought of that idea, by taking the bus from outside the parish boundary to play Bingo in Leighlinbridge. He got his come-uppance then, but it was like water-off-a-duck to him.

I was proud as a peacock when Nancy took my name when she joined the nuns. Sister Brendan. The lads in the pub were impressed too, and would snigger here comes Sister Hackett, when they saw me coming in the door. I didn't care what they said, I was chuffed to say the least, and I'd pretend to bless them, saying they were the Devil's Disciples, and needed a lot of praying for.

Then poor Breeg's passing away really knocked me for six. Only a few short years after me retiring from the job in the beet factory. Her dying laid me as low as you can go. My best friend and love of my life gone, and me left alone, disconsolate. Every room in the house was haunted by her spirit. I spoke to her every day, all one-way talk, but I felt the better of it. Life didn't seem worth living anymore for a while, a long while. Eventually I got over it, but life was never the same again.

Then lo-and-behold, came me later falling sick and being stuck in a wheelchair, but thank God for having Nancy back now to look after me. She's the silver lining in my clouds of grey. I'm so lucky, and I'm sure Breeg's prayers from on high had something to do with Nancy's return. She's made a difference for sure. Not only has she nearly got me walking again, but she's got me crazed about that infernal game of cricket after me reading that book, and it being against all my principles. I do hope she stays, she lights up my life. It's like having a new lease of life in later years when any of your children come back to stay with you, no matter for how long. Loneliness is the Devil's companion. I hope she feels happy to be home.

Nick called today, wanting to see Nancy, but she'd gone shopping with Kitty. Was it anything in particular? I'd asked him. I knew Nick was under pressure in his job, and also because his girl friend Sheila Hynes had left him. Nothing really, he'd replied, but as he turned to leave, fidgeting with his hat in his hands, he spoke again saying, there is something Dad. Ned Rooney is back in town, back again after all these years, the worse for wear too, and in some trouble. What kind of trouble? I enquired. Can't say any more Dad, please keep the news under your hat, I'll speak to Nancy another time. He put his hat on then and left. Afterwards I worried about this development, thinking it might affect her staying at home, just when everything was going so well.

I like looking at the pictures on the mantelpiece. I do it every day, it brings back memories. There's a framed one there of Nancy and me, on the day she became a nun. Pride of place. Beside it there's one of Breeg and me on our wedding day. Next to that is one of me retiring after 40 years working in the beet factory in Carlow, and they presenting me with a silver watch. I still wear it. By God I earned it. Never late a day in my life, and rarely missed a day through sickness, and proud of it.

Also framed on the wall are the three medals my father had got for serving in the First World War with the Royal Irish Rifles. He never liked to talk about the war. After he died, I'd found an envelope in with his private papers. It was marked on the outside "How it was." Inside was a letter. I'd taken it out and read it.

The rain is relentless, non-stop since we got to France. We're scampering around in the mud like rats. They're bombing the trenches mercilessly. The Germans have us trapped. If we leave the trenches their machine guns just mow us down. Take your pick. We drove them out of Le Pilly a few days ago, but at a huge cost of lives. Now they have us surrounded. Our only hope is to pray that the promised help from the British and French battalions arrives in time. If they don't come, we'll be crucified. Dear God, I pray, save us. The noise pounds my ears. I hear the whine from the shells in the air before they land. Wheeeeeeeeeeeh. I feel a pain in my gut. It must be fear.

I pray a bomb doesn't land nearby and blow me to Kingdom Come. But that outcome might be better than ending up like some of the poor wretches nearby, lying askew in the mud, limbs and minds half-blown away. I can see my friend Andy Lee nearby in the trench, now with that thousand-yard stare. He's all into himself now, hardly talks. How will he be if he survives? I pray I don't end up like that. But you can't blame the poor lad with the hell all around. Nobody told us it would be like this. Nobody knew. Nobody knows even now. The bombardment is smashing the trench to smithereens. I flatten myself against its side and pray. Dear God, get us out of here safe, please make the shelling stop. Inside my pocket I feel the rosary beads my mother gave me, and put my hand back on my rifle. And the rain keeps falling, dripping slowly onto my mud-spattered face. And the shells keep screaming down. And the men keep dying. And I feel like crying. Dear God, make it end. Soon.

Sometime later, after reading it many times, I'd lit a match and burnt the letter, dropping it into the fireplace, afraid my mother would find it and read it, afraid it would affect her the way it had affected me.

My father had worked in the beet factory in Carlow before me, since it opened in 1926, Bishop Foley turning the first sod. Father was a fitter, and so was I. He said the factory was the lifeblood of the people of Carlow from the word-go, and also a cornerstone of the economy for the new Government in Ireland, set up in 1922. The factory had a towering 300 foot chimney, and was fully built and operational within one year. It was a sugar factory, but from the word go everyone called it a beet factory. He was a hard worker, my father. He used say work was good for the soul. The Government, he told me, had picked Carlow for the first sugar manufacturing factory, as it had the best hinterland for growing beet, and accessing the factory, and they'd even got international advice from Belgium in their decision to locate there. Transport by the river Barrow was also a factor.

Most farmers in the county grew beet. Many people in Bagenalstown also grew it on small holdings. We even had a few acres under beet at the back of our house on Kilree Street up by the railway bridge. Beet farming was the most soul-destroying, back-breaking work you could think of. The beet had to be "thinned", that is there had to be a gap the size of a man's hand (mind you women did this tough work too) between each beet plant. To do this people had to crawl on their hands and knees through the drills, sacks tied around their legs, weeding out the thistles and scutch grass. Every Autumn, the beet had to be pulled by hand

and "crowned", that is, all the leaves cut off. Then the beet would be taken by horse and cart to the factory. It was hard work all the way, and we all worked like slaves.

I left school early on, serving my time as a fitter and started in the factory in the mid-thirties, cycling the ten miles into Carlow town each day with my father. No complaining, you got on with it, you were lucky to have work, he always said. He passed away eight years later from pneumonia. Ma blamed it on all the wettings he got going to and from the factory. I missed his company on the bike, and him puffing away on his pipe, regaling me with his stories of the hurling and the football. The journeys seemed longer after he was gone. I missed him, but I kept the flag flying for him and the family by working there the rest of me days. In a strange way I would've liked if Nick had followed in our footsteps in the factory, a third generation of Hacketts there, but he had the education, and he made other plans for his life, ending up in the Guards.

Many of my friends worked with me in the factory, even Ferdia Hynes, the father of Nick's ex-girlfriend, and there was a great team spirit there. We'd a huge Social Club for the workers. It was called Coset (the name of a small head of beet). I was secretary for a few years. We had football and hurling teams, and played games against other sugar factories over the years. We did charitable works in the community. My proudest achievement was when we established a "utility housing project committee" to help people purchase homes. Later this type of housing was known as "Co-op Housing." I've started writing a history of Coset, and intend to continue on it when I'm back on my feet.

When Nancy gets back from her shopping, we'll be going for our daily walk down by the river. I'd better tell her the news about Ned Rooney then. The weather today is fine, windless, an autumnal rust on the leaves, and the swallows are on-the-wing, readying themselves for their long travels to warmer climes, and people getting ready to harvest the beet. I long for the day I'll be able to do the walk on my own. I hope and pray it will come soon.

Chapter 16

Borris

Ned Rooney sauntered into the Railway House Bar and glanced about. Twilight dim and shadowy inside, the pub was sparsely populated, with no one he recognised drinking there. Neither did he expect anyone to remember him after all his years abroad. He went to the bar, sat on a stool, put his elbows on the counter, and ordered a pint. He felt the barman staring at him for an instant before turning to get his order. Stranger in town, down at heel, hope he's not going to be trouble later, Ned imagined him thinking.

No point in hiding in a corner, Ned reckoned, hard to make contact drinking in a corner. People think you want to be alone and stay away. Sit up at the bar and they'll come to you eventually. The mountain will surely come to Mohammed. In his pocket, he'd barely enough for four pints. He'd have to make the money his step-sister Mary lent him stretch for the week. The next day he'd sign on the dole, but knew it could be a few weeks before he got any money from that quarter. He knew there was no one in the town he could borrow from.

He'd three weeks left to raise the cash to pay Aengus Hynes and he felt the pressure mounting each day. He could feel it in his bones. As he lowered his first pint he relaxed, but the futility of his position struck him. Even if he got a job, the most he could save would barely be a quarter of what he needed. He'd have to sell the house. It was the only way, he reluctantly realised. But that would take maybe six months or more, much too long to get him off the hook with Hynes. He sighed, realising there was no easy way out of the fix he was in. It was either a rock or a hard place. He racked his brains.

There was nothing he could think of in the house that was worth selling. Maybe an old Singer sewing-machine, or a brass-lamp, or an oak table. But he knew deep down he wouldn't be able sell any of them, the memories of his Ma were too strong. It wouldn't solve the problem either. He rued the day he'd ever got himself into this mess. He knocked back another mouthful. It was his only solace.

Halfway through his second drink a small, lean man in a cap sidled up to him, placed his pint on the bar, took off his cap, revealing a greying, receding hairline, and held out his hand.

"Ned Rooney, it *is* yourself. It took me a few minutes to be sure I recognised you. It's me, Tom Keogh from Leighlinbridge. Remember when we used hunt rabbits together many moons ago? There were four of us then that went hunting every Sunday after mass, always meeting at your house. We used call ourselves The Four Musketeers. God, I remember them days well, those times were some of the best memories of my youth."

"I sure do remember them times, you old son-of-a-gun. You haven't changed much either Tom. What're you having?" Ned drawled, grasping Tom's hand hard in a John-Wayne-like grip.

"No, it's my treat tonight Ned, great to see you back again old son, it's been a long time."Tom Keogh replaced his cap and called the barman.

A real friend, one of the old stock, Ned thought, he could see I was down on my luck. Ned remembered how Tom used proudly regale him, when they were out rabbit hunting in the old days, about his home-town Leighlinbridge's most famous inhabitant and ancestor of his family, Captain Myles Keogh(see Note 1), and how he'd fought and died a hero's death with General Custer at the battle of Little Big Horn, against the Sioux. A real hero in Ned's mind. Ned always wanted to go down that way, if he had to die, a hero against the odds, just like in the movies.

Later, sipping their drinks, they reminisced on past exploits, especially the lore of hunting rabbits, before Ned finally blurted out what was on his mind.

"Look Tom, between the two of us I'm in a jam. I've borrowed some money and have to pay it back pronto, if not I'm in trouble, and I mean big trouble. I need to get a job, or work of any kind. I'm kinda desperate, you know what I mean?"Ned's brow furrowed as he spoke.

Silence followed, as Tom scratched his head, alarmed by the look on Ned's face and the tremor in his voice.

"Jobs are scarce as hen's teeth Ned. I work in the Foundry, and there's nothing doing there, definitely. But there is some work here and there. Are you happy to do any kind of work?" Tom asked, as he saw the worried frown still etched on Ned's face. Ned had always been the boss in their group, and Tom couldn't believe he'd fallen so low.

"Hell yes, I'll take anything Tom. There's nothing you can mention *amigo*, that's worse than some of the work I've already done. You know me of old, I work hard. Work hard, play hard, that's me." There was an edge of desperation in Ned's voice.

"Sure I do know that Ned, but time takes its toll on us all. I've heard there is some work in Borris. Are you prepared to travel there? It's about ten miles away."

"Didn't we hunt rabbits near there many a time, do you not remember?" Ned replied.

"Will I ever forget? But we were young then and could walk that far. I suppose you could cycle there."

"I could *amigo*, there's an old upstairs jalopy at home in the shed. I'll check it out when I get home."Ned's heart filled with hope as he spoke.

"Ok, here's the deal Ned, Sean Gough's a neighbour of mine and he works in Borris House. He told me they need someone for seasonal work, general labouring and the like. You're in luck, I saw him come into the pub just a while back. Will I talk to him?"

"Sure Tom please do, the money is not that important, I just need something to get me going." Ned felt relieved as he sank another mouthful, hoping he might get the break he needed.

Within minutes Tom was back, smiling.

"You're fine Ned, Sean remembered you of old, and said he'd been asked to hire someone soon by the Kavanaghs. They're good people. Want to go over and shake Sean's hand?"

Ned nodded and followed Tom across the pub. Sean Gough, a strong blue-eyed six footer in a red lumberjack shirt, with a mop of wiry, greying hair, stood up from the table he was sharing with another man, grasped Ned's hands, and spoke.

"Yes Ned, I remember you and your mother from way back. My younger brother Frank hunted rabbits with you. Remember Patch, his little brown-and-white terrier? Now the work in Borris is hard but I heard you're hungry for it, and that's what I like to hear. I want somebody who really wants to work. I'll see you at Borris House in the morning at nine. You'll have to get there under your own steam. I have a small put-put but can't take passengers. I hope to rise to a scooter next year."

"Thanks Sean I'll be there. And I do remember your brother and the dog."Ned replied, smiling, before returning to the bar with Tom, where he polished off his drink, and stood up.

"Thanks Tom me ould segosha, you've got me a last chance. I'll not forget it. Got to get home now and get ready for tomorrow. Saddle the horses."

"You do that Ned. Good luck." They shook hands, and Ned left the pub.

The old Raleigh bike was in an unlocked shed at the bottom of the garden. Not worth stealing Ned reckoned, as he inspected it. It obviously hadn't been used in years and was rusted in parts. He found an old tin of three-in-one oil on a shelf. The bicycle pump was still in its place beneath the crossbar. He oiled the chain and wheel axles before pumping up the tyres, holding his breath in case either had a puncture, as he couldn't find a puncture repair kit. They inflated ok. He exhaled, relieved. After making some sandwiches and wrapping them up, he placed them in a plastic bag on the table and retired to bed, hoping the next day would be the start of him solving his financial woes. He knew it wasn't really going to solve them but it was a start. Dang sure it was, he thought.

***

Pushing the pedals along the tar road to Borris, Ned gazed at the sun lifting above Mount Leinster to the East, drying morning dew from the fields and the blackberry-laden hedgerows. He stopped and sampled a mouthful of the berries. They tasted good. They brought back memories. He remembered picking cans of mushrooms in the nearby fields and flogging them for the price of the cinema. In some fields he spotted rabbits hopping about. He hadn't realised they'd made a comeback from the Myxomatosis. His spirits lifted then.

High above him in the big trees, raucous rooks ranted. He'd brought a raincoat, clipped to his back carrier along with his sandwiches. He smiled, realising he'd not need it. Shorn wheat stubble fields flitted by, yellowed in the morning sun. Rusted leaves lay on the roadside, floating from the high trees in leafy showers. Only an occasional tractor or car passed him on the road and in less than an hour he was freewheeling down the neat and tidy main street of Borris, resplendent with granite-fronted buildings bedecked with flowers. The backs of his legs ached after he'd pushed up the street to the Step Hotel. He dismounted opposite it, and entered the Borris estate through the high, wrought-iron gates.

Ned gasped when Borris House suddenly came into view. Stately, splendidly majestic in its Tudor Gothic grandeur, redolent of bygone eras, bordered by graceful gardens. Mount Leinster and the Blackstairs Mountains loomed in the background. The Barrow flowed below, and in the near distance was the ancient 16-arched railway viaduct.

Sean Gough met him near the gate and brought him to the stables at the rear of the house, where Ned would spend the day shovelling and cleaning-out. No problem said Ned, surveying the scene. Later, Sean warned him that the next week would see the beginning of the beet-harvesting, and the work would get a lot harder. Ned grinned saying it wouldn't be a problem, he'd done it in his youth and he was stronger now. Inwardly he felt whacked but was determined to make a go of the job.

Ned and Sean met at lunchtime, sitting in the sunshine, admiring the resplendent gardens. Ned wolfed a sandwich, washed down by a cup of tea.

"How's it going Ned?" Sean asked.

"Grand Sean, it's going grand for sure, but there's one thing annoying me."

"What's that?"

"For all the years I lived nearby in Bagenalstown, and even coming out this neck of the woods to hunt rabbits, I never got to know anything about Borris, its history and all that. I know fuck-all about the history here. I'd love to read a book about the place. I used read a lot, just like my Ma, before I went to England, you know."

"I didn't know that, but I'll see what I can do Ned."

Later that afternoon Sean came back to the stables and handed Ned a small, dog-eared book.

"With the compliments of Missus Kavanagh, the Lady of the House. She said she was delighted that any of her staff would want to read about her ancestors."

"That's nice of her. Thanks Sean."Ned stuffed the book into his pocket.

Wheeling his bike out the gate at day's end, he mounted it and headed home, passing a few enticing pubs on Borris's main street on the way. He noted the names, *Joyce's, O'Shea's,* and *de Barra.* He was tempted to try one but resisted, afraid he'd never get home. His only stop was to buy a puncture repair kit. Strange what fear does to you, he thought. That night he fell into bed, too tired even to go down to the pub, but not too tired to read the small book he'd been given, anxious to learn about the place that had given him a job, given him hope, maybe given him a lifeline. Ned started reading.

Borris House was once a Castle guarding the Barrow whose history went right back to the High Kings of Leinster, to Diarmuid Mac Murrough, who'd brought the Normans to Ireland, and whose daughter Aoife had married Strongbow in Christchurch Cathedral in Dublin. In the lineage ruling Borris House one man stood head and shoulders above all others, Arthur MacMurrough Kavanagh. In fact he didn't stand head and shoulders over anyone, being born limbless. By amazing spirit and willpower, and the help of his mother Harriet and his nurse Anne Fleming, Arthur had miraculously overcome his disabilities.

Amongst his many achievements, he was a skilled horseman, huntsman, and sailor, and in 1853 at 22 years he became Squire of Borris, when his father and two brothers had predeceased him. Arthur was a good Landlord, and transformed the fortunes of Borris House and the town, building a sawmill, getting the viaduct built for a railway line through the town, and designing houses for the town of Borris, using locally-quarried granite.

When he married, his bride Frances was 21 years old. Before they married, she'd worried that any of their children might be born deformed. He promptly drove her around Borris town in a horse and carriage, pointing out several fine children he'd already sired. Frances was re-assured, and they went on to have seven children and a long and happy marriage.

Arthur donated land to the railway company to entice the railway to run through Borris, and helped his wife develop a world-famous Borris Lace industry. As an MP he travelled to London in his own yacht, mooring it under the Houses of Parliament.

Ned was stunned. This was a man in a million, reflecting a ray of hope to anyone in distress with disability. Anybody with a complaint should read this story, Ned thought. No more whining or whinging for me. He placed the book on the bed table, said his prayers, and put out the light.

Sean Gough wasn't kidding with his warning about hard work. The next day was one of the most gruelling Ned had ever spent. Things had changed a lot since he'd first worked in a beet field as a teenager. Dang right they had, he muttered ruefully. There was a two-hour training period, including knife-sharpening on the grindstone, followed by demonstrations of procedures, and finally he was presented with written instructions. He gazed at these as he held them in his hands:

Pulling and Piling beets:

1. Straddle a row and walk it to minimise bending.
2. Pull and pile beets in a stooped position. Don't lift beets any higher than necessary to knock dirt off.
3. Always knock beets together to remove dirt.
4. Grab at least two beets in each hand before pulling and piling.

Topping :
1. After picking beet up with a knife, do not straighten up to top it.
2. Do not raise the beet any higher than the knee to top it.
3. Prevent cutting fingers with knife by placing hand underneath beet to hold it,
4. Hold the beet directly in front of you to prevent striking the leg with the knife hook.

5. Don't raise the knife higher than is necessary. Keep knife sharp.

There were further instructions for loading the topped beet into the trucks.

He weighed up the beet knife, an eleven inch blade with a hook at the end to snag the heads of beet. Dangerous weapon, he muttered, makes me feel like Jim Bowie. By the end of the day he'd become proficient at wielding it. There was also a selection of smaller gardening knives at his disposal. During the day he took a six-inch bladed knife, sharpened it, and slipped it into its scabbard, before putting it inside his coat pocket. Handy to have on you when you're working, he thought, I'll leave it there all the time. Handy for skinning rabbits too, maybe. That night his body ached in places it never had before.

Each day, his work on the beet harvesting improved, and Sean Gough complimented Ned as he handed him his week's pay packet on Friday. The Master's pleased with your progress, Sean said, he told me to inform you. That's good to know, Ned replied, it's a new experience for my body, but I think I'm gettin' the knack. Dang right I am.

Ned realised it was the last week of his deadline to pay his debts. It weighed upon his mind. He'd seen Aengus Hynes around the town in the distance, and suspected he'd have someone spying on him at night in the local pub. Aengus won't be leaving Bagenalstown just yet for the North, Ned thought. He's got unfinished business. *Me.*

Ned put his savings into a bag that evening. It wasn't much, he knew, but it was a start. Better get it over with, he muttered, and walked up the road to Aengus Hynes' house on the Crescent. Aengus himself opened the door, grim-faced, and ushered Ned into the parlour, saying he'd been expecting him.

"Jesus Ned, is this all you're giving me?" Aengus asked, shaking his head, incredulous.

"Shite Aengus, I broke my back to get that much, broke my back so I did. I've got a job, I just need more time. I'm doing my best can't you see?"Desperation edged Ned's voice.

"I'm sorry Ned, but you just don't seem to get it. This is out of my control, unfortunately for you. I've stuck my neck out already, I'm afraid I can't do anymore for you. It's out of my hands now."

"Look Aengus, there's three acres going with Ma's house. It's planted with beet, and set for the year. When the year's over, I'll sell the field an' pay you in full, I swear on my mother's grave."Ned pleaded as he blessed himself.

"Ned, your mother was a fine woman, so don't go bringing her into this, and she's got you a reprieve so far, but what you've just paid me is derisory, and I'm afraid that's how it'll be seen by those who now make the decisions. Sorry Ned, I must go now."As he spoke Hynes' face was impassive, cold, his eyes glazed. He stood up, indicating the meeting was over.

Ned left the house, fuming. Aengus Hynes is doing the Pontius Pilate act, he muttered, washing his hands of the matter. I'll show them. He headed towards the Fairgreen, then up to the Garda station on Kilree Street. The Garda attending noticed his agitated state and motioned him inside to a private room.

"What exactly is your problem Mister Rooney?" The young guard asked, filling in a sheet before him.

"You can call me Ned, guard. I want to report that my life is under threat."

The guard's eyebrows rose above his narrowed eyes as he wrote down the details. At the end he assured Ned they would do their best to protect him but due to lack of resources would be unable to guarantee anything. They would pay Aengus Hynes a precautionary visit in his home. He added that Ned was right to report the matter.

Ned stumbled out into the sunshine, relieved, then went to the church and prayed, before heading for the Railway House Bar.

Note 1:

Captain **Myles Keogh**, from Leighlinbridge in County Carlow, left Ireland in 1860, at twenty years of age, to fight in the Papal Wars in Italy, on behalf of the Pope. He was awarded a Papal medal for his bravery, and thereafter always wore it around his neck.

He later fought with valour on the Unionist side in the American Civil War.

Afterwards, he served under General Custer in the 7th U.S. Cavalry. Before embarking on the ill-fated expedition which ended in his death in 1876 at the battle of Little Big Horn, Keogh had become engaged to a lady in Albany, New York. He was second-in-command to Custer in the battle, and fought with much bravery. The only survivor of Little Big Horn was Keogh's horse, Comanche.

Some years later, Keogh's fiancé had his body re-interred in Albany, New York. She never married, and for the rest of her life, visited his grave every week to lay flowers in his memory.

Chapter 17

Graiguenamanagh

After leaving the new school, Nancy turned left towards the Fairgreen, treading with a lighter step. Earlier, she'd arrived, a bundle of nerves, to apply for a temporary teaching post. The Mother Superior, Sister Cecelia, Head of Music, had interviewed her, explaining the difficulties involved in co-ed teaching. The nun's stern demeanour had at first disconcerted her. Nancy had decided it was better *not* to mention she'd once been a member of the Presentation Order. She *did* however speak of her experience in singing and training choirs.

The mention of *Monteverdi's Vespers* had made Sister Cecilia's eyes sharpen with interest, and when she mentioned that Sister Roberta had been her aunt, the nun's face lit up in a smile. Ah Sister Roberta, she exclaimed, and her lovely flowers festooning the river, such a shame to see the state of the river now, such a shame when something of beauty dies, don't you agree Miss Hackett? Nancy had nodded, her spirits rising, thinking things were now going her way. Her hopes were confirmed fifteen minutes later when told she'd got the position, starting the next Monday. She'd thanked Sister Cecelia, bowed and left the room, elation tingling through her bones. She'd got it. She couldn't wait to tell her family.

At the Fairgreen she turned left, heading down towards the river, to where the dilapidated, deserted convent building stood. Dallying there, she gazed into the swirling waters, mesmerised by the tendrils of weeds weaving beneath the water, delighted by the ducks and water hens busy about their business on the surface.

She said a prayer of thanks to her dead aunt before walking towards the lock beside the drawbridge. At the metal grill where the waters gushed into the millrace of the defunct Mill house, plastic rubbish and detritus had gathered against the bars in an unsightly mess. She resolved to do something about this disgrace, angry that nobody else seemed too bothered. And she vowed she'd do it in Sister Roberta's memory. *And* she would start the next day.

Her heart lifted when she turned to see a pair of swans elegantly arrowing their way down the river towards her, noiseless, heads haughty and high as they eyed her. Her mind went back to her schooldays to the story of *The Children of Lir*, who were turned by magic into swans and lived for 900 years. She recalled then that swans mated for life and thought it a pity that in her world things didn't always work out the same way. The serene stillness and beauty of the swans took her thoughts away from the rubbish in the river. She guessed by their silence they were mute swans.

Arriving back at the house, she put the kettle on. Kitty had taken her father downtown to collect his pension and do some shopping and was due back soon. But it was her brother Nick who arrived first, standing before her in the dining room, fidgeting with his Garda hat.

"Ah Nick, how are you? Will I put your name in the pot? I'm over the moon, I've just landed a job, temporary mind you, in the new school on the Royal Oak road, starting next Monday."

He put his hat down, and grabbed her in a bear-hug.

"Halleluiah, that's great news Nancy, great news altogether, well done." He said, as a frown furrowed his face.

"Anything on your mind Nick? You look worried."

"Well yeah, there is actually…look Nancy, I don't want to spoil the day for you, but there's some news I've just heard that you might find worrying. I think I should let you know about it, while we're here alone."As he spoke he fidgeted with the buttons on his uniform.

"What news is that?" She held her breath, expecting the worst.

"It might be nothing, but it's just that Ned Rooney's back in town. After everyone thinking he was dead and buried. He's now living back in his mother's house and working in Borris. He's alone, and has had a rough time of it in England. Most people say they'd hardly recognise him now. They say that it was the drink that dragged him down."

"Well, that's a bit surprising all right, but hardly disturbing news."She replied, unperturbed.

Nick was surprised she seemed unmoved by what he'd told her. He continued.

"I suppose not. The disturbing bit is that he's gotten into trouble with Aengus Hynes, a local IRA honcho. Ned owes him money, and he can't pay it back quick enough. He's been threatened with bodily harm. Grievous-bodily-harm. He's obviously worried, and has complained to the Garda about it."

"Oh, that's bad… and…and what's going to happen? Hynes is the brother of your girlfriend Sheila isn't he?"

"Ex-girlfriend you mean? Yes, he is her older brother. They're a dyed-in-the-wool IRA family. I called to their house today, and when Aengus opened the door, I told him of the complaint against him."

"And what did he say?"

"He became belligerent, and virtually blew up. Told me it was a pack of lies, and then told me to fuck off and not be annoying people who were putting their lives on-the-line for their country, not like me, and wasters like Ned Rooney. I warned him then and there, and told him to watch out or I'd book him. He spat on the step outside the house, went in and slammed the door. He's a very nasty piece of goods. Though I suppose his IRA bosses are pulling the strings."Nick said, shrugging.

"No doubt they are. Mind you, your ex-girl friend might think you're just out for revenge, hassling her brother."

"She can think what she likes, but I'm just doing my job."

"Of course you are, now please sit down while I pour your tea."Nancy surmised his ex-girlfriend was still a touchy subject with Nick.

Minutes later Kitty arrived with her father and joined them at the table. Nick drained his cup in one gulp, stood up, excused himself and left, citing work pressure for a pending meeting in Kilkenny with an Inspector Doogan.

"Nick should take a break, he's been pushing himself too hard. That Inspector's giving him a hard time, and he hasn't got over that Hynes colleen. He'll crack up if he's not careful." Brendan Hackett spoke from his wheelchair, scone in one hand, teacup in the other.

"You're spot-on Dad, but he's a bit like you, he doesn't throw-in-the-towel easily. Anyway let's celebrate only good news today, Nancy's new job, and you taking ten steps today in the Post Office on your own, without a stick." Kitty said, holding up her cup.

They all smiled then, clinking their cups.

"Just as well I'm getting' around better, I won't have Nancy here to nursemaid me anymore, she'll be off earning a buck or two."Brendan Hackett sighed.

"No you won't Dad, but I'll be around though, and Nancy will be home early every day." Kitty patted his shoulder as she spoke.

Nancy was halfway through her first week teaching when a letter she was half-expecting and half-dreading arrived from Marty. Brief and to the point, it had been posted in Graiguenamanagh, and said he'd arrived home for a summer break, later than expected, but he still missed her company and would love to meet her and gave a telephone number, asking if she could call him at six o'clock on Thursday. It was decision time, she realised.

That night in bed she lay awake, in a dilemma, pondering her relationship with Marty. Yes, she'd enjoyed his company, but that was in a foreign country. Her life had now settled into a more sedate pattern, and overall she was content. So why should she complicate it? She felt more confident now, her enclosed convent life behind her. But Sister Veronica's warning words still churned in her mind. Sleep came hard and only after much praying, after which she decided that next morning she *would* ring him.

And she did, and after some chit-chat agreed that he'd collect her in his hired car on Saturday at ten and they'd travel to Graiguenamanagh for the day. The weather was promised fair, he said, so pack your togs, *and* walking boots. He also said he had a surprise to show her. He remembered she liked surprises.

She put down the phone, nerves jangling, glad she'd rung him. Something to look forward to, she muttered as she started packing. She told Kitty of her decision, asking if she'd keep-an-eye on Daddy while she was away.

"Of course Nancy, you go and enjoy yourself. Are you stayin' the night in Graiguenamanagh? Don't worry about Daddy, I'll spend the night here with him."

"I hadn't thought about staying, but you never know, maybe I'll throw in a few extra things to wear."

"You do that Nancy. Be prepared, just like the Boy Scouts." Kitty laughed.

Saturday came and Marty arrived on the dot, dressed in holiday gear. She remembered his Panama hat and sun glasses from Milan. A flowery shirt and khaki shorts completed his rigout. In the distance she saw the sun rising above Mount Leinster's pointed top in an indigo sky, and felt it was a good omen for the weekend.

"They'd never take you for a priest Marty, dressed like that." She said, lugging her bag out the door.

"When I'm on holidays Nancy I'm a priest incognito. I like to do my own thing, keep a low profile. Here, let me take your bag."He threw her bag into the boot of the Fiat Bambino.

"Sorry I don't have a more salubrious means of transport, but it gets me around, and it's all I can afford."He said.

"Its fine, I'm right used to shank's-mare anyway." She replied, sitting tight beside him in the passenger seat.

***

At Graiguenamanagh, he parked beside the river. Leaving the car, she stood in awe, admiring the seven-arched bridge straddling the river, eye-mirrored in the water by the sun dazzling down.

"I'd forgotten how charming and beautiful this place is." She exclaimed, remembering her first visit on a school outing in her teens.

"It's quite something for sure Nancy, more so on a day like this. Let's start by visiting Duiske Abbey. I like to go there every day. It's my daily fix, my Irish equivalent of visiting the *Duomo*."

She followed him up the road into the ancient portals of the Abbey. Inside she was taken to another era, the sun shining through the arched, stain-glassed Lancet windows as she walked along the medieval tiles. She was transfixed by the life-sized effigy of a 13th Century Norman Knight. She knelt and prayed, before joining Marty, who stood beside a statue near the exit.

"Who's he?" She whispered in Marty's ear, pointing at the statue.

"I'll tell you over a cup of coffee." He smiled back.

Later on High Street, outside a clean and pleasant café, they sipped coffees beneath an umbrella, admiring the sun's shiny ascent over Mount Brandon.

"And now what about that statue, I'm dying to know?" She enquired.

"*St Fiachra*. He founded the early Christian church of Ullard near the town, in the sixth century. Later he moved to France, and is known there as *St Fiacre*. He built a celebrated monastery at *Meaux*. In France he's the patron saint of gardeners and taxi drivers."

"Really?"

"Yes. In fact French cabs are often known as fiacres in his honour."

"Well, I never knew. And pray tell me, what about the word Duiske?"She asked.

"It's from the Irish name for a local river *Dubh Uisce*, meaning black water."

"You're a well of information, Marty."She laughed.

"Speaking of wells, *St Fiachra* has a holy well near Kilkenny. Each year at the end of August there's a Pattern there, where sick people pray to be healed, and others pray for special intentions. Many take bottles of holy water home, believing it will cure their ills."

"That sounds like a pagan ritual."

"Maybe, but there *have* been many cures. You must admire the people's faith. It not only moves mountains, but it can cure the sick. If nothing else, it gives people hope."

"I suppose. We all live in hope."She said.

"And I have hopes that you will grow to like me Nancy and maybe someday love me, and feel the same way about me as I do about you."He spoke, reaching across the table, grasping her hands, looking into her eyes.

"The age of miracles is not over yet Marty. Don't forget your vows either. Anyway, what about this surprise you mentioned? I can't wait to know what it is. I love surprises."She said, withdrawing her hands.

"Ok, let's go and I'll show you."

He stood up, called the waitress, and paid the bill. She noticed he'd left a generous tip on the table. They walked down to the quay on the river where the boats were moored. There was a buzz about the place as people swam and frolicked in the sunshine, some diving in off the river bank.

"There it is, there's the surprise." He said, pointing to a barge, moored at the quayside, red on top with yellow sunflowers all along the sides. The name *St Fiachra* was painted on the bow.

"Wow Marty, do you own it?"She exclaimed.

"No, I rented it for a few weeks. I normally only hire it by the day, but this year the owner was abroad, so I took the chance to get a good deal and also save on my accommodation expenses. It has two bedrooms. Let me show you around."

"Yes, I'd like that."She replied, excited.

He scrambled aboard and held out his hand. She grabbed it, and leapt onto the deck. As well as the two bedrooms, it had another room that was locked, a neat galley and a living-area. He said the locked room was reserved for his friend Henry, a priest, who often came to visit. He continued.

"There are two bedrooms, if you'd like to stay the night Nancy. The choice is yours. I understand you have to look after your father, and I respect your wishes if you cannot stay."

"Thanks Marty that's kind of you, but not tonight I'm afraid. I have to be home by eight, my sister is looking after Daddy until then."As she spoke she realised she wasn't ready yet for an overnight stay, even in separate bedrooms. Maybe next time though. She remembered then Sister Veronica's advice, *Festina Lente*.

"I understand completely Nancy, in fact it's what I was half-expecting you to say. I respect your wishes and live on in hope, so let's get cracking while the sun's still shining. It's a special day for me and I want to make the most of it."

"Me too, so what's the plan?"She asked.

"What about a walk along the river to Clashganny, a picnic there, a dip, then back to the barge? We may even have time for a meal before heading back to Bagenalstown."

"Sounds great, let's go."

They took her bags from the car to the barge. Onboard, she dressed in her walking gear, putting her togs and water-bottle into her rucksack. Outside, he handed her a walking stick and they set off on the towpath on the Carlow side of the bridge.

As they walked, trees towered above them, mottled in tawny autumn hues. The scene had a tranquillity she normally found only in a church. It seemed a sin to break the spell with idle talk so they walked mostly in silence. The noise and smells of cars and roads were far away, with birdsong the only sound. They moved briskly, admiring the river curving on its smooth, silent path towards the sea.

She wondered what animals had their lairs hidden in the dark recesses of the trees. In the rushes on the far side of the river, a heron stood one-legged, rigid, waiting. The wet head of an otter surfaced in the water beside them, paddling along in curiosity for a while before vanishing. Marty said then that when the otter plunged the light of Tuscany had wavered. Nancy said nothing. Along the riverbank blackberry-bushes laden with berries dipped down towards the river. They paused to pick some, which he put into his Panama hat, laughing, and they ate them walking onwards.

Rounding a bend, Clashganny's lock and weir came into view, the sun's sheen on the water there. Soon they'd peeled off their clothes, she modestly behind a bush, put on their togs and plunged into the river, swimming across to the weir. They reclined on the mossy stones letting the white water bubble all over them, immersed in its dizzying roar and its silty smell. Sometimes a fish jumped nearby, leaving a circle behind it in the water.

As she lay in the sun at the weir, she became aware of Marty gazing at her body. She said nothing, sensing his stare, avoiding any eye contact. Secretly she felt flattered, knowing her body was still in good shape. It was not a time for conversation. Words would break the spell. Later they swam back and dried out on the bank, with the evening sun glinting the water gold. Behind the bush she put on a pair of jeans and a white, short sleeved blouse, modestly covering her body. Don't want Marty getting any ideas, she thought, as she put her long-sleeved cardigan on over her blouse.

"If you like Nancy, we could dine in the Step House in Borris on the way back home. I made a provisional booking anyway, as it's usually booked out on Saturdays. Finish off the day in style."

"I'm afraid my style is lacking a bit today Marty, what I'm wearing is all I have with me."

"From where I'm looking that's pretty ok, it's what inside the clothes that counts. You look gorgeous. You'd be stunning even in rags. Well, are you on? Yes or no?"

"Well yes in that case."

"Good, if we push hard we can make the early sitting at six." He smiled, lifting the rucksack onto his back.

***

During their meal, she sipped her second glass of white wine while Marty drained the dregs of his only glass of red wine, before switching to the tumbler of water before him.

"My duck was delicious and how was your sea-bass?"He enquired, gazing into her eyes.

"Divine. It was the perfect end to the day, just as you said, Marty."

"Yes, I couldn't fault it. All things must end, and the perfect end of the perfect day for me would be you staying the night. But as Shakespeare says, the course of true love never does run smooth. Your father's calling, and I respect your devotion to him, and whenever you want to go, I'm ready to roll. Just say the word." He seemed downcast as he spoke.

"Thanks, I will surely Marty, but before I go there are a couple of things on my mind. Things I'd like to talk to you about, if you don't mind. I feel I know you well enough now to discuss them with you. I hope you'll understand." She said, hesitantly.

"Of course Nancy please do, I deem it an honour to be your confidante. And the fact that you were a nun is not a problem at all, if that's what's worrying you. "

"I knew you'd understand Marty. It's actually nothing to do with me being a nun. Well the fact is.... I....I have a son. It happened before I became a nun. He was adopted. I'm trying to contact him, and hope to do so in the near future. He's actually somewhere in Ireland."

In the ensuing silence he twiddled with his glass, a faraway gleam in his eyes, before speaking.

"Thanks for telling me Nancy. I hope you get to meet him. That would be really wonderful. I do mean that, and believe me I'm speaking from experience."

"What do you mean Marty?"She asked, surprised.

"I mean I never met my own father. I really regret that."

"Oh, how sad that is for you. At least you have your mother."

He paused again before replying.

"Yes, I idolise my mother. She was my hero.....I mean she *is* my hero."

"There's something else on my mind that I need to unburden to someone." She continued.

"Please tell me Nancy, no one else will know, you have my word." He said, reaching across the table and touching her hands momentarily.

"Well, it only happened recently, but the father of my son has now returned to Bagenalstown. Ned Rooney is his name. He'd emigrated to England before my son was born. I haven't seen him since. He was a handsome devil then and I fell for him I suppose, but that's all water under that bridge now. He went on hard times over there through drink and gambling habits, and now he's in trouble with an IRA family in Bagenalstown, due to some money matter. They've threatened him with bodily harm or worse. I've no real feeling for him now, but he is the father of my son and I worry he'll come to some harm."

"And who is the IRA person?"Marty asked.

"Aengus Hynes, he lives on the Crescent in the town."

"And what about reporting it to the Garda?"

"Ned did report the matter, my brother Nick is in the guards, he told me. It's a bit complicated, you see Aengus Hynes' sister is Nick's former girlfriend."

"Oh, and who is she now going out with?"

"An Inspector Doogan from Kilkenny, Nick's boss. I told you it was complicated."

"It is for sure. I can understand why you're worried Nancy. Let me know if anything happens. You have my phone number now. I'm glad you confided in me. It means a lot to me, more than you know. We'd best make tracks now, its seven thirty."He looked concerned as he put his hat on, paid the bill, and escorted her outside to the Bambino.

"This is my Bambino, you have a real bambino. I wish I had one like yours."He joked, standing beside the car, his arms embracing her. She looked up into his grey eyes, pulled his face down, and kissed him lightly on the lips.

"Thank you for a lovely day Marty and thanks for taking a weight off my mind."As she spoke she felt an attraction to Marty for the first time. He had lightened her load.

"My pleasure Nancy. Now what about next weekend? We could take a barge trip to St Mullins."He said as he unlocked the car.

"I'd love that." She replied, sitting beside him in the cramped seating, searching for the seat belt which had fallen down beside the door.

"That's great, same time same place. Allow me Nancy, that bloody belt is always getting stuck there."He spoke, stretching across her body, his hands searching down the side of her jeans until he retrieved the belt, his head nudging her breast as he did so. There, presto, he said, clicking the belt together, starting the engine and heading home as the light faded.

Kitty was at the half door, chatting to a neighbour, when they returned. Nancy grabbed her bag, opened the gate and walked up to the house waving goodbye as the car took off.

"So you didn't stay the night? I hope you had a good time?"Kitty said as she opened the half-door.

"Yes Kitty, a wonderful time. I was tempted to stay but not this time, and thanks for minding Dad."

They embraced, and Kitty got her hat and coat and left, saying she'd get all the gossip from Nancy the next day. That night Nancy felt happy and she was glad she'd once more renewed her acquaintance with Marty Maher. He'd behaved impeccably, just like a real gentleman, and already she was looking forward to seeing him again. She fell asleep feeling happy.

Chapter 18

Reckoning

"I was dyin' all weekend to hear how you got on in Graigue with your man. I came early before Daddy woke, hoping we could have a good natter, including all the juicy bits." Kitty said, grinning.

"Good thinking, it's great to have someone to bounce things off. Not that there was anything world-shattering to relate, as you would expect with an ex-nun and a priest involved."

"Well, how did it go then? Give me the lowdown. Was he nice? Were you tempted to stay the night? I told you to bring extra clothes, didn't I?"Kitty asked excitedly.

"Yes you did give me some advice, even if I didn't heed it. Graiguenamanagh was a magical place, a place that bamboozled you under its spell. There wasn't half enough time to take in everything. A virtual Eden on Earth it was, perfect for walking and river-adventures."

"I'm sure the place is all of that, but you didn't answer my question about him, did you? How close did you get?"Kitty asked.

"No, I suppose I didn't answer it. Nosey-parker, don't go letting your imagination run riot. For God's sake, he's a priest, and a proper gentleman to boot, and I'm a former nun."

"Good heavens, I didn't mean you sharing a bed with him, did I? You could have stayed in a B&B."Kitty said.

"Yes I suppose I could, and I *was* tempted. He had rented a barge on the quay with two bedrooms, you know. There was plenty of space there for an overnight stay, and comfortable too."

"No, I didn't know that, well now isn't that something. Two bedrooms, ready for visitors. Jeepers, I think I'd have stayed. I'm getting jealous by the minute. So, it was just a bit of kissing and cuddling then?" Kitty grinned.

"I suppose we're just different Kitty, It's not all about that. I had other things on my mind, and I hardly knew the man, but I think I do now, at least I know him better. *Festina Lente*, that's what the nuns taught us. Make haste slowly. Now that I *do* know him better we're going next week on a barge trip to St. Mullins. I'm looking forward to that."Nancy smiled at the prospect.

"Great stuff. Fair play to you. In a way I envy you. Your life seems so much more interesting than mine. Anyway you know I do love you, whatever."Kitty said, laughing.

They embraced, just as their Dad came shuffling into the room, tapping the flagged floor with his walking-stick. Kitty hugged him and left, saying she had to go to visit a neighbour who had taken ill. After giving her father his breakfast, Nancy left for her job in the school.

***

Ned Rooney had left his bike in the shed in the garden of his house, and made a bee-line for the Railway House Bar. He breathed a sigh of relief when he got there, the almighty thirst on him. He'd arrived home at dusk, with no lamp on his bike. He'd have to buy one the next day, he thought. It was Tuesday, and he'd got paid after another week slaving on the beet harvest in Borris. He knew he had to call on Aengus Hynes the next day, and pay him some money to show he was serious about paying it all back, even though the deadline for the full amount was over two weeks gone. Maybe the visit from the Garda would make Hynes be more patient, Ned thought. Maybe Hynes was bluffing a bit with his threats. First he was going to sink a few pints. He'd earned them. He'd keep a few bob to back a few nags the next day as well. His luck was on the up, he felt it in his bones. Yes, the tide had at last turned for him. Dang right it had.

Not long later he'd fallen into bantering with some of his old pals in the pub, and the night and the pints flew. They reminisced on their old rabbit-hunting days, and talked of starting a new era of hunting rabbits in the area. They agreed they'd now call themselves the Three Old Musketeers. Only problem was none of them had a dog, never mind one trained to kill rabbits. They laughed a lot about that, and the matter was adjourned.

Around mid-night he stumbled home, turning off Kilree Street by the light at the end of the car-road. A few steps on he'd left the light behind him, and become enshrouded in darkness. Before he reached the gate to his house a man stepped from behind a telegraph pole, shining a torch into his face.

Dazzled, Ned stepped backwards and put his hand over his eyes. Squinting through his fingers he saw that the man with the torch was wearing a balaclava and had a short club, like a truncheon, in his other hand. Then he saw two others at the man's side, also wearing balaclavas and with the same short sticks, slapping them in their palms, eager to get stuck-in.

"You Ned Rooney?" The Torch man growled.

"Yeah, and who the fuck are you?"Ned snapped back.

"None of your fucking business. We're here about the money you fucking stole, Rooney. Money needed in the cause to free Ireland from the Brits. Money you never fucking paid back. Money you've obviously spent in the pubs, by the smell off you. Call yourself an Irishman? Huh." The Torch man sneered.

"Yes, I do fucking call myself an Irishman. My father fought in the First World War, and the house behind you, the house where I was reared, was given to him by the English government. My father was proud to call himself an Irishman and so am I." Ned replied, bristling, his blood rising. In all his life he'd never felt so insulted.

"I'd call you both fucking traitors to the cause. We have ways of dealing with traitors, Rooney, medicinal ways we call them. We give them a cure in three doses. The first dose is a warning. The second, a last chance. The third, final." The Torch man snapped, running his hand across his throat to emphasise the last one.

Ned was hit from behind on the back of his neck, someone shouting fuckin' traitor, as he struck the blow. He slumped to the ground, stunned, and got kicked in the head and groin as he lay there. Ye won't be doing any more fuckin' work in fuckin' Borris for a long fuckin' time, a voice yelled, high-pitched, as someone else smashed his club onto Ned's shoulder. He winced with shock and pain.

Ned slipped his hand into his pocket and felt and unsheathed the beet knife he carried there. He slashed out blindly into the blackness with the blade. If he was going to go, he'd take some of them with him, just like Jim Bowie in John Wayne's movie of the Alamo. He felt the knife sink into soft matter, and warm blood oozed over his hand. The man he'd struck swore loudly, screaming he'd been stabbed.

Dazed, Ned grabbed the wire in the hedge behind, hauling himself upright, teetering against the telegraph pole. He saw another shadow come at him, club hand held high and lunged forward, plunging the knife hard into the person's midriff. The blade was short and sank in up to the hilt. Fuck, he stabbed me, the fuckin' bastard's got a knife, someone roared. That was the last Ned heard, as another blow from behind knocked him unconscious. He slumped to the ground and stayed there in a heap.

Two shots rang out into the night sky afterwards. Then someone shouted you fucking eejit, I toldya there was to be no shootin'. After that someone swore and shouted he had a knife and could've killed me, and the reply came that he'd be fucking lucky if someone else didn't finish the job, now let's get the fuck outta here.

Ned's next-door neighbours ran out and saw Ned lying beside the telegraph pole in a pool of blood, and heard the footsteps and shouts of men running away fast in the darkness. The ambulance and Garda arrived not long afterwards, sirens screaming.

***

After reading it, Nancy placed the letter on the table before her. Her pulse was racing. She'd been startled to find the letter, written in a strange hand, addressed to her, lying on the hall floor, after she'd arrived home from the school. It was from her son Liam. His father James had contacted him, and given him her address. His music group had a gig in Carlow town the coming Friday night and he wondered if he could meet her there. They were staying in the Royal Hotel, the venue where they were performing. She couldn't believe it. Recent events had pushed it out of her mind, but now the Holy Grail of seeing her son seemed within reach. She searched the envelope in case he'd enclosed a photo. She found nothing. He'd said to post her reply to him at the hotel, as they'd be there a few days before the gig for rehearsals, and to survey the scene. He'd heard the Barrow was good for kayaking and fishing and he might give-it-a-whirl, weather permitting. He finished saying he couldn't wait to meet her, and hoped she felt the same.

I do I do, she muttered as she scrambled through the drawers, looking for a writing pad and pen. After replying, she sealed the letter, stamped it, and rushed downtown to catch the last collection at 5.30.

When she returned home she flicked the radio on, and sat down to hear the news. She froze at the end of the bulletin when it was announced a man had been shot in Bagenalstown in County Carlow the previous night, a local man, and he was in hospital in a serious condition. She started, fearing it was Ned Rooney. It had to be, she reasoned, after what Nick had told her. Just then she heard a car pulling up outside, and looking out the window saw Nick jumping out of a Garda car. She opened the door and they went inside. She stared at him, afraid the worst had happened.

"It was Ned, wasn't it?"She asked, praying it wasn't.

He nodded. They sat on the sofa.

"Tell me what happened?" Her voice was choked, as she crushed her hanky in her hand.

After a silence he spoke.

"Well, it happened around midnight last night. He'd left the Railway House Bar, and was attacked by three thugs in the dark outside his house. They had clubs and guns. He put up a helluva fight, they say. He'd only a small knife, one used for topping beet, and it seems he wounded two of them. Our forensic team are working on the blood samples at the crime scene. Then he was shot twice in the legs, and they scarpered. The neighbours were great and raised the alarm pronto. Even so, when the ambulance arrived he'd lost a lot of blood. He was taken to Carlow hospital. Its touch-and-go Nancy, he's very low. I suggest you start storming heaven with prayers. I am sorry the way this has panned out."He wrapped his arm around her as he spoke.

"It's not your fault Nick, there's nothing more you could have done."She said, sobbing.

"No, but I do feel guilty. By the way Nancy I would have rung earlier but I knew you were in the school all day, and I didn't want to upset you there. I believe we should've kept Ned under protective surveillance for a while, especially at night. But Inspector Doogan wouldn't have any of it."

"Why?"She asked, incredulous.

"Deployment of resources was his reason. Said we had more important priorities. Basically Ned Rooney didn't count in his scheme-of-things. A human being all right, I suppose, but not an important-enough-human being in Doogan's book. Me, I think he didn't want to upset his girlfriend's brother, Aengus Hynes." Nick handed her a daily newspaper, and she scanned it.

"There's no mention in the paper that Ned had been threatened by the IRA and had sought Garda protection."

"No there isn't, I know that. All information released to the media is done centrally, and would be finally vetted by Doogan."

"So you're doing the Pontius Pilate act, washing your hands of it." She fumed.

"I'm not. There's nothing I can do, Nancy. That's the system. That's how it works. I can't change it."He said, shrugging.

"Well it may not be possible to print the whole truth the right way, but I'm going to contact the media and tell them the true story. This is a free country. The truth is the truth. It must be told." She retorted.

"So be it, you're entitled to do that if you wish, but I wouldn't advise it. It won't change anything. Doogan will have it suppressed anyway. Sleep on it, no knee-jerk reactions." Nick said, rising to leave.

"You're obviously worried about your career prospects. Are you afraid Doogan will make life difficult for you? When there's someone lying near-dead in a hospital, someone who might have been saved his ordeal. I'm afraid I'm not too pushed about this Doogan guy, not too pushed at all." Her eyes blazed as she spoke.

"Nor am I a fan of Doogan's, but I have to go now to visit Aengus Hynes. Our team will be working on the blood samples. All the hospitals are being checked for admissions with knife wounds. I expect something will develop by the weekend. I'll let you know if anything does. I think you should wait until then. Say a prayer for Ned Rooney, they say prayer can work wonders."As he spoke he put one arm around her, gently hugging her, and then left for the waiting squad car.

That night in bed she prayed for Ned, and for heavenly guidance. She racked her brains. Although she'd no close feelings for Ned, she raged at the lack of honesty by Inspector Doogan. She knew that if the cover-up was reported Nick's career prospects might be harmed. It was a principle though. Dammit, a principle is a principle. Until it affects you close to home, I suppose. She thought and prayed and prayed and thought. It was a restless night.

Next morning, having no teaching class, she rang the Carlow Nationalist office, giving her name and asking to speak to the reporter on the Bagenalstown shooting case. She got through at once, and said she had something relevant to relate about the shooting.

"Are you related to Ned Rooney, Miss Hackett?"The voice on the line wheezed.

"No, distant friends you might say. I live near him."

"Please tell me what information you've got?"

"Not on the phone, sorry it's confidential. I can meet you this morning in Bagenalstown. Are you interested? You can view the crime scene too. I'll see you only in my house, for security reasons."

"Ok, I'll be there within the hour, please give me your address. My name is Purcell, by the way. Ignatius Purcell."She gave him the details and the phone clicked dead.

Purcell arrived promptly in a battered blue Peugeot. She was alone. She'd got Kitty to look after her father, saying she'd explain later. Purcell was tall and thin, late-fortyish, hook-nosed, sparse red hair, narrow-faced. A cigarette, long-ashed, hung from his lips. His red tie was loose, his brown suit threadbare in patches. He sat on the sofa, declining her offer of tea, and took out a notepad and biro.

"Let's cut to the chase then, I've a busy day ahead. I've been to the crime scene and it's cordoned off, so there's nothing to relate there. What news have you got Miss Hackett?"

"Ned Rooney went to the Garda a week ago, looking for protection. There was no mention of this important fact in your newspaper article."

"Why did he want protection?"

"He owed money to a local man, Aengus Hynes, and was in arrears in paying it back. He'd paid some, and was trying to buy more time. He went to visit Hynes about it. Hynes said it was out of his hands. Ned was afraid, as Hynes was in the IRA, and had warned him there could be dire consequences. So he reported it to the Garda. Did you not know this?" She asked, shaking her head in disbelief.

"No." Purcell said, scribbling fast on his pad in shorthand.

"Hynes is active up North in the IRA, so death and danger are nothing to him."Nancy continued.

"Ok. Anything else that's relevant?"Purcell asked, pausing to scratch his nose with his biro, as ash fell from his cigarette onto the floor.

"My brother Nick works in the local Garda. His boss is an Inspector Doogan. Nick's ex-girlfriend is Hynes' sister and is now going out with Doogan." She said, putting an ash tray in front of him.

Purcell ignored the ash tray and continued jotting down notes.

"Quite a complicated scenario, I must say. What do you want me to do?"Purcell asked, as he lit another cigarette and pulled on it.

"Report the truth. Do your job. Say that the man had gone to the guards for help."

"What corroboration will I have for the story? It looks like a sin of omission all right. But the guards won't be happy. They'll deny everything."Purcell said, inhaling his cigarette.

167

"How would you feel Mr Purcell, if it was your brother that was shot?"

"I'd want the full facts printed in full. The whole truth, unadulterated. So I'll have to check with the guards. If they deny Ned Rooney ever came to them my editor will pull it. What evidence will I have?"He eyeballed her.

"You have my word and my brother Nick's. He even went to see Hynes about the matter. For God's sake he's a Garda Sergeant, why would he make it up?"

"Perhaps because he was wanting revenge on his ex-girlfriend. But I believe you. We've got to make our Public institutions accountable for their mistakes. That's one of the roles of the media. Look, there's only one way we can get this fact into the newspapers, and that's by me *not* ringing the guards about it, thereby not tipping them off, and by your brother swearing to me that what you've told me is true. Then I can publish it and I've covered my ass. Your brother could be putting his neck on the block but that's his funeral. Anyway you speak to him, and let me know tomorrow. And thanks for contacting me."After speaking, Purcell stubbed his cigarette butt in the ashtray on his way out, and soon was driving his jalopy down the road, black fumes spewing behind it.

Next day she spoke to Nick before he left for work, about her meeting with Purcell.

"Well Nick that's it, will you confirm then to Purcell about your visit to Aengus Hynes?" She asked him at the end.

He'd listened in silence and now paced the floor saying nothing. After what seemed an age, he answered.

"You're putting me on the spot Nancy, and no mistake. I don't know, it's a rock and a hard place. I've been going through things in my head, remembering all the reasons I joined the Garda. It's a few years back I admit and I was wet behind the years then, but the aspirations are still there. But the Force is bigger than any one person. I've worked hard to get where I am, and I can't jeopardise everything for a principle at this stage. It'd be political suicide, I'd be ostracised and pushed out of the Force. Those are the hard facts of life. Much as I'd like to stick one up Doogan's arse, and the fact that I love you, I just can't do it. I'm not proud to say this but I hope you understand."As he spoke he continued pacing the floor.

"I do understand, you've a lot more to lose than I have. That's the way of the world in Ireland these days, I suppose." She said, hugging him. As he put his hat on, ready to leave, she spoke again.

"I wasn't going to mention it Nick, nobody else knows, and I'd like to keep it that way for now, but I'm meeting my adopted son for the first time on Friday in Carlow. He'll no doubt ask about his father and I'll have to tell him the bad news. Hopefully Ned will pull through." After she spoke they hugged again.

"That's great news Nancy, I really mean it. I hope it goes well. Maybe someday I could meet him. I'd like that. By the way Aengus Hynes wasn't home yesterday when I called. He's either hiding in the long grass or up North on a mission."

"That's strange. And what about those three thugs who ambushed Ned?"

"We know who they are from the forensics. They're all from this county and in Hynes' IRA unit. No records of them attending a hospital, but probably they were looked after by a sympathetic doctor."

"Or nurse?"

"Maybe."

"What about Ned?"

"We've a 24 hour watch on his room in the hospital. He's in critical shape, touch and go. Nevertheless, they might want to finish him off. If he recovered he might be able to identify them."

"Hardly, it was dark when they attacked him."

"Who knows? Anyway there's a risk, and we can't afford another cock-up in security. Visiting is out until further notice. Be careful, this is a small town."

"I will, don't worry."

When he'd left she rang Purcell, telling him Nick was *not* prepared to take on his boss, Inspector Doogan, in the media, but she *was*, and he could print her name if he wished, she didn't care. He said he'd have to speak to the Editor, and put down the phone.

That night she wondered if Purcell would print the article the coming Friday. But mostly her thoughts were about her imminent meeting with her son. She'd arranged a day's holiday with the school, and bought a return ticket for the train to Carlow. She'd have to get her hair and nails done, and what would she wear? Next day was going to be a busy day.

Chapter 19

Reunion

On the train to Carlow she fretted, fields flitting by, doubts nagging her mind. What might he look like? Would there be any resemblance at all? What would he think of her? Would he be disappointed in her? What would they talk about? After a while she realised it was a wasted exercise. Better to just play it by ear, she reckoned. She joined her hands and prayed it would go well.

In the Royal Hotel she was informed a Mr. Jones was waiting for her in the lounge. Inhaling sharply, she entered the crowded room and looked around. In the corner a young man sat on a sofa, reading a newspaper. It *had* to be him. Her heart raced as she approached him. He turned his head, saw her coming, and stood up, holding out his hand. A well-built six-footer, fair- haired, combed back, blue-eyed, handsome like his father had been. Like her in the face maybe, she thought. He wore jeans, a lumber-shirt, and cowboy-boots. Hard to think I'd brought him into the world, the size of him. It didn't seem possible. She stared at him, speechless at first. After a few moments she spoke.

"Liam, so it's you, at long last." She smiled, grasping his hand. She wanted to hug him, but knew she couldn't.

"Right first time, howdy, I…I must apologise, I..I'm not sure what to call you."He grinned shyly.

"You can call me Nancy if you like. I'm Nancy Hackett from Bagenalstown in County Carlow, and I'm your biological mother."She felt awkward as she uttered the words.

"Please sit down awhile Nancy, until I get my head together, and tell me what I can get you?"

"Just a cup of tea and a scone, please." She sat down, still in a daze.

"Hey, that's just what I fancy myself." He said, calling the waitress, and ordering.

"Do you feel half as jittery as I do?" He asked, nervously stuffing a notepad in his shirt pocket.

"Yes Liam, more so I'd say, though it probably should be the other way around. I've had butterflies in my tummy all the way here." Close up to him she could see more resemblances, the high forehead, and bushy eyebrows, arching closer when he spoke.

The waitress came.

"Me too, hell, I'm as nervous as when I'm waiting to go on stage. Like some milk or sugar?" He grinned.

"No thanks. I hope you're happy with your life. The Jones's are a lovely family."

"I sure am. Mum and Dad couldn't have done any more for me, they spoilt me rotten. I've been so lucky to have them."

She felt the urge to say, but I'm your Mum, but said nothing, sipping her tea instead.

"What made you come to Ireland?"She asked.

He paused before replying.

"I suppose the idea started when my parents told me I was adopted, and had Irish blood in my veins. I was about eighteen then, and it planted the idea in my mind. That was about four years ago. Mind you I loved living in Manchester as a kid, growing up, following United, and playing cricket, but Dad's job meant we had to move house a lot. Anyway, a year after they told me I was adopted, I asked if I could go to Trinity College in Dublin to study music. They agreed. I was delighted."

"You could have studied music in many great places in England, *and* played cricket."

"I suppose so, I can't quite explain it. Maybe you can. Maybe it's Ireland's musical heritage, the image of the harp or something like that, I don't know. I was drawn to the place. Or maybe I just wanted to try to meet you, probably it was a bit of all those things. My parents never objected to me studying in Dublin. I couldn't believe it.

And they actually play cricket here too. The fact my parents are now living in Dublin is a bonus."He smiled broadly, shyly, reminding her in a way of Ned when he did so.

"I'm well aware they play cricket here Liam, they even have a club in my home town. I'd love to know all about your love of music. Do you sing or play?" Secretly she was proud of his decision to pursue a career in music. It was what she once yearned for herself, but the money for it was never there, and she would've loved one of her children to be a musician, if she had married and had a family. If her life hadn't turned out the way it did. But don't look back, only forward, don't be sentimental, she thought ruefully.

"A bit of both I guess. I always had an interest in music, and was in all the school choirs. I did all the piano grades, picked up the guitar from a friend, and learned the flute. I twiddled around with the concertina too. I'd love to master it. My parents are tone deaf, so they say. Say, tell me Nancy, are you musical? I've often wondered where this passion came from. It's usually in the genes, they say. Maybe it's not, or maybe it skips generations. It skipped my parents anyway."

"I suppose I do have an interest in music, and so did my mother. I didn't play, but I sang, and organised choirs. I love opera, but *Monteverdi* was my favourite. I adore his *Vespers*. He's probably not your cup of tea."

"Can't say I've heard of him, he sounds Italian."

"Yes he's Italian, from the Middle Ages, but *Claudio Monteverdi* is still popular. He wrote Madrigals for the Duke of Mantua. Italian ladies loved him. And what kind of music do you play?" She asked, thinking by his rigout it was probably Country& Western.

"Not rock and roll now, though I was in a rock band at school. But when I learned of my Irish heritage, I got interested in Irish traditional and folk music. That's what I'm into. Four of us formed a traditional group in Trinity this year. We call ourselves "The Spalpeen Fawnachs", and we're on our first tour of Ireland.

"That's a funny name, what does it mean? And how is your tour going?" She asked, fascinated, relieved the initial formality had abated, and that they shared a passion for music.

"It means the wandering labourers, called after an Irish poem of that name. We thought it appropriate and we're enjoying the tour. It's tough going though, a hand-to-mouth existence. Music has charms they say, but it's hard on the road. Not much drinking, we don't have the money. We've honed our playing skills and our repertoire, met some nice people, got to visit some great places. I could get to like this life, Nancy. Irish music is like a buried treasure-trove. I'd like to mine it."He smiled.

"I hope you do. But you have to put bread on the table too. I'd love to have played the harp like Mary O'Hara, and sung the songs she sang in Irish, back in the fifties. She's one of the famous voices in the history of Irish music. I just loved it when she sang "Aileen Aroon" or "The Quiet Land of Erin". But we couldn't afford a harp, never mind the lessons, in those days."

"I must research those songs. She's the lady who joined the nuns after her husband died, is she not? And tell me what *you've* been doing these past twenty two years?"

"Well … by some coincidence, I ….I also was a nun, until last year that is. I was in the Presentation Order in Manchester. I….I joined after you were born and adopted."As she blurted it out, tears welled, and she dabbed her eyes. An awkward silence ensued. After some minutes, he spoke.

"Thanks for telling me that Nancy, thanks for your honesty, I appreciate that, it can't have been easy for you." He embraced her, hugging her tight.

A vision of the night in the boat house on the Barrow with Ned Rooney flashed through her head. To think it all began that night. Silence came again momentarily, before she replied.

174

"No it wasn't easy, but here I am talking to you like I've known you all my life. I can't believe it. Life sometimes has a way of catching you out, playing tricks with you almost."She sniffled, raising a hanky to her face.

"It can play tricks for sure. Funny thing, I felt the same as you, when I saw you. Nervous at first, but now it's as if we've known each other a long time."A grin spread across his face.

"I'd like us to be friends for life from here on. Just on-and-off, like. I respect and I like your parents. Can we be lifelong friends, Liam? That's all I pray for."She said, anxiously.

"Of course, and Mum and Dad are of the same mind, they've told me so. He grasped her hands momentarily, before releasing them.

"I can't believe it Liam, they're so kind, your parents, I'm so relieved. It's a dream come true. It may not last, but at least for the present we're living in the same country. Maybe we can meet again, while we have the chance?"

"Why not indeed Nancy? Our next gig is in Waterford, then we travel to Kilkenny by way of New Ross and Graiguenamanagh. By the way, I went kayaking yesterday in the Barrow near Leighlinbridge. It was great fun. Going under the bridge was something I'll always remember. One of my friends came too. The locals said we should try Clashganny and Graiguenamanagh."

"Graiguenamanagh? Maybe we could meet there. It's a magic place, and near where I live."Her heart filled with elation as she spoke.

"Fine with me, we have a gig there in a pub called Doyles. I can fill you in about my research on those songs too. I *do* know that "Aileen Aroon" originated in that area around the 13th century."

"I forgot you're studying music in Trinity."

"Yes, actually I'm doing my thesis on the poetry and music of Thomas Moore, who died in 1852. His "Moore's Melodies" book was hugely popular. He was lionised by the English, invited everywhere. Even worshipped by no less a person than Albert Einstein himself. He's up there with John McCormack, and Mary O'Hara as one of the three greats in the history of Irish music."

"I thought he was more English than Irish?"

"Not true, at heart he was very Irish, a republican, who only left for England when his friend Robert Emmet was executed after the failed rebellion in Dublin in 1803. But you probably know all this stuff already?"

"No I don't, I'm fascinated, please continue Liam."She thought then music would be their bond in the future.

"Well ok I will, in that case. Moore later wrote the poem"She Is Far From The Land " for Emmet's fiancee Sarah Curran. She had married after his execution and gone to live in *Haiti*. She died from TB while still young and is buried in Cork."

He took the notepad from his shirt pocket and read from it.

"She is far from the land where her young hero sleeps,
And lovers around her are sighing;
But coldly she turns from their gaze and weeps,
For her heart in his grave is lying! ....etc."

"I know it almost by heart. It moves me to tears. The poem was later put to music. I sang it once at a gig in Ireland but no-one knew it. It went down like the proverbial lead balloon. Moore's heart was always in Ireland."Liam's voice was animated, and he had a far-away gleam in his eyes.

"Liam, you're so lucky to be working at something you love. Not many do, believe me. And tell me, what do you do to switch off from the music?"

He thought for a moment before replying

"I read a bit, westerns mostly."

She wondered when he would ask who his father was, and if he'd want to meet him.

"I *am* lucky in what I do, I have to say. Hopefully it'll stay that way. I have to meet the guys soon for rehearsal, but there's one last question I'd like to ask before I go, if you don't mind Nancy. "

"Of course, please do."She had a nervous feeling as she spoke, guessing what was coming.

"It's just a family thing I suppose, and if you don't want to answer, I'll understand. It's about my biological father. I have no great desire to meet him but I'm curious to know anything you can tell me about him."

"Of course, I don't mind Liam. I'll keep it as short as I can. His name is Ned Rooney, and like me he's from Bagenalstown. He'd emigrated to London before you were born. I had no contact with him over the years. But he came home not long ago. "

"So he doesn't know I exist?" A frown came on Liam's face.

"Yes Liam, he doesn't know, but that's not the full picture. When he returned to Bagenalstown this year from England, he was in a bad way. After working a lifetime on the buildings over there he'd got drinking and gambling problems. He'd also run foul of someone here in the IRA, and got beaten-up and shot because of that. At the moment he's in St Luke's hospital in Kilkenny, but he's at death's-door, I'm sorry to say. Now you know it all. I'm sorry how it worked out for him, and to have to give you such sad news. I didn't mean to." She wiped her eye with a hanky. Silence. After a while he spoke.

"I'm sorry Nancy, I shouldn't have burdened you with that question. Anyway, we'll meet in about two weeks in Graiguenamanagh. I'll write to confirm." He stood up, looking at his watch, before speaking.

"Gosh, I can't believe how the time flew. I should have bought you dinner."

"No, I much preferred the talking. I'm looking forward already to our next meeting. I have an hour to go, before the train leaves. By the way, I *can* confirm you share a love of westerns with Ned Rooney. It was a pleasure to meet you Liam." She had to refrain from calling him "son".

They hugged, and he left to join a group on the far side of the lounge. She exited the hotel, and headed to the nearest church, where she prayed for Ned's recovery, thought about visiting him in hospital, but then decided not to. She remembered Nick had said visitors were out for the moment. Better not rock the boat, she thought, Ned would hardly be able to talk anyway. Inside her body she felt her emotions churn in a way she'd never felt before.

On her way back to the station, she saw a large chimney towering over Carlow town, belching smoke plumes high into the sky. A lady passing by stopped, and told her it was the beet factory chimney and it was going like the clappers, as the beet-harvesting season was in full swing. She remembered her father and his father before him had both worked there. She decided she would ask him sometime about the factory's history.

Travelling home on the train, she regretted not trying to visit Ned in hospital. Although it was in Kilkenny, Nick might have brought her. It would have been purely an act of charity, and as a former nun she now felt should have done it. Even if she'd not been allowed to see him, at least she'd have had the consolation of having tried. Deep down she had to admit she'd probably shirked it, and felt guilty. She prayed for forgiveness.

Later that evening she remembered Marty was calling the next day to bring her to St Mullins on his barge. What with all of the hullabaloo happening during the week, she'd forgotten about their date. She dashed over to Kitty to ask her about minding their Dad.

"Of course, I hadn't forgotten. Bring your overnight-things. You could do with a good break this weekend, after the week you've had. I don't want to see you back until Sunday."Kitty said.

"Thanks, you're a brick, and I love you." She hugged her older sister, and then rushed home to pack her bag.

Outside the house, she looked up and saw swallows cavorting high in a salmon–pink sky, a sure sign of good weather. In the garden the flowers seemed more fragrant and colourful than before. That night the excitement of meeting her son still swirled through her mind, pushing the thoughts of her coming trip to St. Mullins with Marty into the background.

Chapter 20

St Mullins

They parked by the Barrow quayside at Graiguenamanagh, walked along to Duiske Abbey, and said a short prayer there, before boarding the barge. Marty carried her case. It was heavy. He wore his sea captain's cap at an angle, his face sprouting the early stubble of a beard. Hard to imagine him being a priest, still it does take all sorts, she thought.

She had to admit she enjoyed his company. He made her laugh and seemed intent on pleasing her. Gracious too, and generous. Sympathetic. The Abbey visit and prayer helped ease her doubts about their relationship. God would understand, she hoped. The sun dipped in and out of the clouds bundled above the river. She felt content. Elation tingled through her bones at the prospect of the day ahead.

"Your case seems a bit heavier than last week, Nancy. Perhaps you brought enough clothes this time for an overnight stay? " He said, his face creasing in a smile.

"Perhaps, you never know."She replied, thinking she'd keep him in suspense for a while longer. In reality she wasn't sure if she'd stay or not. She'd just play it by ear.

"I've stocked up just in case. There's a nice salmon in the fridge, wild of course like myself, and I have a fine Chablis to wash it down. Might that be enough to tempt you to stay?"He asked, grinning.

"Maybe, it's been a tough week."She replied, relenting.

"Oh, has it? I'm sorry to hear that. Want to talk about it?"

"No, not now thanks, maybe later."

"Ok, hold on, we're on our way."He said, steering the barge away from the quayside, under the seven-arched bridge, left of the weir, downriver towards Tinnahinch Lock.

He stopped there, unlocked the upper gate of the lock with a lever, and pushed the gates open on both sides. When the barge was inside he closed the gates behind them, waiting for the water to release from the lower gate, until they were at the lower water level. Then he opened the lower gate, driving the barge through, and stopped again beside the river bank, before closing the lower gates and locking both gates again with the lever.

Continuing, they chugged onwards, passing the ruins of Tinnahinch Castle, repeating the lock procedure at Lower Tinnahinch. The barge moved lazily along the water, and she felt herself relaxing to its pace.

Before her the river dropped to form a gorge. Above the steep sloping banks on either side were high slanting woodlands, some evergreen, some in rusty autumn colours. She stared at the water, mesmerised, as a kaleidoscope of river life unfolded before her.

Far away the Blackstairs Mountains jutted above the tree tops. An angler on the riverbank waved to them, and they waved back. Cattle lazed in passing fields. The sun broke through in patches, before the clouds vanished in the rising heat. The sky soon became a cobalt blanket, mirrored in the river, the sun shining on the giant Willows and Ash trees, some growing in the water.

It was hot. She put on a wide-brimmed hat and sat at the rear beside Marty. He was silent, concentrated, holding the wheel tightly. The worn towpaths evoked in her mind memories of a bygone era, ruins of horse stables and grain stores still standing there. With each bend of the winding river, the tension of the week eked from her body.

At St. Mullins, he berthed the barge at the quayside near the ruins of an old granary store.

"It's an uphill walk to the monastic ruins. Fancy something here first?"

"Sure thing Marty, I'm parched, I'd love a coffee."

She sat inside the barge as he brought coffee and scones from the galley on a tray, putting it on the table before her.

"There you are, like to chat now about the things on your mind?" He asked as he filled the mugs.

"Perhaps. But just give me a few more minutes."She replied.

They waited, relaxed, gazing out the porthole at the moving mass of water.

"The river's tidal here, coming up from New Ross. Sometimes salmon are caught here." Marty informed her.

"Really?"

"Yes, along with a lot of fresh water fish. I like fishing. It makes me unwind and forget the things that gnaw inside your head, things that get you stressed. Things like the evil that lurks in the world. I love this place and the fishing. They're what draw me back here. Those things, *and* my mother, *and* now you." He smiled, and a distant look came in his eyes.

"And tell me, how is your mother? I'd love to meet her."

"She's actually not great, sorry to say. She took a stroke recently. She gets befuddled at times. Hopefully you can meet her when she recovers, before I return to Italy."

"You seem to get home to her quite a lot."She remarked.

"The people in the hospital in Milan are most understanding, because of my mother's health. Though they wouldn't normally allow me to be away for this length. The longer break's given me a chance to do some social services in the area. I like that. Want to talk now?"

She nodded.

"Remember I told you before that Ned Rooney had got into trouble with the IRA over a money matter."

"Yes I do."Marty said, frowning.

"Well, he got beaten up during the week and was shot twice in the legs in the fracas, and is now in a critical position in a hospital in Kilkenny. God forgive me, I have no great feelings for the man, but he *is* the father of my son. I have mixed emotions, but it upsets me. It seems so unfair, to be attacked outside your own home. I pray each day for his recovery."

"He's in St. Luke's Hospital?"

She nodded. He scratched the stubble on his chin.

"Your brother's in the Garda, is he not?"

"Yes he is."

"You must warn him the IRA will make every effort to finish the job off, in case Ned Rooney can identify any of his attackers. I've seen this in Italy with the Mafia. Anyone who might spill the beans on them becomes a dead duck. Pronto."

"I'll pass on your words. Nick said the Garda *are* guarding Ned. Thank you for the warning anyway, I'm beginning to feel better already."She felt relieved she'd shared her troubles with Marty. He *did* seem genuinely concerned.

"That's good Nancy, I'm glad you told me. Let's stay here a little while and relax. You can tell me when you're ready to go see the ruins."

Soon she stood up, saying she was now ready to go, and they went up the winding driveway.

Standing on top of a grassy mound that had once been a Norman Motte, they looked down on the tidal limit of the Barrow. She tried to imagine what life there might have been like back in St Moling's era thirteen centuries earlier.

Drifting smoke, lay workers scurrying about, monks pacing, cocks crowing, dogs barking, church bells clanging. All beside the castle, palisade, and tollhouse for the river.

Around them, a stone wall enclosed the weather-worn stubs of old monastic buildings rising from a mossy sea of grave slabs and crucifixes. They walked towards the Abbey church, then on to the High Cross and the remains of a Round Tower.

"Many of these ruins date from way after St Moling." He said.

"You seem to know a lot about him."

"You would too if you lived in this area as long as I have. I could write a book."

"Tell me about the man, I'm curious."She said.

He paused a few moments before speaking.

"Well, St Moling was a remarkable man, unlike most of the hermits who founded the early monasteries. They were poorly educated men filled with fierce convictions, but with fish scales in their beards. Moling was born a prince and ended up an Archbishop. A poet and a thinker too, a man useful with his hands. He dug his own mile-long mill-race, taking seven years to do it. He ground corn, built his own raft and ferried folk across the Barrow. He also got rid of a penal cattle tax paid to the Kings of Meath. There's a holy well called after him which people swear by, saying many cures come from it. I could go on."

"He sounds like a remarkable man all right. Many people today in high places could learn from his example."

"I agree. "Marty said.

After walking through the graveyard and viewing some graves dating back to the 1798 rebellion, they returned to the barge.

Marty loosed the tow rope, turning the barge in the middle of the river, moving upriver towards Graigue.

On the way she felt the sun burning her skin, looked up at the azure sky, and turned to Marty.

"It's so lovely here Marty, the weather's perfect, I'd love a swim to cool off. Otherwise I'll pass out with heat exhaustion."

"Sure thing, the weather's perfect for a dip, but we're nearing the tidal currents of St Mullin's so I can't join you. I've never swam here before, so I'll keep the boat steady for you in the middle. You go right ahead, I'll just watch. You can wear a bikini if you like, I won't object." He laughed.

She dashed into her bedroom, opened her case and put on a new, blue, one-piece bathing costume she'd bought in Carlow earlier in the week. Pink polka dots. A bit more revealing than the old one, but not too much, she mused.

"Lovely outfit, lovely lady in it. *Bellisima.*"He said when she re-appeared.

She thought his eyes seemed glued on the curves of her body in her new swimsuit, as she moved to the stern, fixing her swim cap on her head. She felt good that he found her attractive.

"Flatterer, can I dive in here?"She asked.

"Sure, no problem, it's quite safe here."He replied, cutting the engine.

She plunged in from the back of the barge. Cleaving the surface with strong, clean strokes, she swam over to the west bank, then back to the centre of the river. Marty tracked the barge in her wake. As she reached the middle of the river, going against the current, she flipped onto her back to float. It was then she felt the weeds trailing over her body, entangling her, before being caught in a surging eddy that sucked her below the surface. She gasped and struggled to resist the unseen force that was dragging her down, deeper into the streeling weeds. She held her breath until forced to inhale. She gulped water, sank deep, and fought back again. Forced to inhale again, some water entered her lungs. She felt her body being dragged below again. The Second time. She panicked as she'd always heard that in drownings the third time under was the final and fatal time.

Marty spotted her difficulties, cut the engine, dropped anchor, and threw a lifebuoy on a rope towards her. Her hands flailed to grasp it but missed, and it floated down the river. He shed his shoes, grabbed another lifebuoy, put it over his neck and under one shoulder, and jumped in feet first. When he reached her, she was about to sink for the third time. She grabbed him in desperation.

He felt the undertow and her weight bringing him under. He hit her hard on her face and she released her grip,dazed, allowing him to get the lifebuoy over her head and shoulders. He had to keep her head out of the water as she was inhaling water, her eyes closed. He got his left elbow under her chin, and kicked out with his right hand

185

and feet.

He could still feel the pull of the vortex. The terror he felt seemed to give him extra strength, and the downward drag began to recede. He swam one-armed back to the barge, tied the lifebuoy rope to the rudder at the back, to keep Nancy above water, while he climbed aboard.

He removed the lifebuoy, laying her on her back on the deck. There seemed to be a purple tinge on her face and lips. Panicked, he felt her pulse. Faint, but there. He immediately applied mouth-to-mouth resuscitation. After a few minutes her body shuddered, and her eyes flickered open. He continued doing the resuscitation, until her eyes stayed open. After a while they closed again.

When she woke she was in her bed in the barge. She saw her swimsuit lying in a pool of water on the floor, and realised she was naked beneath the bedclothes. Marty entered the room. He held her in his arms and kissed her lightly on the cheek.

"How are you Nancy? God but you had the life scared out of me."He said, his brow wrinkled with worry.

"What happened? I…I dreamt I was drowning, it was like some nightmare."She whispered.

"It was no dream Nancy I'm afraid, you very nearly *did* drown. A very close call. We're in Graigue, I've called the ambulance to take you to the hospital in Kilkenny. They'll check you out there, as there might still be water in your lungs. They'll keep you in overnight most likely. I'll follow with your suitcase, and tell your family what happened later. Here's a bathrobe you can wear. I can hear the ambulance's siren. You were very lucky Nancy. Very, very lucky indeed. Somebody up there was praying for you." He pointed to the sky.

"I can't thank you enough Marty."She coughed as she spoke.

"You don't ever have to Nancy, because I love you."He held her hands in his.

"But you can't love me, you're a priest, you can only love God."She gasped.

"Yes, I know, it doesn't seem fair. You know, the Church says there are three things only in life that last. Faith, hope, and love, but the greatest of these is love."

As he bent over her something on his body caught her attention.

"Marty, what's that purple mark on your arm?"She asked.

"Oh that, it's just a small tattoo. It's a scorpion, my birth sign, remember? I had it done years ago. Like it?" He smiled.

"I don't like tattoos."She shuddered.

"A lot don't, but it's pretty discreet."

Later he kissed her lightly on the lips as he slipped the bathrobe around her, helping her out of the barge and into the ambulance, saying he would follow it to Kilkenny. On the way she slept, dreaming about her nightmare in the river, and Marty saving her life.

When Marty got to her ward in the hospital, a tall, pretty nurse with the name Sheila pinned to her uniform met him. She smiled and said the doctor had advised that Nancy must remain there for at least two days for tests, and she was presently sedated and asleep. He gave her the suitcase, thanked her, and left to inform Nancy's family.

When he reached her house, a young man in Garda uniform opened the door, saying he was Nancy's brother Nick, and invited him in. Marty went in, introduced himself and explained about Nancy's near-drowning experience, and that she'd been detained in St Luke's hospital as a precautionary measure. He gave the nurse's name as a reference.

"Tell me was the nurse tall and slim, with long black hair?"Nick asked.

"Yes."

"I think I know her. Her second name is Hynes." Nick said.

The name rang a bell in Marty's head.

"Thanks for letting me know Marty, and also for saving my sister's life."Nick said, standing up, and extending his hand.

"It's nothing, I feel somehow responsible for letting her swim there. I should've known better." Marty replied, shaking hands, and departing.

Three days later Nancy completed the tests, and the doctor confirmed she could leave. Nick had visited a day earlier, saying he'd bring her home when she recovered. He informed her Marty had told him the news, and that he seemed a decent guy. She agreed. Later, as she lay in her bed, reading a magazine, it hit her that she could be in the same hospital as Ned Rooney. When Sheila Hynes arrived to take her temperature Nancy asked her if Ned *was* there.

"Yes, he's been moved from the Intensive Care Unit to a private room not far away. Are you related?"Sheila replied.

"No. We're old friends you might say. But I'd love to see him, if only for a few minutes."Nancy pleaded.

"I'm afraid the poor man's in a bad way. He can't talk and he's got tubes coming out of everywhere. It'd be a one-way conversation at best, but he's awake, I've just been in his room. I could allow you in if you insist, for five minutes maximum, but I'd be breaking all the rules."

"I insist, oh please break the rules just this once, I beg you."

"Ok then, just this once. Mum's the word though, I could lose my job you know."The nurse said, a worried look on her face.

Nancy thanked her and said she'd keep her mouth shut, then put on her bathrobe and followed the nurse outside.

The room was dim, lit by a monitor, and in the dimness she heard the door close behind her. Ned lay on the bed, tubes protruding from his body, breathing in gasps, but his sunken eyes were wide awake. She barely recognised him. Emaciated, he'd aged beyond recognition, his skin gaunt on his cheekbones. He stared at her.

"Ned, do you remember me? Just nod if you

understand"

He just stared at her.

"Ned, it's me, Nancy Hackett. We went out together many years ago. Do you remember?"She asked.

After a while he nodded slowly.

"I want to tell you that after you went to England I had a baby, a son. He was adopted. You were the father. Do you understand me?"

He nodded again, this time quicker.

"Tell me, if you were able to, would you like to see him?"

Ned nodded immediately. A knock came on the door then and Nancy left with the nurse.

The next day Nick brought Nancy home, stating she must rest a few days. He'd spoken to the school, who understood and said they wouldn't expect her back until the following Monday. He said Kitty was coming shortly with her father, and he'd wait until they arrived. She sat on the sofa, picking up the newspaper. She told him about visiting Ned Rooney.

"Sheila the nurse was very helpful."

"That's good, she's a grand girl. She's Sheila Hynes, my ex-girlfriend, you know."He said nonchalantly.

"Really? But Nick, I thought you said Ned Rooney was on twenty-four-hour security protection. There was nobody guarding his room."

"What! Christ, this is fucking Doogan's handiwork. Damn him to Hell and back. I've a meeting with him tomorrow, and it's not going to be pleasant. There'll be blood on the floor over this. I'm going to the hospital now to check for myself. Seeing is believing. I hear Kitty at the door, I'd better be off." He said, picking up his hat, fuming, and storming out, excusing himself to Kitty, saying he'd just got an urgent call.

Chapter 21

Meeting

Nick Hackett arrived at the Garda station an hour early, washed out after a fitful night's sleep. He was intending to read up on his notes before his follow-up meeting with Inspector Cornelius Doogan. Outside, Kilree Street was damp and deserted, murky in a morning drizzle. Inside, a pall of smoke hovered around the bare bulb dangling in the meeting room. He realised someone was already there.

Doogan looked up from the pile of papers on the table before him. His raincoat hung on the back of the door behind him. He seemed bright-eyed and alert, a grin splitting his face, his pipe tight between his teeth. Smug bastard, Nick thought, he thinks he's the master of one-upmanship. I'll show him.

"Ah, Sergeant Hackett, so glad you came early. I've actually put the main meeting with the others back a few hours. Thought we should first have a few words together in private. Face-to-face. *Mano a mano*, as they say in Spain." Doogan smirked as he leant back, pulling hard on his pipe, puffing a tobacco cloud towards the ceiling. He then took the pipe from his mouth and scratched the dimple on his chin with the pipe stem.

"Ok Inspector, what exactly do we need to discuss?" Nick muttered, irritated, feeling he'd been caught on-the-hop, feeling this time Doogan really had got under his skin.

"Well, first there's this local incident involving Ned Rooney, but let's have a coffee to kick-off. Black as the ace of spades, eh?" Doogan grinned, displaying his clean, white teeth.

Nick nodded, and Doogan went to the kitchenette, returning within minutes with a tray holding two mugs of coffee, and some Marietta biscuits. As Nick ate his first biscuit, Doogan leered at him and spoke.

"Have the forensic boys come up with anything regarding Ned Rooney's attackers?"

Nick shook his head.

"That article in the newspaper, alleging Ned Rooney came here to this station looking for security, has been very damaging to the Force. I've been in all kinds of shit with the people up in the Park in Dublin over it." Doogan spat the words out, slit-eyed, teeth tightening on his pipe stem.

"But that's the truth Inspector, there's no alleging, he came into this station and made a formal complaint. It's there in black and white. It's a documented fact."Nick felt comforted by Doogan's apparent discomfort.

"I've just been through the records Sergeant, and there's no vestige of any such complaint, and nobody here recalls meeting a Ned Rooney around the alleged date. I suggest you go out now and check for yourself." Doogan growled, pulling on his pipe.

"Ok, I will."

Nick rose and left the room. Going to the administration office, he took the log book out, and checked it. There was no entry about Ned Rooney around the time in question. He also realised that as the log book was changed and archived annually, it could have been re-written for the year to date, omitting Ned Rooney's complaint. A cover-up. Not normal procedure, but if the order came from the top, he knew it would be obeyed, or someone's neck would be on the block. He returned to the meeting room.

"I admit I can't find any mention of it in the log book." Nick said, feeling foolish and outwitted.

"Because it never happened, that's why. This woman who fabricated these lies, this Nancy Hackett, who the hell is she?"Doogan snarled.

"She's my sister."

"What, so it was you who put her up to it?" Doogan's voice had become strident.

"Excuse me, but I didn't put her up to anything Inspector. She makes her own mind up. She's a big girl. She was a friend of Ned Rooney years ago, before he went to England."

"What does she do? Has she a job here?" Doogan barked.

"She looks after my father who's recovering from a stroke." Nick said, sussing Doogan's game.

"Ok Sergeant, this matter will be pursued. Onto another matter, what the fuck are you up to, harassing Aengus Hynes, a powerful force in the local IRA? We've enough problems on our hands here, what with the fallout from Bobby Sands, and dealing with the "Vanished" cold-cases, without bringing more trouble on our heads."Doogan stabbed the table with his pipe, his eyes bulging.

"I was doing my duty, actually. He was the one who had it in for Ned Rooney, over some money debt."

"You have no evidence that he did anything. There's no record of any complaint." Doogan hissed.

"I'd hardly have gone up to Hynes' house on my own bat, without a shred of evidence. Why would I do that?"

"I don't know, but I have my suspicions. Sheila and her family are very upset. They think it's a vendetta by you against their family."

"Inspector, I requested that Ned Rooney be given a twenty-four-hour security guard at the hospital, and was this not agreed? After apparently not protecting him before he was shot, I felt the least we could do was to protect him afterwards." Nick had it in writing, a fax copy kept secure at home. Doogan knew that too. Nick was relieved he'd taken the precaution.

"Yes, it was agreed." Doogan said grudgingly.

"Well, I'm afraid it's not happening Inspector. He's getting zero Garda protection in the hospital. The media would love to hear about that."Nick sat back, satisfied, feeling he'd landed a punch to Doogan's solar plexus.

"How do you know?" Doogan asked, taken aback.

"My sister, Nancy Hackett was in the hospital in Kilkenny a few days ago, and was brought to see Ned Rooney by a nurse there. She reported there was no Garda presence anywhere."

"And who was this nurse?"Doogan's mouth sagged in surprise.

"Sheila Hynes is her name. I know her well, and she was very helpful to my sister Nancy."

"She broke strict security procedures, there was no visiting allowed, the man was in Intensive bloody Care, for God's sake." Doogan looked shook as he spoke.

"But what about the lack of Garda security, surely it's obvious he's a potential target by the IRA?" Nick demanded.

"We've been under great strain all this week. One of our members, Garda Timothy Laker, a personal friend of mine from Kilkenny has gone missing. There had to be a re-deployment of our resources."Doogan appeared unsure, on the back foot for once.

"So you decided Ned Rooney's life wasn't all that important?"

"I wouldn't put it like that. We're under-resourced, and at full-stretch, you should know that. Although Garda Laker wasn't married, it's important that members of the Force get priority."

Especially if he's a personal friend of the local Inspector, Nick thought grimly.

"So is Ned Rooney still unguarded?"Nick asked.

Doogan nodded. Nick suspected Ned Rooney had never been guarded.

"And how long has Garda Timothy Laker been missing?"Nick asked.

"Three days."

Nick knew Ned Rooney had been in hospital over a week. He had to act now.

"Can we adjourn for a few minutes Inspector, while I go to the loo. It's a urinary infection."

Doogan agreed, and started sorting through the papers before him, while Nick dashed to his office and rang Nancy.

"Hi Nancy, I'm in the middle of a meeting with Inspector Doogan, its daggers-drawn stuff. Can you do me a favour? It's urgent."

"Sure Nick, what is it?"

"I think Sheila Hynes works late shifts in the hospital in Kilkenny. She should be at home now. Please buy a bouquet of flowers and give them to her at her house, 14 St. Brigid's Crescent, thanking her for everything she did for you in the hospital. But try to find out if Ned Rooney ever had a Garda on duty protecting him at the hospital. Got that, I have to hurry, please do it now and ring me back as soon as you find out."

Nancy said she would. He put the phone down and hurried back to the meeting room. When he returned Doogan was standing at the table, refilling the coffee mugs. He was a big man, handsome, about mid- thirties. Strange he'd never married. Nick wondered if he was one of those guys who reckoned he needn't buy the book when he could just join the library. He couldn't see what Sheila Hynes saw in Doogan. To Nick he seemed sly and slimy, not to be trusted.

"We're all a bit stressed these days Sergeant, makes you forget sometimes whose side you're on." Doogan appeared conciliatory, as he handed Nick a mug of coffee.

"I suppose Inspector, any ideas about what happened to Garda Laker?"

"None, it's a mystery I'm afraid. Laker's a keen angler. He plies his rod up and down both sides of the Barrow. Pardon the pun, the whole thing sounds fishy, in fact it stinks. It may have been a fishing accident, but you never know when you're in the Garda, you're a target for any nut-case in the town. It worries me." Doogan's brow was wrinkled, his face sombre, as he spoke.

This is not like him, no, not like him at all, Nick mused. Doogan sat back, took out a tin of St Bruno tobacco, stuffed the bowl of his pipe with it, struck a match and lit up. Soon he was puffing away like a steamboat on the Mississippi, smoke billowing behind him. His face still had a charming smile, but somehow Nick thought he seemed a worried man beneath his smiling façade. From time to time Doogan twitched nervously. This made Nick feel better. They drank their coffee in silence, reading their notes. Later Doogan rose and spoke.

"We've a half-hour left before the main item on the meeting agenda…the Missing People. I'm going out for a short walk beforehand to clear my head. See you shortly Sergeant." Doogan then left the room, tipping his hat, taking his raincoat from the back of the door.

Nick reckoned Doogan was off to make a few phone calls to cover his lack of security on Ned Rooney at the hospital. He rushed back to his office and rang Nancy. She answered, sounding breathless.

"How did you get on?" He asked.

"Sheila Hynes was there when I knocked. She's a lovely girl, and invited me in for tea. She confirmed she was there each day since Ned was admitted, and there was never a Garda presence at any time. A ban on visitors, that's all."

"Anything else?"

"Yes …yes there is…while we sat there in the house, a call came from the hospital….an…an urgent call."Her voice became distressed. He heard her sobbing.

"Yes, what was it about?" He asked, holding his breath.

"Ned…Ned Rooney is dead. Someone entered his room last night and unplugged all the machines that were keeping him alive. He..he's dead. He…he was murdered. It's horrible." She broke down, sobbing for a few minutes.

"God Nancy, I'm so sorry about that, and for putting you through all this and you not in the whole of your health. I really am sorry, I'll ring Kitty and she'll come to you straight away. I didn't mean to put you on the spot like that, and I'm really sorry, but there's no way you can hide bad news. Still, it might and should have been prevented."

"It wasn't your fault Nick, the deed was done before I got to Sheila's house."She sighed as she spoke.

"One last question though, was anyone spotted entering or leaving the hospital by the staff, or on the security cameras?"

"Yes there was someone, a Garda, or someone dressed as a Garda, apparently entered and left the hospital within half an hour of when it happened. God, I don't know why I feel so upset, but I do. "

"Nancy, I'm truly sorry to keep questioning you, but was any name given?"

"No, none asked for or given, seeing he was a guard."

"Thanks Nancy, you're a brick."He put the receiver down, rang Kitty, telling her about Ned Rooney, asking her to call on Nancy straight away, before hurrying back to the meeting room, feeling sorry for Ned Rooney, but also feeling he now had Inspector Cornelius Doogan by the short and curlies.

Back in the room, people were filing in the door for the main meeting. Doogan sat at the top of the table, puffing away, a worried look on his face. Nick asked to speak to him privately. He nodded, and they adjourned to Nick's office. When Nick looked into Doogan's eyes, he knew he knew the news.

"You know Ned Rooney is dead?"Nick asked.

Doogan nodded, looking downcast.

"Are you going ahead with the meeting?" Nick continued.

"Why the hell not? Everyone's here, and they're not related incidents."

"There was a Garda involved."Nick said.

"It may have been someone disguised as a Garda. Most likely it was."Doogan retorted.

At that moment, a young Garda knocked and entered the room, saying there was an urgent call for Inspector Doogan. Doogan told Nick to wait there, and left the room. He returned within minutes, ashen-faced.

"They've found Garda Timothy Laker somewhere near Goresbridge. He's dead too. A burnt-out car was found in a remote place. The meeting's off. Definitely. Tell everyone it's postponed due to a possible double murder, apparently unrelated. Then you better come with me in my car to the crime scenes. Also, grab all my files and my raincoat while you're there."As he spoke Doogan looked visibly shaken. Nick was surprised to see him like that, and he'd put his pipe away.

Nick followed instructions and within minutes the squad car was on the road to Kilkenny, siren blaring.

They drove first to the Garda Laker scene. On the way, Nick asked Doogan when Laker was last seen.

"He left the station Tuesday evening, two days ago, saying he had a call about some petty burglary, said he'd deal with it on his way home."

"So he was alone. Was there any record of where he was calling?"Nick asked.

"No."

The scene of the incident at Goresbridge was cordoned off with ambulance and squad car lights flashing. It was in a clearing in a wood near the Barrow. The burnt-out car was beside a large rock in the centre of the clearing. They parked, got out, and looked around.

"The forensic team will have their work cut out. He's cremated already, there's nothing to work on. Ashes to ashes. The car is buckled beyond recognition. It must have been an inferno. It's a miracle there wasn't a forest fire, or that no one saw the blaze. He must have hit the rock, but how the hell did he not see it, unless he reversed into it in the dark. It's strange. The fuel tank must have ignited with the impact. Self-combustion. Something doesn't add up."

Doogan muttered, nervously scratching his dimple with his pipe.

They walked around the area. Not far away was an idyllic spot on the river, ideal for fishing. Nick wondered if Laker had decided to take in a spell of fishing there on that ill-fated evening. He suggested that the forensic team check that area for footprints. Doogan agreed, seemingly distant, shot-to-pieces by the incident. Nick remembered then that Doogan and Laker had been close friends.

They moved onwards in silence. One side of the river was mainly woodlands, but on the far side of the river were fields and meadows. One meadow had some cows grazing in it, and at the far end of it stood a bull, massive, ring in nose, aroused, surveying the scene.

"Who first discovered the accident?" He asked Doogan. Nick wasn't really convinced it had been an accident. He felt there was something strange about the whole set-up.

"Apparently it was the farmer who owns those fields over there, including the one with the bull. He'd left the bull into the meadow early in the week, then went for a few days visit to Dublin. We know he has IRA sympathies, and is an associate of Aengus Hynes. When he returned, he came into the field where the bull was, in his tractor. While driving it near to the river, he looked across, and thought he saw something odd, brown-coloured, through the trees. He drove his tractor across the bridge to the far side, and found the charred remains of Timothy Laker's car. He reported it immediately." Doogan informed Nick.

"Did he leave footprints anywhere?" Nick asked.

"No, he stayed on the tractor."

Smart move, Nick thought.

They left later for St Luke's hospital in Kilkenny city. Nick was relieved Sheila Hynes wasn't there when they arrived. Things were awkward enough. The crime scene was cordoned off inside. Ned Rooney's body lay beneath a sheet. Nick lifted it, glancing at Ned Rooney's face, emaciated, covered in bruises, but serene and defiant, lips tight, one of the lads, but now no more. A soft target, but he'd fought the good fight. Nick vowed to get whoever did it, as much for himself as for his sister, and replaced the sheet.

While Doogan was immersed in conversation with the forensic team, Nick left him to search for the doctor who'd looked after Ned Rooney. He tracked down a Dr David Clohessy, a young and bespectacled man, who said Ned's relations in Dublin had been informed of his death. Funeral arrangements would be deferred until a full autopsy and police investigations were complete. Nick thanked him, before asking the question bedevilling his mind.

"Would Ned Rooney have recovered, if this incident had not occurred?"

"Unequivocally the answer is yes. His quality of life would have been reduced, but he would have recovered. His body had suffered from the affects of alcohol and nicotine over the years, but yes, he would have lived on."

"Hmmm, so its murder, full-blown, then?"Nick asked.

"Yes it is, and I hope you find those responsible."

"You think there was more than one involved?"

"I do, but crime is not my area. I leave that to you guys. Good luck. "The young doctor replied, saying he had to attend an urgent call.

Nick thanked him and left, arranging a lift back to Bagenalstown. He spoke to Doogan before he left.

"I'm off home now, Inspector."

"Ok Sergeant Hackett, thanks for your input today. I would ask you to warn your sister against any knee-jerk reaction to Ned Rooney's death, while investigations are ongoing. I understand she works as a part-time teacher in the new school on the Royal Oak road. Ned Rooney would not have survived his prior injuries anyway."

"That's not what I've been told by the medics." Nick retorted.

Doogan scowled, saying he was glad Nick's urinary infection had cleared up so quickly. Nick knew they were now sworn enemies, and Doogan knew it too. But Nick didn't care.

Chapter 22

Conflict

News of Ned Rooney's death made front page in *"The Carlow Nationalist"* the next day. Nancy read the article word for word, written by Ignatius Purcell, who'd done the article about the Garda's previous lack of security for Rooney. Riven with remorse, she wondered what Purcell would make of the Garda's no-show at the hospital where Ned Rooney was murdered, and the fact that the murderer had entered the hospital disguised as a Garda. How ironic, she muttered, how ironic indeed.

The paper also covered the discovery of Garda Timothy Laker's body and burnt-out car in Goresbridge. The Garda were quoted as saying the two incidents were unconnected.

Mid-morning that day, she received an unexpected delivery, a bouquet of flowers from Marty, with a note enclosed hoping she was fully recovered from her near-drowning experience, and sending his understanding and sympathy about Ned Rooney's death. He'd just read the bad news in the paper. He's really so thoughtful and nice she reflected, as she unwrapped the flowers and arranged them in two water-filled vases. Twelve flowers again, probably symbolic of the Zodiac, she mused. A perfect gentleman, I do owe him. He saved my life too. His message lifted her spirits.

Nick arrived not long later, bleary-eyed, sallow and unshaven.

"God, I'd give my right hand for a coffee." He said, throwing his Garda hat onto the sofa.

"Ok. By God you're a sight for sore eyes, what ails you?"She asked, startled at his appearance.

"A long day's journey into a night of liquor, after a helluva day yesterday. A lot of crap at the meeting with Inspector Doogan, then visiting two possible murder scenes. It'd wreck the head of a saint. I don't know what Sheila Hynes sees in that guy. Wouldn't trust him as far as I'd throw him. What I wouldn't do for a hair of the dog." Nick sighed.

"Don't be crazy, drinking on the job is foolish. What you need is a good sleep. Here, get this into you, it'll help you sober up." She said, filling his mug.

"Thanks. I've been over to Aengus Hynes' house again. He wasn't there, same old story as before, up North on business. Lying low in the long grass, I'd guess. We have people tracking his henchmen who attacked Ned Rooney. We'll track Hynes down too. He'll have some explaining to do. Strange, Inspector Doogan still protests the man's innocence."

"How could he? There was a formal complaint to the Garda of intimidation against Hynes by Ned Rooney himself."Nancy said, shocked.

"Yes, but I believe Doogan's had the records altered. All references to Ned Rooney have been deleted."

"What, how could he get away with that? And what about the time you visited and spoke to Aengus Hynes at his house?"She said, indignant.

"Doogan says it's just me getting my own back. A grudge by me personally, a vendetta because he stole my girl friend Sheila Hynes. I believe he has a conflict of interests. A serious one."

"He's out to get you Nick, you must be careful. I don't care for the man, I've a bad feeling about him. I'm worried by him." She leaned over nervously and hugged Nick. She sometimes forgot he was her kid brother.

"That's only the half of it. He's out to get more than me. You'll have to tread carefully from here on Nancy. That article you had printed in the newspaper really got under his skin. Poor fellow ended up in all sorts of shit with the Big Boys up in the Phoenix Park in Dublin.

Hopefully it's banjaxed his ambition of becoming a Superintendent. Boo, hoo, I'm in bits for him. By the way he told me to tell you not to write any knee-jerk articles in the newspaper about Ned Rooney's death. He said it could hinder Garda investigations into the murder."

Nancy raged at the nerve of Doogan thinking he could browbeat her into silence.

"We've got him over a barrel. Sheila Hynes confirmed to me there definitely was no Garda cover at the hospital. It's a fact." Nancy exclaimed.

"But he'll get her to retract that statement. Mark my words. Then it'll only be your word against his. He'll fabricate lies, like he did with Ned Rooney's request for protection. He's a wily bastard. He tried to pump me about where you worked. I gave him no information, but I'm marking your cards. He has it in for me, thinking I've a grudge against the Hynes family, because he wiped my eye with Sheila, and he hates you for the newspaper article. That really upset his applecart."Nick cracked his knuckles as he spoke.

"And *have* you a grudge?" She asked, eyeballing him.

"No, I just hate his guts."

"I'm with you there. But we can't let him intimidate us, he's a bully, and he'll try to have his way. Anyway, I'm prepared to sacrifice my job for the truth. Are you?" Again she glared into his eyes.

There was a pause during which he circled the room, cracking his knuckles again, before replying.

"Yes." Nick said, sighing, picking up his hat and leaving, saying he was going to rest. She guessed that inwardly Nick had a conflict, but had decided now was not the time to reveal it.

The funeral was held a week later. The cortege left the hospital in Kilkenny, after Mass in the oratory there. Nancy followed behind in Nick's car. The final place of rest was at the cemetery in Carlow town, near Dr. Cullen G.A.A. Park, where Ned Rooney was interred in the family plot beside his mother.

Ned's step-sister and some of her family from Dublin attended the funeral, as well as some of Ned's former rabbit-hunting friends from Bagenalstown. Nancy paid her respects to Ned's family at the graveside, saying she was an old friend of his, before heading back towards the car.

On her way, she was startled when a figure appeared from behind a large tombstone. It was Marty Maher.

"Jesus Marty, you frightened the living daylights out of me. What are you doing here?"

"Sorry Nancy, I'm here to pay my respects to you. I've already done the same with Ned Rooney's family. I just wanted you to know you have my sincere sympathies. Even though you and Ned Rooney were only like long-separated friends, I know there's still a sense of loss. I like to attend funerals when I'm home from Italy, as part of my social services. I do have a special empathy with the Departed. We must all take our leave for the Hereafter sometime. We know not the day or the hour, do we? Anyway, in this case I must admit it was also a chance to see you. May I give you a lift home?"He smiled at her.

She hesitated a minute.

"Let me speak to Nick first, I came here with him."

"Of course."

She left him waiting beside the huge tombstone of an itinerant family, returning minutes later.

"Yes Marty, that suits him fine, Nick's just been drafted urgently to Kilkenny, to the scene of Garda Laker's accident. You probably read about that in the papers. He has to interview a farmer who owns a meadow with a bull in it, near the scene. I think he said the farmer's name was Summers."

"Yes, I read the article. So they think it was an accident?"

"They don't know, they have an open mind. That's why they're interviewing the farmer. The man apparently has republican sympathies. By the way, thank you for the flowers Marty, it was a lovely surprise."

"My pleasure dear Nancy. Fancy a coffee on the way, and we can discuss more pleasant matters, like your next visit to Graigue. Our unfinished symphony." He smiled as he studied her face.

"Ok, that would be nice."

She squeezed into the front seat of his Bambino. They stopped at The Lord Bagenal Hotel in Leighlinbridge. After serving themselves with sandwiches, they found a quiet nook by the window, and ordered coffees.

"Such lovely paintings." She said, admiring the many pictures decorating the walls.

"None as beautiful as you are Nancy. You're my *Mona Lisa*." Marty said, glancing into her eyes.

"Go on Marty, flatterer, you'd say Mass if you knew the Latin." She grinned.

"I *do* say Mass, and I *do* know the Latin." He grinned back.

"Nick is under fierce pressure from his boss, Inspector Doogan. And the same Doogan now has it in for me."She said.

"Really? Why is that? He's the one who stole your brother's girl friend, is he not?"

"Yes, that's him."

She told him of Doogan's doctoring of Ned Rooney's complaint in the local Garda station, and his lack of protection for Ned in the hospital, and his fury at her for publishing the newspaper article. He listened intently, speaking when she'd finished.

"You have a conflict, Nancy. If you blow the gaff on Doogan's behaviour, you'll jeopardise both your careers. Inspector Doogan has an ungrateful heart. What will you do?" His forehead furrowed in a frown.

"The truth must be told, whatever the outcome. I owe it to Ned Rooney and his family. Nick and I are agreed on that. We'll not kowtow to a bully."

"You're brave, both of you. Some would say foolish, but I say brave. I admire you Nancy, but then I've always admired you, now more than ever. In fact it's more than admiration. If there's anything I can do, please call me, I'd love to help." He leaned across the table and hugged her gently.

She didn't mind him doing that. After all, he'd saved her life. And she needed a shoulder to lean on. Still, he was a priest, even if no one in the restaurant would have known it.

"Thanks Marty, you never know."

"And will you come to Graigue this weekend?" He asked, hope in his voice and eyes.

After pondering a few minutes she replied.

"Yes Marty, I will."

They left the hotel then, walking hand-in-hand along a flower-bedecked street, across the ancient six-arched bridge spanning the Barrow. Half-way over they stopped, looking down at the water gushing through the arches beneath the bridge, and the reflection of the bridge in the water. Elated, she looked into his eyes.

"What a lovely place, have you ever taken your barge this far?"

"No, it's on my list of things to do. I'd love to travel all the way up the Barrow right to its source, somewhere in the Slieve Bloom Mountains I believe. That's my dream. I've always dreamed of taking the barge upriver to Monasterevin, where the river Barrow coincides with the Grand Canal, Ireland's Venice they call it. As we're not likely to get to the real Venice together, maybe you'd come with me to the Irish one?"

"Maybe, I'd have to think about it."

"Please do."He smiled.

They walked on across the bridge, turning upriver to the graveyard. There they looked at the names on the headstones. Many buried there were casualties of WW1. She saw a gravestone to Major Myles Keogh, a local hero of three wars, dying with Custer at Little Big Horn.

"Graveyards are fascinating. So many stories buried in one place." She said.

He nodded, his eyes staring up the river with a faraway look in them.

They returned to the car, and soon were back and parked outside her house in Bagenalstown, at the end of Kilree Street, before the railway bridge.

"Say Nancy, that's a strange kind of wall over there. " He said, pointing across the road from her house. There were pillars of granite mounted on top of each other, with spaces in between, all along that side of the road up to the railway bridge.

"It's called a Carlow Fence. They were built from granite by the Quakers years ago. Carlow is the only place in Ireland that has them. We're proud of that fact."

"Impressive. *Ciao* Nancy, until Saturday then. *Bella Ciao*." He waved as he drove away.

She waved after him, and opened the gate, walking to the front door, opening the latch on the half door, inserting her key in the lock of the main door, and entering. Her father was asleep beside the Stanley range fire, which had gone out. Childhood memories crept into her mind.

The times she'd turned the bellows wheel to keep the fire alight under the skillet pot, when the sparks would fly up from the turf, and sometimes fill the room with smoke. And the times the hens flew up onto the half door in the summer months, and when she'd collect eggs for her mother from the laying hens. And when they'd go picking mushrooms early in the Autumn days with the dew heavy and the mist lifting off the meadow, and the many times they went up to the Sliding Rock and slid down on their bums, yipppeeing with delight, and the fun they had milking the spancilled goats in the meadow, and they trying to puck her as she held the metal jug under them. And the lovely lady, Annie Conway, who lived next door, married, who had no family but once had a Bonham piglet living in the house with her. She called the piglet her baby, and when they took the baby pig to market a few months later, Annie herself cried like a baby. Her baby was gone. They'd taken her baby. And she remembered the times she'd gone out with Ned Rooney, and him the handsomest fellah in the town, and him now buried and gone in the cemetery in Carlow. Forever.

So many memories, so long ago, she sighed, wiping a tear from her cheek. If only she could turn back the clock. She climbed the stairs, lay on the bed and in minutes was asleep.

Next morning early, she rang Ignatius Purcell in the Carlow Nationalist.

"Nancy Hackett here, do you remember you wrote the article for me about Ned Rooney's lack of security?"

"I do indeed. It ruffled a few feathers, I can tell you. Quite a few feathers indeed. No harm done though, they needed ruffling."The voice wheezed.

"Really?"

"Yes, the Editor afterwards got some threatening phone calls from people in high places."

"Oh, I'm sorry about that. What did he do? Did you get into hot water?"

"No. I'd cleared it with him beforehand. He defended the freedom of the Press, as I knew he would. He called me in and briefed me on everything. He's an honest man. And a decent one too."

"The Garda know I gave you the information."

"Not leaked from me or my boss, I can assure you. I hope you didn't get into trouble over the leak. It's a small town. Tongues wag."Purcell coughed after speaking.

"No, no trouble so far. Look, let's cut to the chase. I have an even better follow-up story. Are you interested?" Nancy asked.

"You bet I am, my pencil is in my hand already."

"Can you come to my house now?"

"I'm just back from Kilkenny, and I have to write something about the accident concerning Garda Laker. Give me an hour or so."

"Ok, I'll be waiting."She put down the phone.

Purcell's jalopy arrived almost an hour later. She heard it coming up the road. Through the laced windows, she saw him park it beside the Carlow Fence across the road. She met him at the gate.

"Please come in Mr Purcell. Can I get you a coffee? "

He nodded.

"Yes thanks. You can call me Ignatius by the way. It's been a rough day." He said, and sat on the sofa, taking a pad and pencil from his frayed jacket.

"Sugar or milk?" She asked.

He shook his head.

"So what have you got this time?" Purcell asked.

She gathered he was in a hurry, and got to the nub of it.

"After Ned Rooney was assaulted, he was taken to St. Luke's Hospital in Kilkenny. He was obviously in a serious condition and was put in the Intensive Care Unit. There was to be 24 hour Garda security on him, as there was a clear danger someone might try to finish him off, in case he identified his attackers. I was in the same hospital by chance last week, and asked my nurse if I could visit Ned. She agreed, and I saw him briefly. There was *no* Garda cover on him then. Definitely none. Nor had there ever been any, the nurse confirmed it."

"What was the nurse's name?"Purcell asked.

"Sheila Hynes."

"Any relation to Aengus Hynes?"

"Yes, she's his younger sister. And to add irony, the man who broke in and killed Ned, he was dressed as a Garda."

Purcell stopped scribbling and looked up.

"I've just come back from the scene of Garda Laker's accident. It just occurred to me now, what if Laker was killed, and his uniform taken for use in gaining entry to the hospital?"

"If that was the case he *was* killed by the IRA, by someone the same size as Laker."Nancy said.

"Yes. But you'd think they could've got a uniform by some other method. However, I understand the man who owns the meadow with the bull in it, across the river from the accident scene, is the same height and build as Laker. And he's a republican. His name is Summers and he's the prime suspect. It looks like another murder case. They've also found a clue at the scene."

"Really? What is it?"

"In confidence, for your ears only?" He leaned closer, putting his finger to his lips.

"Yes. What is it?"She asked again, intrigued.

"The forensic team were trawling through the bushes in the vicinity of the scene yesterday, when they came across something a trifle gruesome."

"What was it?"She held her breath after she spoke.

"Looked like some human entrails, maybe leftovers from wild animals. They're being analysed in the lab. You never know. It could be a double murder case."

"Then the two murders might be connected?"

"Maybe, we have to wait and see." Purcell muttered.

"Ok, so what about my story?" Nancy asked.

"Coming on top of the earlier article, there could be blue murder, no pun intended. You and your brother could be put under almighty pressure. Sheila Hynes might deny your story. Selective amnesia, we call it in the trade. You'll not be popular, to put it mildly, but I admire your pluck." He downed his coffee after speaking.

"The truth has to be told, Ned Rooney deserves it. Will you print it Ignatius? It can't affect Garda investigations, particularly after what you've just told me." Her voice trembled as she spoke.

"I'll have to run it pass the boss. I'd say yes we will, probably in a few days." Purcell replied, wheezing as he rose to leave.

They shook hands and she told him she'd say a rosary that he was successful. He said it might more likely need a miracle, as he put his pad and pencil back in his pocket. Soon his car was spluttering down Kilree Street, exhaust fumes billowing behind.

The next Friday before leaving the school, Nancy was summoned unexpectedly to Sister Cecelia's office. Her heart raced, pulsating with panic. Good news, bad news, she wondered, knocking on the office door, and entering.

"Please be seated Miss Hackett, it's over a month since you started with us, and time for a review of your progress." Sister Cecelia said, smiling as she removed her pince-nez glasses, and rubbed them with a tissue.

Nancy felt her heart palpitate.

"I..I hope you're happy with my work."She stuttered.

"Personally I'm very happy, I'm glad to say. You've fulfilled your teaching duties really well, and worked wonders with the choir. *Monteverdi* himself would be proud of your efforts. And you've helped in cleaning up the river Barrow, where Sister Roberta's flowers once blossomed. That last action particularly, has not gone unnoticed by me. Unfortunately, I'm only one of eight on the Board of Management of the school. Recently, others on the Board have brought up issues." The nun replaced her glasses, and her face hardened.

"What issues?" Nancy asked, a hollow feeling coming in her stomach.

"Well, for one, you never mentioned you were an ex-member of the Presentation Order."

"Oh, I...I.. didn't think it relevant at the time, as it was just a temporary teaching post."

"It might be relevant in the future, if a permanent position arose, or in the renewal of your contract.It also could be construed that you had something to hide."

"Yes Sister Cecelia, I was a member of the Order in Manchester, for over twenty years."

"And why did you leave?"

"I..I felt I no longer had a vocation, and I was not happy in my life there, and my father was invalided at home here in Bagenalstown."

"Anything else you'd like to tell me?" The nun said, peering over her glasses.

A pregnant pause came then. The nun stared at her in silence. The penny dropped.

"I had a baby before I joined the Order. It....he was adopted." Nancy's voice shook as she spoke.

"Good. I'm glad you mentioned that. I'm with you Miss Hackett, but that fact could be used against you by others. I will be prepared to fight on your behalf, but only if you tell me the truth. Just be careful whom you antagonise in the future. I can only do so much. That's all for now Miss Hackett. I'm looking forward to the *Monteverdi* concert in the church next month." Sister Cecilia smiled, her eyes peering knowingly above her glasses.

Nancy breathed a sigh of relief after she left the nun's office.

That night she reflected on Sister Cecelia's words. At least she was on her side. Nick was right too, Doogan was dangerous. The week had been stressful. At least she had her weekend on the Barrow with Marty to look forward to. He'd helped her cope with stress before. She felt she'd earned the break with him. Sleep descended like a dark fog.

Chapter 23

River

Kitty called before Marty had arrived to collect Nancy for their trip to Graigue on the next Saturday. She'd agreed to mind their father for the weekend.

"Packing an overnight case?" Kitty grinned.

"Yes, jealous?"

"You bet. Now don't do anything I wouldn't do."

"That gives me plenty of scope."Nancy laughed, enjoying the banter, eager to be on her way.

Minutes later Nancy heard the letterbox snap shut, a letter hitting the hall floor. She rushed to pick it up. It was from Liam, she recognised his handwriting. Her heart pounded as she thumbed it open. The music tour was going grand he said, and he'd be in Graiguenamanagh the following Wednesday for a gig.

He'd got plenty of info on the songs she'd enquired about. He hoped to get in some kayaking on the river, and wanted to meet up with her again, if possible. He gave the name and address of the pub where he hoped they could meet in Graiguenamanagh. He said he'd understand if she couldn't make it. Their final gig was the following weekend in Kilkenny city, in Langton's pub. Her hands trembled. Of course I'll be there, she thought, I'll be at both places, by God I will, wild horses won't keep me away. Don't worry son, I'll be there, she vowed. She smiled then, elation filling her heart.

Soon Marty arrived. He wore a pair of khaki shorts, and a peaked sea captain's cap, which he doffed to her. His beard was gone, and over his mouth a moustache was beginning to sprout. A smile crinkled his face.

"Today your every wish is my command. I hope it is a lovely one for you. I'm so happy to be here, and I hope to make you happy. I know you've had a difficult week."He said.

"Thank you, I'm sure my troubles will be blown away."The news from Liam had already helped to blow them away, she thought.

"Don't worry they will, I'll see to it." He said, picking up her case and putting it in the boot.

She squeezed into the passenger seat, fastening her seat belt. The car sped over the railway bridge onto the Borris road in the brightening air, patches of blue breaking up the clouds, Mount Leinster rising large in the distance, a few fluffy clouds covering its apex. Excitement tingled through her veins. The river was always an adventure for her.

"The weather looks promising, mostly dry and sunny. Did you bring your togs?"He asked.

"Yes, but not for swimming this time, only sunbathing. I've learned my lesson, once bitten." She smiled ruefully.

"I agree, that's a wise decision. I think we should do something different this weekend, after your last escapade in the river."He frowned as he spoke.

"And what have you in mind?"

"Well, I thought we'd leave the barge in Graigue, drive to Goresbridge, then travel by kayak back to Graigue. I've dinner prepared for us later aboard the barge. After that, I can drop you home. Or if you choose to stay the night, we could travel back to Bagenalstown on the *St Fiachra* on Sunday. The choice is yours. I hope you stay. Naturally." He smiled, hope etched on his face.

Silence. She hesitated a few minutes before replying.

"Yes, well ok, that's a good idea Marty. I would like to stay the night. Providing of course, there are no disasters on the kayak trip."

"Great, I'll make sure there aren't. Everything will be fine, just like the weather." He smiled, looking to the heavens.

Aboard the barge, she changed into shorts, t-shirt, sandals, and a cap. He packed a picnic and stopped to admire her figure when she appeared on deck.

"O beautiful body, lead me not into temptation." He joked.

She ignored him.

"We pick up the kayak and life jackets in Goresbridge. I'll leave the car there, and collect it on Monday. The kayak will be picked up in Graigue later, by the hire company." Marty informed her.

Within the hour they were sitting in an Indian-style canoe for two in Goresbridge, gliding downriver. The river's surface, smooth as glass, mirrored the tall trees on both banks, guardians of the river's ancient towpaths, mills, and lock-houses. She felt more secure sharing the canoe. Her near-drowning experience had shaken her to the marrow. She knew she could rely on Marty now. She trusted him, he'd saved her life.

As they passed Lower Ballyellen lock, he pointed out Barrowmount House, home of the Gore family who built the bridge in the 18th century. She nodded, captivated by the beauty all around her. She felt her doubts about having a relationship with a priest start to slip away on the journey. What harm could it do after all? She mused. Even Jesus was friendly with Mary Magdalene.

They paddled on with clean, strong strokes, the sun beating down. Beads of perspiration moistened her body. Soon they were at Ballytiglea weir. The weir water level was shallow, giving a backdrop to a flood plain. They navigated between granite boulders, dropping low and left into farming pastures. Ahead lay the ancient, five-arched structure of Ballytiglea bridge. Passing under it, they entered the Borris Demesne, taking the navigation channel where the river ran smoothly past the oak forests.

They stopped there, pulling the canoe onto the bank, and had their picnic. Later, paddling on in silence, broken only by birdsong, they reached Clashganny weir's rapids, where they'd swam weeks earlier. They rested there, breathless, enthralled by the scene. She loved the music of the water gurgling over the weir. A while later they moved on again, passing a pine forest, and soon the seven-arched bridge of Graigue appeared before them. They continued onwards, relaxing, letting the current do the work, pulling in beside the *St Fiachra*, moored by the quay.

After lifting the canoe out of the water, they turned it upside down, placed the paddles underneath, unfastened their life jackets, and placed them beside the paddles. The heat of the afternoon sun still blazed down on the river, relentlessly, as shadows slanted from the old Mill building, creeping towards the river's edge.

"I hope you enjoyed the journey. I did. The barge can be our river home for the rest of the weekend."Marty said.

"Yes I did enjoy it, it was magic. And now I need to relax and get in a little sun-bathing."

"Good idea, I'm perspiring from all the paddling. You can go down and change, if you like, and shower later. I'll set up two deckchairs, and get two glasses of wine from the fridge." Marty said, wiping his brow.

Below deck, she changed smartly into a pink, one-piece bathing costume she'd bought during the week. She hoped it wasn't too revealing, but when she glanced in the mirror, she felt good about it and herself. Maybe I'll wear a silk shawl on top, she thought, just for modesty's sake, searching her case. Yes, I'd better do that, she muttered.

"Down the hatch. *Salute, bella bambina*." Marty raised his wine glass to her, as they sat on the deck.

"*Salute*." She replied.

They clinked their glasses and sipped the wine. She glanced about. In the background, the sun was a ball of fire above Mount Brandon. Nearer, the river was busy with people frolicking in the water, some diving in off a board and swimming to the far side. Further up the towpath, anglers were casting barbed flies to lure unsuspecting fish. Kayaks arrived downriver in droves, while barges chugged upstream from St. Mullins. Swallows were swooping low in a tangerine sky, feasting on insects flitting above the Barrow's surface.

Soon the swallows will be off to warmer climes, she mused, and that's sad, the end of summer is not far away. And soon Marty will be off to Milan. She sighed. Will that make her sad? Probably, she liked predictability, and constancy, happy to lean on familiar things.

Yes, she preferred a sense of order, and predictability, and familiarity. They gave her a feeling of security, but she knew that in life they were hard to find. She felt that today she may have got a taste of what she was looking for, even if the man she was with was a priest. I'm just a home bird, when all's said and done, she muttered. She put her sunglasses on, and lay back in her deck chair, closing her eyes. As she did so, her top slid off her shoulders.

Through half-closed eyes she saw Marty gazing at her body. She didn't mind. She knew him better now. He'd saved her life, and helped her cope. His time was running out, she knew, he'd told her the people in Milan were putting pressure on him. The *Ospedale Maggiore* had been calling him weekly. When would he be returning? They needed him, they were very busy. The excuse of blaming the delay on his mother's health was wearing thin, he'd said. She remembered him saying that he hoped to get another two weeks out of it. Maximum. Her eyes became heavy with sleep. She nodded off.

When she woke the barge was shrouded in shadow, and she had goose bumps on her skin. She shivered, and pulled her wrap around her. An aroma of Italy wafted from the galley, and memories of Milan came to her. Marty appeared in a chef's hat and chequered apron.

"The dead arose. It's *Spaghetti Bolognese*, just like *Mamma Mia* made, *Tortellinis* to kick off. *Vino da casa* is *Montepulciano*. Pretend we're not on a barge Nancy, but a gondola gliding along the Grand Canal in Venice. Now that *is* heaven on earth. You want to shower and change for dinner?"

She nodded. He was charming, she thought, always trying to please her.

"Ok, please go ahead then, I should be ready when you return."He said.

She showered, dried off, and put on her new red v-necked dress. A string of pearls that had belonged to her mother hung around her neck. Then she discovered she'd forgotten to pack an extra bra, and the one she'd worn kayaking was in no fit state to wear again. To hell with it, she decided, I'll just have to wear none. Go bra-less. She knew she was lucky to have kept her figure so well, and reckoned her lack of a bra shouldn't be too noticeable with the pearls on. She put a smidge of red lipstick on her lips. No makeup. No high heels, just sandals. After one last look in the mirror she was ready.

The small table was covered by a red and white chequered cloth. A candle flickered in the centre of the table, spreading eerie shadows about, and a bunch of wildflowers sat in a vase before her. For you, he said, I picked them while you were asleep. He smiled as he spoke, pressing the button on a cassette machine, filling the place with Italian music. He poured her a glass of red wine.

"*Montepulciano*, my favourite." He said.

She sipped some.

"Hmm, is this the wine we had that night in that restaurant in Milan?"She asked.

"Right Nancy, right first time. I'm impressed, your memory for wine is good."

"It is good for some things. That tune, I love it, it sounds vaguely familiar, what's it called?"

"Right again my darling. *Pietro,* the restaurant owner sang and played it that night for us in Milan, on his mandolin. He knows it's my all-time favourite, and usually obliges me when I'm there. It's probably one of the reasons I keep going back to his restaurant. He *has* a grateful heart."

"What's it called?"Nancy asked.

"*Core Ngrato.* Ungrateful heart. A Neapolitan song. Sung by all the most famous singers from Caruso to Callas. Caruso's version is my favourite."

"It's so beautiful. I wonder what the words mean in English."

"I'll do my best to translate for you Nancy, if you like. I'm thrilled you like it too."

She nodded, saying she'd like that. After a pause he spoke.

Caterina, Caterina, why do you say these bitter words?
Why do you speak, and torment my heart, Caterina?
Don't forget, I gave you my heart, Caterina
Don't forget.

Caterina, Caterina, why do you come and
Say those words that hurt me so much?
You don't think of my pain,
You don't think, you don't care.

Ungrateful heart,
You have stolen my life,
Everything is finished,
And you don't care anymore. " When he'd finished he stared at her.

She felt the words stab into her heart.

"It's very moving I must say, very moving indeed."She said.

"Yes, the words get right inside my being, and also into my soul. In my mind I change the name Nancy to *Caterina*, but I do know you have a grateful heart."He winked at her as he smiled.

Maybe I'm more grateful than you realise Marty, she thought. At that moment, she had an urge to hug and kiss him, but before she could do anything he excused himself, and returned to the galley. Just as well, she mused, I've never felt like doing that before. He might get ideas, and the night's just beginning. I must keep saying to myself that he's a priest. Glancing out the window, she saw the Harvest moon hover over the trees, a giant orange balloon mirrored in the river, while higher up early stars had started to flicker forlornly. Her reverie was broken by Marty returning with the food. After the first course, he returned holding a silver tray with a lid. *Spaghetti Bolognese*, he proclaimed, lifting the lid.

"It goes perfectly with the *Montepulciano*, and that's important. *Buon Appetito*."He continued.

"*Buon Appetito*"She replied.

He raised his glass at the end of the meal.

"*Salute*."He toasted her.

They then touched glasses before entwining hands, each now sipping the other's drink. He gazed at her eyes and face, seeing her blond hair still curling at the edges. She gazed back into his eyes, grey, piercing, and his greying, grinning face and hair. They uncoiled their hands and sat back. After a while he leaned across the table, and took her hands in his.

"*Bella notte*, my *bella bambina*, the stars look down on us. God must surely approve of our happiness. He knows I am your Guardian Angel, and I take care of you. Always I do and always I will. Tell me, is there anything worrying you dear Nancy, has Inspector Doogan been making life difficult for you?"He asked.

"As a matter of fact he has."

She told him then of her meeting with Sister Cecilia, and Nick's warning regarding putting another article about the Garda's lack of security for Ned Rooney, leading to his death, in the media, and of her decision to publish anyway and be damned.

"The truth must be told, Marty. I couldn't pray in Ned's memory, if I didn't tell the truth about how he died."

"Yes Nancy, the truth is what life's struggle is all about. Jesus is truth. He gave his life for it. The Devil thrives on untruths. Falsehoods foster evil. We must fight it, or evil will spread like a cancer throughout the world. It's a daily battle, and in this life the Devil often triumphs. This Inspector Doogan fellow, he consorts with the Devil. You must beware of him. He *has* an ungrateful heart."

"Yes Marty, I agree, when all's said and done, all that's left is the truth. Thank you for taking care of me, my Guardian Angel. "She took his hands to her mouth, and kissed them. Looking into his face , she saw him frowning.

"You seem worried Marty, is something the matter?"

"I feel sad because I must return soon to Italy. I'd rather stay here, because you are here. I've never wanted to stay longer before. But it's because of you. I hope you feel the same about me leaving, even a little bit. That would mean so much to me."He sighed, a solemn look on his face.

"Yes Marty, I will miss you. But maybe you'll return now and then to visit your mother?"

"Yes, I'll come back as often as possible, even at my own expense if I have to."

"That's not too bad then, is it?"

"No Nancy. But before I go, I want to apologise for my behaviour in Milan."

"What behaviour?"She asked, surprised.

"It was on the night of the Opera, that night I had too much to drink. I may have misbehaved in the booth while you were engrossed in watching the opera. I'm afraid I did not behave like a gentleman that night. For that I am truly sorry. And I'm not surprised you avoided my company afterwards, and left for home a day earlier."His eyes seemed moist as he spoke.

She remembered the lie she'd told him in Milan about when she was leaving, and felt a twinge of guilt.

"I'm afraid I don't remember too much about the later parts of that night. I think the mixture of the atmosphere of *La Scala* and the champagne proved too much for me. I crashed out completely in the hotel. In fact I felt quite ill the next day."She said.

"Oh, I am sorry, I didn't realise that. It's my fault. I thought you were a bit wobbly leaving the taxi outside your hotel, so I escorted you to the lift. You said you'd be ok, so I left you there. What happened then?"

"I have no recollection Marty. I must have tripped or fallen in the room. I had a bruise on my thigh, nothing much really, but I felt terrible the next day."

"I understand now how you must have felt. Again I apologise."

"Don't worry Marty, it's all water under the bridge now."

He moved over to her side of the table, and sat beside her on the bench seat, putting his arm around her, pulling her close to his body. She felt again the urge to kiss him, but held back, remembering he was a priest.

"Nancy, I have to tell you I love you. You must believe me. Ever since I met you, I was smitten, head-over-heels mad about you."He said, breathing heavily.

His lips were inches from hers, his body touching hers.

"But you're a priest Marty, you can only love God."

"Yes I know, it's crazy but I can't help it. But you're different, maybe it's because I know you were a nun, Nancy, I can't help it. I want to marry you, and yet I can't. Will you marry me, a priest?"

Before she could reply he had kissed her, deep and lingering. She felt his hands embracing her, and her body crushing against his, his fingers pressing the back of her neck, pulling her tighter to him, and exploring beneath her dress, soon sussing she was without a bra. She realised she could get carried away, and felt it already, just like when she was sucked into the eddy in the river, the time Marty rescued her. And she felt so grateful to him for saving her, that she didn't care if he swept her away in his arms. Then a vision of Sister Veronica flashed into her mind, and she remembered the old nun's words of warning. Nancy pulled away, stood up, straightened her dress, and tidied her hair.

"Pull yourself together Marty, you mustn't forget you're a priest."

"Yes, you're right, I...I..I forgot, I'm sorry. I think you have that affect on me. You make me forget I'm a priest." He seemed breathless as he spoke.

"That's all right. Beneath our skins, we all have a heart."

"A grateful heart?"He asked, a twinkle in his eye.

"Yes, a grateful heart."She replied.

And then she embraced him again, and kissed him goodnight, and made it all right for him, feeling she owed it to him, and afterwards they retired to their separate beds.

Later in bed, after praying, she felt herself drifting into a cosy cocoon of relaxation before falling asleep. She was happy that Marty had apologised, and that he'd behaved as a gentleman all that day and night. Even if they didn't end up sharing a bed that night, they did have close moments of intimacy towards the end. Very nice moments indeed. And he'd proposed marriage, she'd nearly forgotten that. My God, how could she? What would she do? Soon dark veils of sleep enveloped her.

Next morning dawned grey, and after breakfast they attended Mass in Duiske Abbey, neither of them taking Communion. Afterwards they returned to the barge, the sky filled with low-scudding clouds, raindrops peppering the river. They decided to return to Bagenalstown by car.

As she lifted her suitcase from the car, Marty took her hand in his.

"Nancy, remember I asked you to marry me last night?"

"Yes Marty I remember. But you're a priest, how can such a thing happen?"

"Rome wasn't built in a day. We can find a way. Love will find a way. Tell me you will try to find a way."

"Ok Marty, I appreciate your proposal and I will try. I need to think about it, I need time."

She kissed him lightly on the lips, closed the car door, and waved him off. Just then the nun's advice of *Festina Lente* flashed into her mind.

Chapter 24

Update

Kitty arrived early at Nancy's house on Monday morning saying that she'd slept little the night before, her mind bedevilled by what Nancy might have got up to in Graigue with Marty, saying too that she envied Nancy, and wished her own life was half as exciting.

"Get on with you, I'll put the kettle on." Nancy laughed as she replied. She enjoyed her *tete-a-tetes* with her sister.

"Honestly, I really am excited for you. I simply can't wait to hear all the news about you and Marty. I want a complete update, no omissions."Kitty said, grinning.

They sat side by side, sipping tea, facing the window, the morning sun filtering through the lace curtains. Nancy described the canoe trip from Goresbridge, Marty's Italian meal and afterwards, her voice tinged with excitement. Kitty listened intently.

"Well, it sounds wonderful, a real adventure, wish it was me, and how did it go? I mean how far did you go, if you know what I mean? I don't mean to be prying, but the suspense is killing. Did you stay the night?"Kitty asked.

"Now you are prying. I did stay the night, but don't go reading too much into that. He is a priest, after all, dedicated to God."

"He's a priest who sends flowers to his beloved one, brings her to the Opera, cooks her exotic Italian dinners, serves her wine, and saves her from drowning. Sounds like a priest who's besotted with someone. But no, I suppose I shouldn't be reading too much into that at all, or should I? Oh, but the thrill of it all's got to me. And did he kiss you?"Kitty's eyes twinkled as she spoke.

"None of your business really. But as a matter of fact, he did."

"And did you resist?"Kitty persisted.

"Again, none of your business, but the answer is yes. Initially, that is."

"And…and….. did you go any further?"Kitty's asked, startled at the response.

"Did I what? *Absolutely* none of your business. No, we did not end up sleeping together, if that's what you're insinuating. As I said before, he's a priest. We ended up in our separate beds. But we did have an enjoyable time, in fact more than enjoyable, you'll be glad to hear."

"Thereby hangs a tale. I bet he was up for it. But you were right, love is sometimes like climbing a mountain, you have to do it in stages."Kitty sighed, her eyes glazed over.

"Yes, *Festina Lente*. That's what the nuns preached in the monastery. But time is running out for climbing that mountain, and for Marty. He has only two weeks left before he returns to Italy."

"Oh, that's sad."

"But he says he'll be back occasionally to visit his mother."

"And you too, no doubt. That's good anyway. "Kitty said.

"Oh, and there is one more piece of important news I nearly forgot to update you on."

"And what's that?"Kitty asked, agog.

"Marty proposed marriage to me." Nancy replied, smiling.

"He did what! Hey that's wonderful, but why didn't you tell me before?" Kitty jumped up and hugged her.

"I don't know, it must have slipped my mind. I still can't quite believe it."

"And what did you say?"

"I said I'd think about it. It's complicated. He is after all a priest, bound by vows of celibacy and chastity. He'd have to renounce all that and leave the priesthood. It kind of makes me feel guilty, like some Jezebel tempting him from his calling. In fact it's *very* complicated. I don't know what to do."Nancy sighed.

Their conversation was interrupted by the noise of the front door opening. Seconds later Nick had entered the room, twirling his Garda hat in his hands, before throwing it on the sofa.

"They used say Bagenalstown was a sleepy backwater of a place, but now it's anything but. It puts Hawaii Five O in the shade. I've a meeting here with Inspector Doogan at noon. It sounds just like High Noon to me, and I feel the way Gary Cooper did in the movie. Isolated." Nick fumed, pacing the floor, fiddling with his buttons, his face haggard.

"I'm putting on a fresh pot. You look like you need a cuppa."Nancy said.

Kitty excused herself and left, saying she'd shopping to do, and she'd see Nancy again soon.

"Daddy still in bed?"Nick asked.

She nodded.

"Purcell's article about the lack of security for Ned Rooney in the hospital was published in "The Carlow Nationalist" today." He said ruefully, handing her the newspaper.

She glanced at it. The front page had a picture of Ned Rooney. The headlines were "**Lack of Garda Security at Murder Scene**". Ignatius Purcell had written the report. Her stomach tightened as she read on.

"Doogan will be on the warpath today over that article, and also over developments in the Garda Laker case, so you better watch your back."Nick's face creased with concern as he spoke.

"We both better take care. The truth will out. Sooner or later we have to face the music and dance." She said. Inwardly she had a hollow feeling, though outwardly she put on a brave front.

"I suppose we'd better watch out, anyway we'll fight it out together, through thick and thin."Nick said, as he put his arm around her and hugged her. He gulped his tea down and spoke again.

"I've got to leave now, I've got lots of stuff to prepare for the meeting with Doogan. Thanks for the tea Nancy. Be careful, watch your step."

***

He stood up, put his hat on and left, walking down Kilree Street. He needed a walk to clear his head. He was worried about the meeting with Doogan, and walking always helped him relax. Turning left at The Railway House pub, up the Royal Oak Road, he went right at the Fairgreen, down to Connolly's shop, then right again onto Main Street.

He liked the way the town was laid out. It has a certain charm, he mused, streets wide and parallel to the river. Halfway up Main Street he stopped to admire the Court House building, built years before by Lord Bagenal himself. He walked on to the Bank at the corner, turning right onto Kilree Street, and entered the Garda Station's granite façade.

He checked the time as he walked towards the Meeting Room. Fifteen minutes to go, just enough time to prepare. He was wrong. Opening the door he saw the raincoat hanging from a nail, while Inspector Cornelius Doogan sat at the top of the long table, the room lit by a bare bulb dangling from the ceiling. The ashtray before Doogan was clogged with butts, and the air stank of stale smoke. A copy of "The Carlow Nationalist" was in his hands. Wrong-footed again, I should have known, Nick fumed.

Doogan looked up from reading the newspaper, the fury in his face palpable, but Nick was startled by his appearance. Normally so immaculately dressed, Doogan now looked dishevelled, buttons opened on his shirt and uniform, a stubble beard covering his dimpled chin and his face. But it was when he stared into Doogan's eyes he got the biggest shock. Black bags sagged beneath each, and etched into them was something he'd never seen before. Fear. There was no mistaking it, Doogan looked scared.

"Sergeant Hackett, I trust you've read this newspaper today." Doogan sneered, shoving it into Nick's hands.

"Yes Inspector, I have."

"A pack of drivelling lies, the whole of it. I warned you Hackett, I won't stand for anymore of this scurrilous slander in the media. In the Force we all sing from the same hymn sheet. Using my girlfriend to stab me in the back. By God, I won't stand for any more of this. It's a downright vendetta." Doogan's voice rose to a crescendo. Nick felt Doogan was losing it.

"Your girlfriend confirmed that there was no Garda presence in the hospital."Nick said.

"She did no such thing, it's a complete fabrication. I've spoken to her. She denies she ever said such a thing. And here's a copy of the Garda roster assigned to protect Ned Rooney in the hospital."Doogan growled, throwing a foolscap sheet on the table.

Nick picked it up and read it. They all seemed like people Doogan could manipulate one way or another. He was sure too Sheila Hynes *would* retract her story under duress from her boyfriend. Doogan had a very persuasive manner. Still, the whole affair seemed to be taking its toll on the Inspector. Probably not sleeping, maybe hitting the bottle, Nick mused. He'd never seen Doogan so drained. Something must be getting to him, he reckoned. He wished he knew what it was.

"I agree it's a serious charge Inspector, without a doubt. Nevertheless, a person lost his life."

"Not through any negligence of the Garda. Anyway, it's not as if Ned Rooney was anyone important." Doogan snarled, baring his teeth, pressing his face closer to Nick, who got a whiff of nicotine mixed with whiskey from his breath.

"Ned Rooney was a human being just like you or I, Inspector. We're all equal at birth and death. I suppose the reporter has his sources, and once they back him up it's the Court that will, in the final analysis, be the arbiter." Nick was surprised at how calm he felt as he spoke. Up to then he'd never spoken to a superior in this manner.

Nick suspected that beneath Doogan's bluster lay a worried man. He felt the Inspector was in some kind of trouble. It gave Nick strength. He felt he had the upper hand for once.

"I think a retraction, with a full apology is in order by the newspaper. I'll attend to that matter today. The sooner the whole thing is put to bed the better. We have other more important matters to examine. Let's kick off with a coffee before we get stuck into the Goresbridge incident." Doogan snapped.

Nick nodded, ambling over to the kitchen area to put the kettle on. Within minutes, there were two mugs of steaming coffee before them.

"Well Sergeant, let's move onto the Goresbridge affair. This has now been upgraded to murder status. The forensic feedback confirmed the intestines found near the scene *were* human. We have to conclude that they were Laker's remains, and that foul play was involved. Forensics are checking this out. Tim Laker was a friend of mine, you know. We must get the murderer, and quickly. What's the latest update?" Doogan spoke anxiously, taking a drag from the cigarette hanging from his lower lip, tipping it afterwards into the ashtray.

Doogan seemed nervous. He *is* nervous, Nick thought, but why? He commenced the update.

"I'm glad to report progress *has* been made Inspector. In a spot search of the outbuildings of Sean Summers, a bachelor farmer living near the Laker crime scene in Goresbridge, an intact Garda uniform has been uncovered. The number on it showed it belonged to Garda Laker. It was hidden beneath the floorboards, and only discovered when an alert detective thought the boards had creaked abnormally. After checking them he saw some boards had loose nails, and prised them up. Both Laker and Summers are roughly the same size. Summers is also a committed Republican. Everything points to him being the killer of both Garda Laker and Ned Rooney. When I called to

Aengus Hynes's house a while back, Sean Summers was there. I distinctly remember his face from that time. I believe we should arrest Summers now, and charge him with both murders."

"Good progress Sergeant, but I think we should treat each murder as a separate incident. We also need to do forensic tests on the uniform. The hospital evidence will be viewed as circumstantial, and won't stick. We should arrest Summers now, only on a charge of murdering Garda Laker. He may crack under questioning about the Rooney murder." Doogan gave a sigh of relief after he spoke.

And it means Aengus Hynes will be off-the-hook for the moment, Nick thought, and then Doogan can muddy the waters, and ingratiate himself further with the Hynes family. But although Doogan seemed to have perked up, his voice still lacked confidence.

"The hiding by Sean Summers of a Garda uniform on his premises points to the probability of him wanting to use it, and given that the person who entered the hospital also wore a Garda uniform, the two incidents have to be linked."Nick said.

"Not necessarily Sergeant. You're still a bit wet behind the ears, when it comes to prosecuting a criminal charge in Court. The legal beagles will eat you up and spit you out, if you don't have watertight evidence. So far all we have is circumstantial. The forensic evidence will be conclusive." Doogan muttered.

"We know that Aengus Hynes is Sean Summers' Commanding Officer in the IRA. Should we not question Hynes as a matter of course?" Nick asked, enjoying Doogan's discomfort and defensiveness.

"No. There's no connection between the two murders at the moment, except in your head Sergeant Hackett. I suggest you drop the connection. Immediately." Doogan snapped, irritated.

There was a knock on the door. A young guard entered the room, looking ruffled.

"S…sorry to interrupt Inspector Doogan, there's an urgent call holding for you."

"Damn, what's it about?"

"Sorry sir, it's top priority, he gave the IRA codeword."

Doogan left the room, swearing. When he returned ten minutes later he said nothing, slumped in his chair, lit a cigarette, and downed the dregs of his coffee.

"Is there any chance of a fresh top-up, Sergeant?" Doogan enquired, looking disconsolate, like a beaten man.

"Anything wrong Inspector?" Nick asked as he refilled Doogan's mug.

"Yes. There's been a new development."

"Is it relevant to our case?"

"Well, you won't be interviewing Aengus Hynes for starters." Doogan stated.

"Why's that?

"He's gone missing. AWOL for three days. Confirmed by the IRA themselves. He returned last Sunday from the North, and went for a walk that night down by the Barrow. Never returned." Doogan replied glumly, his eyes with a faraway, haunted look.

"Well now, that's a turn-up for the books." Nick said, shocked.

Doogan pulled hard on his cigarette, and exhaled smoke clouds towards the ceiling, before taking a slug of coffee. He looked like a pummelled boxer who'd just beaten the count, back in his corner, who was dreading the sound of the bell when he'd have to go out again for more punishment. Nick silently had to admit he was enjoying the moment. He felt like the boxer waiting in the other corner, anxious and waiting to land the killer-punch.

"Sounds suspicious Inspector, but there could be many explanations." Nick spoke as he leaned inwards, adopting a concerned pose.

"Such as?"

"He might be hiding low, afraid of some retribution, courtesy of the IRA. He vanishes in the long grass, and hey presto, a few months later he miraculously reappears.

It's happened before."

"Maybe so, anything's possible. Anyway it's another bloody investigation, as if we didn't have our hands full already." Doogan muttered edgily.

"I agree with you Inspector. But now it's back to Sean Summers. Permission requested to arrest and interrogate him. Presumably the IRA is not aware of this development with Summers?"Nick asked.

"No they're not. Yes, you can go ahead and arrest him." Doogan replied.

As he left the room, it occurred to Nick that Sheila Hynes might not be over-the-moon with Doogan following the disappearance of her brother, and she after changing her story about the lack of Garda security for Ned Rooney at the hospital. This thought perked him up. And it also occurred to him that Doogan might not now be as likely to seek retribution on Nancy for the latest newspaper article. Doogan's career was in tatters and so was Doogan, and Doogan knew it. Nick smiled as he left the building, stepped into the waiting squad car, and sped to Kilkenny to arrest Sean Summers.

Chapter 25

Song

Next morning Kitty arrived early, asking Nancy if she'd join her for a walk by the river, the weather being set fair, and there being no Physio that day for their father. Nancy agreed as she had a free morning from the school.

As they walked and chatted, Kitty said she had to ask Nancy the question that had been intriguing her thoughts the previous night. She hoped Nancy wouldn't mind her asking.

"Of course, do please go ahead, sure why should I mind?"Nancy asked.

"You told me that Marty asked you to marry him. Nick came into the room yesterday before I could ask you the burning question… that is… well…are…are you going to accept?"

"I told you my answer before. I said I'd think about it, and that's what I'm doing. I'm thinking about it. It's not a straightforward matter." Nancy replied calmly.

"Yes I know, but…well… you've had time to think about it now, have you not?"Kitty continued.

"Not long enough I'm afraid, it's a big decision. It needs more time. There'll be no knee-jerk reactions. I haven't even met his mother for God's sake, and she living nearby. I need more reassurance. Is he going to leave the priesthood? I'd feel guilty if he didn't. We'd both be living in sin."Nancy replied. Sister Veronica's words of caution still troubled her mind. Her heart and head were locked in turmoil. However, she had to admit privately that Marty was charming and she enjoyed his company. And he'd saved her life. She owed him that.

"I suppose your life as a nun has made you suspicious about men's motives. And I don't blame you. Anyway if you ever want to kick the question around with someone, you know your big sister is always available."Kitty said, her face solemn.

"I *do* know that big sister, and I do appreciate it." Nancy grinned, enfolding her in a hug.

"To change the subject, Daddy is doing so well since you started bringing him to the Physio. He's now nearly walking without the stick."Kitty said.

"But only with your help. Since I started teaching in the school you've been bringing him. It's a team effort."

"A task shared, you got the ball rolling. That Nick did nothing, he's a waster." Kitty fumed.

At the end of the walk they parted, Kitty saying she had shopping to do, and would call later.

When Nancy got home, Nick's squad car was outside.

She noticed the worried frown on his face as soon as they met in the kitchen.

"Tea Nancy? The water's boiled. My treat today."

"Well, how did your meeting with Inspector Doogan go yesterday?"She asked.

"Interesting to say the least. "

"Did he mention the newspaper article?"

"Yes. He was furious, bellowed like a bull on the rampage. He threatened hell and damnation, but strangely I wasn't worried by his bullshit. No, not one bit."

"Why not?"

"Because I thought he seemed worried, deeply worried. I've never seen him that way before. Despondent too, and he looked wretched. A touch too many late night drinks I suspect. And then something happened towards the end of the meeting, something that threw a giant spanner into his works." Nick smiled grimly as he remembered.

"Tell me what happened."Nancy said, leaning forward.

"News came in that Aengus Hynes had vanished."

"Well, that's a shock all right, but he might just be hiding low. People in the IRA do that from time to time don't they? There may be nothing sinister about it."

"True. But on the other hand you never know, strange things are going on. Anyway it knocked Doogan off his stride. Completely. I had to leave him then and go to Goresbridge. He looked utterly shattered as I left. I don't think we've anything to worry about from him at the moment."

"I hope not. On another matter Nick, would you by any chance be going to Kilkenny tomorrow? I'd like to cadge a lift to Graigue if you are."

"Sure thing, I have to go to Goresbridge everyday at the moment. I can go via Graigue, no problem. I'll drop you there after mid-day, and call back about four o'clock. Meeting Marty?"

"No, just a friend. I might look Marty up, if I have time." She didn't feel like telling Nick just then the details of her meeting with her adopted son in Carlow, and her rendezvous with him the following day in Graigue.

***

Next day in the car, on the way to Graigue, excitement coursed through her body. She wondered would Liam feel the same towards her as he had at their first meeting. Or maybe the novelty would have worn off? She'd also have to tell him about the murder of Ned Rooney, his father. That was going to be difficult. She wasn't looking forward to that. Best leave it to the end, she decided.

Nick left her outside Doyle's pub in Graigue, the venue for Liam's gig that night. He wound the car window down as he left and waved, shouting he'd pick her up at four, before pulling away, tyres screeching. What a show-off he is, she muttered, waving back. When Liam rang the previous day he'd said he'd meet her in the lounge of the pub at lunchtime, and this time he would buy her dinner. She'd accepted, saying she'd be happy to see him with or without dinner. She entered the pub, nerves jangling.

Inside the lounge, she spotted Liam in a corner reading a book. He looked up. Their eyes locked. Still blue-eyed as the heavens, she thought, hair blonder and longer, same jeans, different coloured cowboy shirt, boots, and hat this time. Denim by God, that's a change. I wonder who looks after his laundry? Most likely no-one. I'm sure the smell doesn't bear thinking about, with all the heat and sweat from a music session. She shuddered at the thought.

Liam ambled over, doffing his Stetson hat.

"Hello, good to see you again."He said, squeezing her in a bear hug.

He seemed taller than she remembered. Could be the cowboy boots, she thought.

"Fancy something to eat?" He asked.

"Just a sandwich and a pot of tea in a quiet corner. I'd rather talk than eat."She replied.

"Me too. Let's stay in my corner, its quiet there, and I'll go get some grub."

He escorted her to the table before sauntering over to the bar. She gazed after him, fascinated. She looked at the name of the book Liam had left on the table. *O'Neill's 1001 Irish Tunes*. She picked it up, browsing through the pages. She read that O'Neill had emigrated to Chicago from Cork, becoming Chief of the Chicago police. A traditional Irish musician, he'd recruited many Irish musicians into the Force there, compiling an archive of Irish music, afraid if he didn't write the tunes down they'd be lost forever. Liam arrived back just as she finished reading.

"I decided on self-service in the end. Chief O'Neill was some man, wasn't he? There should be a statue of him somewhere on O'Connell Street in Dublin."Liam said, nodding towards the book, placing a tray on the table.

"Maybe someday there will be, Liam. Tell me all about your tour."She said, anxious to break the ice.

"So far so good, I'm glad to say. Good crowds and fine receptions everywhere. We're improving at the music too. Chief O'Neill's tunes do help too, we've used quite a few. I can't tell you how much we're enjoying it, the music and the craic. But for me the icing on the cake was meeting up with you here."He replied nervously.

Her heart leapt at his words.

"Really? That's nice of you to say. For me to meet up with you here was a huge thrill, one that's hard to describe."She blushed as she spoke, and her heart seemed to somersault inside her body.

"And Nancy, I have a little present, or presents, for you."

"Really? What for?" She asked, excited.

"Well, remember you said when you were young you were taken by two songs sung by Mary O'Hara, the beautiful harpist who later became a nun."

"Oh yes, I remember now. I had forgotten."

"Well I did some research on your behalf."Liam said.

"Oh thank you, you shouldn't have gone to any trouble."

"I didn't, it was a pleasure, an experience I learned a lot from. It's also what I'm studying. Before I start into the history, let me pour you some more tea." He filled their cups, took a notebook from his back pocket, and continued.

"The first thing to say is that Mary O'Hara is up at the top in the history of Irish music."

"That's some accolade. And why did she become a nun?"Nancy was fascinated.

"Her husband died very young. He was a poet and they were not long married. She entered the Order soon after his death. How sad that was to lose him so young. Having listened a lot to her recordings recently, I can assure you she was something special. Many of her songs were in Irish. "

"She probably could have become a very rich person."Nancy said.

"Yes, but money didn't interest her. Love and happiness were more important. Anyway the two songs you mentioned would rank as my favourites too, you want to hear about them?"

"I do indeed, please go ahead."

"The song "The Quiet Land of Erin" is an English translation of the traditional Irish song "Airde Chuain". It's an exile's lament gazing back from Scotland to the remote Irish coast, probably towards Carrickfergus. A beautiful song, but "Aileen Aroon" wins the honours for the best Irish song, and wins it by a country mile or two."

"Why's that?"

"I can't exactly say. It's been popular for many centuries, and Mary O'Hara's original version in Irish is special. Even Handel the German composer, when he heard the song on a visit to Dublin in the 18th century, said he would rather have written that one tune than all his own compositions put together."

"Where did it originate? She asked.

"Actually, it comes from this area. At one time it was thought that the air "Aileen Aroon" dated back to the 12th or 13th century, and that the title was another name for Ireland, and its message was that when all is lost, all that remains is truth itself. Truth is a fixed star, Aileen Aroon."

"But was that not the real story?"Nancy asked.

"No, the real story is fascinating. Although the original air most likely goes back three or four centuries earlier, *Aileen Aroon* was written by Carol O'Daly, a poet and Harper of the early seventeenth century. It was addressed to his lady-love, Eileen Kavanagh, daughter of Sir Morgan and Lady Kavanagh of Clonmullen Castle, in the County Wexford. The family were related to the Kavanaghs of Borris Castle. Aileen was to be married to another man in an arranged wedding. O'Daly mingled with the wedding guests, disguised as an itinerant Harper. He sang this song to her in Irish on the harp. She saw through his disguise and eloped with him. There are a number of English versions of the words of the song, the most popular being by Gerald Griffen. His verses, though beautiful and sung by all, are not a direct translation of the original Irish words of O'Daly, which certainly tie in with the story of the elopement. Therefore Mary O'Hara's version rings true, and hers is the definitive version of what is acknowledged as Ireland's most memorable song. Amen." He closed his notebook.

"Thank you Liam, that was fascinating about the song. And did Mary O'Hara stay in the convent?"

"No, she came back into the outside world many years later, taking up her musical career again."

"And did she find happiness and love?"

"I believe she found happiness, as she had not been happy in the convent in her later years there. As for love I'm not sure, but if she hasn't found it yet I'm sure she will in the future."

Nancy felt happy when she heard her hero had left the religious life and found happiness. In a way, she felt she was following in her footsteps. Nancy wondered if she herself would find love and happiness. So far she reckoned she had found happiness. Her mother had always told her love was an elusive will-of-the-wisp.

Liam filled her in on the details of his music tour in Waterford.

She looked at her watch. Nick was due to collect her in half an hour. She had to get it over with. It was now or never.

"Liam, there's something I need to tell you. Bad news I'm afraid. There's no easy way to say it."As she spoke she grabbed his hands. Tears came in her eyes.

"Ok Nancy, spill the beans whatever it is, get it out in the open."

"Your father.... your real father.......Ned Rooney, was murdered last week in St. Luke's Hospital in Kilkenny." She sobbed as she said the words. Why am I feeling this way? She thought.

"Hell, that's awful, and I'd hoped to visit him next week. What happened? Who did it?"He asked, shocked.

"Nobody knows. The Garda are investigating. The IRA is implicated. Ned got entangled with them when he was in England."

A silence followed, the previous mood of magic vanished. Finally Liam spoke.

"I guess he and I weren't meant to meet. I would have liked to see him and talk to him. It feels strange, the whole thing, him dying just before I got to meet him. But so be it, I suppose. Hopefully the police will get the culprits. Tomorrow I'm going kayaking with the lads down to St. Mullins. That should blow the cobwebs away, help to clear my head and try to take in what you just told me. I really like this place, there's something special about it." Liam said, stood up, and embraced her.

"There is for sure Liam, but be careful tomorrow, the river can be treacherous."As soon as she spoke the words, she regretted saying them, thinking she was behaving like a typical mother.

"I will, don't you be worrying and thanks for coming."

"My pleasure Liam, good luck with the gig tonight."

"Thanks Nancy." He put his Stetson on and embraced her again.

She liked when he put his arms around her. It will hit him later, she thought, that he'll never meet his father. God moves in mysterious ways.

Nick arrived at four o'clock sharp. Liam escorted her to the car, shook Nick's hand, and hugged Nancy, saying he hoped she'd be at their final gig in Langton's on the weekend. He said he'd play a special request for her if she came. She realised she might have a decision to make if Marty rang. She nodded, saying she'd be there for sure. In the end she knew blood was thicker than water, and Marty would have to wait. Liam would probably pass temporarily out of her life after the next weekend, and then she'd have time to ponder Marty's marriage proposal.

"Nice young man, your friend. Good-looking too. I like your taste, Nancy." Nick said, grinning.

"Of course he's good-looking, he's my son you *amadawn*."

"What Nancy, are you having me on?"Nick said, gob-smacked.

"No, I don't joke about things like that. He's studying music in Trinity College in Dublin. Remember I met him for the first time in Carlow a few weeks ago. It was a strange experience, but I'm hoping we can develop some kind of ongoing relationship in the future."

"I'm sure. I'm sorry Nancy, I'd forgotten with all the goings-on. I didn't realise." Nick mumbled, embarrassed.

"That's ok. It all happened so long ago, when you were too young to know and care. He was adopted, and afterwards I joined the Presentation Order in Manchester. I've found it hard to talk about all that up to now, you understand. "

"I do understand Nancy. I'm sorry, I had forgotten."

"To change the subject Nick, please tell me how your investigations are going."She liked to be his sounding-board.

"Well they're ongoing, that's all I can say. Sean Summers, that man we arrested for the murder in Goresbridge of Garda Laker is proving a tough nut to crack. Swears he's innocent, that he's been set-up but doesn't have an alibi. We're continuing with the forensics. If the blood on the uniform proves to be that of Garda Laker then we have him, even if his fingerprints aren't on the uniform."

"How come?"She asked.

"He could have worn gloves."

"And what about Aengus Hynes?"

"He'still missing. I think Doogan's losing his marbles. He's got a scared look about him, and acts nervous. Still he's dangerous, and you know what they say about rats when they're cornered?"

"I think I do." She replied, nodding.

"Then don't underestimate Doogan."

"I won't."

In the hallway back home, Nancy picked up the post. She recognised Marty's handwriting on one envelope, and tore it open. It was a short note saying he would be busy at the weekend tying up some loose ends before his return to Italy. Anyway it would give her more time to think about his proposal, and they would definitely meet before he left. She sighed with relief. She liked Marty and *did* want to meet him again before he left the country. She knew she had to straighten out their relationship before he left. She couldn't leave it up in the air, but now she was free to see her son perform his final gig. That night she prayed that his gig would be a success, and thanked God again for letting her meet her son, something Liam had now been denied with his own father.

Chapter 26

Quest

Later that week while Nancy was waiting for Kitty to arrive, the phone rang. She rushed into the hall, wondering if Marty was on the line, trying to arrange a farewell meeting. Anxiously, she picked up the receiver. She was in a dilemma. She still hadn't made up her mind about Marty's marriage proposal, and she'd promised Liam she'd attend his final gig in Langton's pub in Kilkenny the coming weekend. She didn't want to tell white lies to Marty, but relaxed on hearing the voice of Ignatius Purcell rasping on the line.

"Miss Hackett, you remember me, Ignatius Purcell from "The Carlow Nationalist"?

"Yes Ignatius, you can call me Nancy."

"Have you read today's Nationalist paper?"He asked.

"No."

"Then I suggest you do that straight away."

"Ok, thanks for the advice. Should I be worried?"She asked.

"I don't think so, possibly the opposite. Is your brother, the Sergeant, there? "Purcell wheezed.

"No, but he'll be here in an hour or so."

"If you could tell him that I'll be a little late, say an hour, for our mid-day meeting at the Garda station. He might be glad of the extra time. I hear he's a busy bee these days. Cheerio."

"Goodbye." She muttered, then left down the phone, grabbed her handbag, and dashed down Kilree Street to Madden's newsagent shop. When she returned, Kitty had arrived.

"Sorry I was out for a few minutes, I had to go get a copy of the local paper in a hurry."

"Something important?" Kitty asked, as Nancy stood reading the paper.

Nancy gasped at the headlines in the paper. **Garda Inspector Missing. Uniform fished out of the Barrow. Investigations ongoing to ascertain his whereabouts.** A head-shot photo of Inspector Cornelius Doogan, displaying his white teeth and dimpled Kirk-Douglas chin, grinned at her from the front page. Kitty looked over her shoulder and asked.

"Is that the guy who threatened to get you fired from the school, and stole Nick's girl friend?"

Nancy nodded.

"Looks like neither of you will be bothered by him anymore. Strange goings on indeed. I'm sure our shopping trip is off. Anyway I'll let you and Nick chat about that news on your own. I'm more interested in whether you've made your mind up about Marty's proposal. And when is he actually returning to Italy? I can't believe that you're taking it so cool, I'd be all in a tizzy about it."Kitty grinned as she spoke.

"Actually I'm not that cool at all, I'm nervous as hell really. The truth is I'm still thinking about it, and Marty's busy finalising everything for his departure, and he hasn't told me if he's leaving the priesthood so we can get married. He may be thinking about it, but actions speak loudest. He does lots of charitable work here, you know. He'd like me to get involved in these activities in the future. He's also got to organise his mother before he leaves. They're very close you know, and she gets upset whenever he goes, and he does too. I'd like to meet her. But the real reason I'm not pushing things with Marty is because of my son Liam."

"Tell me more."

Nancy briefly informed Kitty of her meeting the previous week with Liam in Graigue, and her plans to see his final gig in Kilkenny, and ended up inviting Kitty to come too, saying Liam would love to meet her. She would understand if Kitty couldn't make it. Kitty replied without hesitating.

"I'd love to go. Jim's away in Waterford following the work. A carpenter's life is like that as you know. The older kids can hold the fort, they'll probably be glad of the chance to get up to a bit of devilment. We'll go in my car, it's an old banger but it won't let us down." Kitty's eyes sparkled, excitement coursing through her body.

"Maybe we could stay the night there Kitty? The gig could run late, and we could have a drink and relax."

"Great idea, a sister's fun night out, let's do it, we deserve it."Kitty responded.

"Wonderful, I'm so delighted you're coming."Nancy said as they embraced, her sister's perfume filling her nostrils.

"Life's for living. I'll try to book a double-room in Langton's. I'll have to get my hair done, and I might need something new to wear."Kitty said.

"It's only your sister you're going out with, not Cary Grant."

"I know but I'm so excited already, I haven't had a good night out for years, what with Jim being away so much."

"Will Jim mind you spending a lot of money?"Nancy asked.

"What Jim doesn't know won't worry him and anyway I don't query him about what he does every night when he's away."

Nancy heard the front door open.

"Nick's coming in now Kitty. I have to give him a message."

"Ok, I'm off, tell Daddy I'll collect him at twelve for his Physio."

They hugged and Kitty left, waving to Nick who was on the phone in the hall. After a few minutes he put the phone down slowly, hung his hat behind the kitchen door, and entered the living room.

"Seen the papers Nancy?" His face was haggard, his hand clutching a newspaper.

"Yes I have. Tea?"

He nodded, and read the paper while she cleared the table.

"The plot thickens Nick, what's going on?" She asked, filling his mug.

"I wish I knew, and now I'm in charge of the whole investigation. I got a call from Superintendent Donoghue in Dublin. He's hoping I'll have some convictions soon, no pressure though, he said. He said the media were like hounds baying for blood, and he had to give them something to get them off his back. And it was now *my* quest to get to the bottom of this conundrum involving four people, two dead, one murdered in a hospital, one killed in a burnt car, and two missing. He said he had every confidence in me, and of course he dangled the carrot of me doing a good job etcetera being good for my future prospects, hinting he hadn't been too happy with the way Doogan had been handling things. And now Doogan himself has become a possible victim. And all I've come up with so far are two Garda uniforms. At least I'm getting some help. Sergeant Greg Foley is being seconded from Waterford to help me. He arrives today, and I have a briefing meeting with him this afternoon. That should make a difference. The Super says he's going to assemble a crack team in Dublin as well, and send them down to help me straight away. He'll let me know soon about it."Nick seemed anxious to get his worries off his chest. She was glad he trusted her with his worries.

"That's good Nick. More?"

"Yes." He nodded. She refilled his mug. He continued.

"Then after that, as if I hadn't enough going on, I got a call from Sheila Hynes."

"Really? What did *she* want?" Nancy's eyes narrowed as she spoke.

"Probably just a shoulder to cry on. She was distraught, first her brother goes missing, now her boy friend. You have to feel for her."

"I suppose, but she left you in the lurch."

"That's history now, you have to move on. I can't forget the look of fear on Doogan's face over the past weeks. It's been haunting my mind. He was a strong swimmer too. He was worried about something. I wonder what it was." Nick scratched his head.

"It's none of my business, but are you any closer to solving these mysterious goings-on?"

He shook his head. She refilled his mug.

"I've got to go Nancy, thanks for the tea. It's nice to have someone to talk to. Someone you can trust to keep their mouth shut. "

"You're welcome Nick and please be careful, we don't want you disappearing too, and don't go too heavy on the drink. By the way Ignatius Purcell rang to ask if you could put your meeting with him back an hour."

"Ok Nancy got that, I'll heed your advice, and don't worry I have no intention of doing a vanishing act."

Nick hugged her, put his hat on, and left. The thought that Nick might be implicated in Doogan's disappearance then flashed into her head, after all he had a motive, but she quickly dismissed it out-of-hand.

That night she prayed long and hard for Nick's safety, and for guidance on Marty's proposal of marriage. She wondered if he would invite her to visit him for a holiday in Milan, and what would her decision be if he did. After all she was a free-agent now, with no Sister Veronica looking over her shoulder.

***

Nick decided to have the media meeting with Purcell in the Interrogation Room. It wasn't a salubrious room but was private and had no phones. Can't be too careful nowadays he muttered, what with phones being tapped and thin walls. He remembered his father's phrase from WW2 about loose-lips sinking ships. From now on he had to watch every word he uttered to the media, or *he* could be sunk.

His first test would be his meeting with Purcell. Purcell had rung him the previous day and said "The Carlow Nationalist" newspaper wanted to do an interview with him as part of an in-depth article about the recent strange happenings around the river Barrow. The article would appear the following Saturday. It might help uncover new evidence, Purcell said. He would say that, Nick thought, reluctantly agreeing, knowing he had no choice, aware he still hadn't a clue as to what was behind the strange goings-on on the Barrow.

Yes, they'd arrested Sean Summers on suspicion of murdering Ned Rooney, but so far Summers hadn't broken under questioning. Time was running out. In a matter of days they'd have to release Summers, due to a lack of evidence. If that happened he'd be in the manure business for sure. It would not be a good start in his new role. The Super wouldn't be impressed. And he had the" A" Team, on their way from Dublin, to deal with. He sighed, lifting a glass of water to his lips.

"Hmm, plastic chairs, is this some new form of interrogation-torture Sergeant?"Ignatius Purcell grumbled as he entered the room, cigarette dangling from his mouth. His spindly legs took his thin body to the trestle table in the centre of the room, where he placed his worn, leather briefcase.

"It's done to discourage visitors from overstaying their welcome. I can get you a cushion if you like. "

"Don't bother, I'll offer it up as penance Sergeant. I do appreciate you meeting me. By the way, congratulations on your new promotion following Inspector Doogan's demise,..... sorry disappearance. Not official yet, I believe. Now, let's cut-to-the-chase. First I have some questions." Purcell croaked as he took a wad of papers from his briefcase, ash falling from his cigarette onto the table.

"I'll do my best to answer them, but you appreciate confidentiality is paramount as investigations are ongoing. Also I'd like to review the final draft before you go to print." Nick said, shoving the ashtray across the table towards Purcell.

"Sorry, can't do that Sergeant. We have our own editor, and freedom of the press is paramount and all that. Starting in reverse order, what are your comments about Inspector Doogan's disappearance, and his uniform being found in the river?"

"Three possibilities. A swimming accident, suicide, or something sinister."

"By sinister, do you mean murder?" Purcell asked, scribbling furiously in shorthand.

"Yes."

"What do *you* think Sergeant?"Purcell wheezed, looking up.

"It's too early to say. Doogan was a good swimmer, but the river can be treacherous. We're trawling for a body around where the uniform was found. That could take days, as the river divides in two outside the town, and it's swollen after the recent rains. Suicide can't be ruled out either. Doogan seemed under pressure in recent weeks."

"Yes, I've been told he was. What do you think really happened, Sergeant?"

"I told you already it's too early to say."Nick snapped. Purcell was getting under his skin.

"I understand there was no love lost between you and Inspector Doogan."Purcell smirked as he spoke.

"In a professional capacity we worked fine together. And we're not here to discuss my private life."Nick said, irked, his patience stretched, feeling he was being goaded.

"No need to get defensive Sergeant, even the dogs on the street know that privately both you and Doogan were at each other's throat. In fact he thought you had a vendetta against him and the whole Hynes family."

"Who told you that?" Nick's eyes blazed as he spoke.

"I usually protect my sources but I've worked with you

and your sister before. So I'm prepared to tell you in confidence it was members of the Hynes family."

"Predictable. It's well known the Hynes family are IRA sympathisers, and up to all types of shenanigans, so I'd take anything they say with a pinch of salt. I also believe Inspector Doogan's judgment may have become clouded when he got involved with Sheila Hynes. It's not good practice for a Garda to become involved socially with an IRA family. As you ran the newspaper article about the lack of Garda security for Ned Rooney on two occasions, the second time in the hospital proving fatal, you're familiar with the details. A police officer must never step over the invisible line which could allow himself and his judgment to be compromised. But I believe Inspector Doogan stepped over that line."After speaking, Nick studied Purcell's face. Inscrutable as a Sphinx.

"Got that Inspector, I mean Sergeant. Speak no evil of the dead or the missing, so I won't be printing any of that about Inspector Doogan. What about Garda Laker and Aengus Hynes? Have you made any arrests yet? I suppose a coffee is out of the question?"Purcell rasped.

Nick left the room to order the coffees, glad to get away before his temper exploded. Purcell continued chain-smoking.

When Nick returned, a pall of smoke hung in the air, clouding the room, an acrid smell everywhere. He opened the sash window before sitting down.

"Yes, we have made progress, but as the case is ongoing, the information is confidential."Nick said.

"So there's nothing to relate? What about Sean Summers? He's been arrested, hasn't he? Will he be charged with murder?"

"I can't comment I'm afraid. Investigations are ongoing and confidential. A decision on him is imminent, that's why I'd like to delay things, or leave him out of the article." Nick replied.

"We must put him in. If he's charged by mid-night we can change the article. It's the only development we've got so far. It won't look good for you if Summers is released." Purcell eyeballed Nick.

"I'm aware of that."Nick glared back.

The door opened, and an orderly brought in two mugs of coffee on a tray and left it in on the table.

"What, no biscuits?" Purcell growled, taking a long drag on his cigarette before squashing it into the ash tray.

"Looks like it."

They had their coffees in silence, Purcell poring over his notes, Nick looking agitated, seemingly anxious to get the meeting over. After a lull Purcell lit up again, scratched his nose with his pencil, and continued.

"To sum up we have one arrest with a potential link to two murders, involving Laker and Rooney. And two other missing persons where investigations are ongoing. I have to warn you Sergeant, your so-called vendetta against the Hynes family may make you a figure of suspicion."Purcell remarked, squinting at Nick.

"I had no vendetta against the Hynes family. I did not step over the line. My conscience is clear. Be careful what you print."Nick wagged his finger at Purcell.

"We're always careful Sergeant, we've been in the newspaper business far longer than you've had birthdays. I'm just marking your cards for you. Thank you, I must go now."Purcell retorted as he stood up, stuffing papers into his briefcase.

After Purcell left, Nick stormed back to his office and rang Garda Pat Nolan, one of his team in Kilkenny.

"Pat, what's happening on the forensic tests on Garda Laker's uniform?"

"They're still not back from the lab."

"Why not? They should be well finished by now."Nick fumed.

"I agree. Apparently there were been some technical glitches in checking for fingerprints."Nolan replied.

"What about the blood tests?"Nick asked.

"No news yet either."

"Typical bloody bureaucrats, Pat, get your ass over to the lab pronto, and stay there until you've got the results in your hand. Its 2.30 now. I have a meeting at four o'clock with my new assistant Greg Foley. I need these results by six o'clock. This is your chance to make an impression. It's a matter of life-or-death."

"Ok Sergeant, I've got the picture. I'll ring you by six, latest."Nolan said.

The phone went dead. Nick sighed, drumming his fingers on the desk. Maybe I laid it on a bit thick, he mused. Life and death? Of my career probably. With that, his new assistant entered the room.

Greg Foley was blocky, dark haired, close-eyed with bushy eyebrows meeting in the middle, hairy nostrils, who had played in goal for Waterford's minor hurling team in his youth, unmarried, in his thirties, and barely came up to Nick's shoulder. Must have just made it on the height, Nick thought. Foley listened carefully as Nick briefed him. He said little, and took notes diligently. I think I'll get on fine with him, Nick reckoned at the end. I'll get an unofficial check done on him as well, can't be too careful these days. Foley said he'd hang around to hear the forensic lab results. Nick glanced at his watch. Five thirty, still nothing from Pat Nolan. At six thirty Nolan rang.

"Well?" Nick's hand shook on the phone.

"I had to kick ass Sergeant, but we've got something at last. Those latchicos have to be sat on to get results out of them."Nolan said.

"What was the outcome? Get to the point."He should have been kicking ass anyway, Nick raged inwardly.

"The blood samples proved positive. The blood on the uniform was a match with Ned Rooney's." Nolan said.

Nick sighed with relief. They now had a case. They could now formally charge Summers with the murder of Ned Rooney. The pressure was off. For the moment.

"Well done Pat, that's good news. What about the fingerprints?"Nick asked.

"Nothing I'm afraid so far. You would have expected Summers' prints to be all over the uniform, but they only found those belonging to Garda Laker. Summers must have worn gloves."Nolan replied.

"Probably, but he slipped up with the blood."

"It was only a very small stain, splashed onto the inside of one cuff. There had been a scuffle beside Ned Rooney's bed, glass broken and blood spilt on the floor. Anyway, that's Summers' funeral."Nolan said.

"Good job Pat, well done. Listen, Foley and I will be over in Kilkenny at ten in the morning to formally charge Summers. Please have him ready and be there yourself. After Summers is charged, I'll be giving Foley his first assignment."

"And what's that?"

"I want him to give Summers a robust interrogation about the murder. The full works. Up to now we've only been pussy-footing around. I want to try and link the murder to Aengus Hynes."

"Ok Sergeant, got you, all will be ready."Nolan replied.

The phone clicked off. Nick then rang Purcell, and told him the news. Purcell said he would insert it straight away into the article. It would give the Carlow newspaper a scoop, Purcell chuckled, saying Nick himself would be smelling-of-roses. Nick smiled, relieved, and put down the phone. Better to be smelling-of-roses than lilies, he muttered under his breath.

He briefed Greg Foley of the developments, and his assignment the next day. Greg said he was rarin' to get going. Nick headed home for an early night. He needed it.

***

Next day Nick lazed around the station reading Purcell's article in the *Carlow Nationalist*, chuffed. Good balanced reporting, and he'd come out with his reputation enhanced. For the moment anyway, he muttered, better not get ahead of myself, one false step and they'll jump on me.

That morning when they'd formally charged Summers with the murder of Garda Laker, Summers had gone ballistic and spat on the ground, swearing he didn't do it. Nick was taken aback by his vehemence. He checked the time. Greg Foley had already been grilling Summers for two hours non-stop. That *was* robust. The door opened and Foley entered, grim-faced, in his shirt sleeves.

"How's it going?" Nick asked, looking up from the paper. He could see it wasn't.

"He's some tough bastard. A psychological break was needed. And a coffee."Foley looked tense as he spoke.

Nick poured two coffees.

"Ok Greg, it was never going to be easy. Let's try new tactics. You continue with the hard approach, and after another 45 minutes, call me in. I'll try another tack."

Greg nodded in silence.

When Nick entered the dimly-lit room, Sean Summers was slumped over the table, head between his hands.

"Sean, this is Sergeant Hackett, he wants to have a friendly chat with you." Greg said and left the room.

"Whaddya want? I didn't fuckin' kill anyone, I'm being fuckin' framed."Summers snarled, glaring bleary-eyed at Nick.

Summers was short, squat, grey-eyed, muscular, fair haired with a crew cut, and had nicotine-stained fingers.

"Just a friendly natter Sean. Fancy a fag?"Nick asked, assuming nonchalence.

"Yeah."

Nick handed him one and lit it for him. Summers tilted his head back, sucking the smoke into his lungs.

"Look Sean, this questioning could go on quite a while, so why not be reasonable and maybe we can find a way to end it in a way that's to your advantage?"Nick suggested.

"Whaddya mean? I told yeh I wanted to see my lawyer. I'm being fuckin' set up." Summers spat the words out.

"You'll get life for the murder of Ned Rooney. The forensic evidence is conclusive Sean, believe me I'm not bullshitting. And that's not mentioning the murder of Garda Laker where investigations are ongoing, and the fact you used Garda Laker's uniform to gain entry to the hospital to kill Ned Rooney, thereby implicating you big-time in Laker's murder."Nick said, feigning concern.

"What's your fucking deal? I didn't kill Rooney and I didn't kill Laker, I fucking told you. I'm being set up. I want to see my lawyer. Are you fucking deaf?"Summers growled.

"You will see your lawyer later Sean. I want to be fair to you. I believe also that you *are* being set up. For Ned Rooney's murder that is. I believe you were acting under instructions from Aengus Hynes. If you are prepared to testify to this fact, I believe we could get your sentence mitigated, and pin-the-rap on Hynes. Also we could possibly drop any Garda-Laker-related charges, unless new evidence emerges. That's the deal. What do you say?"Nick spoke in a conciliatory tone.

"Why should I believe a fuckin' word out of your fuckin' mouth?"

"Because I believe you don't have many choices Sean. I suggest you sleep on it. Your lawyer will see you later. We will suspend questioning for the moment. Sergeant Foley will be disappointed."

"Fuck Foley." Summers sneered, as he ground his cigarette-butt in the ashtray.

Nick left the room. Foley was waiting outside.

"How did it go boss?" Foley asked.

"Ok Greg, a hostile meeting, but I left him with a proposition to chew over. He's a tough boyo. We'll suspend questioning for a few days, so he can sleep on it. Now let's head on to Goresbridge, and investigate the Laker crime scene again."

Foley exhaled, seemingly glad of the respite from questioning, buttoned his uniform, and they boarded for the squad car parked outside. As the car sped away from the station, Nick concluded that Summers was one hard bastard. But was he a stool-pigeon, *or* had he done the deeds? Nick was undecided, he needed more proof.

Chapter 27

The Gig and After

"Where are you off to?" Nick asked as he entered the room.

"Kitty and I are heading to Kilkenny for the night, our bags are packed and we're ready to go. We're off to see Liam's group perform a gig this evening in Langton's. We're staying the night. Will you keep an eye on Daddy we're away?" Nancy replied.

"Sure I will Nancy, no problem. The last place I want to visit now is Kilkenny. I seem to be spending every waking hour there. And I'm off to Goresbridge again on Monday to interview a Travelling Community leader. I've some files to plough through over the weekend. This case sure has my brain shot-to-pieces. I envy you both in a way. Give Liam my regards, I do hope his gig goes well."Nick smiled.

"I will, we're having a sisters' night-out. Listen, I can hear Kitty's car coming."

"You'd hear that exhaust a mile off." He grinned.

"Don't overdo the work Nick, you've had a lot on your shoulders since Inspector Doogan did his Houdini act."

"I've been assigned an assistant, a Sergeant Greg Foley from Waterford, he's already proving a help. And there's also an" A" team coming down from Dublin to progress the case."

"That's good, you *do* need some help." Nancy said, inwardly worried Nick might crack up. She wondered if he knew of the rumours flying about of him being a suspect in the disappearance of Aengus Hynes. She hoped not.

"Let's go Nancy, I've left the engine running, and the battery's been acting-up lately. Chitty Shitty Bang Banger I've christened it." Kitty said, flouncing into the room. Red hair bouffant-style, red lipstick, red dress v-necked with pearls hanging, red stilettos.

"Stop the lights Kitty, you'll cause a traffic jam in Kilkenny dressed like that. Red for danger is right. And you can't drive in those shoes, it's against the law." Nick laughed, scratching his head.

"To hell with the law, I've a pair of walking shoes in the car. I wanted Nancy to see my full regalia. Ok?"She grinned at Nancy.

"Wow, I'll be beating the men off you all night with you dressed-up like that."Nancy replied.

On the way to Kilkenny, Kitty enquired about Marty.

"No news to relate and in a way I'm glad of that, I need more time to mull over things. He's probably packing his bags for Italy as we speak. I was wondering, Kitty, if we could return home on Sunday by way of Graigue back to Bagenalstown. I love the drive by Bennetsbridge and Inistioge, its bridges all the way, and I could call into Marty's barge on the way and say hello. He might be there, and anyway it's a beautiful drive."Nancy said.

"No trouble at all, I haven't done that trip for years."

Nancy thanked her, realising how much she enjoyed Kitty's positivity, that it made her feel better, glad she'd come home, glad she'd made the decision to change her religious family for her real family. Not sorry to have been in a convent all those years, but glad to have moved on in her life.

"I'm worried about Nick. He's under pressure big-time since Doogan vanished, and now Sheila Hynes has started ringing him up again."Nancy related.

"Has she by God, the nerve of her, after ditching him for that Garda Inspector. The climbin' bitch, the Hynes family are not to be trusted."Kitty fumed.

"In spite of all that, Nick's still besotted with her and she might just be seeing him in a new light now that she's all alone. Still, I can't get over how she lied about there being Garda security in the hospital the night Ned was murdered. I'll never forgive her that lie." Nancy raged, her voice shaking with emotion.

They parked the car, checked into Langton's, had a light lunch, agreeing no alcohol would be drunk until the sun was below-the-yardarm, and set off to spend the afternoon exploring the medieval City. After visiting Kilkenny Castle first, they later moved on to view the ancient St. Canice's Cathedral, before finally calling into Kyteler's Inn for a coffee. The infectious rhythyms of Irish traditional music pounded away upstairs.

"Boy am I glad to sit down Kitty, my feet are killing me. What a quaint place this is, lively too."

There was a plaque on the wall. Nancy stood up and read it.

"They say this is one of the oldest inns in Ireland, going back to the 13th Century. Apparently its original owner Alice de Kyteler was accused of being a witch and sentenced to be burnt at the stake."Nancy said.

"Oh, and was she executed?"Kitty asked.

"No, she was well connected locally and escaped to England."

"Good, we'll drink to that later, Ireland's first suffragette."Kitty said.

After returning to their hotel, they showered, dressed, and headed for the restaurant Kitty had booked for six o'clock, *Ristorante Rinnucini* , opposite Kilkenny Castle. They chatted during the meal.

"God Kitty, well chosen, that seafood risotto was superb, and the black sole off-the-bone was an Italian meal Marty would be proud of. He'll be mad jealous when he hears about it. And the Chianti I had was his favourite. What a charming place, a real Italian treasure."Nancy said, elation tingling her bones.

"And what about my ravioli stuffed with lobster and prawns? It was heavenly. God, I sound like one of them food-connoisseurs. And I thinking you'd taken a wine-tasting course unbeknownst to me. Marty certainly knows his wine. Do I detect a certain longing for Italy in your voice?"Kitty giggled as she spoke.

"No, more likely it's the wine talking."Nancy said, laughing.

The restaurant buzzed and the time flew.

After eight o'clock they wandered up to Langton's, expecting it to be half-empty, the show not starting until half-nine. When they got there the place was jammed. Nancy panicked, thinking they'd have to stand all night, or maybe not get in at all. They pushed their way into the room where the stage was set. It was packed there, the excitement palpable. Then Nancy saw Liam sitting near the stage with two seats beside him marked "Reserved". Her heart skipped with pride. He wore an Australian bushwhacker's hat with his cowboy-boots and shirt. He spotted her, waved, and ambled over, embracing her.

"That's my special hug, reserved for special friends. Glad to see you again Nancy, I knew you wouldn't let me down. I've been sitting here awhile, hoping you'd come. There's a big hurling game in Nowlan Park tomorrow, Wexford are playing the Cats. The place is jammed, so I was holding a few seats for you. I had to fight a few locals off to hold onto them. It's great to have a full-house, we've had the opposite you know in some places on our tour."He laughed.

"Thanks Liam, that's kind of you. Let me introduce you to my sister Kitty. She wanted to meet you and has come with me on a girl's-night-out. We're staying the night here."

"That's the proper way to do it. So you're my aunt Kitty. Great to meet you and you know you're the spit of Maureen O'Hara, and I mean that as a compliment, your hair being like hers, and you're both beautiful.

261

He smiled as he bent down to embrace Kitty, she saying she was flattered to be likened to a Hollywood legend, and so delighted to meet him.

"And now ladies, let me get you both a drink before I retire to do a last minute check with the guys on the sound and what we're playing tonight. We'll have to put in a few Wexford ballads, *The Boys of Wexford, Boolavogue, Bunclody*, and the like, along with *The Rose of Mooncoin*. Give the punters what they want, that's our motto. Mind you, early in the week in Waterford all they wanted was Country& Western music."

They ordered glasses of red Italian wine. He returned within minutes with the drinks. When he'd left Kitty spoke.

"My God Nancy, you never told me he was such a fine fellow. And a gentleman to boot, properly brought up, so mannerly, you must be proud of him, and you always so good at school with the singing and the music, taking after Mammy, she had a great voice, and him now following in your footsteps. I'm so delighted for you." Kitty said and hugged her.

Inside, Nancy felt herself exploding with pride after Kitty's words, reassured she'd made the right decision to come home.

The buzz about the room was palpable and at half-nine sharp the lights dimmed, and the *Spalpeen Fawnachs* took to the stage, playing non-stop for two hours. Liam did most of the vocals and played guitar, while the other three did sets of Irish traditional music, mixing it up so much that the night flew. Nancy noticed a hush coming on the crowd whenever Liam sang, no mean achievement she thought, when the beer was a river flowing, and the craic ninety.

When they left the stage the crowd cried out for more. Liam returned alone with his guitar, and stood staring at Kitty, and winked before he spoke.

"This song is for the lady in red in the third row. In case any of you start gettin' ideas, *don't,* she's my aunt Kitty. It's a song I hadn't planned on singing, but here it is and it's by Robbie Burns."

"O my Love's is like a red, red rose,
That's newly sprung in June:
O my Love's like a melody,
That's sweetly play'd in tune...........

The song went down rapturously, and Kitty blushed. Liam smiled, put up his hand for silence, and spoke, as he re-tuned his guitar.

"This one is for my Ma, also down there in the third row."

He smiled and winked at Nancy. She held her breath. The crowd was hushed.

Youth must with time decay,
Eileen aroon,
Beauty must fade away,
Eileen aroon,
Castles are sacked in war,
Chieftains are scattered far,
Truth is a fixed star,
Eileen aroon.....................

When he finished there was a moment's silence, as if the audience was spellbound. Then the applause lifted the rafters until Liam left the stage. They wanted more but there was no more to give.

"God Nancy I don't know what to say, I don't think I've ever felt this way before, it's as if someone pierced my heart. I'm speechless, so I am. How did he do it? It was a surprise but a wonderful one. He's a revelation."

"Yes Kitty, I'm proud of him."She felt as if her heart could burst.

"And so you should."

They embraced, and ordered drinks, and toasted Alice de Kyteler and Liam, and people came and shook their hands, and congratulated them, and offered to buy them a drink.

Kitty thanked them but declined their drinks offers, saying afterwards to Nancy that she didn't want to get too involved with them, in case some of the males, being hot blooded, might have other things on their mind, apart from a bit of banter. She was glad to know that men were still interested in her, she said, but she'd rather they were interested when they were sober. Nancy agreed, clinking glasses.

About an hour later, Liam joined them, a drink for them in each hand, and placed them on the table, apologising for being so long, saying he needed at least an hour on his own to wind-down after each performance. Some people came and shook his hand. He smiled back and thanked them.

"I can see they loved you Liam, can I get you a drink?" Nancy asked.

"No thanks Nancy, water's fine with me, I don't drink after performing, it's a dangerous habit you know, I just like to savour the atmosphere and I do stay up late. I hope you ladies enjoyed the show and your songs."

"It was beautiful, I cried right through mine. It was a great night, one I'll always remember." Nancy said, dabbing her eyes with a hanky.

"Funny, so many have said they were moved by that song, and that they'd never heard it before, even though it originated in the area. I'll have to include it in my repertoire." He smiled, lifting a tumbler of water to his lips, saying here's to *Aileen Aroon*.

"And thank you Liam for singing that lovely Scottish song for me, it's one of my all-time favourites, and it made my night. I feel like someone famous, so many people have spoken to me, some of the men even making insinuating remarks with a twinkle in their eyes, but all in good fun. Nancy and I are sticking together in case some of those amorous males start getting ideas, in fact we're heading off soon."

"A wise decision, I have to meet the guys soon backstage. What time are you leaving tomorrow?"Liam asked.

"About noon, Nancy wants to take the scenic route back to Bagenalstown, through Graigue."Kitty replied.

"Don't blame her wanting to return that way. Kayaking in Graiguenamanagh was one of the highlights of our trip, as well as meeting you both of course. See you tomorrow morning ladies."

He grinned, hugged them both, and left the room. They went soon afterwards.

After breakfast they checked out, and met Liam in the foyer. He gave them both handwritten cards with his address in Trinity College, and his phone number, saying he'd love to meet them both again in Dublin. They hugged each other, all agreeing it was a wonderful idea, and soon they were in Kitty's car, waving goodbye as it chugged away, with Liam standing outside Langton's, waving back at them.

Nancy felt a pang of emptiness inside her as they left Kilkenny city. Liam had left her life again. Temporarily, she hoped. Their paths had crossed at last, and for that she was grateful and said a silent prayer, and vowed to try to make it happen soon again. Their passion for music would bind them, she hoped and prayed.

Silence reigned in the car. Kitty seemed emotionally drained as well. After a stop in Inistioge, and a visit to Woodstock House and a walk around the gardens there, the mood of gloom lifted. They stopped at the ruins of the house, once beautiful, but burnt by the IRA in the 1920's.

"Why did they do it?" Nancy asked.

"Apparently the owners were accused by the IRA of helping the Black and Tans. The family said the Tans had forcibly occupied the house, and there was nothing they could do about it. Sixty jobs were lost locally. A thing of beauty, part of our heritage destroyed, lost forever."Kittty murmured bitterly.

Nancy shrugged, and continued staring at the ruins. All that remained of the building was the façade of the house. After a while they moved on to finish their tour of the garden.

"What a wonderful time we're both having. Last night was one I'll remember forever. I'm so glad you came home Nancy."

They hugged, and Nancy spotted a tear trickling down her sister's cheek.

"It was for me too last night, and I'm overjoyed about coming home, it's all working out for the better." Nancy spoke, a lump in her throat.

They left the car in Graigue, outside Duiske Abbey. Evening-shadows shaded the river. In the stillness of twilight the birds sang their evening song.

"I'd like to take a wander around the ruins, and say a few prayers. I feel in the mood. I haven't had the urge to say a prayer in a long time. Take your time Nancy if Marty is there at the barge, I'm not in any rush."Kitty said.

Nancy nodded and walked along by the river to the wooden jetty where the barge was moored. All was silent. She called Marty's name. Silence. She stepped down into the barge, and walked around, calling his name again. Silence again. Everything neat and tidy. The silence eerie. She recalled the night they'd had their romantic Italian meal there. As she passed the room Marty had told her was reserved for Father Henry, she noticed a key in the door. She remembered that before it had always been locked. Maybe Marty was asleep in there? Anyway she was intrigued as to what might be inside and decided to find out. She turned the key and entered.

It was gloomy in the room, and the porthole window onto the river was open. Under the window was a sofa, and in the centre a table, rectangular and fixed to the floor. Strange, she thought, no bed, maybe the priest didn't stay overnight. The room furnishing was Spartan to say the least. A smell of incense wafted in the gloom. Perhaps the priest performed religious services there? Maybe Marty was doing last-minute cleaning before handing back the boat? A large wardrobe stood alongside one wall. As she passed by it she started, hearing a scratching sound from inside, like a mouse or a rat. She shuddered. She hated rodents and left hastily, vowing to tell Marty of the infestation. As she stepped onto the boardwalk, a bearded man, middle aged, medium sized in wellingtons and a cap, was standing there. He tipped his cap.

"Evening ma'am, Walter Gough's the name, Wally to my friends. I own the boat next to Marty's. We're good mates. If you're looking for him, he's gone off to St. Mullins for a walk. Can I give him a message?" He squinted as he spoke.

"Thank you Walter, I mean Wally, you can tell him Nancy called. I was on my way back from Kilkenny with my sister, and decided to drop in for a surprise visit. I'd better be going now, as my sister will be waiting for me."She couldn't wait to get back to the car, and turned to leave.

"I'll do that surely ma'am." He said, tipping his cap.

As he hurried to the car, she turned and glanced towards the bridge one last time and saw the golden glow of evening glinting on the water. When she reached the car, breathing hard, Kitty was waiting there.

"I just had ten minutes in the Abbey before it closed. I'll have to come back again. I presume Marty wasn't there?"Kitty said, starting the car down the road and across the bridge into Carlow.

Nancy nodded, shivering still at the memory of the room on the barge.

That night she found it hard to settle into sleep, restless with the scratching rodent sound in the boat gnawing into her head and mind, eradicating the earlier magical, musical memories of Liam.

Chapter 28

The Net Tightens

At the start of the following week Nick received a call from Superintendent Donoghue in Dublin, enquiring how the Barrow investigations were going. His voice was polite but demanding.

"We're making good pressure sir. The net's tightening. We've arrested someone, a local farmer, for the Ned Rooney murder."Hopefully that will placate him, Nick thought.

"That's good Sergeant, but I'm most concerned about the missing Garda. It doesn't look good if two of our own vanish, and we still can't unravel what occurred, or even come up with a definite line-of-enquiry. Not good for morale in the Force, and pressure is mounting from within, and from the media, although recent happenings up North have taken the headlines. I'm sending a crack team of three of my best men; Detective Sergeants Sean Philpott, Tom Rogers, and Ed Cassidy, to back you up. They'll arrive in Kilkenny tomorrow, staying in the New Park Hotel. They'll report direct to me as you do, and you will brief and advise them on all relevant matters. It's a team effort, and this should help getting the matter sorted. And how is Sergeant Foley working out?"

"We're also working on the Hynes case sir, the missing IRA man. Sergeant Foley is a big help. We're interviewing someone in Goresbridge later this morning about the Garda Laker case. He's a Travelling Community leader, his name is Richie Doran." Pressure is mounting here too, Nick thought.

"The new resources should help."Donoghue stated.

"Yes, they'll make a difference, without a doubt."Nick replied, not really sure if they'd be a help or a hindrance.

"Ok Sergeant, good hunting, and keep me informed."

The phone clicked dead. Nick now felt caught between a rock and a hard place, suspecting any progress he made on the case from hereon could be attributed to the new team.

Around mid-morning a squad car pulled up by the river near Goresbridge, close to the crime scene. Nick and Greg Foley got out, and walked across the clearing to the burnt-out car wreck. They gazed for some minutes at its grey metal shell and the circle of ashes around it, before entering the trees, and heading towards the Travelling encampment.

Nick glanced around, seeing at least twenty caravans in various stages of dilapidation, some with paint peeling off, litter blowing about the place, mongrel dogs roaming wild. Probably no running water or electricity, he guessed. No ragamuffin kids that he could see. They must be at school. Careful where you walk Nick, Foley growled, there's dog-shit everywhere. At least they don't have horses these days, Foley added.

Nick got the impression that Foley wasn't enamoured with the Travellers' set-up or their habits. Strange, he thought, given the country was trying to get Travellers to give up their wandering ways and integrate into the community, and with special schools being set up to assist this process. Foley's attitude seemed out-of-date.

An entourage, all male, fronted by a large man in a fedora hat, left the encampment, heading in their direction. The group stopped about ten yards away, and the big man came forward alone, a stick in his left hand. Over six foot, with wellingtons, a high colour, curly hair down the back of his neck, dressed in a sleeveless lamb's wool jacket, big-bellied, weighing in around twenty stone, Nick guessed. He stood before them, slapping his hand with the stick. He was massive.

"Pleased to meet you gentlemen, I'm Richie Doran. I hope you've come to visit us with good intentions, for we bear no ill-will here to anyone, living or dead." Doran spoke softly and shook hands with both of them, crunching their fingers like a vice.

"I'm sure you don't, and thanks for your time Mister Doran, we do appreciate your co-operation. We're here as part of an investigation, a murder investigation we believe, into the disappearance of Garda Laker, the driver of the burnt-out car over yonder." Nick pointed towards the river.

"Yeh, but what's that to do with us? We had no hand, act, or part in any of that."Doran said, eyes squinting, forehead furrowed, lips set tight, restless on the balls of his feet.

"It's just a routine investigation, so there's no reason to get excited. We're looking for clues that will help us get to the bottom of what has happened here. We need to ask you a few questions. Ok?" Nick asked, eyeballing Doran.

"All right then, if that's the case I'll do my best, tell me what is it yeh want to know?"

"Did you, or any of your community, know Garda Laker?"Nick asked.

"Yeah, I suppose you could say yes we did."Doran grimaced as he spoke.

"Really, in what way?" Nick asked, eyebrows arching, as Foley scribbled in his notebook.

"He often used come visit hereabouts. He swam near here. He wasn't too popular with me or any of my community. Bad cess to him." Doran spat on the ground.

"Oh really, and why was that?"Nick continued, excited, feeling at last they were getting somewhere.

"It was the way he was carrying on, his disgraceful behaviour, the bastard. I warned him about it. When I told him he got agitated and threatened me, said he had a lot of stuff on us Travellers, drunken brawling, stealin', being a nuisance, litterin' the landscape, and the like. And here we are, working hard, just trying to do the best for our families, sending the children to the local schools, and

271

behaving ourselves as best we can. I was mad with him, I can tell yeh. I wanted to teach him a lesson. I wanted to land one on him. Give him a black eye at least. I used be a boxer yeh know. Heavyweight. Champion." As he spoke, Doran's face was granite-like, grey eyes bulging, stick slapping in his palm.

"Really? I didn't know you were a boxer. How did your meeting with Garda Laker end?"Nick enquired.

"I restrained meself, though it was hard goin'. He was goadin' me like I was a bull, actin' the maggot like, but I knew his game, he wanted to get me on an assault charge. I didn't fall into his trap. No sirree."

"So you nearly assaulted him, and you threatened him?"Nick said.

"Well, so would you if someone told you a pack of lies, and behaved in the way he did."Doran snarled.

"And how did he behave? What did he do that was so bad?"

"Well, as I said before he came here swimmin' a lot, sometimes wearing his Garda uniform, sometimes dressed ordinary-like. "Doran scowled as he spoke.

"And what's wrong with that?"

"Nothing except...he... he liked to swim in the nude, in his royal pelt, a bit upriver from where our families would go. The women weren't happy at all about it, complainin' to me at first, saying it was scandalisin' them and the children. At first I ignored their complainin', hopin' the problem would go away. But it didn't go away, it got worse and he took to exposin' himself to the children in the woods. When this scandal came out, I had to do something about it, so I met Laker one day by the river, and told him this was no fuckin' nudist camp, and I told him if he didn't stop his fuckin' filthy ways they'd be changed for him, and that afterwards he'd wish he'd been a woman from the word go, and that would be the least of what might happen to him."Doran growled, worked up, eyes glazed, dropping the stick, punching his right hand into the palm of his left.

272

"What did he say then?"

"He said it was all a pack of lies I was telling him, that I was out for revenge because he'd got me arrested over a fight last year in Borris."

"And what happened in Borris?"Nick continued.

"There was a fight there alright with another family, but I didn't start it. I got off with just a warning and the Probation Act."

"How did you end up your meeting with Garda Laker?"Nick asked, on edge.

"He said it was a free country and he'd swim where he liked, and he'd not be frightened by a crowd of Yahoos living in the trees. I told him he was a fuckin' cunt, that I'd have his balls for breakfast, and on his head be it. That was the last time I saw him alive, as God is my witness. I swear I never laid a finger on him."

"Thank you Mr. Doran, you were very helpful, I appreciate your co-operation." Nick said, ending the meeting, happy with what they'd learnt.

They shook Doran's hand and returned to the car.

On the way back to Bagenalstown, Nick asked Foley what he thought of Doran's story.

"I wouldn't trust a word out of his mouth. I've read the reports about what supposedly happened in Borris, and he's a dangerous man, he nearly killed a man with a punch there. I wouldn't put anything past him."Foley replied.

"Ok, we have a suspect. Let's have a no-holds-barred meeting when we're back at base. There seems to be more going on here than meets the eye. Time is running out, we may need to involve our new resources in this area pronto. See what they can dig up." Nick felt Foley was biased against Doran, but Foley might be right. Better to get a new face involved with Doran. This was a chance for the" A "team to show their mettle. He knew Doran had an explosive temper and the strength to kill someone with a punch.

While Foley got the coffees, Nick set up a blackboard on an easel in his office, took some chalk and wrote four names on it....Rooney....Hynes...Laker....Doogan.

"Let's get the little-grey-cells working Greg." Nick said, pointing at the names as Foley handed him a mug of coffee. Nick spoke then.

"Let's start with the easy one....Rooney. Here we have Sean Summers as the guilty party, but the real culprit is Hynes. He orchestrated the killing, according to Summers, and I believe him. But Hynes goes missing, and we can't arrest him, so it's stalemate. Why? Is it a coincidental IRA revenge killing? Or is Hynes lying-low in the long grass, knowing we're after him, afraid Summers is going to spill the beans on him? He could be in the North of Ireland, waiting for the heat to die down. The IRA wouldn't like to lose him, he's an experienced campaigner. What do you think, Greg?"

"It doesn't make sense. We have informers in the IRA, and they swear he's gone AWOL. They wouldn't make up a story like that unless it was true. It could be just an accident, but there's no clue so far to indicate Hynes is lying-low."

"OK, let's park that, there may be a connection between the two incidents. We need more information. I need the new team to review everything about Ned Rooney's murder in the hospital in Kilkenny, including the Sheila Hynes testimony about Garda cover, and they also need to do a forensic analysis of Hynes' last movements and whereabouts. We also need to give Sean Summers full Garda protection, something Rooney never got. The IRA never cared too much for informers within their own ranks."Nick muttered ruefully.

Foley nodded and wrote in his notebook. Then he looked up and spoke.

"I have some news regarding Ned Rooney."

"What's that?"Nick asked, eyes alert.

"It's about the three thugs who attacked Ned Rooney. I checked the security camera footage at the hospital in Kilkenny, and saw three youths entering the hospital the day after Rooney was attacked. It could be them. They were treated by a nurse there. I checked the hospital records yesterday, and discovered the name of the nurse. The hospital records also showed two people were treated for stab wounds that day."

"And who is the nurse? Nick asked, holding his breath.

"Someone you're acquainted with Nick. Her name is Sheila Hynes." Foley replied, his face impassive.

"Ok Greg, I'll speak to Miss Hynes myself. I want you to find and arrest the three people in the security camera pictures on a charge of assault and GBH, and question them individually. Tell them we know Hynes put them up to it, and if they are prepared to testify that he did, they'll get a reduced sentence for co-operating."

"Righto chief, but there's a lot of work involved in that, and they're not likely to dish-the-dirt on their IRA boss, even if he's gone missing. A prison sentence might be better than swimming-with-the-fishes."Foley muttered.

"Ok Greg, I agree it's an unlikely outcome but we have to try, and I can deploy our new help in the matter."Nick felt frustrated as he spoke. Every which way he turned in the investigation he seemed to arrive in a cul-de-sac. Maybe Sheila Hynes would provide the key? He doubted it, but he'd give it a try, he'd nothing to lose.

Then they went onto the details of the missing Garda. There was little uncovered so far. But as of today they had at long last, a lead pointing towards the Travelling community to follow up in the case of Garda Laker. *And* Doogan's uniform had been found in the river the previous day by a local fisherman named Fred McDonald. But there was still no sign of his body. Nick scratched his head.

"As far as Doogan is concerned, there is no revenge motive on my part Greg, so we can definitely discount that one. Unless you've unearthed something new?"

"You're not on my list of suspects Nick, in fact I don't have any names on that list."Foley grinned.

"There is a connection between Rooney and Hynes, so maybe there is some link between Laker and Doogan?"Nick stated.

"Like what?"

"I don't know Greg, but we know they were friends. Maybe you could do some probing into that, and see if anything emerges?"

Foley nodded and scribbled in his notebook.

When Foley had left, Nick sighed, picked up the phone and rang Sergeant Philpott of the crack-squad in the New Park Hotel. Another long day loomed.

***

"You'll never guess what happened yesterday in the school."Nancy said, sipping her tea.

"Ok, let me have three guesses. You've either become permanent, been promoted, or got a rise."Kitty replied.

"Wrong on all counts, I'm afraid. One of the teachers, Simon Williams, who teaches English, asked me to go with him to a variety show in the McGrath Hall next Friday. He's very nice. He's a widower, a bit older than me, with two grown-up children."

"I don't blame you. I can't keep up with you. And why would you not go out with him?"Kitty asked.

"Well…..he….he's a Protestant, and was educated in Trinity. His father was the Vicar here in the town."

"So what? His religion is of no concern. If he's nice and you like him, what have you got to lose? Or have you still got Marty on your mind?"A smile creased Kitty's lips as she spoke.

Just then Nancy heard the letterbox snap shut in the hall.

"Maybe I have Marty on my mind, but what have I got to lose? You're right Kitty, God it's great to have someone to bounce things off."She hugged her sister, before rushing to see what the postman had delivered.

It was a large envelope, containing an ordinary-sized envelope addressed to her, and also a medium-sized one addressed to Nick. She recognised Marty's handwriting on both. Breathless, she left the envelope in the hall and rushed back to the kitchen. Kitty was tidying up.

"I hope you got something romantic in the post. I have to fly, must do some shopping, but make sure you accept that invitation from Mister Williams." Kitty said, putting her hat and coat on.

"Don't worry I will." Nancy replied, excitement welling in her veins.

They embraced, and after Kitty had left, Nancy rushed into the hall, grabbed the letters, hurried back into the living room, sliced the one addressed to her open, and read it.

Dear Nancy,

I was so sorry to miss you last Sunday. Wally told me that you called. I was making my final goodbyes to my mother, and it wasn't easy. It never is. I'm returning to Italy this week, and I'd love to say *arrivaderci* to you face-to-face. If the weather is ok, I might go up to Bagenalstown one day in the barge. If you're not there it doesn't matter, I love the trip anyway. Please don't think I'm putting you under any pressure about the marriage proposal, it's just simply that I love your company and I love you, and I always will, no matter what. You must believe that.

I'm enclosing a letter for your brother, and would ask if you could personally deliver it to him. It's very important, and hopefully will assist him in his investigations.

Ciao Bella,

Marty

She rang Nick immediately. He was working in the Garda station in Kilree Street with Sergeant Foley, he said. She told him not to leave, that she had an important letter for him. Within minutes she was entering Nick's office. Inside, she saw Nick and Foley in their shirtsleeves in front of a blackboard littered with comments. They looked stressed. She handed Nick the envelope and left, not wanting to get involved, feeling the angst heavy in the air.

Nick thanked her as she left, and then opened the envelope while Foley went to get more coffee. A letter and two smaller envelopes fell out. He read the letter.

Dear Nick,

Enclosed are two letters which I think will assist you in the work you are doing, although the contents may not make you particularly happy. The truth in life is sometimes hard to take and believe. The two letters are from families in the vicinity of New Ross, not far from where I live. I have been helping these families in their difficulties for some time. In it they state that both Garda Laker and Inspector Doogan have been abusing children in that area.

Ciao,
Marty.

Nick gasped in disbelief, shocked to the core. After some seconds he thumbed both letters open and read them before Foley returned. He felt the bile rise in his gut as he spoke.

"Greg ,I think we've found a link between Laker and Doogan. Maybe it's the break we've been looking for." Nick spoke, dazed, throwing the letters on the table, writing another note on the blackboard.

Chapter 29

Twist of Fate

Nick swore Foley to secrecy about the paedophile letters, despatching him straight away to visit the two families involved. Twilight shadows were glooming the room when Foley returned, looking pale and forlorn. Nick was startled by Foley's appearance and motioned him to sit down.

"So it's true?"Nick spoke first.

Foley nodded, grim-faced.

"I'm shot-through, mentally and every other way Nick, and begging your pardon but could we please adjourn until the morning? We both need to be fresh in mind and body to deal with this shit."

"Is it that bad?"Nick asked.

"Yeah, I'm afraid it is."

"Ok Greg, let's call it a day and continue tomorrow a.m., and well done."Nick patted his shoulder as he left. Foley muttered it was all in a day's work, as he put his hat on and left.

It was a day's work, Nick reasoned afterwards, one he was glad to have avoided, happy to have let Greg Foley do the dirty work. Divide and conquer, that's the way to do it, or so he tried to convince himself. The deeper you dig the dirtier it gets.

In bed that night his mind raced in contrary directions. He was facing a showdown meeting with Sheila Hynes, one he couldn't avoid. He had to face the music this time and do his job right, even though he was still beguiled by Sheila. Her raven hair and ravishing body always made him feel weak-kneed. No, there'd be no passing the buck this time. He couldn't get his head around the latest Laker and Doogan bombshell either, hoping he'd wake up to discover it was all a nightmarish dream. Richie Doran flitted in and out in the background of his mind, like a giant shadow. Sleep was sporadic.

Next morning he woke to the birds' dawn chorus, feeling anything but chirpy, dressed, took a light breakfast, and went for a stroll along the river to clear his head. Watching the river flow always relaxed him. It was his fix. Birdsong banished the melancholy mood in his mind. A song thrush sang from the trees. His favourite melody. The trees had a russet autumn tinge. Overhead, a wispy mist and rising sun promised a fine day, and his spirits rose too. He sucked fresh air into his lungs and headed back to the station.

He'd arranged for the new team to visit Goresbridge, check the crime scene, interview Richie Doran again, before visiting the hospital in Kilkenny. He was glad of the team's arrival, his workload was escalating by the day.

The blackboard was set up, updated, and the coffee made when Foley shuffled into the room, haggard and bleary-eyed.

"Up before your breakfast, Chief?" Foley's lips cracked in a grim smile.

"Sort of Greg, sleep ok?"

"Kind of, you know what it's like."

"Sure do, like a coffee to kick-off?"Nick asked.

"Yeah, no milk or sugar."

Nick poured two mugs, took off his jacket, and hung it on the back of his chair.

"Let's cut-to-the-chase Greg, give me the lowdown on yesterday. I want the gory details and don't spare anything. Let's have it no-holds-barred."Nick had a hollow feeling inside as he spoke, wanting to get it over with.

Foley paused, fished his notebook from his pocket and read his notes, before he started talking.

"Yesterday's discovery has me sick to my stomach. To think that the perpetrators are members of the Force, colleagues you'd put your trust in, who've let the uniform down in the most despicable manner. Anyway, both families' stories follow a familiar pattern, and tie-in with Doran the Traveller's story, for which I must apologise as

I did Richie Doran, not to mention the whole Goresbridge Travelling Community, a disservice. Both Gardai were keen swimmers, and swam in isolated places, mostly buck-naked. They gradually enveigled some young children of both families into their spider's web of perversion, giving them treats and rewards for joining in games with them in the water and out of it, swearing them to secrecy. They lured these innocents into a spiral of depravity that somehow went on for years with the parents unaware that anything was amiss. Each family had many children, so I suppose the parents had their hands full in coping anyway, but it's incredible to think it went undetected for so long."Foley sighed, as he stopped speaking.

"Ok Greg, I know it's hard but keep going. But just because there are two bad apples in a very large barrel doesn't make them all bad. Most of the Force are genuine and doing a fine job."

Foley paused to gulp some coffee, wiped his mouth with the back of his wrist, inhaled, and continued.

"I suppose. It looks like a conspiracy of silence. Maybe the families were in awe of the Garda uniform, thinking those who wear it could do no wrong, or else the two Garda had something on the families in question. Tit-for-tat like. That doesn't bear thinking about, nor does the abominations got up to with the children. I can't repeat them but I've got them written down, most of them anyway. I'm sick to the teeth the way that the Garda uniform's been let down, not to mention the damage done to these children, mentally and physically. How will they ever get over it?" Foley sighed again and took another swig of coffee, checked his notes, and then continued.

"Anyway the person we have to thank for uncovering this scandal is a priest called Martin Maher. Apparently one of the children was serving Mass for him one morning in Graiguenamanagh church about two months back. Maher thought the lad looked a bit down and quizzed him about it, and after a while the child, a twelve-year old lad, blurted out his story about being perverted by the two guards. This happened this year in the time after Maher came home on holidays from Italy. Maher pieced the depraved jigsaw together, visited both families last week with letters drafted for them to sign, and convinced them to do so and to be prepared to swear in court that the contents of the letters were true. He told them that this was probably only the tip of the iceberg, that there were most likely other families implicated, a ring of evil he called it, and that the evil would spread like a cancer to other families if nothing was done now. Thankfully the families involved listened to Maher's advice and signed the letters."Foley paused.

"So it's Marty Maher we have to thank for this revelation?" Nick asked.

Foley nodded.

"Now, at last we have a link between the two probable murders. I can remember now, clear-as-a-bell, how worried Doogan seemed when Laker disappeared, that look of fear on his face." Nick spoke, wrote on the board, then turned to Foley and continued.

"Importantly, thanks to Maher, we now have a motive, child abuse."

"Yes Chief, we now have a motive as to why someone might want to kill them. Certainly the Travelling Community hated Laker's guts with a vengeance and had grounds for killing him, but that's purely speculation, and speaking of which some of Laker's entrails were found near the burnt-car scene, so there's now a question mark over the Travellers there. A pretty big question mark. And then what about Inspector Doogan's disappearance? And does this ring of evil consist of more than two people? Mindboggling stuff. Definitely progress though." Foley muttered, scratching his head.

"Yes, progress alright Greg, but we need to find the bodies. You must review operations on the Barrow straight away. Check the river where they're trawling for Inspector Doogan's body, and report back. In the meantime I'll inform Dublin HQ of developments."

"Certainly Chief ."Foley said, a forlorn look creasing his face as he put his hat on and trudged out the door.

Nick paced the room, his mind in turmoil after what Foley had just told him. How was he going to handle the vitriolic news that two members of the Force were child molesters? It wasn't what they'd want to hear in Garda HQ in Dublin, no, not by a long shot. He still hadn't a clue as to how they died, but the evidence he'd received was damning, and murder seemed now more a probability than a possibility. The finding of human entrails near Laker's burnt-out car sent shivers up him. What the hell was going on? He had a motive for their murders, but no bodies and no arrests.

His mind envisaged him becoming entangled in a spider's web of perversion and depravity, and the spider being the invisible face of the Garda itself. He feared the paedophile letters incriminating Doogan and Laker would be suppressed on some pretext or other to avoid adverse media coverage, especially as no bodies had been found. And it hit him he himself could be in the firing line and be dismissed as incompetent just to silence him, especially as the case was still unsolved. He continued pacing the room, worried, hands clasping and unclasping, occasionally staring out the window. Self-preservation rules supreme, he muttered. It's a rock-and-a-hard-place, and he needed to cover his ass.

Later he wrote a letter to Superintendent Donoghue, outlining developments, enclosing copies of the two child-abuse letters. Once he retained the originals he felt he was safe from dismissal, and he'd do his damnedest to keep them. He'd hide them safely from harm's way. He smiled to himself thinking if he played his cards right, the promotion that he'd normally only earn after many years of toil and grind, might come his way sooner, a lot sooner. Then maybe he could afford to buy a house and settle down with Sheila. His mind raced. Don't get carried away my son, he cautioned himself, remembering there's many a slip between the cup and the lip, words his father had always spoken.

Back in his office he took an old Remington typewriter from the shelf and used it to bang out his case update for his files. It was mid-afternoon when all the documents were despatched by courier to Dublin. Afterwards he rang Superintendent Donoghue, informing him important data was on the way, and that they should be read before they had any further discussion of the case. As soon as he'd put the phone down, Foley burst into the office, breathless, looking distressed.

"What's up Greg?"Nick asked, startled.

"I've just run all the way up from the lock down by the old drawbridge." Foley gasped.

"Well out with it, what is it man?"Nick snapped.

"I'd been down at the Minch Norton Mills where the river-search was going on for Doogan, when a hullabaloo arose about a barge being sunk in the lock by the drawbridge. I ran up there, fast as I could, but the barge was below the water-line and was sinking fast when I got there.

"What happened? Was anyone on board?"

"I don't know, there probably was, someone had to open the lock-gates."

"Jesus. Have you any other information?" Nick said, dumbfounded.

"Yes, somebody was on the scene quickly, a fisherman named Fred McDonald. He said it went down fast but he spotted the name "*St. Fiachra*" on the side of the barge before it sank."

"Strange, the barge's name sounds familiar. Better check out the barge owner's identity Greg, while I get sub-aqua assistance, and find out how to get the barge lifted out of the lock pronto. It's blocking the passage on the river. Let's hope there's no fatality involved, we've enough on our plate already."Nick sighed, stunned, his thoughts still on the courier message he'd sent to Dublin. Foley rushed from the room.

Within two hours Foley was back, saying the barge's owner was a Martin Maher from Graiguenamanagh. Nick froze, realising it was Nancy's friend, the priest who'd saved her life, and had helped expose the child-abuse scandal, and whom he'd met before. Surely he wasn't the latest victim? A feeling of shock hit him. It didn't make sense. He shook his head.

"Are you sure?" Nick eyeballed Foley.

"Yes."Foley nodded.

"Did anyone see him at the lock?"

"There were no witnesses of the incident. It happened around two o'clock. Maher had left Graigue in the barge about two hours earlier, heading for Bagenalstown. I've confirmed that from his friend Wally in Graigue."

"So what do you think happened, Greg?"Nick asked, his mind churning.

"Well, he had to leave the barge to open and close the lower-gates of the lock, then get back on board as the barge rose when the lock filled. He may have been trapped below deck when it sank, or else fell from the lower-lock gates and got swept away."

"So you think maybe he drowned?"

Foley nodded, saying the sub-aqua team would soon find out.

"What do you think caused the barge to sink?"Nick asked, still dazed by the news.

"Who knows Chief? And why should it happen in an enclosed space like a lock? It could be just a case of bad luck, just a simple twist of fate."

"Let's hope there's nothing sinister involved, we've enough to deal with already." Nick grimaced as he spoke.

"You're right there, Nick."

"Greg, can you keep tabs on the search for Doogan's body, and the lock incident?"

"Sure thing Chief." Foley nodded and left the room, scurrying back to the river.

Nick then picked up the phone and rang Superintendent Donoghue in Dublin.

"Just wondering sir, if you'd had time to read the update and letters I couriered to you today?"

"Yes Sergeant Hackett, only got to it in the last hour. I was about to ring you, but you beat me to it. I needn't tell you the allegations in the letters are dynamite, incredible stuff, and must be kept completely confidential until they're checked out and proven. Does anyone else know about them? I notice too that the letters are copies. I need to see the originals. Have you checked directly yet with the families to verify the letters? I note also there's no progress on recovering any of the three missing bodies."

There's the rub, Nick thought, gritting his teeth before replying.

"Apart from the families themselves, and Father Maher from Graiguenamanagh, Sergeant Foley, you and I are the only ones who know about the allegations in the letters. It will be kept that way. Yes, we've checked with the families and they've corroborated the contents. I need to keep the originals here for legal reasons in the case file. We're scouring the river and following up on all angles that might lead to the whereabouts of the bodies. The picture has changed again this afternoon. A barge has just sunk in the lock in Bagenalstown. The owner is missing, possibly drowned. His name is Marty Maher, and he's the same priest from Graiguenamanagh who was instrumental in obtaining the abuse letters."

"Good heavens, not another missing person? Could this be connected to the other fatalities?" Donoghue seemed astounded.

"I don't think so, it seems just like an unfortunate accident, and the sub-aqua team are on the way. They may uncover something. On the other hand it could be retribution for what he uncovered. It's an incident we could've done without."Nick said ruefully.

"Yes I can see you're flat out Sergeant Hackett. Well done in what you've uncovered so far, it will be noted on your file. The new team are impressed with your work, by the way. Don't worry about the original copies of the letters for now. Make sure they're safely locked away at all times. Keep up the good work."

"Thank you sir." Nick stood staring at the silent phone in his hand. Now he had to make a call he hated making, to his sister Nancy. He dialled her number.

"Hi Nancy, you home alone?"

"Yes, Daddy's just gone to bed. What is it Nick?"

"Just want to have a chat Nancy, put the kettle on, I'll be there in five minutes."

He put the phone down, and rushed home.

Nancy had the table laid when he arrived. She looked up as she poured the tea, a frown frozen on her face.

"Is everything alright Nick? You don't usually come visiting this late in the evening."

"No I don't. I'm sorry but I'm afraid it's bad news I'm bringing."He said, sighing.

She put the tea pot down, startled.

"What is it? Please tell me, please get it over."Her face had creased with worry.

"There's been an accident down at the lock by the drawbridge this afternoon. A barge has sunk, and the owner's missing. The barge is called the *St. Fiachra.*"

"Dear God that's Marty's barge. He said he'd try to come in the barge to say goodbye before leaving for Italy. Oh God, please tell me it's not true, how could it have happened?" She gasped.

He hugged her, as tears streamed down her face.

"It's a mystery I'm afraid, we'll know more tomorrow. I really am sorry Nancy. Look nothing is definite, he's just missing at the moment, who knows? He might show up yet." He tried to comfort her, wrapping his arms about her.

"It doesn't look good, I can't believe it, Oh God, first Ned Rooney, now Marty, I must have a jinx on me." Nancy sobbed as she spoke.

"I'm sorry to have to give you the bad news, but please don't give up hope, nothing is definite at the moment. I just wanted you to hear about it first from me."He said.

"Thanks Nick, I appreciate your kindness. I know you

sometimes have to bring bad news, and it can't be easy for you. I'll say a rosary tonight that Marty turns up somewhere." She kissed his cheek, and dabbed her eyes dry.

"I'll call over to Kitty and tell her the news, I'm sure she'll be over straight away."Nick said, and left soon afterwards.

On his way back to the station he saw Greg Foley coming up Kilree Street, dressed in civvies, and called across to him.

"Didn't recognise you out of your uniform, Greg."

"Yeah, I'm heading for a pint in the Railway House Bar, Nick. I feel I need one, fancy one yourself?" Foley called back, grinning.

Nick hesitated a moment, before replying.

"Yes, seems a good idea. I've a call to do, and then I'll get out of this uniform, and join you in an hour."After a day like today I might need more than one pint, Nick muttered to himself.

Chapter 30

Outcome

"Let's start with what's hopefully good news. Tell me how it went with Mr Williams the other night when you both went to the concert in the McGrath Hall. What was the outcome? I'm dying to know."Kitty spoke as she poured the tea.

She'd stayed with Nancy the night before, helping her cope with the shock of Marty's barge sinking and his body not being found. Nancy had resisted at first, saying she was fine, but Kitty had insisted and stayed, saying she had to bring their father shopping the next day anyway, not to mention her husband still being away working in Waterford. Nancy was secretly glad of her company, and soon relented.

"Actually it went very well. He was the perfect gentleman and brought me flowers and chocolates. The show was enjoyable and the night passed most agreeably. It's nice to go out with someone and find you get on with him. Believe it or not he's a cricket aficionado and plays for Bagenalstown. He played at Trinity and in a Dublin cricket club at a high level some years ago. I'll have to introduce him to Daddy, and they can bore the socks off each other talking cricket."Nancy said, smiling.

"And?"

"And what?"

"And how did it end?" asked Kitty, staring at her, eyebrows arched, eyes twinkling.

"Formally and friendly, much as you'd expect from a gentleman and son of a vicar, but he asked me out again next weekend to the cinema. He likes films. He's away in Dublin for a few days to visit his son in Trinity College. I wonder if his son knows Liam. God it's a small world."Nancy sighed.

"Indeed it is, and did you agree to meet him?"

"I said I'd let him know. I'll see him sometime in the school."

"And was his religion ever a problem on your date?"

"No, not at all."

Deep down, Nancy had to admit she hadn't been swept off her feet as much as she had been by Marty. He lacked Marty's flair, *frisson*, and Italian charm, but seemed solid as a rock, dependable, someone you could grow fond of over time, she reckoned.

"So your pre-conceived notions about Protestants were all in the mind?"Kitty enquired.

"Yes, I must admit I got it wrong there."

"Let's hope there'll be some positive news today about Marty. There could be some simple explanation as to his whereabouts. "Kitty said hopefully.

"I have a bad feeling about the whole thing, I mean the barge sinking in the lock. My stomach's in a knot, and I prayed long and hard last night. It's not like Marty to vanish into thin air. He's a priest, and he has to keep in touch at all times of every day and night."Nancy said ruefully.

"But who would want to harm a priest?"Kitty asked.

"I don't know, it could be an unfortunate accident, but to change the subject I got some good news myself yesterday."

"Great, tell me more." said Kitty, glad to divert to another topic.

"In the middle of a class I was called to Sister Cecilia's room. I was nervous as a new-born lamb. What could it be? It's a big deal to be summoned to your Superior's office, especially after Inspector Doogan's threats when the newspaper article came out about the Garda not protecting Ned Rooney. Of course with Doogan now gone missing I'd forgotten all about his threats. Nick had assured me they'd vanished along with the Inspector. I still felt nervous. Anyway Sister Cecilia said she was very happy with my work, and offered me a permanent position. I was over-the-moon, I can tell you. She said there was a sting in the tail though, as she wanted me to produce a school concert in the autumn in the McGrath Hall, and wanted it to become an annual event. I assured her it would be my pleasure. I came out of her office in a daze. A happy one."

"Wonderful news, wonderful, it's great for you. God I'm so glad you came home Nancy, everything's been so much better here since you arrived, and Daddy's health is so much improved. He's only weeks away now from a full recovery. The doctors are amazed at his progress. Care in the home by the family is best, when all's said and done, you've proved that." As Kitty spoke she embraced her younger sister, tears of joy trickling down her face.

***

When Sheila Hynes walked across the foyer of St. Luke's hospital in Kilkenny, Nick held his breath. Elegantly tall, black hair and eyebrows, her eyes sky-blue in an oval face with lips that always seemed poised to smile. And with her shapely body tucked inside a nurse's uniform, it was more than a man could resist. Well he couldn't anyway, he'd been smitten when first he'd seen her, and she was out of uniform then. But he had to admit the uniform added to her allure. He wondered if she was impressed by *his* uniform. He'd rung her that morning, saying he'd like to ask her a few questions about incidents concerning Ned Rooney, expecting a hostile reply, but surprisingly she was quite affable. She said she'd meet him at the hospital at mid-day, when she came off-duty. She strolled towards him, smiling.

"Hello Nick, let's find a more salubrious place to chat. There's a nice coffee shop beside the river, near the Castle, and you can park anywhere for free with your squad car, can't you?"She grinned.

"Good idea, you guide me there." He followed her outside, aware of prying eyes following them.

A short time later they were ensconced on the balcony of the coffee shop, admiring the swirling river beneath them, the sun flitting in and out of low-scudding clouds, and Kilkenny Castle majestic in the background.

"I take it your visit is more business than pleasure, Nick. God, my feet are killing me. Eight hours on the go." As she spoke she slipped her shoes off.

He held his breath, her legs always excited him. He remembered when she used ask him to massage her feet when she came off-duty. It always turned him on. He felt his blood rising.

"It could be a bit of both. Let's have lunch first." He said, calling the waiter.

"They say there's no such thing as a free lunch, so let's get the hard bit over now." She said when they'd finished eating.

"Firstly Sheila, I want to assure you I'd no involvement in the disappearance of either your brother Aengus, *or* Inspector Doogan for that matter, even though some people might say I had a motive for the latter."

"I never thought you did anything Nick. I know you too well."She said softly, looking earnestly into his eyes.

"Thanks for those kind words Sheila. It's reassuring. But it must have been hard for you though, the shocks coming one after the other."

"It was for sure. Even when you've been reared with danger and death in an IRA household it hits you. A tidal wave of grief, when hey presto, someone you know, have lived with, has gone out of your life. For good."Her face was pensive as she spoke.

"I understand Sheila, and my job is to solve these mysteries, and that's why I'm here. So I hope you won't take offence at any of my questions."

"I'll try not to, I promise, so go on ahead, get it over with."She said nervously.

"Firstly, when my sister Nancy was in your hospital after her near-drowning accident, she mentioned that you informed her that there was no Garda security on Ned Rooney, who was in the Intensive Care Unit. Later you denied you said this."He stared into her eyes as he spoke.

"Yes, I recall the incident."She replied, frowning.

"Why did you change your opinion Sheila? Was it pressure from your brother Aengus? I know blood is thicker than water but Ned Rooney was murdered, and there was no Garda presence at the hospital to save him. My sister Nancy said you were very understanding and helped her to speak to Ned Rooney. He was the father of her adopted child, you know. I'd like you to tell me the truth Sheila, you've no one to protect now, and this conversation is strictly between the two of us."

Silence. Minutes crept by, before Sheila sighed and spoke.

"I suppose I was weak. Yes, it was Cornelius Doogan who persuaded me, saying it would help my brother Aengus's situation, because Aengus was the number one suspect. Aengus did ask me as well. I've had plenty of time on my own lately to reflect on those things and realise how weak I was, and I know now I should have spoken the truth. But I didn't. I'm sorry."Her face was set grim, eyes moist, as she spoke.

He decided then it was better to avoid saying anything about Inspector Cornelius Doogan's sexual perversions.

"Are you prepared to tell the truth now Sheila? Even to swear it in court if necessary?"

After hesitating for several moments she agreed she was.

"Ok, then there was another incident at the hospital, where the three thugs who assaulted Ned Rooney were treated for their wounds, shortly after the assault. You were seen on security cameras, treating their injuries. Do you accept this as a fact? And if so, did you help them because your brother asked you to? Because he knew you'd keep your mouth shut afterwards?"Nick felt uncomfortable as he spoke, fearing she might blow up and end their relationship.

She shuddered, looking forlorn, and replied.

"Yes, my brother Aengus asked me to help them. I was weak again, and blood is thicker than water I suppose, and I like to help anyone suffering, that's why I became a nurse. I'm sorry, I realise I shouldn't have done it. They were criminals, but I just treated them as human beings. I suppose I shouldn't have done it, but someone else would probably have helped them anyway."She snuffled into a handkerchief.

"I understand Sheila. I know you were co-erced into doing these things against your better judgment, and I appreciate your honesty."

"Can you really appreciate it Nick, especially after me walking out on you?" She asked, looking into his eyes, appealingly.

"Yes I can, and now that I'm finished the interview, I'd like to drop you wherever you're living now Sheila. I've got all the answers I need."He stood up and got ready to go, relieved it was over, happy they were still on talking terms.

She put on her shoes as he paid the bill, and he then drove her to where she was staying with another nurse from the hospital. At the door of the flat she turned to face him, her face red and splotchy, eyes rimmed with tears.

"Nick, I feel a huge load's gone off me. The flat's empty now, my partner's working, so would you like to come in for a cuppa?" She asked, winking.

He didn't hesitate.

When he entered, she shut the door behind him, kicked off her shoes, and rose on her tiptoes to kiss him long and languidly, her hands behind his neck pulling him down, his hand slipping inside her uniform, feeling her breasts. Within minutes they were in bed together, both uniforms in a heap on the floor, making love as they'd done many times before, but with a hunger that surprised them both, ending with a promise to each other they'd never part again.

When he emerged from her apartment an hour later, he felt happy for the first time in a long while. They had made a date for her next free night. Afterwards he reckoned he might start looking forward to his trips to Kilkenny in the future.

***

Within the hour Nick was back again in the station in Bagenalstown, writing notes onto the blackboard in his office, while Foley made the coffee.

"What's the story with the sunken barge Greg?"He asked as Foley put the tray on the table.

"We searched the river high-and-low around the lock, and finally found this item in the reeds, half way down to the Royal Oak Bridge."

Foley took something out of a bag he'd left on the floor, and placed it on the table. Nick picked it up and stared at it. It was a sodden sea captain's peaked cap, similar to the one Marty had worn when they'd met. He was stunned. He placed the cap on the table, gulped his coffee, and spoke.

"The cap looks like the one Marty usually wore on the barge, and judging by its condition, it can't have been in the water for more than a day. Its ominous though, looks like he must have drowned."

"I'd agree about the time in the water, and also your conclusion about drowning." Foley replied.

"Any other developments?"

"No, we're still searching. No other items of clothing were found near the barge. The number of missing bodies we're searching for in the river has now risen to three. We're at full stretch searching, but so far it's to no avail. We may need to bring in more help" Foley replied, looking anxious.

Nick jotted down notes, his mind in a quandary.

"Yes, things have escalated further, I'll ask for more

assistance from HQ. It doesn't look good for Marty Maher. It looks like a drowning accident, but I suspect there's something sinister going on. Something just doesn't add up. What's happening with the barge?" Nick asked.

"The lifting company are going flat out since they arrived first thing this morning. They expect to have it out of the lock this evening, before nightfall."

"That's good Greg, keep the pressure on, we need to clear the river for navigation urgently. Hopefully that will be by tomorrow. I have to update Dublin in the next hour. We could do with finding some missing bodies in the interim."Nick muttered ruefully.

"We'll keep looking, something will turn up. It always does. Eventually." Foley said, saluting as he left the room.

Nick wrote some more notes on the board before sitting down. It's bad news for Nancy for sure, he thought, running his fingers through his hair. Not conclusive though, no body found yet, but not good at all. He decided to wait another day before telling her about Marty's cap, hoping for better news in the meantime. He glanced at his watch. Time to ring Superintendent Donoghue in Dublin. Better get it over with. He sighed and picked up the phone.

"Well Sergeant Hackett, what's the news? I've a media briefing in less than an hour, and I need to have some progress to report on." The Superintendent's voice was brusque.

"We found an item of clothing in the river, sir, which almost certainly belonged to the person manning the barge that sank in the lock in Bagenalstown. Marty Maher is his name. Our river search has now been expanded to a search for three bodies. We need more resources urgently, on top of the team you sent already. We're flat out to breaking point at the moment. The barge has just been lifted from the lock, and will be searched as soon as possible. Normal traffic can resume on the Barrow from tomorrow."

"Ok, that's something I suppose. But there's no bodies found so far. Not good. Anything else?" Donoghue asked, disappointment edging his voice.

"Well actually yes, there is a development which is very worrying, and could prove extremely embarrassing for the Garda, if it ever got into the public domain."Nick lowered his voice then.

"Well, what is it Sergeant Hackett?"Donoghue demanded impatiently.

"Sir, I'm worried about discussing it on the phone. I'm afraid in case someone might be listening in. The line might be tapped. The information is classified."

He heard a sigh on the line, followed by a silence, before Donoghue spoke again.

"Ok Sergeant, good point, I like your awareness. Just to be sure to be sure, call me back straight away on this number, it's completely confidential." Donoghue read the number out, and within minutes Nick had rung back.

"Right Sergeant Hackett, you've got me on tenterhooks with all this cloak-and-dagger stuff, now tell me what's on your mind?"

"Sir, do you remember the newspaper article about lack of security for Ned Rooney before he was beaten up? And that this happened in spite of him reporting to the Garda that his life was under threat."

"Yes, I do recall it. It was highly embarrassing, but I understood from Inspector Doogan that this allegation was untrue, and that he was about to take action in the matter. That was of course before Inspector Doogan himself disappeared." Donoghue retorted.

"Correct. But following a recent interview with a nurse from the hospital involved in Kilkenny, I can confirm that no Garda security was provided to Ned Rooney while he was in the hospital. She says she's prepared to testify in Court to that effect."

"What? Surely not? Incredible, it was obvious Rooney was in serious danger after the previous incident. Inspector Doogan must surely have been aware of that?"

"I cannot fathom either why it was not done. Only Inspector Doogan himself can answer that question."Nick stated calmly.

"In his absence we'll have to deal with it, Sergeant Hackett. This could be a disaster for the Force if it got out. What do you suggest?"

"Sir, I believe I might be able to get the nurse involved to stay silent on the matter. It'll be tricky, but I think it can be done, a sort of a *quid pro quo*. Yes, I believe I could pull it off."

There was a pause before the Superintendent replied.

"Good man Hackett, that's what I like to hear. That's the kind of initiative we need in the Garda if we want to progress. I'm afraid Inspector Doogan sadly lacked the specialised skills required for the job. I'm prepared to recommend you for promotion to Doogan's position, on the condition that you *do* pull it off, and for the moment the matter lies between just the two of us. Understand?"

"Yes sir, t...thank you sir, I won't let you down." Nick's voice trembled as he said the words.

"I know you won't, I'm counting on you. And there is one other condition."

"Of course and what is that?"

"Those letters that you sent me from the two families, concerning Inspector Doogan and Garda Laker, I'd like you to have the original copies sent to me. Obviously we wouldn't want these letters falling into the wrong hands, would we Inspector, sorry I mean Sergeant Hackett? The fallout would be disastrous for the Force, morale would be damaged. We wouldn't want that now, would we?"

"N...no sir...absolutely no way. I'll despatch them by courier to you tomorrow."Nick replied. And then I'll get Foley to get another set signed by the families, just for insurance purposes, Nick thought. He smiled inwardly.

"A good day's work, well done, I can see we're going to get on famously Sergeant Hackett. Soon I'll be calling you Inspector Hackett. Now please find those bodies."

The line went dead.

Nick looked at his watch. Seven o'clock. Greg Foley would be in Railway House Bar by now. He decided he'd join Greg for a pint or two, and leave his bad-news conversation with Nancy until the morrow. He changed out of his uniform and headed for the pub, feeling things were now on the up-and-up. He'd achieved a promise of promotion in his job if he played his cards right, plus a reconciliation with Sheila, and all in the same day. Yes, life was definitely on the up. He knew Sheila would follow his advice, and he resolved to save straight away for an engagement ring. No, he wasn't going to let her slip through his fingers a second time, once bitten twice shy. And after that they'd save for a house of their own. He'd rather it that way, living in his parent's home wasn't what he longed for. He wanted to be his own man in his own house, with his own woman, and if Superintendent Donoghue delivered on his promise that outcome was now possible. He smiled, thinking he was going to enjoy his drinks with Foley.

Chapter 31

Confession

My mother was my saviour and I thank God for her. She'd lift me up when I'd sunk low, and give me hope when my world had run wild. Love was all when you were young and growing up in a small town like Graiguenamanagh, in the nineteen forties. Without it you had nothing, you'd nothing to strive for. You were nothing. She *was* love.

Graiguenamanagh was a poor place to live in then, people scrambling for whatever food they could get with the rationing. No doubt mother spoiled me a bit, me being an only child." Martin Maher", she'd say, "you'd take the bit out of my mouth, but I wouldn't have it any other way, and I hope someday you'll find a good woman who'll spoil you the way I do, someone who's grateful to have you." Someone with a grateful heart, just like her, I suppose. Yes, love *was* all, when all was said and done.

I can't remember much about my father. He'd left when I was only three years old. I learned later he was a drunkard, and a blaggard to boot, who sometimes beat my mother. When finally she'd had enough, she packed her bags and left him. Good on her I say, but she didn't get much sympathy from her own family. The stigma of a broken marriage in a small town in Ireland in those days didn't sit too well with the community or the church, and the woman involved was usually blamed. When love is gone everything's gone, there's nothing worth clinging on for, mother always said. Father had a small farm holding he'd inherited, but every few years he'd sell off a few acres to pay for his drinking habit. Mother scolded him about this, saying he'd soon have nothing left, but he ignored her, thinking he knew better. He didn't respect my mother, he wasn't grateful he'd married her. He didn't have a grateful heart. Mother said she never regretted leaving him one little bit. She never re-married.

She got work in a milliner's shop in the town, and knitted baby-things for people at home at night. That helped make ends meet in the small cottage she'd rented in the town. Work can make you happy if you get your mind right about it, she used to say, you need a goal, something to aim at, or else life can be just boring. I discovered later that her goal was to have enough money saved for me to become a priest, but only if I wanted to, of course.

She was happy in the cottage, had a circle of friends who met every week for a cup of tea and a chat. Being an avid reader, the library was her most loyal friend. It took her on mind-trips all over the world at no expense, she said. Once a month she'd play Bingo in the Church Hall. Her daily vice was a flutter on the nags, sixpence each way being her top bet. I know, because I placed the bets for her. When she backed a horse, she'd be on tenterhooks all day until I got a copy of the evening paper with the late racing results, and she could check if she'd won anything. Sometimes, if she'd backed a few winners, she'd give me the price of the pictures. She never smoked, saying it was a disgusting habit. I loved her.

She kept mostly to herself, being happy with her own company. And mine. Men didn't feature much in her life, or so I thought when I was young. Being attractive and bright, she was not short of male admirers. Sometimes, when I was older and could mind myself, she'd leave me alone and go to the cinema in Kilkenny with a local man who had a car. After she'd returned I'd notice her lipstick sometimes was smudged, or her nylons had run or were crooked. Once, the day after she'd gone to a dance in New Ross, I saw that the nylons she'd worn to the dance were rolled up in a ball in her handbag. That made me mad. I don't know why it did, but I thought someone had done something nasty to her, or taken advantage of her, and I wanted to hurt him in some way in case it happened again. That night a fury came over me when I thought back about it. Every time from then on when mother went on a date with a man, I took to rummaging through her used-clothes the next day after she'd put them in the laundry basket. I think I was about twelve at that time.

When I was in secondary school, I played on the senior school hurling team. We were coached by a local priest, Father Tom Devine, who'd played inter-county hurling in his youth. Around this time I'd begun serving Mass in the church where he officiated. Once, on a hot summer's day after a schools' under seventeen hurling game, Father Tom insisted on all the team taking a shower, saying he would give us all a rub-down afterwards with wintergreen. Individually. This happened when there were no other adults about, and we had the use of a club ground with shower facilities. One by one, clad only in a towel, we lay on the table as he performed the massage. The odour was overpowering, and I remember getting a shock at the end, when his hand slipped under the towel for a moment, and he touched me. I blushed and felt uncomfortable when he did this. I wasn't sure afterwards if it was accidental or deliberate. Later when I spoke to them, some of the lads reported a similar experience. Others maybe didn't want to talk about it. Neither did I. I don't know why.

About a week later, I served Mass alone for Father Tom. In the sacristy afterwards, he beckoned to me to help him take off his vestments, as the church clerk who normally did this task was sick that day. After I'd helped him, he turned to me and spoke.

"Thank you Martin. Well done, you did a fine job today, serving on your own. All the Latin words perfect, and you rang the bell just the right length of time, I do hate when it's rung too long or too loud."

"T...t...thank you Father."I stammered.

"You know you'd make a fine priest. Your mother told me she hopes and prays that you'll have a vocation when you're older. Tell me, would you like to become a priest?"

"I...I.. don't know Father, I haven't thought about it much."

I wondered then about how he knew what my mother thought, and how he knew her at all.

"A wise answer, my boy. It's a big decision for any young man to make these days. To be sure you need to think long and hard about it. Maybe I can help you make that decision. Please let me know if I can, Martin. I'll pray that you will make the right decision, and also for your intentions." He patted me on the shoulder after he spoke, and I blushed as a thrill shot through my body. I felt privileged that he was so interested in my welfare. I'd always looked up to him as if he was an angel on a pedestal. I thanked him and left.

Over the following months the other altar boys became jealous, saying I was Father Tom's favourite, as he'd regularly stay back to talk to me in the sacristy when everyone else had left. I quizzed Mother too about how well she knew Father Tom, and she said she usually met and spoke to him at the Bingo Hall every month. I was relieved to hear that.

Afterwards I used look forward to my meetings alone with Father Tom, as by then I'd decided I *did* want to become a priest, and felt he could help me. One day after Mass, he informed me he was an amateur photographer, and asked if I'd like to see some of his photos. I agreed, and he told me to call that evening to his house. When I arrived, he ushered me into the living room, saying his housekeeper had gone out to the pictures, to see Doris Day and James Garner in something or other. Next he took out a folder from his desk, sifting through the photos inside. The first ones he showed me were of buildings and animals. Then he produced a bunch that he said were a bit risqué, and that he might have to censor them sometime. I gasped when I saw that many of them were nude pictures taken in dressing rooms, with the people photographed obviously unaware he was snapping them. Many photos featured male and female genitalia. A lot of the female nude pictures were taken as the women were bathing in a river I recognised instantly as the Barrow. He said they were taken with a long-range lens from a distance. I reckoned they were taken from a nearby vantage point unknown to the women. He must have noticed the look of amazement on my face, before he spoke.

"Don't get too excited by these pictures, dear boy. All great artists portray the naked body in their art. These are just amateur efforts, I will get better. Anyway Martin, I'd appreciate if you stayed quiet about seeing these, as I've never shown them to anyone before now, and some people just don't understand real art anyway."

I said I'd say nothing, and left. That night in bed those photos revolved in my mind like a moving picture, blood pulsating through my body.

He continued to invite me to his house about once a month, always when there was no one else in the house, always on some pretext or other, always related to me becoming a priest. Something inside warned me not to go but I always went. Evil attracts. I'd tell my Mother some fib or other, not letting on I was going there. He and I became intimate over a period of months. He used say that what we were doing was not sinful, and that God would understand that we were doing it for Him. And I believed him, after all he was a priest, and would be on more intimate terms with God than me. I trusted him.

When I was attending Maynooth University, studying for the priesthood, Father Tom would visit me every month, sometimes bringing my mother with him, saying it was too far for her to travel alone. She seemed happy to take lifts from him, and I was delighted to see her more often. When he came alone we took advantage of the situation in my room. It was in the third year of my studies that my mother's health began to deteriorate. Before that year was out, she'd been diagnosed with an aggressive form of Dementia. I was devastated. I always thought she would stay the same forever. She kept her looks but her mind went downhill rapidly. Father Tom brought her to my ordination, and though she was heavily sedated I was delighted she was there, and wept to see her. Her dream

304

had come through, I was ordained a priest. Father Tom was so thoughtful, like a father-figure to me.

My life as a priest was varied initially, and I took temporary positions in parishes up and down the banks of the Barrow. Building up my experience, they told me they were doing, so I could soon get my own parish. But all I wanted at that time was to be near Father Tom and my mother. I had my own car, and got home to see her most Saturdays. Her health got worse, and I had to place her in a Nursing Home, for all the good that did her. I continued to visit Father Tom discreetly, after the visits to my mother. He would visit her too in the Nursing Home, and I was glad of that. He was a friend not only in need but also in deed, or so I thought until the night of the revelation.

After visiting my mother one night in the Nursing Home, I left feeling depressed and headed for Father Tom's house as arranged. When I got there I rang the bell but to no avail, then used the knocker. Ditto, so I entered with the key he'd given me. A note lay on the hallstand, saying he'd gone on an urgent sick call and would be back in an hour or so. I was to make myself at home and have a cup of tea and wait in the living room, as there was nobody else in the house that night. How convenient, I thought.

While I waited, sitting on the sofa sipping my tea, whiling away the time, I decided to browse through Father Tom's photos. Taking the folder from his desk, I emptied the contents onto the table beneath a naked light. It soon hit me that Father Tom had not previously shown me the most explicit nude pictures, a lot involving men and women together, and I gasped as I gazed at them, finding it hard to see the art involved. Before I'd gathered and sorted the photos back into the folder, I noticed an envelope marked "private, not to be shown". Curious, I opened the envelope, a batch of pictures falling onto the table. Picking them up, I grimaced as I flicked through them. They were all in colour, and showed a man and woman, both naked, cavorting in various sexual positions. I wondered how the photos were taken, and surmised a cine-camera must have been used. I picked one up, holding it beneath the bare light, immediately recognising the man's face as Father Tom's, and the woman's as my mother's. At first I couldn't believe it, I was stunned and scrutinised more photos, but the outcome was the same.

A wave of nausea hit me, and I rushed into the bathroom, vomiting into the toilet. For a while I was in a state of shock, unable to think or act, and sat on the toilet seat, my head in my hands. All I could think of was how I'd been betrayed by both of them. Gradually I returned to my senses, and came to blame Father Tom for what I'd just seen, thinking that he had preyed on my mother, just as he had preyed on me over the years, and on God knows whoever else. Realising he could return at any minute, I hurried back to the living room, put the private photos back in the envelope, but not before taking one photo and putting it in my pocket. When everything else was back in the folder I replaced it in the desk, and wrote a note to Father Tom, saying I'd taken ill and had to go home. Placing the note on the hall table, I dashed out the door, slamming it behind me.

As I drove home a fury welled within me, it's a miracle the car stayed on the road. That night I stormed heaven for guidance. No sense in over-reacting, I reasoned, God would tell me what to do, don't panic, but panic I did, hands trembling as I prayed. More and more I saw Father Tom in the role of the devil. He had seduced my mother, she being vulnerable on her own, just as he had seduced me and probably many more. My mother was an innocent victim and so was I. He was evil. He was the devil. Every so often I'd take out the photo I'd kept and stare at it, then weep bitterly afterwards.

Over the next weeks I became convinced Father Tom really was the devil incarnate, a person who was a danger to society, someone who was going to lead innocent people astray, in a word a pervert, and I knew something had to be done about him. And I realised it was I who had to do it, as nobody else would. I wanted revenge on him, and thought of suitable ways of doing it. He was a disciple of Satan, and I wondered how I might defeat him.

I prayed harder and harder. One night in bed it came to me in a moment of inspiration, a message straight from God, spelling out how I might sort out this menace to society. The message came loud and clear. I was to be God's appointed Avenging Angel, and my role would be to protect the world from the evil of Satan, and people in his employ, starting with Father Tom. The prospect excited me. My mind filled with ideas on how I could do it.

Whenever I thought of Father Tom being with my mother, my blood coursed like a river in tumult. It was clear to me he was also entirely to blame for her ill-health. He tried to meet me a number of times in the following weeks but I avoided him. Gradually a plan grew in my mind, and I reviewed it over and over until it was honed to perfection.

At a meeting with the Office of the Bishop of the Diocese I applied for a temporary posting abroad, stating that my mother's Dementia was affecting my own mental state, and that I needed a temporary spell overseas. At first they did not respond to this idea, asking me to think about it for a few months. This I did, before applying again, saying my decision hadn't changed. Then they asked me to put the request in writing, and it would be considered, saying the process could take some months. Once more I followed procedures and waited. I reckoned they were trying to dissuade me from my decision, but I persisted. Finally, after a four month's wait I was summoned to the Bishop's residence, and told by His Eminence's secretary that my application for a position abroad had been reluctantly granted. His demeanour was disinterested and grim as he spoke to me, obviously unsympathetic as to why I should want to leave the country.

"Father Maher, we are aware of the pressures our priests must endure these days, and at all times their health, mental and physical, is of paramount importance to the Church. Have you any particular place you would like to be assigned to? You had mentioned Italy previously. Can you please be more specific? Rome, Naples, Milan, Florence, or wherever."

After a few minutes thought I chose Milan. His eyes arched in surprise before he replied.

"By chance there is a position available, attached to a large hospital in Milan. Not the normal priestly duties mind you, more a counsellor to people who are dying, and to their families. Are you still interested?"He asked.

"Yes, it sounds perfect."

"I will process the relevant forms and advise you in due course, Father Maher. By the way, who will now keep an eye on your mother?" He asked, his lips curled in a sneer as he snapped the file shut.

"I hope to get home on holidays as often as I can. I also have a friend, also a priest, who has kindly agreed to visit her weekly, as I don't have any relatives in the area."I replied.

"You are truly lucky to have such a friend, and so is your mother."

"Yes, I suppose we are." How wrong you are my friend, I thought grimly to myself. How wrong indeed.

After I left, satisfied with the outcome, I knew there was a lot to do before I left for Italy. On my way home I called to see my mother. Unfortunately she was sedated and I didn't stay long. The nurse said her condition was unchanged. That night I prayed she would improve, and thanked God for my job in Milan. Now I could progress on my real career in the world, and fulfil God's wishes. Now I was embarking on my real mission for God. My destiny was clear, and I couldn't wait to get on with achieving it.

I'd managed to avoid any one-to-one meetings with Father Tom since the night of the photo revelations. He didn't seem to suspect anything was amiss, ringing me at least once a week. I didn't inform him of my decision to leave for Milan, keeping it simple. Shortly before I was due to leave, he rang saying he'd taken his holidays, and would leave Ireland in two days time, alone, touring the continent, ending up in Rome, and suggested that maybe I might join him for a few days in one of his destinations, or at least that we have a last get-together before he left. It was mid-summer, with the weather hot and muggy, so I suggested kayaking to St. Mullins, and having a picnic and a dip nearby in a secluded place we'd used before. As we would be there mid-week, I said it was bound to be quiet, and we could go skinny-dipping if he wished. He jumped at the idea, saying he couldn't wait. Neither could I.

When we reached St. Mullins we pulled the kayak onto the less-frequented west bank. The sun was hot in a sultry sky, dappling the grass through the trees, but the foliage and trees gave lots of privacy. Father Tom said his bags were packed and left in his house, ready for his departure the next day, and his housekeeper had already gone on her annual leave, so the house was empty if I wanted to stay the night. I said I'd think about it. He opened a bottle of red wine and we filled our glasses, soon emptying the bottle. After a while he peeled off his clothes, asking if I'd like to join him for a plunge in the river. I said yes and suggested a bit of fun beforehand, maybe bondage, which I knew he liked. He nodded, aroused, and we retreated into the shadows of the trees, where I tied him up with the rope I'd brought, stuffing a gag into his mouth, binding his feet together. He seemed a bit alarmed at the severity I used, and the gag, but on the other hand seemed to be enjoying himself. Father Tom's eyes bulged with terror when I produced the photo of him and my mother in *flagrante delicto*, shoving it in front of his face.

309

"So I see you enjoyed my mother's company. Well there's a price to pay for all evil deeds in this life. I suggest you say your final prayers and ask for God's forgiveness, because you sure aren't going to get mine."I snarled through clenched teeth. He blanched.

I took a bucket I'd hidden nearby in the bushes, filled it with water from the river, and stuffed his head into it, only pulling it out when he'd nearly drowned. After doing this about six times, I finally put him out of his misery by slitting his throat. I had previously contemplated doing worse things to him, but relented later. Then I grabbed his legs and dragged his body deeper into the undergrowth.

I buried his remains, including his clothes, in a grave I'd previously prepared deep in the bushes. The grave was deep, and I covered it with rocks, to prevent wild animals unearthing the body. I said a short prayer afterwards but inside felt no remorse, the world was now a less dangerous place with one less of Satan's disciples in it.

On the way back it rained heavily. Thank you God, I muttered, relieved that it would wipe out any traces of blood in the area. That night I took his packed bags from his house, and burnt them in his garden. His planned holidays gave me time to be in Milan before the alarm was raised. He would become just another missing person. And so it proved.

Settling smoothly into life in Milan, I took to the city, the people, the weather, and the job. Although I missed my mother, I realised from a distance that she was no longer the person that I'd grown up adoring and worshipping. Dementia is the devil's own illness, and all the Nursing Home staff seemed to be doing was sedating her so that she slept most of the time. Her quality of life seemed to have sunk into nothingness, day-in-day-out. I prayed for a miracle cure, but deep down I despaired of that event ever happening.

After attending classes, I became fluent in the Italian language, finding it easy after studying Latin at school. In my first year overseas I got home on several occasions, but each visit saw my mother's health sliding further downhill, and I returned to Italy each time feeling more depressed than ever.

During my fifth year abroad, a friend from the Milan hospital where I worked invited me to a meeting of people dedicated to fighting the evils of Satan in Italian society. They were called the Friends of God. He was a middle-aged doctor, *Paolo de Rossi*, and he told me there was an unseen battle raging in Italian life between the forces of good and of evil, and at the moment Satan was in the ascendancy. Intrigued, and aware of my own new-found role as an Avenging Angel of God, I attended the meeting. The attendees were male and female from all strata of Italian life, including a cell from the hospital itself. A number of incidents involving cult murders were discussed at the meeting. I was astonished at what I heard, at what was going on below the surface in Italian society, and after six months attending these monthly meetings, I was initiated into the group.

One of their major tenets was a belief in the Signs of the Zodiac as a way of combating the forces of evil, and also as a guide to conducting one's life. This was in contrast to what I had previously believed, and I soon became immersed in studying all aspects of this credo.

I was also asked to become an Exorcist, and be at the frontline in combating Satan, there being a rising number of Exorcisms in Italy, and a shortage of priests in this area. I agreed, and after a period of training and assisting in a number of Exorcisms, eventually became qualified to fight Satan head-on. Every Exorcism left me drained for weeks afterwards, and I soon realised why there was a shortage of people wanting to work at it. Some of the things I experienced doing them left me shocked to the core, but I found out I was good at this work, and soon became hardened to it. I had found my reason for living. I was fighting against the hidden evils of Satan in the world.

Milan is a beautiful city, resplendent with wonderful architecture, abounding with beautiful women. Maybe it was a reaction to my experience with Father Tom, but after being there for some time I became attracted to Italian women. There were many alluring women in the hospital, tempting and beautiful in their uniforms, low-hanging fruit, inviting. And just like Adam in the Garden of Eden, I was tempted and fell. Many times.

In spite of my priestly vows, I didn't worry too much about these affairs, feeling my new role as an Avenging Angel allowed me to question existing church rules and mores, and then make up my own mind. God would understand, I felt. Although I had many relationships, none was lasting. I often wondered why, as in many cases it was not my decision when it ended, but I always made sure the parting was on a friendly basis. Looking back on these liaisons, I often wondered if I looking for someone like my mother, someone you'd sell your soul for, someone with a grateful heart. I was thankful for all the women I met, for their time and friendship, but the kind of love I sought was elusive. I kept searching.

My involvement with the Friends of God brought me into contact with some gruesome, ritual killings in Italy. Resulting from my exposure to these grisly events, and from my work in the hospital with sick and dying people, I became inured to physical pain and discomfort. It was probably a gradual process over a period of time. It was like developing an alter ego. I believed it was something that happened to you when you became one of God's Avenging Angels.

After a visit home one summer, I became depressed about my mother's mental health. It had gone down so much that her quality of life was zero. I couldn't bear it any longer. On my next visit a few months later, I signed her temporarily out of the Nursing Home, brought her home, administered the lethal dosage I'd got from a friend in the Milan hospital, and buried her in the undergrowth near the Barrow, not far from Father Tom's grave.

At last she was at peace. I performed the normal funeral rites for her after the interment. It was euthanasia, but I felt no guilt in helping her to enter heaven a little earlier than the rules allowed. We hadn't had a real conversation in years. You can be alive but not living. Anyway my plan was to pretend she was still alive, but now in a different Nursing Home. It worked a dream. When I informed her Nursing Home that my mother would not be returning, as I had made private arrangements for her at home, they seemed relieved, glad to hear the news. I gleaned from the conversation that my mother had been a difficult patient, having been guilty of anti-social behaviour with other patients and staff, and I was re-assured that what I had done for her was the right thing. Every week, when I was in Ireland that year, I would visit my mother's grave, and say a rosary in her memory, thanking God all her trials were over.

Back in Italy, I continued my search for that elusive true love, that someone in the image of my mother, who would replace her, someone with a grateful heart, someone who would fill my life with happiness and love, while I continued with my mission as God's Avenging Angel. Finding this person proved impossible, despite the many beautiful women I met over the following years, some actually working near me in the hospital. Everything would go well, until I reached the time for commitment, then I would baulk, afraid if I revealed my true role as God's Avenging Angel, they would panic and run for the police. My being a priest didn't help in many cases, as I normally didn't divulge this fact at first to the women.

I'd almost given up on finding that right person, when Nancy Hackett happened into my life on that day in Milan, that auspicious day when I'd gone for the umpteenth time to view *Da Vinci's* masterpiece, The Last Supper. That day I'll never forget, and I've recorded it for posterity in my diary. Straight away there was something about her that attracted me, something perhaps that brought back memories of my mother. She was beautiful, intelligent, modest, elegant, having an air of calm dignity like the Virgin Mary. And she was born near the same part of Ireland as I was. What more could I ask for? Not much. I was smitten. Head-over-heels.

In retrospect, I must confess my behaviour to Nancy at first was not that of a gentleman, and for that I am truly sorry. That night at the *La Scala* theatre I panicked that she would leave Italy and go out of my life forever. I thought if we made love it would cement our relationship, so I put a draft I'd taken from the hospital into her drink. I now regret bitterly doing this, it was unforgiveable behaviour, but I wasn't thinking straight then, and wanted to fast-track our relationship before she left my life forever. My plan backfired when she fainted in the foyer of her hotel, and I had to help her upstairs to her room.

As she lay slumped on the bed, I spotted a set of Rosary beads and a Missal lying on the bedside table, and realised Nancy was a nun. Like a bolt from the heavens it hit me that she was the person I'd been searching for, someone who might understand my role in the world, and live with me, and grow to love me. I'd already sensed she had a grateful heart, that she might be the special one for me. The fact that we'd both taken vows of chastity didn't seem to enter into it, as these were matters that could somehow be sorted if we were both in love with each other. God would understand. He had selected me. She *was* the one.

Then the fact that I had behaved despicably caused panic to surge through me. What if she woke up? What would I say? More lies? I needed time to build on our relationship. As I undressed Nancy, and laid her beneath the sheets, my emotions got the better of me, as I viewed her beautiful body. I exited the hotel, leaving a note for her at reception, relieved she hadn't awoken. On the way back to my apartment, I vowed to make up to her for my behaviour. That night in bed, her face was constantly in my thoughts, as I pondered how I might win her heart and mind. It was a long night.

When I discovered Nancy had left Milan without further contact, I was distraught. I felt guilty. Normally, as a Scorpio man, I'd be in control of these situations, but this time I'd been left high and dry, on the receiving-end for once. Deservedly so. It hurt me to the core, but this woman was special. If I stayed patient and persistent like my Star sign advocated, I believed it would work out in the end. A pearl-of-great-price indeed, worth striving to have. I wouldn't give up. I would protect her like a Guardian Angel. I would be her Knight in shining armour. I knew she was my Holy Grail. My Madonna. I prayed to God for forgiveness.

That next summer in Ireland, when I met Nancy again, I became even more besotted with her, although I tried to mask my feelings behind a façade of flattery and jollity. When I discovered she had left her Religious Order, I felt half of the problems in our relationship had been resolved. There was still the other half, mine, the matter of me being a priest, but I reckoned I might be able to cajole her around this problem, though I knew it wouldn't be easy.

Around this time I'd been approached by a family from Owenmore, a village near the Barrow, on the way to New Ross, who claimed there was a ring of child abusers operating in the vicinity, and it involved two Garda. I was shocked at this, and said I would investigate the matter straight away. After all, I thought, this was part of my new role as God's Avenging Angel.

When Nancy told me about Ned Rooney being beaten up and hospitalised by an IRA gang, I saw how it affected her and I was moved, vowing vengeance on anyone who tried to harm her, or make her unhappy. I swore to myself I'd protect her, like an angel. When Ned Rooney was murdered in the hospital, it was clear to me Aengus Hynes was the instigator and culprit. I had to act, it was part of my role, and I hoped it would eventually endear me to Nancy. Straight away I made investigations into Aengus Hynes' social habits, and discovered that he went to his local pub in Bagenalstown, late each night for a nightcap.

315

On the night in question I lurked in the shadows on his route home, invisible in my priest's garb, my car parked nearby on the roadway. As I heard his footsteps, I sussed he was alone. Stepping from the shadows, I spoke as I approached him.

"Excuse me sir, I wonder if you could help me, the blessings of God on you. I was on my way to an urgent sick-call, when I got a puncture."

"Of course Father, which tyre is it?"Hynes replied.

"The back rear one, beside the kerb."

As he bent down, I smashed the spanner onto the back of his neck, bundled him into the back seat, and drove off. The incident lasted only a few minutes, I couldn't believe my luck. Back at the barge all was eerily quiet as I manhandled him aboard and into Henry's room, where I strapped him to the table just as he started to come-to. After taping his mouth I checked if there was anyone about. It was after midnight, dark as pitch, the moon smothered by clouds. There was nobody around, all was quiet, a night fit for banshees. Better to get it over with, I muttered to myself.

Back in Henry's room I pulled the tape from Hynes' mouth and asked him what day his birthday was.

"Fuck you and your birthdays whoever you are, you'll be sorry you were ever born. I'll have your guts-for-garters. When my men are through with you you'll be sorry you tangled with me." He snarled, spitting at me, eyes bulging as he pulled against the straps.

"Perhaps I will, but in the meantime maybe Henry will make you change your mind."I said and went to the wardrobe and took out a small cage.

After disrobing him, I placed the cage on his chest. Something scuttled around inside the cage.

"Who....what the hell's in there?" Hynes shrilly cried, sounding scared.

"It's a scorpion. It has a nasty bite. So now, for the final time, what's your birthday?"

"It..its....the 31st October." Hynes stammered.

"Another Scorpio, how very coincidental. Water sign."
I informed him.

Soon Hynes had confessed to organising Ned Rooney's murder. No big deal, he seemed to think. There was no remorse in his voice. That was all I needed to know. After putting the tape back on Hynes' mouth, I lifted the latch on the cage and Henry scurried out, tail cocked. After his tail had done the business, I lifted him back into the cage with gloved fingers, and replaced the cage in the wardrobe.

Although Hynes had slumped into unconsciousness, I knew the sting was not fatal, as, contrary to popular opinion, a scorpion's sting normally does not kill its recipient. It's serious enough though, and I guessed Hynes would most likely remain unconscious for at least a day. Henry had proved a valued ally in fighting the evils of Satan, and I was glad I'd bought him a few weeks earlier at a market in Belfast.

Next morning I took the barge downriver towards New Ross, past the tide-line, and after the ritual stomach incision, deposited Hynes' body in a plastic sack, weighed down with rocks, and dropped it into deep water, re-uniting him with his Sign. The tide would soon do its work, and no trace would be found of him, I reckoned, as I watched the remains vanishing into the river in a vortex. The world was rid of another of Satan's henchmen, and I felt satisfied. And I was doing it on behalf of Nancy, atoning for my past misdeeds with her. Maybe she would understand someday when I explained it all to her. That was my hope. Anyway, I'd struck a blow against Satan and the forces of Evil, against the Devil without the D. God would be happy. I blessed myself.

Soon my investigations into the ring of child abusers led me to Garda Laker. I brought the St.Fiachra upriver to Goresbridge one Wednesday afternoon, near where I'd discovered Laker swam most Wednesday evenings, near a Traveller's camp. After parking the barge a little upstream from the swimming area, I returned to where Laker had left his squad car, and hid nearby in the trees. There was nobody about. Perfect, I rubbed my hands and waited. When Laker returned later to his car, dripping water in his royal pelt, he opened the door, and bent over to retrieve his towel and clothes. It was easy to sneak up behind him, bang him with the spanner across the back of his head, and bundle his inert, naked body onto the back seat, then speed back to the barge, where I lugged his body into Henry's room, and strapped him to the table.

With Henry crawling about in the cage I'd put on his stomach, Laker confessed quickly to his child abuse habits after he'd come-around, implicating Inspector Cornelius Doogan as the ringleader, hoping that fact might save his bacon.

"What's your birthday?" I asked him.

"The first of August. Why?"Laker replied, bewildered.

"Leo. Earth sign fire, that's all I need to know."

He gave me more information on Doogan's involvement, before I released Henry from his cage. Henry's tail struck, and Laker lapsed into unconsciousness. As a decoy, I hid his uniform in the barn of a nearby farm.

Afterwards I dragged Laker's body from the barge back to his squad car, sliced his stomach, and deposited his body on the back seat, then drove back to the swimming area, doused the car with petrol, and threw a burning newspaper from a distance to ignite the conflagration. Hellfire, I mused grimly as I stared at the inferno. Blessing myself, I said a short prayer for Laker's soul, before rushing back to the barge and getting out of the area pronto, back to Graigue. I couldn't believe how easy the whole thing had been.

That night I felt pleased. Another of the Devil's army despatched to the flames of Hell. God would be pleased too. I'd also got the lowdown on Inspector Cornelius Doogan, Laker's accomplice, who was giving Nancy's brother Nick a hard time, and who had been at fault for Ned Rooney's death. Everything was falling into place. Surely I was pleasing God, I thought, my relationship with Nancy was blossoming, and I was certain she would be pleased even more on the day when I'd inform her of the deeds I'd done to prove my love for her.

Then, on second thoughts, I decided on discretion. I wouldn't divulge all the details to her, but let it be our little secret, until the right time came along, if ever. Some things are best left unsaid, best left in the mind. Things that are hard to explain, and might be misunderstood. God would know, He would understand. I prayed He would.

Taking care of Cornelius Doogan was a piece-of-cake. I felt I was getting better all the time in my avenging role. Doogan had a favourite spot on the Barrow where he liked to fish early in the morning every Friday, quite near his house. Perfect for the ambush, which I executed on a misty Friday morning, after tailing him to his fishing-place near the weir, and taking him from behind with a knife, the noise of the rushing weir water muffling my approach. I had no need of any help from Henry on that occasion. Garda Laker had already spilled the beans completely on Doogan.

Doogan's birthday designated his star sign as Earth, and that's why I buried his body deep in a field nearby after the ritual slicing of his stomach, guessing everybody would assume he'd accidentally drowned into the river. And that's how it proved. As a red herring, ha, ha, I threw Doogan's uniform into the river, in a place where I knew it would be found. And so it was, afterwards. Lo and behold. God was truly on my side.

Not long later, my bags were packed for my return to Italy, and Nancy still hadn't made her mind up about my marriage proposal. In desperation I finally decided to do something about it, and, two days before my departure date, I bought an engagement ring, before setting off in the St. Fiachra for Bagenalstown.

It would be a surprise visit, ostensibly to say farewell to Nancy, but in reality an excuse to present her with the ring, and help her make her mind up. Surely she wouldn't say no, I thought. Then I could return to Italy a happy man, knowing the love of my life loved me. The more I went over my plan the more I liked it. I prayed she would say yes.

As I set off on my journey, my nerves jangled. Nothing could go wrong, I kept telling myself. And nothing did, until the bloody barge began to sink in the lock beside the hand-operated drawbridge in Bagenalstown. Rapidly.

I couldn't believe what was happening, the best-laid plans sinking before my eyes. Then I remembered a smell I'd got in Henry's room from below the floorboards a week earlier, which I'd meant to check out, but had forgotten, with all the goings-on. And the barge was overdue for a maintenance check. I cursed my stupidity, guessing that it was a leak. Before the barge submerged beneath the lock-waters I jumped clear, glancing about in panic. Luckily the place was deserted.

The possibility of the secrets of Henry's room being discovered shot through my mind. There was no time to concoct any elaborate plans. I had to vanish. Pronto. My disappearance would be linked to the other recent ones around the river, unexplained and mysterious, or so I prayed. Running towards the Royal Oak Bridge, I threw my cap into the river, along the way. Another red herring, I hoped.

Deciding it was a safer option, I flew back to Milan from Belfast. I realised it was unsafe to return to my work in the *Ospedale Maggiore*, and contacted my friend *Dr. Paolo de Rossi* in the Friends of God, telling him the IRA were after me, for a perceived breach of trust, similar to what the Mafia called *Omerta* in Italy. I needed a new identity and a new job. Urgently. Incredibly, he believed my story, spoke to his friends, and soon had me fixed up in a similar position in a hospital in Treviso, near Venice.

That's why I'm writing this epistle from a small café in the corner of St. Mark's square, sun-shaded in the morning glare, observing the teeming tourists thronging the square where the water seeps up from the flagstones at high tide, where the Campanile rises to the heavens, where the crowds gather on-the-hour to watch the marvels of the renaissance Clock when the two figures hit the bell with their hammers, beside the Oriental façade of the Basilica, behind which lies the Church where I attend early morning mass each time I visit Venice.

The café is located where I can listen to my favourite orchestra, ear half-cocked for when the tenor might sing *Core N'Grato*, and whenever he does, I revel in the times shared with Nancy in Ireland, happy times, and I remember the river, always the river, constant on its course to the sea.

I like to spend most weekends in Venice, staying in the *Albergo San Marco*, just off the square, beside a canal where gilt-adorned gondolas glide by in silence. There's nothing I like better than to travel in a gondola, with a beautiful lady, past the house of Marco Polo or Casanova, ideally in a private cabin, with mandolin music playing away outside. It kills the longing for home and for Nancy, my one and only true love, but only for a while.

The women and Venice are so beautiful, but my heart longs for Nancy. It's like before I first met her, no one is the right one, and now that I have found the right place, Venice, she's not here. I'll have to devise a plan to lure her here. I know she'll love the place, and the romance in the air. I know it. Venice is heaven on earth, I'm her Guardian Angel, and I want to mind her for the rest of my life. Every day I look at the ring I bought her, a diamond scalloped in gold, and long for the day I can put it on her finger.

But for now the best thing I can do is to let the hare sit, do nothing, lie low in the long grass. When the heat has died down, I'll have my plan perfected, I'm a *Scorpio* for God's sake. It's not a bad place to be in the meantime, and I can continue my work in fighting Satan and his cronies. And this wine I'm drinking from the Veneto region, it isn't half bad either. I already have the bones-of-a-plan to entice her to my side. I know she loves the music of *Claudio Monteverdi*. This is his area, born in *Cremona*, working in *Mantua* for the Duke, and then spending his later years in Venice as *maestro di cappella* at the basilica of *San*

Marco. I'm sure she'll want to come.

But hark, the singer, now he's singing my song, our song, *Ungrateful Heart*. My eyes are becoming moist.

"Caterina, Caterina, why do you say those bitter words?
Why do you speak and torment my heart, Caterina?
Don't forget I gave you my heart Caterina, don't forget.
Caterina, Caterina, why do you come and
Say those words that hurt me so much?
You don't think of my pain,
You don't think, you don't care.
Ungrateful heart,
You have stolen my life.
Everything is finished,
And you don't care anymore."

Now, more than ever, do I enjoy listening to that song, because I feel it's *our* song. Now, more than ever, does it make me sad, because everything in it is the opposite of reality. Nancy *does* have a grateful heart, she does care, and she's given new meaning to my life. She is the truth in my life of subterfuge. I know I'm not worthy of her, but each day I pray for when we will be together again. Surely God will not deny me the love of my life? But nothing in life happens unless you make it happen, and soon, with God's help I will commence my plan to be re-united with her. That is my desire, and that is what I pray for now. And I am a *Scorpio*.

I recently replaced Henry, my pet scorpion, who perished when the barge sank, with a new scorpion, Harry, whom I bought recently at a market near the *Rialto*. I like to talk to him daily, as I did with Henry, about Ireland, and the river Barrow, which brings back happy memories of my times with Nancy, and my mother. He gives me solace in my solitariness.

Chapter 32

Sting in the Tale

Nancy stared numbly at the discoloured sea captain's cap in Nick's hand. She recognised it as Marty's, remembering the time he told her he'd bought it in Italy. Stifling tears, she thought about him on the barge when he'd worn it, his face always smiling. She couldn't believe he was gone forever, though it now looked inevitable. She now regretted her hesitation in deciding about his proposal of marriage, wondering if Sister Veronica's words of caution had unduly influenced her. The irony of it, to think Marty, who had saved her from drowning, was now drowned. Maybe she'd let her head rule her heart too much? Maybe her procrastination had somehow led to his demise? A wave of guilt hit her. Her eyes filled with tears. The whole thing didn't make sense, she muttered, sometimes life doesn't make sense. She twisted her handkerchief in her hands.

"It's Marty's cap, I can vouch for that. It looks like he must have drowned. Or does it?"She asked forlornly.

"It does, but it's not conclusive at this point." Nick shifted uneasily from foot-to-foot as he spoke.

"And to think it happened here in Bagenalstown, in the lock, when he was coming to visit me."She muttered, drying her eyes with her handkerchief.

"Yeah Nancy, look I'm really sorry for your trouble. It was unfortunate, the whole thing happening like that, the coincidence of it. It's a mystery for sure, but we'll get to the bottom of it. We have to. By the way we got the barge lifted from the river this morning."

"Oh, did you? And was there anything or anyone on board?"Her heart leapt with hope as she spoke.

"I'm afraid not. But...but there was one thing though, one thing that has us all a bit flummoxed."

"And what was that?"

"In a wardrobe in one of the cabins, we found a small cage with a dead scorpion in it. Rather an odd pet to have, we all thought. A sting in the tale, you might say. Sorry, that wasn't meant to be funny. A bad joke. Did you by any chance know Marty had a pet scorpion?"

"N..no."Even as she spoke, the memory of the scratching noise she'd heard that night on the barge in Graigue entered her mind. She felt faint, and sat down, her face blanching.

"Are you ok Nancy? You don't look well. Can I get you a drink of water?"Nick asked, shaken by her reaction.

"Thanks, but I.... I'll be all right in a few minutes. I need to rest awhile. This whole thing has been such a shock."

"Of course it has, I'll leave you in peace. Give me a ring if there's anything I can do for you. I'll be down at the lock checking out the scene."Nick rose, hugged her and rushed outside.

After Nick left she went upstairs and lay on her bed, feeling faint and fatigued. Her mind raced. A scorpion as a pet, strange, but then again some people have unusual animals as pets, she reasoned, as a way of expressing their own individuality. Then she recalled the time in Milan when he told her his star sign was Scorpio. He'd also seemed overly immersed in the Signs of the Zodiac. She recalled the scorpion-tattoo on his arm after he'd saved her from drowning. Nothing wrong with that, she thought, but not what you'd expect a priest to be interested in. Weird indeed. Then the scratching noise she'd heard on the barge, in the room he kept locked, came back to her, haunting her mind, as she realised it was a scorpion not a rat. She felt edgy. Why hadn't he told her about his pet? Maybe he'd have been embarrassed, thinking she might consider it an oddball-thing? The hair rose on the nape of her neck at the memory of that evening on the barge, but then she always had a phobia about creepy crawlies. It's all academic, she tried to convince herself, as Marty was now dead, and from here on life would follow a more predictable pattern. But deep down she had an uneasy feeling about the scorpion revelation. It's probably just me and my phobias, she muttered, and will be gone after a good night's sleep.

There was another question deep-down dogging her mind, but it wouldn't come to her. Leave it and it might come later, she thought, frustrated. What was it? She sighed as she checked her watch, realising she had a music rehearsal in thirty minutes. She left a while later, her heart heavy, after praying for Marty's survival, but feeling it was a lost cause.

That afternoon, after returning to the house, she was met by her sister Kitty and her father. They told her they'd been to the library. He said he'd got a book on cricket to read, and Kitty an Agatha Christie mystery. Her father then announced that he'd got the all clear from the Physio, and he could now walk unaided.

"I'm as happy as a pig in you- know- what." He added.

"So am I, sure there'll be no stopping your gallop now." Kitty laughed.

"That's great news, I'm delighted for you both." Nancy said.

"Are you feeling alright Nancy? You don't look yourself." Her father said.

"I'm fine Daddy, it's just the stress of Marty's barge sinking, and not knowing the outcome yet."She didn't mention Marty's cap being found, not wanting to worry him. When he'd departed upstairs for his afternoon nap, she told Kitty about the discovery.

"Don't give up hope yet."Kitty replied, grabbing her sister's hands.

"I won't, I'm still praying. I feel partly responsible. Maybe I should have accepted his proposal, and not dilly-dallied."

"Don't be so silly Nancy, it was probably just a freak accident. You're not clairvoyant you know."

"Maybe, God it's great to have someone to pour your heart out to. When you're on your own, your mind can play tricks on you."

"That's what sisters are for. And are you still going-out with your Mister Williams?"Kitty asked.

"I am. We're going to the pictures next Friday. He said there was a good one on, a musical. Knowing my luck it's probably Calamity Jane. I'm half-thinking I should cry off with this hullabaloo going on down on the river. What do you think?"

"I think you should go. It's nothing to do with him. You're not going to get that many offers in a one–horse town like Bagenalstown, believe me. So don't be getting any high-falutin' notions."

"How unromantic of you Kitty, but you're probably right."Nancy smiled.

As they laughed together, Nancy remembered the question about Marty that had been bedevilling her mind.

"Excuse me Kitty, but I have to ring Nick urgently about something."

"Of course, I have to be heading anyway, I'll see you tomorrow."Kitty rose, hugged Nancy and left.

Immediately Nancy rang Nick, getting straight through to him at the station.

"Hi Nick, can you talk?"

"Sure, I'm alone in my office, fire away."

"I've been racking my brains since I last saw you about Marty. There's an obvious thing I overlooked, in fact we may both have overlooked it."

"What is that?"

"It's Marty's mother. I've never met her. I'd love to speak to her. She hasn't been well, but Marty had been looking after her, and was making arrangements for her before he left. She may be unaware of what's happened. Have you contacted her?"

After a short silence Nick replied.

"In fact no, we haven't got around to that yet. We've been flat-out here with the local goings-on. I have a review

326

meeting in an hour with Sergeant Foley. I'll get him to follow up on Marty Maher's mother as soon as possible. And thanks for bringing up the matter. We would have got around to it eventually, but not as quickly. It's important, but, you understand the situation here is unprecedented."

"I do understand Nick, and I hope I'm not putting you under more pressure."

"Not at all, that's what we're paid for. I'll let you know when we contact her."

"Great, I'm looking forward to meeting her."Nancy put down the phone, thinking it would be nice to meet Marty's mother. She wondered if Marty resembled her. Strange he hadn't brought her to meet his mother before he left, she mused. Later she rang Simon Williams to confirm their date that Friday for the Astor cinema.

Lightning Source UK Ltd.
Milton Keynes UK
UKHW012143230521
384249UK00003B/111

9 781789 558470